Liz Byrski is the author of seven other novels and a number of non-fiction books, the latest of which is *Getting On: Some Thoughts on Women and Ageing.*

She has worked as a freelance journalist, a broadcaster with ABC Radio and an advisor to a minister in the West Australian Government.

Liz has a PhD in writing from Curtin University where she teaches professional and creative writing.

www.lizbyrski.com

Also by Liz Byrski

Fiction
*Gang of Four*
*Food, Sex & Money*
*Belly Dancing for Beginners*
*Trip of a Lifetime*
*Bad Behaviour*
*Last Chance Café*
*In the Company of Strangers*

Non-fiction
*Remember Me*
*Getting On: Some Thoughts on Women and Ageing*

Jane Harrap

# LIZ BYRSKI
*Family Secrets*

MACMILLAN
**Pan Macmillan Australia**

First published 2014 in Macmillan by Pan Macmillan Australia Pty Ltd
1 Market Street, Sydney, New South Wales, Australia, 2000

Cataloguing-in-Publication entry is available
from the National Library of Australia
http://catalogue.nla.gov.au

Typeset in 11.5/15 pt Palatino by Post Pre-press Group
Printed by McPherson's Printing Group

The characters in this book are fictitious and any resemblance to real
persons, living or dead, is purely coincidental.

Papers used by Pan Macmillan Australia Pty Ltd are natural, recyclable
products made from wood grown in sustainable forests. The manufacturing
processes conform to the environmental regulations of the country of origin.

*For my family, with love*

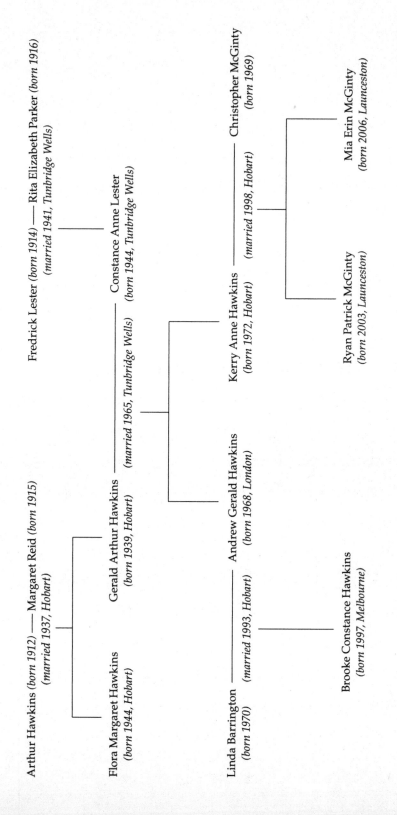

**HAWKINS, Gerald Arthur**
Passed peacefully at his home in Hobart on
25 January 2012, aged 73.
Beloved husband of Connie, father of Andrew and
Kerry, grandfather of Brooke, Ryan and Mia,
father-in-law of Linda and Chris.
Peace at last after a long and painful journey.
So many happy memories.
We will miss you terribly, but you will live forever
in our hearts.

**HAWKINS, Gerald Arthur**
25/01/12
In loving memory of my brother Gerald, who
always tried to do his best.
Love and deepest sympathy to Connie and family,
my thoughts are with you.
Flora.

# One

It begins exactly as Gerald had predicted it would, but much sooner than either of them had anticipated. It begins a few days after the funeral, on the morning of the day they plan to scatter his ashes. Connie, back from her usual early-morning walk, opens the side gate and lets Scooter off his lead. The dog pricks his ears at the sound of voices and darts around the side of the house towards them. Connie pauses to listen; the children are up – Andrew and Kerry, and their respective spouses, Linda and Chris. There is laughter, the chink of crockery, the softer voices of her grandchildren and the thud of a ball against the wall. She hesitates, feeling she should join them but, wanting a little more time to herself, takes a deep breath and slips in through the laundry door and up the stairs.

When she'd called she'd feared that they might not make it in time, that despite what she said about urgency, Gerald had been dying for so long they might think there was time to spare. But they had come at once – Andrew, Linda and Brooke on the first available flight from Melbourne, and Kerry, Chris and the kids driving down from Launceston

3

---

that same afternoon. They were all there with him at the end and since then they've been on their best behaviour; the minor spats and jealousies, the scuffles for supremacy that flare at other times, have been stilled by grief and replaced with meaningful hugs, bursts of crying and conversations scattered with tender reminiscence. Gerald would have been proud of them.

Peeling off her shorts and t-shirt Connie perches uncomfortably on the edge of the bath, remembering conversations she and Gerald had had about the children, their fine qualities and their frequently inexplicable and irritating habits. Then she steps into the shower, turns on the taps and lets the hot water stream over her as though it might wash away more than just the sweat raised on the steep climb back to the house.

Back in the seventies they had chosen the Sandy Bay house for its location, perched high in the hills with unbroken views across the water – Hobart to one side, open water to the other, and the reassuring bulk of Mount Nelson in the background. Andrew had just started school; Kerry was a robust, fractious toddler. The big, two-storey house, white-painted and with curves instead of corners, had been built in the early fifties. The rooms were flooded with daylight from windows that captured every vista, and there were more cupboards than Connie had thought she could ever fill. And up a narrow staircase from the second floor there was a sixth bedroom with its own tiny bathroom. She'd thought it impressive.

'It looks like it's meant to belong to important people,' she'd said, awed by the style and size.

'It will if *we* buy it,' Gerald had said.

And Connie had known then that he wanted it. Important. Gerald was determined to make a name for himself, to stand out from the crowd. That was why he had wanted to come back to Tasmania, where he believed he could become a big fish in a fairly small pool, and do it quickly. The competition in London was fierce, but here his old family connections gave him a head start. Gerald's parents had moved back home to Hobart from England a few years earlier when his father retired from the Australian diplomatic service. His more than twenty years at the London embassy meant they were financially comfortable and when Gerald had written that he and Connie were thinking of joining them, his father had stumped up a very generous deposit for a house, in a glorious location.

'You might as well have the money now, when you need it,' he'd said. 'No point waiting 'til we're dead.'

But for Connie, it wasn't ever about status – she loved the house for itself. It was in many ways an oddity at the time, an impressive, elegant oddity. And she loves it more now because she has made it her own, and among the mix of homes that have sprouted up nearby it seems like a slightly worn but grand old lady; solid, safe, a little run down but still stylish.

Connie wraps herself in a towel and wanders into the bedroom, pausing by the open window to look out across the river glittering in the sharp morning sunlight. The mild air is heavy with the scent of the old roses she planted in her first spring here. Out on the lawn Brooke, elder stateswoman of the grandchildren by six years, is lying in the hammock reading, while her cousins Ryan and Mia argue over a ball. From the paved terrace beneath her window, the raised voices of her two adult children and their spouses drift upwards and Connie, who can hear but not see them, realises they're talking about her. She leans further over the windowsill to eavesdrop. And so it begins.

'She'll need to move of course, she can't stay here on her own.'

'Yes, a smaller place, easier to manage.'

'Has she said that? Have you asked her?'

'No. Not yet . . . obviously not.'

'She should move nearer to us,' Kerry says. 'She could see more of the kids – in fact she could have them in the holidays and after school.'

'That's typical, Kerry,' Andrew says irritably. 'Near *you*! Has it occurred to you that Mum might not fancy Launceston? She loves Melbourne, she'd be better off nearer to us. She could get a little unit in Fitzroy or Carlton.'

'Your ma loves it here,' Chris, Connie's son-in-law, cuts in. 'She loves this house. Don't you think she might like to be left alone to do her own thing?'

'It's not practical. It's never been a practical house,' Kerry says, her voice rising an octave. 'And anyway, she hasn't really got a *thing*. We should talk to her, while we're all still here.'

'But do you even know what arrangements Gerald made about the house?' Chris asks.

'The house is in Mum's name,' Andrew says. 'Dad told me that years ago.'

'So Connie could sell it and get one of those places that are going up just near us,' Linda says. 'You know, Andrew, those townhouses on the corner. Downsizing at Connie's age makes a lot of sense for her and, well . . .' she hesitates, awkwardly, 'well, for all of us, I mean financially . . .'

Connie hears Kerry give a snort of derision, the one that she seems to save for her sister-in-law. 'I hardly think a townhouse is the answer,' she mutters.

'Nothing wrong with a townhouse,' Andrew says. '*We* live in one in case you hadn't noticed.'

'Oh give me a break! Stairs, Andrew, stairs! Mum's only a few years off seventy, she shouldn't be moving to anywhere with stairs.'

'She's used to the stairs here,' Chris points out, 'and that back-breaking walk up the hill. This is her home and, anyway, she might have plans of her own.'

'It's just not practical for her to stay here,' Kerry snaps back at him. 'And she *won't* have plans, she doesn't do plans, *we'll* have to do them for her. And how come Dad told *you* about the house, Andrew? Why did he tell *you* and not *me*?'

'I *don't know*, Kerry, he just did. It's not like he made a thing of it, just mentioned it and said he'd done it for tax reasons.'

Connie steps back from the window. So much for peace and goodwill, she thinks, things are back to normal already – Andrew and Kerry, both so strong-minded and opinionated, and Linda too, although her opinions are always identical to Andrew's. Connie runs her hands through her wet hair and plugs in the dryer. Chris is different though, far more reasonable. Why, she wonders, switching on the hair dryer and drowning out their voices, is her son-in-law the only one who thinks she has a mind of her own?

She has known for years that this time would come but, now that it is here, it feels quite sudden. Three, maybe four years, the consultant had said when he'd delivered his diagnosis of motor neurone disease, but that was nine – almost ten – years ago. He hadn't counted on Gerald's legendary tenacity, which, in the last couple of years, had begun to feel more like sheer bloody-mindedness in a man who could do nothing, signal nothing, say nothing, not even blink his eyes in recognition. And so it's over at last, but Connie has been focused on Gerald for so long that, although there is an element of liberation, she really has very little idea how to use it. What is she supposed to do now? There is just one thing she's sure of, sure that she will do as soon as she can. And she finishes drying her hair, pulls on her clothes and hurries downstairs to email Flora about it before she starts on breakfast.

\*

'I think it all went very nicely,' Andrew says as they sit down for lunch later that day after scattering the ashes at Gerald's favourite spot on Mount Nelson. He strips the gold foil from a bottle of Moët. 'And isn't it typical of Dad to want us to celebrate his life rather than mourn, even down to the champagne?'

'Absolutely typical, he was always so thoughtful,' Kerry says, her eyes brimming with tears again. 'You were so lucky, Mum.'

'I'm sorry?'

'I said you were so lucky to have married Dad, he was so thoughtful.'

Connie, in whose opinion thoughtfulness had not been particularly high on Gerald's list of good qualities, wondered why they thought Gerald had decreed the nature of this event when he hadn't been able to communicate anything to anyone for years.

'That's one interpretation,' Chris murmurs, and Kerry flashes him a warning look.

She's edgy this morning, Connie thinks, even more so than she has been through the years of watching her father deteriorate. Kerry had idolised Gerald, constantly craved his attention, but too often saw it turned elsewhere: on his work, on her brother, then on his grandchildren, and finally, on nothing at all. So much effort for so little reward.

Andrew fills the last of the adults' glasses and then pours cordial into two champagne flutes. 'Come on, kids,' he calls, 'come and drink a toast to Granddad.'

The 'littlies', as Connie thinks of them, though with Ryan nine and Mia six they aren't really that little anymore, race towards the promise of something they are not normally allowed, and Brooke sighs, closes *Hunger Games* and saunters slowly over to join them.

'Right then,' Andrew says, 'on your feet everyone.'

And they push back their chairs and raise their glasses.

'To Dad,' he says. 'The best father in the world. A magnificent life – you'll always be with us. To Dad!'

And they chorus his words, drink the toast and then fall into awkward silence.

'Is there cake?' Mia asks. 'Did Granddad want us to have cake too?'

'I'm sure he'd want that, darling,' Connie says, drawing Mia towards her. 'There's a passionfruit cake, but we'll have lunch first. Come and sit here with me.' And Mia clambers onto a chair and unfolds a paper napkin.

Connie leans back, watching her children talking together, passing food, clinking glasses, and wishes that she could freeze the moment. Andrew, so much like his father, tall and rangy, the same grey-green eyes and the clear golden skin that both he and Kerry had inherited and which she, with her pale English complexion prone to blushes, has always envied. He leans over to talk to Ryan, heaps some ham onto his nephew's plate and gives his shoulder an encouraging squeeze. She watches as Chris tops up Linda's glass, then turns to Kerry, holding the bottle out, gesturing her to hand him her glass. He is such a blessing, Connie thinks, a warm and loving man who thinks the world of Kerry and his children. Kerry pushes her glass towards him; her expression is tense, her manner stroppy – it seems to be her default setting since the early stages of Gerald's illness, and it's worsened as time has dragged on. But Connie, exhausted by the task of keeping Gerald alive and as comfortable as possible, has lacked the physical and emotional energy to try to talk to her about it. Kerry has inherited Gerald's stubbornness, that's for sure.

Here they all are, her family, unobscured now by the blurring lens of Gerald's condition. For more than half of Brooke's life, most of Ryan's and all of Mia's, Connie knows she has been a semi-detached grandparent; too exhausted and distracted to participate in their lives in the way she had wanted. Lost years that can never be recaptured. Connie feels a lump in her throat as reality bites. And it's not just about the grandchildren; Gerald's illness has driven over all of them like a bulldozer, leaving them crushed and resentful, the family ties fraying and disconnected. Love has been numbed in the face of so many other painful emotions, it has slipped too often between the cracks of time and distance, and the wanting, all of them wanting so much from each other, but unable to give or receive. Time to rebuild all that, she thinks, but I can only start on it once I've rebuilt myself. That's why she needs to be with Flora, the only person still living who can take her back to her youth, to the time before Gerald moved into her life and made it his own. Flora, who can remember who she was and who she might have become.

*

It's an hour or so later, when they've finished lunch on the terrace, that Connie emerges from the kitchen with the coffee pot, that the conversation takes the turn she's been dreading.

'We've been thinking about you, Mum,' Kerry says. 'About your situation. Now that Dad's . . . well . . . now he's no longer with us, you'll need to think about what comes next.'

Connie opens her mouth to speak but Kerry cuts across her.

'We've had a family conference and we all agree . . .'

'Er, excuse me,' Chris interrupts. 'A family conference?'

'Yes, to decide what's best for Mum.'

'Do you mean that brief conversation this morning?'

'Well, yes, but there was a conference after that.'

'And who was at this *family* conference? Not me, for a start,' Chris continues.

'Me neither,' Brooke chips in.

Kerry's expression is all irritation, she sighs and rolls her eyes. 'Of course *you* weren't there, Brooke, it's none of *your* business.'

'Well, I *am* part of the family, Auntie Kerry,' Brooke says. 'In case you hadn't noticed.'

'Brooke, cut it out,' Andrew says. 'This is serious.'

'What about *you*, Connie?' Chris asks, turning to her. 'Were you at this family meeting?'

'Well, no . . .'

'So it was just you, Kerry, and Andrew presumably? When you hopped in the car this morning and said you were going to Battery Point for a coffee.'

Andrew nods.

'And you, Linda? Were you there?'

Linda shakes her head. 'Um . . . not exactly. I wanted to look in the antique shop so they dropped me off, but Andrew told me what he thinks and I agree entirely.'

'Right,' Chris says in a soft and steady voice, turning back to his wife. 'So just before you go on, Kerry, there was a general conversation this morning while Connie was out walking the dog, and then you and Andrew chewed it over in the café. There hasn't actually been a *family* meeting.'

'For goodness sake, Chris . . .'

'Well, has there?'

Kerry sighs. 'I suppose . . . no . . . not *exactly* . . .'

'Right, just as long as we're all clear about that.'

Kerry hesitates and Connie's stomach clenches. She loathes conflict. As an only child she never had to compete for anything at home, never had to negotiate with siblings, and survived school by keeping a low profile. Politeness, good manners, never putting oneself first, deferring to the opinions of others and never saying outright what you think, had been the ruling code. Once, in anger, she had told Gerald that it was the ideal training for the job of being the wife of a control freak like him.

'Well, you're saying what you think now,' he'd replied.

'And you simply haven't a clue how often I hold back.'

Kerry leans forward in her chair, fixing Connie with a steely gaze. 'Anyway, Mum,' she begins again, 'it's like this, we all . . .'

'You mean, you and Dad?' Brooke says.

'Yes, *okay*, Brooke,' Andrew intervenes. 'Kerry and I think that you should consider moving somewhere smaller, Mum.'

'You'd enjoy it,' Kerry says. 'You can move nearer to us. It'd be lovely. We can help out . . . it'd be more convenient.'

'D'you mean it'll be more convenient for *us*, Kerry?' Chris says, leaning towards her, putting his hand on her arm. 'And, Connie, just so as you know, the helping out probably means that *you* could help *us* with the children.'

Connie's throat has gone dry. 'Look, I don't . . .'

'That's not it at all,' Andrew says. 'We all want what's best for you, Mum. Linda and I think you should come somewhere nearer to us. You know how you love Melbourne.'

'You should stay here, Nan,' Brooke cuts in again. 'It's where you were with Granddad.'

'Granddad's ghost might be here,' Ryan says, and he begins some ghostly howling.

'Stop it, Ryan,' Kerry snaps. Her cheeks are fiery red and Connie is reminded how much her daughter hates the flush that rises when she's agitated. 'And, Brooke, this isn't up to you. Keep out of it.'

'Actually, Kerry,' Chris says quietly, leaning across the table, 'I think it's up to Connie to decide what to do, and personally I think it's pretty insensitive to be talking about this right now.'

Kerry shakes her head irritably. 'We're just trying to help, Chris, stop being so difficult.'

A great surge of something hot and fierce, something stronger than the anxiety, rears up in Connie and she pushes back her chair and gets to her feet. 'Stop it, at once, all of you,' she says, in a voice that sounds entirely unlike her own. 'We've just scattered your father's ashes, for heaven's sake. How do you think he'd feel if he could hear you arguing like this? How do you think it makes *me* feel?' They're looking at her now, Kerry and Andrew, visibly shaken and embarrassed, Linda flushed and awkward while Chris studies the tablecloth with a deadpan expression on his face. The silence is deafening.

'Woohoo, Nan! You rock,' Brooke says, a huge grin spreading across her face.

'Shut up, Brooke,' Linda hisses.

'No!' Connie says. 'Don't shut up, Brooke dear. I do indeed rock and now I'm going to rock on upstairs for a rest which will give you all time to sort yourselves out and do the washing-up.'

'We're just trying to help . . .' Kerry cuts in, crimson-faced.

Connie holds up her hand. 'Kerry, I said, stop! Stop it now. If this is your idea of help, I don't want it. Remember why you're here.' And she turns into the house away from the mix of anger and hurt that Kerry has carried with her since childhood and which nothing – not love, or encouragement, success or motherhood – ever seems to resolve.

*

It's Brooke who wakes her, tapping on the bedroom door.

'It's me, Nan, can I come in?'

'Of course, dear.' Connie struggles to sit up.

Brooke opens the door and crosses the room clutching a mug. 'I made you some tea.' She puts it down on the bedside table and perches on the edge of the bed.

'Thank you, darling, just what I need.' Connie yawns, resting her head against the bedhead. 'I must have fallen asleep. Have they stopped arguing?'

Brooke nods, twisting a strand of hair. 'Just about.'

'And have they stopped making plans for me?'

She grins conspiratorially. 'Not really. They're so bossy, Dad and Mum and Auntie Kerry.'

'Except for Chris.'

'No, but he's not one of them really, is he? Like he's not . . .' she pauses, turning her fingers into inverted commas, 'not a blood relative, as Dad says.'

'Your dad said that?'

Brooke nods.

Connie looks at her, searching for something of herself in her granddaughter. Brooke certainly has the Hawkins gene – the height and the strong, rangy build – but her dark hazel eyes belong to neither of her parents nor her grandfather. Those are my eyes, Connie thinks, as she reflects on how surprised she'd been when Brooke had spoken up so bravely during the earlier argument between the adults. She had grown up a lot in recent years; years Connie has largely missed due to nursing Gerald.

'Anyway, they all reckon they know best. Are you coming down soon?'

'In a minute. Did you mean what you said – about my staying here?'

"Course I did. It's your home, you wouldn't like living in a townhouse. It's like living in a big posh box and everything has to be tidy all the time.'

Connie laughs. 'Well, I'd be hopeless with the tidy bit, but I think that's more about who's living there than the place itself.'

'Yeah right! Mum and Dad are so anal . . . it's like they're always expecting a magazine to turn up and photograph them.'

'Well, your father's changed. He was an absolute grub as a kid. I never knew what I'd find when I cleaned under his bed or tried to tidy his cupboard.'

'Mum's worse though,' Brooke says. 'Anyway, you were cool down there today, Nan. I never saw you do that before, like, tell people off.'

Connie swings her legs off the bed and crosses to the dressing table to brush her hair. 'I used to do it quite a bit when they were younger,' she says. 'I thought I'd lost the knack but perhaps I haven't. What are Ryan and Mia doing?'

'Ryan is in the big tree throwing stuff at Mia, and she's screeching, but standing right under the branch he's on and won't move away.'

'Oh dear, it never stops, does it?'

'I'm never going to have children,' Brooke says. 'They're evil.'

'*You're* not,' Connie says, picking up her tea.

'Well, I quite often am, really,' Brooke says, turning to face her. 'When I'm feeling really, you know, shitty and stuff.'

'Knowing that is a good thing,' Connie says, following Brooke out of the bedroom. But then what do I know about it, she thinks, giving in all my life and mostly not minding about it, too comfortable to take a stand, happy to leave everything to Gerald. And she wonders suddenly what her granddaughter really thinks of her.

'Mum, I'm sorry,' Andrew says as they reach the kitchen. 'Really, it was unfair, today of all days.'

'It was,' she says, smiling but determined to resist the temptation to tell him it's okay and not to worry. And she walks on out to the terrace, where Kerry jumps immediately to her feet.

'Mum,' she holds out her arms, 'very bad behaviour, really sorry, you need more time, of course you do. Big hug?'

Connie allows herself to be hugged but refrains from hugging in return. 'Ryan!' she calls sharply over Kerry's shoulder. 'Come down from that tree immediately. I will not have you throwing things in my garden. Mia, stop snivelling and go and wash your face.' Mia complies immediately. Connie had forgotten what it was like to have people do as they're told. How long can she keep up this assertiveness, she wonders. Long enough to tell them about her plans? She has a horrible feeling that they're not going to like them at all.

*

An hour or so later it's clear she was right.

'Going away? But why?' Kerry says before Connie has begun to explain. And before she has time to answer continues, 'Shouldn't you be sorting things out here? Making plans for the future? And why France, why Auntie Flora?

Dad didn't want anything to do with her. I don't think it's . . .' she stops, colours up again and looks away.

'And after that,' Connie continues, ignoring her, 'I'm going to England. I've never been back, not since Dad and I moved here.' She waits, hoping they'll show an interest, but there is just an awkward silence.

'So I suppose you'll be away for about three weeks?' Andrew asks eventually.

She laughs, irritated, and hurt by their lack of interest in what she wants and needs to do. 'Oh for goodness sake, you think I'm going to do that horrendous journey, spend time in France with Flora and then go back to places in England that I haven't seen in decades, and be back here again in *three weeks*? I'll be gone a couple of months at least.'

'Sounds good, Connie,' Chris says. 'You need to go back and touch the past. You could go to Ireland too, you'd love the west coast, Galway – I can just see you in Galway.'

'But you're not used to doing things alone, Connie,' Linda says, 'and that's a very long time . . .'

'Far too long,' Andrew agrees. 'I think you should . . .' he stops abruptly. 'Sorry I . . .'

Connie gives him a long and steady look. 'I've been waiting to go home to England since before you started high school, Andrew. Gerald went back for work but I couldn't go with him because I couldn't leave you two. This is my time now and I'll take as long as I need.'

There is another awkward silence.

'I can understand that you'd want to go to England,' Kerry says, 'but really, Mum, I hope you won't mind my saying this, but staying with Auntie Flora hardly seems very respectful to Dad considering that he had virtually disowned her.'

'Is Auntie Flora *my* auntie?' Mia asks.

Connie takes a deep breath. 'She's your *great* auntie, Granddad's sister.'

Chris gets to his feet and takes Mia's hand. 'Come on, sweetheart, let's go and see if the goldfish are awake. You too, Ryan.' And he leads the children away from the table towards the overgrown pond.

Kerry gets to her feet. 'Well, I'll go and make some fresh tea.'

'Sit down please, Kerry,' Connie says, struggling to keep her voice low and steady, and she waits until Kerry is back in her seat. 'First of all, I *do* mind your saying that, in fact it's really offensive. Flora and I go back a long way, back to before I met your father; we were at school together. You know nothing about what happened between the two of them, so I suggest you keep your opinions to yourself. I've spent years looking after your father with very little help from any of you, and now that it's over I feel absolutely free to do what I want.'

'Oh yes, and you were wonderful, Mum,' Kerry says, 'we all knew that. I was always saying to Chris how wonderful you were looking after Dad, I . . .'

'Absolutely,' Andrew joins in. 'Kerry's quite right. We all thought you did an amazing job.'

'Stoic,' Linda adds.

And Chris, poised halfway between them and the fish-pond, says nothing, just turns to look back at her over his shoulder.

The silence is tense. No one exchanges even a glance. Andrew clears his throat. Kerry's cheeks flame crimson and she stares down at her feet.

'So . . . er . . . what about Scooter, while you're away, Nan?' Brooke asks.

Connie turns to her. 'My friend Farah will stay here and look after Scooter. She and her children live in a flat so it'll be nice for them to have a bit more space for a while.'

Kerry straightens with the sort of bristling energy that Gerald always said reminded him of a fox terrier. 'Farah? You mean that woman who, the one who . . . ?'

'Exactly, Kerry, the one who *was* here, and who *did* help me, who made it possible for me to have a day to myself sometimes.'

'But she's . . .'

Andrew sucks in his breath. 'Kerry . . .'

But Kerry is quivering now. 'She's an illegal, isn't she? Came in on one of those boats?'

Connie waits, wondering if her daughter is going to dig herself in further or back down. She loves this daughter, loves all of them so much that it hurts, but right now she just wants to smack Kerry, as she had frequently wanted to smack her when she was a troublesome toddler. She wants to tell them all to go home and leave her in peace.

'Farah's husband was drowned when the boat they were in sank offshore. They left Afghanistan in fear of their lives, she and her children are refugees.'

Kerry is silent for moment. 'And she's . . . well, she's . . .'

'A nurse?' Connie asks, deliberately misinterpreting. 'Yes of course.'

'Well, I really don't think it's right . . .' Kerry says. 'After all . . .'

'After all what?'

'Well . . .' Kerry draws up her shoulders. 'Well, I just don't think Dad would've liked it, you know . . . being . . . well, she's not one of us . . .'

Silence. Kerry's blush deepens and she looks around as if for support. 'What I mean is, she's not one of the family.'

Connie pauses, poised between disgust and disbelief. She knows her daughter well enough to know that she is free of racial and religious prejudice, but for some reason Kerry seems determined to win this battle of wills whatever tactics are required. It seems so ridiculous that she throws back her head and bursts into laughter. 'Well, Kerry,' she says, 'Dad was happy to have her sit with him, play chess with him, wash him, shave him and clean him when he soiled himself.

And anyway, I make the decisions about who gets to stay here now, so you'd better get used it.' She gets to her feet. 'Would anyone like any more tea? Brooke dear, come and help me fetch that cake, Ryan and Mia must be desperate for it by now.'

# Two

*T*here is a collective sigh of relief from the pews as the priest genuflects, picks up the altar vessels and departs to the sacristy. He is young and inexperienced, a locum filling in for Father Bertrand, who is in hospital in St Malo recovering from a triple by-pass. This one seems barely old enough to be out of high school, let alone ordained. Flora, irritated by his trembling hands on the chalice, the dropped wafers and most of all the torturous fumbling as he lost his way in the litany, waits impatiently for the right moment to leave. It's not unusual for her to come and sit in the church but it's a long time since she attended a service. This morning, however, she had come to the six o'clock mass and to her own surprise had taken the sacrament, although she had wondered whether she was entitled to do so after such a long absence. It was thinking about Gerald that made her want to do it, and she'd told herself that God would be more concerned about her intentions than in checking up on her dismal devotional record. She'd thought she'd stay on after the service – make the most of the silence for a while – but

21

the young priest took so long that her time has run out, and now she needs to get back home. Silently Flora slips out of the pew, nods to the altar and walks quickly down the aisle and out into the square, letting the church door swish softly to a close behind her.

It's daylight now and as she pulls her bike from the rack the market traders are unloading their vans, and a waiter in a long white apron is setting up tables on the pavement outside Café Centrale. Flora weaves her way between the stalls and heads for the *tabac*, glancing at her watch. The breakfast trade back at the hotel ramps up well before seven as the fishing fleet finish unloading the catch. But while being late is bad, being late without Suzanne's cigarettes would be a cardinal sin. Flora queues for the cigarettes, then squeezes her way out of the crowded little shop, drops the two packets of *Gitanes Bleu* into the bike basket and freewheels down the hill to the post office, where she collects the mail from the post box, and doubles back past the square heading for home. Outside the church the young priest, hands tucked nervously into the sleeves of his cassock, is chatting with members of the congregation. Flora flashes him a killer look; she should have stayed home, practised some yoga as usual, before cycling down for the mail.

As she turns the corner onto the quay, the wind whips into her face tugging at her hair and making her eyes water, but she pedals on along the curve of the harbour where the leisure boats are bobbing at anchor on the high water. At nine she had fallen in love with this place, this harbour, the stone houses that line the quay, and behind them the rocky pine-clad backdrop of the cape stretching out beyond the curve of the sea wall.

It was the fifties; their first ever visit to France, and her father, who had driven the Morris Oxford confidently onto the ferry at Southampton, suffered an obvious loss of confidence as he steered his way off at St Malo and pulled out onto the street where traffic was hurtling towards them on the wrong side of the road. What should have been a forty minute drive to Port d'Esprit had taken two hours because Flora's mother had a problem reading the map.

'For god's sake, Margaret, give the bloody map to Flora,' her father had shouted when they found themselves back for the third time at the same roundabout, 'then we might get there before midnight.'

There were just the three of them that year – Gerald, by then fourteen, had gone with the family of a school friend to Switzerland. Port d'Esprit was smaller in those days, just a neat fishing port with stunning sandy beaches, nothing like the steep and stony ones of the Sussex coast, or the coarse and crowded sands of Southend where the school had once taken them on a day trip. Their father had been posted to London when Flora was five and by the time they made that first trip to France her memories of life in Hobart had all but faded away.

As she cycles on against the wind Flora remembers that first day, more than half a century ago; remembers the moment they pulled up outside the Hotel du Port. She had fallen instantly in love with it, the rough stone walls, the blue shutters and the pavement tables, their blue and white striped sunshades swaying in the wind from the sea. A wave of nostalgia takes her by surprise and she stops abruptly, one foot on the ground, marvelling that despite all that has happened in the intervening years so much about this place remains unchanged.

There are more buildings along the quayside now, several other small hotels, many more leisure boats, a much larger fishing fleet, and both the harbour and the town have been smartened up and their boundaries extended in all directions. But it is still essentially a small fishing port with a good tourist trade in summer. The hotel too has been renovated since the days when Flora and her parents arrived for their holiday and were greeted by Suzanne's parents. White paint, white linen, pale timber floors and furniture have transformed the bedrooms, and a complete renovation of the café–restaurant has almost doubled its size. While still instantly recognisable from the outside, the interior of the hotel is very different from the dull and poky rooms where she, Suzanne, and in subsequent years Connie too, had played hide and seek in the wardrobes and behind the heavy curtains. Suzanne has lived in this place all her life, helping her parents and eventually, with her husband Jacques, buying them out, taking over the business and moving into the big top floor flat.

Flora takes a deep breath of the salty air and starts pedalling again, along past the seaweed coated steps where she and Suzanne had sat that first summer navigating their way to friendship with Flora's schoolroom French and Suzanne's slightly better English. Further on, where the sea wall stretches out away from the land to enclose the port, the fishing boats are returning, the fishers unloading their catch, spreading nets, piling up lobster pots, just as their fathers and grandfathers have done for decades. Fishing has a long and respected tradition along this coast and in this little port, the hotel is part of that. Not simply a haven for holidaymakers, it is also home to fishermen and women, who come here after a night's work, hosing themselves down at the far end of the quay before heading inside for their breakfast.

As Flora slows her pace outside the hotel and swings into the side alley, she can see through the window that the first of the fleet are already ensconced at the tables waiting for their coffee. Suzanne will be racing frantically between the café and the kitchen, cursing Flora's lateness. In the backyard, Nico, the baker's son, is unloading trays of bread, croissants and patisserie from the back of his van. Flora leans the bike against the wall, opens the kitchen door for him, and carries one of the trays into the kitchen.

'*En fin*!' Suzanne is harassed and irritable, her face flushed. She is in that hyperactive state that she thinks is efficiency but actually just makes her short-tempered and accident prone. 'Problems with the coffee machine, Nico is late, *you* decide to go to church.'

'Sorry,' Flora says, pulling off her jacket. 'There was a queue at the *tabac*.'

Suzanne looks up from the tray she is unloading. 'But you got my cigarettes?'

Flora tosses them to her across the table. 'I'll take over here while you get out there.'

'The German couple from room six are down already,' Suzanne says, putting four croissants into a small basket and adding it to her serving tray. 'What is the matter with these people? They're on their honeymoon but they're up and dressed before seven.'

Flora shrugs. 'That's the master race for you.'

Suzanne balances the tray on the flat of her hand with the ease of one who has grown up waiting tables. It's an enviable skill that in all the years they have run this place together, Flora has never managed to acquire. She ties on an apron, rinses her hands at the sink and begins to slice the baguettes and place them in baskets for the tables. In winter the break-fast trade is easy – mainly the men and women off the fishing boats – and in the last couple of years they have saved money by managing it themselves, bringing in Gaston the chef and Pierre the kitchen hand at eight to start on the lunches. The tourists begin to arrive at the start of spring and that's when they need the full staff on duty from six.

Flora makes up more baskets of the still warm bread, decants preserves into dishes, and rolls butter into balls between the old wooden pats that belonged to Suzanne's grandmother and which she won't consider replacing. She piles pastries onto a cake stand, replaces its domed glass lid, carries it through to the café, sets it down alongside the coffee machine, and heads back to the pleasant silence of the empty kitchen.

The café is Suzanne's comfort zone. It's what she does best, socialising with the locals and the tourists, keeping the coffee coming, pouring shots of cognac for the fishers who have returned on the tide. And it is Suzanne who maintains their relationships with the other harbour traders, and generally keeps them connected to the heart of Port d'Esprit. She is part of the town, more so even since the night of the terrible storm when Jacques went out to help secure the boats and was swept off the sea wall and crushed against it by a boat that had broken free of its moorings. Flora had been here on holiday at the time; the friendship that had begun on that first trip had lasted decades. She was almost fifty-two and had just resigned from her job in the sprawling north London school, where she'd been teaching for years, to accept a cushy-looking job as principal of a small, rather posh girls school near Eastbourne. It was the start of the summer holidays and she had planned to spend the first three weeks in France, before going back in time to prepare to take up the new job in the autumn term. But that freak storm came out of nowhere and caught the town by surprise.

'I'll stay on for a bit,' she'd reassured Suzanne in the dark days after Jacques' death. 'And I might be able to negotiate something with the school for a couple of extra weeks.' She had stayed for five weeks and the day before she was due to leave Suzanne had burst into tears.

'I don't know how I'll manage,' she'd said. 'I am *désolé* that you leave. Stay, Flora, please stay. You say always how much you love it here. We can run the hotel *à deux*.'

It had taken Flora only hours to decide. She *did* love Port d'Esprit. Gerald and Connie, her only remaining family, were on the other side of the world and she hadn't seen them for years. Suddenly, taking charge of a school full of assertive, uppity girls and opinionated staff seemed distinctly unattractive. She had withdrawn from her newly signed contract, gone back to London, packed up the contents of her flat and was soon back again, working full-time in the hotel, and sharing the top floor apartment. That was fifteen years ago, and here she still is.

They've had their problems, she and Suzanne. Negotiating the boundaries of live-in friendship with a working relationship has taken patience and tolerance. Most of the time it has worked well, but sometimes Flora burns with discomfort at what feels like an imbalance of power. Suzanne depends on her and says she couldn't run the business without her. She frequently points out that Flora is the one with the freedom to pack her bags and leave. But Flora knows that she has cut off most of her options by staying here. Now in her late sixties and with dwindling savings, starting over is a challenge that she frequently contemplates but may not be able to summon the fortitude to risk. And she often longs for quiet, for solitude, and for a place of her own.

It's after ten this morning before the breakfast crowd thins out and Flora has a chance to draw breath. By now, Suzanne is at a corner table in the café, meeting with people from the Bastille Day organising committee, among them her late husband's younger cousin Xavier. Flora, tidying the stack of menus on the bar, watches the animated group from a distance. She sees the way that Suzanne leans slightly towards Xavier, sees him stretch his arm along the back of her chair, sees their thighs pressed close together under the table. Perhaps, Flora thinks, she is not indispensable after all.

She turns away into the kitchen where Gaston and his staff are peeling and chopping. In the backyard laundry Prudence has the washing machines on the go and is ironing as if her life depends upon it. Flora heads through to the office, flops into the chair by the desk and switches on the computer. There is the usual mix of advertising material, some email reservations, e-bills and last of all a message from Connie with an attachment, both of which Flora opens first and prints immediately.

The funeral went well, Connie tells her, lots of people, lovely flowers, Andrew and Kerry both spoke very nicely, and the priest, who had been very fond of Gerald, did everything beautifully. Strange that, Flora thinks; they had been brought up Catholic and in his twenties Gerald had been particularly devout, but later he had become a fierce critic of the church. Had that changed, she wonders now, had illness and the proximity of death made him think again, or was he just hedging his bets?

There is a tap at the door. '*Excusez moi*, Flora.' Gaston sticks his head into the office. 'The *charcuterie*, they send the ham and the *pâté* but no *saucisson* . . .' he hesitates. 'You are all right?'

'Yes,' Flora says, looking up. 'Just thinking. No sausage?'

'*Non*. I think if you are going into town you can bring some? If not I send the boy . . .'

Flora sits looking at him, trying to focus her thoughts. 'I'm not going into town,' she says, taking Connie's email from the printer and getting to her feet. 'By all means send Pierre, he can take my bicycle. I *am* going out for a while though. When Suzanne's finished with her meeting, would you tell her I'll be back later?'

'Later?'

'An hour, maybe.'

He looks at her with obvious concern. '*Vous semblez un peu . . .*'

'I'm fine,' she says, and she picks up her jacket and heads for the kitchen door. 'Don't forget to tell Suzanne.'

'*D'accord*! You want I tell her where you go?'

'No,' she says. 'I really don't want that,' and closing the door behind her she sets off across the yard where the steam from Prudence's ironing machine is puffing the scent of freshly laundered linen into the crisp air. It's a smell that always transports Flora back to childhood, to Mrs Peacock, her mother's daily help, ironing in the large, rather chilly laundry off the kitchen of the house in Tunbridge Wells, the sheets and tablecloths, and everyone's clothes, all laid out in neat piles on the long shelf, ready to be returned to the linen cupboard, the bathroom and bedrooms. She pauses, savouring it briefly before opening the back gate and heading briskly along the path that runs the length of the cliff behind the buildings, to the steep track that leads up to the cape.

She presses on up to the first outlook point, putting height as well as distance between her and home, and stopping only briefly to catch her breath before slowing her pace as the climb becomes steeper. When she reaches the final section of rough stone steps cut into the rock face she drags on the hand rail to pull herself to the top, where she stops, doubled over, hands on her knees, lungs bursting, her heart pounding so hard she can feel the blood thumping in her ears. She leans against the signpost that points out the pathways to the various coves along the cape, her head spinning, waiting until her heart slows to a more normal rate. Ignoring the side paths she presses on along the unmade road that leads to the sharp promontory of Cap d'Esprit.

The wind is colder here and stronger, and that's all she thinks of as she strides on: the fierceness of the wind, the shafts of brilliant sunlight slicing through the pines, the steep drop of the cliffs and, metres below, the surging blue-green waves crashing against the rocks in dazzling bursts of white foam. The fierce beauty of the landscape, the rush and cut of the wind, the roar of the sea below, blot out everything else as she walks on over flattened earth and pine needles and sinks down on the wooden bench that faces across the bay and beyond it to the next headland, carved sharp and clear in the sunlight.

Leaning back Flora closes her eyes, her own heartbeat pounding in her ears beneath the roar of wind and water. Eventually, she straightens up, reaches inside her jacket, takes out the email and begins to read it again.

Gerald's death hadn't really come as a surprise but when Connie had called with the news a couple of weeks ago Flora was taken aback by the sudden and intense grief she felt. She'd come to terms with her feelings about Gerald years earlier – laid them to rest for her own peace of mind. He had cut her out of his life and she had decided to cut him out of hers. Her attachment was to Connie, and to the idea of her nephew and niece whom she had known only briefly as children. She and Gerald had fallen out for the first time when, a year after leaving school, she had decided to enter the convent and a year later was expelled before taking her final vows. And they were at loggerheads again in the late sixties when she'd turned her attention away from God and onto the Maharishi Mahesh Yogi and announced she was going to India. Gerald had been horrified, angry and disdainful; he called her irresponsible and shallow, and accused her of breaking their parents' hearts. But two years later she came home to find he'd forgiven her, and she'd surmised that his own happiness about his surprising engagement to Connie, originally Flora's closest friend, had made him a more generous and forgiving person, although she was far from happy about this proposed marriage. When he and Connie had been back in Tasmania near their parents in the seventies, Gerald had urged her to join them.

'Come back to Tassie,' he'd said. 'Stay with us.' He'd even sent her money for a ticket. And so she had gone there, to that strange, enticing white house that he and Connie had furnished with second-hand furniture, and some hand-downs from the parents, and where every day was tainted by her unease over how much Connie seemed to have changed – she'd abandoned her planned career in the opera, and committed herself to domesticity.

Still, she'd stayed with them for almost a year and it was starting to feel like home again, she was even thinking of settling back permanently in Australia. But then she and

Gerald had the row to end all rows, and she'd moved out to a tiny bedsitter in Hobart where she stayed for a few weeks trying to decide what to do. This time there was no generosity or forgiveness; he treated her as an alien, as though she had committed some unspeakable crime, and drew their parents into the argument, so that the whole family – with the exception of Connie – had virtually disowned her. Banned from both houses, and cut out of their parents' wills, she finally gave up on her family, bought a ticket and headed back to London by sea. By then she was in her thirties and had lived most of her life in England, so she had felt as though she was going home. Only Connie had stayed in touch, their letters, emails and more recently online conversations had been Flora's only connection to her family. There were many times when Flora found it hard to accept that Connie didn't put up more of a fight for her and their friendship, that she let Flora's estrangement from the rest of the family go on for so many years, but despite that they have always been in close touch. And now Gerald is dead.

Flora returns to the email, and the copies of the death notices that Connie has scanned for her, most of them placed by people Flora has never heard of. But she pauses longest at her own. *'In loving memory of my brother Gerald, who always tried to do his best.'* How ridiculous! How could she have written it? Loving memory, my foot, she thinks now, trying to remember what had been going on in her mind when she filled in the form on the newspaper website, added her credit card details and pressed send. In no way does it represent the utter chaos of her feelings about him that had erupted with the news of his death. Flora sees Gerald now as she did all those years ago, as a ruthless and selfish man who only ever did his best in his own interests.

A biting wind stings the salty tracks of the few tears that have trickled to her cheeks, and wraps itself like an icy scarf around her neck. Flora shivers, turns up the collar of her jacket and returns to the email. They will scatter the ashes later today, Connie writes. Flora glances at her watch – the time difference means they will have done it by now and she pauses, thinking of them somewhere up in those tree-clad slopes on Mount Nelson, standing together, taking turns to send Gerald on to wherever he was destined. She turns back to the email. Connie writes that she needs to get away for a while. Do they have a vacancy at the hotel at the end of March? Flora stuffs the email back into her pocket and gets to her feet. Connie is coming! Connie who goes back to school-days, to fish and lumpy mash on Fridays, to hopscotch in the playground, to hockey and netball, to grazed knees and learning to use tampons, and whispering over fan letters to Tommy Steele and Adam Faith. Connie, who has for so long been a distant but emotionally reassuring presence in Flora's life. Connie is coming. And Flora pushes her windswept hair back from her face and sets off along the path and down the steep steps home to tell Suzanne.

# *Three*

**B**rooke, curled in the window seat in the row behind her parents, feels her eyes glaze over as the flight attendant demonstrates the safety procedures. She sets her iPod to shuffle and stares at the bits of her mother's hair that she can see around the sides of the headrest. Sitting behind them is better than being alongside or even in the row in front, where the desire to block them out competes with the possibility of eavesdropping on their conversation. They're pissed off with each other, have been for ages, but Brooke hasn't been able to work out what's happening. She thinks they're both pretty hopeless, but her mother is the worst, running her stupid gallery – really who cares? People pay thousands of dollars for paintings because her mother tells them some weird guy or one of those drippy women is going to be the next big thing. At least her father actually knows something about art, that's why he gets to decide who gets money from the State Government, at least she thinks that's more or less what he does. He's quite important anyway, lots of people think so, except of course her mother.

Brooke reckons it's school that keeps her sane. She has friends; Donna is probably the closest, even though they don't hang out together much, not like some of the others. Some of the girls call her 'the cat that walks alone' but in a nice kind of way and the school's not bad. Some of the teachers are quite cool, so at least her parents got one thing right. At twelve Brooke had fallen in love with Mademoiselle Marchand, who had arrived fresh from Lyons to teach French and Spanish. French is now her strongest subject and she is obsessed with all things French. Sometimes she makes herself feel better by fantasising that she is not her parents' daughter, but the love child of a glamorous French couple. The philosopher Bernard-Henri Lévy would do fine for her father, she's seen pictures of him in *Vanity Fair*. He was wearing a white linen shirt, open almost to the waist, a cream linen jacket and jeans, and looked more like a movie star than a philosopher. At one point she had thought that Mademoiselle Marchand, with her long dark hair, always slicked back in a neat bun like a ballerina, and with her selection of elegant suits and little black linen dresses, would be divine as a mother. But recently her fantasies have become more ambitious, and she fancies the idea of someone more exotic – a beautiful and eccentric writer or singer perhaps. Brooke hasn't yet decided on a specific candidate for mother, Colette might have been good or Anaïs Nin, but unfortunately they are both dead. She's considered and dismissed Juliette Greco and Simone Signoret, and is now close to settling for Juliette Binoche. But the way she feels now, as the plane reaches cruising height for the flight back to Melbourne, is that anyone would be better than Linda.

Peering down at the Tasmanian coastline still partially visible through the cloud she thinks about her grandmother, getting all stroppy with them the previous day. She'd never seen Nan like that before, it was always Granddad who told people off and got into arguments with her father and Auntie Kerry. This new version of Nan was different and interesting. This morning, just before they left, they'd been in Granddad's old study and Brooke had chosen a paperweight that she wanted as a memento. She'd stood there, watching Connie wrapping bubble wrap around the paperweight, thinking how little she knew about her.

'What did you want to do when you were my age, Nan?' she'd asked.

Connie stopped wrapping and looked up. 'A singer,' she'd said. 'I was a really good singer at school, and the teacher told me I should study music.'

Brooke was amazed, she'd never heard anything about her Nan singing.

'So did you do it?'

Connie had closed the top of Brooke's bag and leaned on it. 'No. Well, yes and no. Mum got me a voice coach and when I finished school I auditioned for the Guildhall School of Music, which was *the* place to go in London in those days. I had to wait around and it was really competitive but eventually I was accepted. It was difficult because by that time my father had raced off to Spain with another woman and Mum and I were really hard up. I had to work part time as well. The only thing I was any good at, apart from singing, was French, like you, Brooke, so I got a part time job waiting tables in a French restaurant. It was the only way we could afford for me to stay on at the Guildhall.'

'Did you want to be in musicals and stuff?' Brooke asked.

Connie laughed. 'No, although I suppose I wouldn't have minded that. I wanted to be an opera singer, I wanted it desperately, and apparently I was quite good.'

'So why did you stop?'

There was a longish pause, then her Nan had looked up and out of the window before turning back to her.

'In the middle of my final year, I had an audition coming up and I'd already done two small solo concerts but then Mum died, quite suddenly in an accident. I was on my own.

Flora, my best friend – your granddad's sister – was in India, and so Granddad stepped in to help. He just sort of scooped me up and took over everything, but I dropped out of study that term and I just didn't go back.'

'But why?' Brooke asked.

Connie sighed. 'I've asked myself that so often, Brooke,' she'd said. 'I still do. It's complicated. Things changed from Gerald just helping me. We started going out together and instead of just being a friend he became my boyfriend,' she'd hesitated then and looked away from Brooke, then back again. 'Then, a few months later, we got engaged.'

The silence seemed awkward suddenly and Brooke wondered if she'd said something to upset her Nan.

'But what about the singing? You must have kept on singing?'

Connie shook her head. 'No, I always meant to but somehow it just didn't seem to fit in with married life.'

Brooke dropped down abruptly to perch on the arm of the sofa. 'But lots of opera singers are married, Nan.'

'Of course they are today, Brooke, and yes, I suppose it wasn't uncommon then, but it was more common for women to give up their careers when they got married. Especially in a family like Granddad's who were rather old-fashioned and conservative.' She paused. 'Anyway, thankfully things are very different now, women have more choices.'

'Yes, but it's so sad for you . . .'

'No, darling, it's not.' Connie looked Brooke in the eye. 'I married a good man, I've been happy and very lucky. I'd always wanted a family, even as little girl I told my mother I wanted two children, a boy and girl. I got them and I got you, Ryan and Mia as well.'

'I suppose.' They are silent for a moment. 'I still think it's sad though. Didn't you ever do any singing?'

'A bit. I joined a choir when we lived in London, and we sang in some little local concerts, but then I got pregnant, and we moved here to Australia, and that was the end of singing.'

Brooke had run her fingers along the worn leather of the sofa arm. 'Didn't you mind?'

Connie smiled. 'It's not as straightforward as that. There were times when I wished I'd gone on with my career, you know, tried to have it all. But none of us gets everything we want, Brooke, you learn about compromise and also you learn to appreciate what you *have* got.'

Brooke nodded. 'I suppose . . .' she hesitated. 'I'm never going to get married.'

Connie nodded. 'Okay, but you may not always feel like that.'

Brooke had zipped up her bag and turned back to her. 'Nan, now that Granddad's . . .'

'Now that he's dead?'

'Yes,' she was sure she was blushing, 'could I come here sometime and stay with you?'

Connie had looked at her then in a way Brooke had never seen her look before.

'Wouldn't it be boring for you?'

She shook her head. 'It'd be so cool to be here and just hang out with you. We could talk French to each other when there's no one else around.'

'I'd love it too, darling,' she said, 'really love it. I've missed out on so much of your life, of everyone's lives while . . . well, anyway, do come, when I get back. In the school holidays. Meanwhile I'll send you some pictures and tell you about the places I go. You don't have to read it all, just . . .'

'I'll read it,' Brooke had cut in. 'All of it, and write about Auntie Flora because she's so mysterious, no one ever talks about her.'

Connie had paused then, and given her that funny look again. 'No, no they don't. But I will – I promise.'

'Come on, Brooke,' Andrew had called up from down-stairs. 'The taxi's here, we'll be late for the flight.'

'I'll write to you, Brooke, and I'll tell you about Flora, I promise,' Connie had said as she led the way downstairs.

'Whatever have you been doing?' her father had asked, taking her bag.

'We were talking,' Connie had said. 'Brooke would like to come to stay with me when I get back.'

Andrew straightened up. 'Really? Won't that be a lot of trouble for you?'

'Oh Andrew, really!' her nan had said. 'Sometimes I wonder what planet you live on.' And she'd hugged Brooke and given her a little push towards the backseat of the cab. And then she'd hugged her father and Brooke heard her say, 'You need to chill out, darling, or you'll be dead before you're fifty.' And she kissed him and he'd got into the car looking as though someone had punched him.

Brooke fiddles with her headphones and sinks further into her seat wondering what she would be willing to give up to marry a stupid man. She wishes she'd asked Connie whether giving up her music to marry Granddad was *really* the right decision, because if she'd gone back to music school and ended up being an opera singer she wouldn't have had to spend years looking after an old man and waiting for him to die. Perhaps she was just being brave.

Brooke thinks of her granddad, and the last time she saw him. She sort of loved him, she supposed, but by the time she'd been old enough to get to know him properly he was pretty sick, hard to talk to, often hard to understand. She'd hated it when his food dribbled out of the side of his mouth, or his nose ran. She knew it was wrong of her to mind those things, but she couldn't seem to help feeling that way. It was hard to think of him as a normal person, hard to try to love him when he slurred his speech like a drunk, and bits of him jerked around as though they had a life of their own.

Brooke shakes her head and skips a couple of tracks on the iPod. I am never going to get married, she reminds herself, and I'll never have children, and I will never ever give up anything for some stupid boy who wants to marry me.

\*

They agree to share the drive home to Launceston and Kerry, irritated and ill at ease after her encounter with an unusually assertive Connie, takes the first shift. Mia is asleep in minutes, Ryan plugged into some game on his iPod, and once out of the city Chris drops his seat to a reclining position. Kerry takes a quick sideways glance at him and sees that his eyes are closed. It's a relief; the last thing she wants is some sort of post mortem on the way home. She's always an anxious driver and so is at her best behind the wheel in an otherwise empty car, or not involved in a conversation. The tension in her body relaxes slightly and she shifts her position and at that moment Chris brings his seat upright again.

'You were a shocker yesterday,' he says. 'An absolute shocker. I can't think what got into you.'

'I was just saying what I thought. I don't see what's wrong with that. It's my father that's died, I'm entitled . . .'

'Grief does not entitle you to be rude and hurtful, love. Your ma is grieving too and she has a perfect right to go anywhere she likes, with whomever she likes, and what she said about us not helping was absolutely spot on.'

'I couldn't face it, you know I couldn't,' Kerry says, 'having to do all that stuff for him, washing him, feeding him, cleaning him up when . . . well . . . sorting out his clothes. He was my father – I shouldn't have to do that.'

'Unbelievable,' Chris says, shaking his head, and he turns away from her, looking out of the passenger window. 'Y'know, Kerry, one of the things I love most about you, always have done, is your relentlessness in telling it how it is. But yesterday you were set on telling it how it isn't, grabbing at straws and turning them to cudgels to beat your mother with. There's a difference between assertiveness and aggression, and you really crossed the line.'

Kerry's heart is pounding in her chest and she feels the heat of the embarrassing crimson blush that always gives her away. She hates it when Chris disapproves of something she's said or done, but she's always been able to handle it and make her case. Now it rocks her because she knows she was in the wrong, but can't admit it. To do so would rip apart the suffocating blanket that has been threatening to smother her for months now, and that simply won't shift.

'I had to say what I thought about the house,' she says, hearing the defensiveness of her tone. 'It's my responsibility to let Mum know my concerns about her staying there alone.'

Chris lets out a short laugh. 'That's bullshit. If that were really a concern for you, you'd have been talking about it with me months ago when we knew your dad was close to the end. Yesterday was not about the house and where Connie should live. And what was all that stuff about Farah? "She's not one of us!" What's that supposed to mean? Not what it sounds like, I hope. You teach Muslim kids at school. You get on all right with their parents, you've signed petitions for onshore processing and against the treatment of asylum seekers.'

'They don't stay in my house,' Kerry says, searching for a justifiable position. 'It's different.'

'No it's not. Don't play games with me about this, Kerry. Anyway it's not *your* house and before your da disappeared into wherever he disappeared to he was okay with Farah doing all the things you couldn't face doing. And now you're spitting chips because she's going to stay in the house and look after the dog? I don't know what's going on with you, but I do know that none of this is really about where Connie lives, nor about Farah.'

Kerry feels nausea rising in her chest. She swings the car sharply onto the hard shoulder, slams on the brakes and snaps off her seatbelt. In seconds she is out of the car and striding towards a wooden bench that overlooks a sweep of fields scattered with a few sheep. Breathing deeply to calm the nausea, she drops down on the bench and sinks her head in her hands. She and Chris have always been frank with each other; she'd demanded that of him from the early days of their relationship. Since she was old enough to understand what was happening between her parents she had watched time and again as her mother bottled her own feelings and opinions and went along with what her father wanted. Kerry had come to understand that this was Connie's well-intentioned effort to keep the peace, to provide a home life free of parental dissent and argument. But it had always irritated her, she had thought her mother worthy and capable of so much more, but she had never broached the subject. Kerry loved her father, but had come to resent the routine acquiescence to his wishes and demands – demands that were still respected when he was no longer capable of expressing them.

'So what's happening?' Chris says, sitting down beside her on the bench.

Kerry shrugs; she feels remote from him, almost numb.

'Look, darlin', you can't go on like this – you really upset your ma. Sure, you lost your pa, but she's lost her husband.'

Tears crawl down Kerry's cheeks and Chris offers her his handkerchief.

'It's the selfishness,' she says eventually, and her voice sounds cold and distant, as though the numbness has taken over. 'The selfishness of it all.'

'Selfishness?'

'Yes, all the time – ever since the kids were born – she's never been there for me. Everyone else's mother is ready to take their kids, ready to help out, but not my mother. No babysitting, no taking the kids overnight, helping out with all the work, nothing.' She knows it's all wrong but she's digging herself in deeper now.

Chris inhales sharply. 'Darlin', we live more than two hours' drive away, Connie could hardly pop over to babysit for the afternoon. Besides, she's been looking after Gerald full-time virtually since Ryan was born, and all of Mia's life. And she *did* drive up for an occasional day and stay overnight when she could get someone to look after him.'

'Oh you always make excuses for her, don't you? According to you she's the bloody perfect mother-in-law, I suppose.'

'I'm very fond of her. I admire her and, yes, as a mother-in-law she's as good as they get. What *is* this all about?'

'Well, she may be the best mother-in-law but she's been a lousy mother and grandmother, so wouldn't you think that now that she's free she'd jump at the chance to put that right? She could sell that place straight away and come up to Launceston, but no, she won't even talk about it. Instead she's going off on this ridiculous holiday for lord knows how long . . .'

'Okay,' Chris says, standing up. 'This is totally unreasonable. Come on, get back in the car, we're going home and I'll drive.' And she watches as he walks back to the car, slides into the driving seat, starts the engine and sits there waiting.

Kerry sighs and rubs her eyes with the heels of her hands. So now she's made things even worse. She gets to her feet and takes a last look out across the countryside. It's all so beautiful, so green, so pure, the sheep grazing peacefully in the distance. Chris always says that Tasmania captured his heart because in so many ways it is so like his home in southern Ireland.

'And you're just like the women in my family,' he'd told her when they first met. 'Formidable they are, smart, feisty women with their feet on the ground, who'll argue the hind leg off a donkey when they believe in something. I love that in you.'

She shakes her head, takes a deep breath and turns back towards the car.

'So I've stuffed that,' she tells herself. 'My feet are nowhere near the ground and I don't seem to believe in anything right now.' And she walks back to the car, gets into the passenger seat, fastens her seatbelt, and turns away from Chris towards the window, wishing she could just reach out and touch him, touch anyone in a way that would help her understand what's happening to her.

# Four

lora weaves her way between the café tables out to the edge of the pavement, screws up her eyes and peers down the quayside hoping for a glimpse of the yellow Renault heading back to the hotel. Nothing. Sighing with frustration she checks her watch again – ten to four. Suzanne had promised to be back by three-thirty at the latest; if she doesn't show up in the next five minutes Flora will have to take the old Citroën van to St Malo to meet Connie's train.

All around her the pre-Easter holidaymakers are sipping tea and coffee or dawdling over wine, and Flora feels a stab of envy trying to remember the last time she had a real holiday. The year-round nature of the hotel business isn't conducive to holidays, although twice a year Suzanne always finds time to spend with her parents, who have retired to the south of France. Flora's occasional trips back to England don't qualify as holidays, being only a few days at a time, and usually packed with commitments. Last time she had stayed overnight in Nottingham with an old colleague from her teaching days, and they had gone together to visit a mutual friend who was seeing out his final weeks in a hospice. From there she'd gone

45

Liz Byrski

to London to squeeze in a film and an exhibition, and the next day a meeting with a solicitor about her will – not that she really has much to leave – and an appointment with the dentist. When she got back she was more exhausted than when she'd left. The days of three-week holidays in a hotel, fed, watered, laundered, and with the freedom to wander aimlessly, paddle, lie on a beach, or sit in a café and read a book, are long past.

It hasn't all been work of course, and much of it has been a very good life, but right now Flora sees herself as she fears others might see her: the willing helper, the dogsbody, making someone else's life work because she has no life of her own. There have been other times when she has glimpsed this but she's always pushed it away. She loves this place, the small and vibrant community, the dazzling scenery, the unpredictable weather, loves living in France. And yes, although she frequently feels irritated by Suzanne, she is very fond of her, otherwise she wouldn't still be here. But looking back over the last fifteen years Flora knows that she has been standing still while, in those same years, Suzanne has grown: recovered from her loss, made changes to the hotel, involved herself in the civic life of the town, had a couple of brief affairs, and now something is happening with Xavier, something serious that could change everything and leave Flora – where exactly?

She clears her throat, holds her hand up to shade her eyes again and in the distance, at the point where the main street turns onto the quay, she spots a glimpse of yellow. Is it? She hesitates . . . yes, thank god, it's five to four, she will probably just make it in time to meet the train. Relief doesn't assuage the complex emotions that are raging in her, but it diverts her attention. The last thing she needs now is to catastrophise her situation; she must concentrate on Connie, on the joy of spending time with her as well as the task of supporting her through her grief, and Suzanne, it seems, is not going to be much help with any of that.

'Why is Connie coming here?' she'd asked that morning.

Flora had put down her coffee cup. 'Well, it's obvious, isn't it? She's coming for a rest, a holiday after years of being a full-time carer. And she's always wanted to come back here. She says those holidays here were the best days of her childhood. She wants to see me, and of course you.'

Suzanne had taken a long final draw on her cigarette and stubbed it out in the ashtray. 'It's a long time ago. So long I barely remember.'

'Well, Connie remembers, and so do I,' Flora had said, feeling almost indignant.

'One thing I remember always though,' Suzanne said, extracting another cigarette from the packet on the table, 'is that Connie has not been a good friend to you.'

'What's that supposed to mean?' Flora asked, although she knew what Suzanne was getting at. 'Connie is my oldest friend, I've known her longer even than I've known you, and we were like sisters.'

Suzanne flicked her lighter and concentrated briefly on her cigarette. 'An *old* friend, yes, but a *good* friend would not accept what Gerald did to you – to throw you out, to turn your parents against you. To accept this situation is not the behaviour of a *good* friend.'

Flora had felt herself flush; the last thing she wanted was to discuss this with Suzanne. 'What else *could* she do? She was married to Gerald and had two young children. Was she supposed to walk out on her family?'

'She can fight for you. She can be like the dog with the bone, refuse to let go of it.'

Flora gave an irritable shrug and got up from the table. Suzanne was venturing into dangerous territory, giving voice to the undercurrent of resentment that Flora has, for decades, managed to subdue within herself. 'Look, Connie had no choice . . .' she began.

'*Pouf!*' Suzanne dismissed that with a wave of her hand. 'Of course she has a choice, there is always choice. I understand it is difficult – she does not want to leave Gerald, she has young children, of course it is difficult. But children grow up, the times change, the world changes, but Connie does not. She still does nothing. She calls you her best friend but does nothing to try to change things with Gerald. She does not even come to see you until Gerald is dead. This, I think, is a weak and selfish friend. You think I am harsh, Flora? Maybe I am but I have never understood how you can accept this without ever any criticism. I know you do not want to hear this, and of course I like Connie in all other ways, but this is not something I find easy to understand.'

'Well, I am not asking you to understand,' Flora had said, feeling far too vulnerable for comfort. 'Just accept her as a friend. I don't need you to be my champion, Suzanne. It hasn't been easy, but when this all happened back in the seventies I decided it would be unfair to rock Connie's boat. I'm delighted she's coming, and I don't want you to mess it up. And I really don't want to talk about this anymore.'

'Of course, if that's how you wish it,' Suzanne had said, getting to her feet and rinsing her cup in the sink. And she put a reassuring hand on Flora's shoulder. 'I don't understand this, but I respect what you say. I will pretend that I am English and I will not speak the truth about the unspeakable.' And she went off down to the kitchen leaving Flora to struggle with the turbulence of her own emotions.

The Renault comes to a halt alongside her now and Suzanne gets out. 'So sorry I forgot. I stopped to have a drink with Xavier. But you still have good time to get there I think.'

Flora nods irritably, slipping into the driving seat. 'Oh for goodness sake, Suzanne, you forgot to fill up with petrol. You said you would and now it's almost empty.' And clipping on the seatbelt she puts the car into reverse, turns it around and heads back down the quay.

\*

'So what do you think?' Flora asks Connie's reflection in the mirror as she flops onto the chair in her room later that evening.

What Connie thinks is that she feels like death. It's really all she's capable of thinking right now after almost thirty hours of travel during which she had only a few hours' sleep. She peers at her face in the mirror; the journey has added at least ten years to the way she looks. 'I think – well, I know – I'm glad to be here,' she says.

'I'm glad you're here too. But what do you think about the place, Suzanne, everything?'

Connie smiles, remembering her first visit to Flora's home in Tunbridge Wells when they were eight. The house, set in a walled garden, was in one of the best and leafiest streets in the town and to Connie it seemed enormous and like something from a history lesson. Victorian, Flora had said, 'That means it was built in the time of Queen Victoria who was also the Queen of Tasmania, where we come from.' Not that this meant anything much to either of them. There was a greenhouse at the side of the house and beside it a peach tree with real peaches growing on it, and as they walked around to the front Connie spotted huge dark red berries, like giant raspberries, growing up a trellis.

'What are they?' she'd asked, as Flora dragged her up the steps to the front door.

'Loganberries, dummy. Come on, I want to show you my room.'

Connie had never heard of loganberries, let alone seen them.

Flora raced up the steps and through the open door into a vast flagstoned entrance hall. 'Do hurry, Connie,' she'd cried, throwing her school hat onto a huge hallstand. And she raced up the wide, curving staircase and stopped halfway, looking back for Connie, who was still standing just inside the front door, shifting nervously from one foot to the other.

'It's all right, dear,' Mrs Hawkins had said, 'you can go up. Give me your hat and blazer,' and she smiled and picked up Flora's hat, which had slipped to the floor, and reached her hand out to take Connie's. 'Flora's so pleased that you've come.'

'So what do you think?' Flora had asked when she had shown Connie the Queen Anne style dressing table with the triple mirror, the patchwork quilt that her grandmother in Australia had sent for her birthday, and practically everything else she owned. The room was flooded with light, and Connie walked over to the window, peering past the perfect lawn, and the white roses in full bloom.

'What's that?'

Flora came over to her side. 'It's a swing hammock,' she said. 'We can have tea out there. But what do you think of my room?'

'I think it's the most beautiful room I've ever seen,' Connie had said wistfully, thinking of her own narrow and rather dark little room in the semi-detached house in a far less desirable area. 'It's like a princess's room.'

'Don't be silly,' Flora had said, 'princesses have much better rooms than this. But I'm glad you like it. Now that we're best friends you can come and stay here whenever you want.'

It really didn't seem that long ago . . . the memory was still vivid.

'Come on, Con,' Flora says now, shifting her position in the chair and edging Connie's suitcase out of the way with her foot. 'Tell me – what you think?'

'The town seems to have grown and smartened up and I've hardly seen anything yet, but as we drove through it seemed so familiar – the pharmacy, the patisserie, the old Café Centrale in the square, the church. So much the same, and here on the quay, a few more shops and cafés, but still a lovely little fishing port. And this . . .' she gestures around the room. 'The hotel looks much the same outside but so much nicer inside. This room is lovely, and the way they've opened up the café – Suzanne and Jacques did a great job, it's all so light and welcoming. Lovely, I'm so thrilled to be here.'

Flora nods in satisfaction. 'And Suzanne?'

Connie laughs. 'She's still Suzanne, rather cool and superior, and so elegant. How do French women do that and make it look so easy?' She leans over and grasps Flora's hand. 'I was thinking back to the first time I came to your house. Do you remember? Your mum made fairy cakes with pink icing, and we had tea in the garden sitting on that big swing hammock.'

'I do remember,' Flora says. 'And I doubt Mum made the cakes, it was probably Mrs Peacock.' She stops for a moment, looking hard at Connie. 'More than half a century, Con, it's a long time.' She glances at her watch and pulls a face. 'We'd better go down, or we'll be in trouble with madam downstairs. She's held the best table for us and she doesn't like to be kept waiting.'

It's an unseasonably warm evening for March and the tables are filling rapidly with locals and tourists. Suzanne pours them large glasses of red wine and joins them as they sit near the doors that open onto the outside tables. Connie feels herself beginning to unwind. Suzanne has organised a meal of local shellfish, a huge salad and a mouth-watering bowl of *pommes frites*, the pungent scent of Gauloises floats in through the doors along with the faint strains of an accordion being played nearby. It really does feel like a step back in time.

'Do you still have the Bastille Day dances?' she asks, the images suddenly clear as yesterday: the crowded square, a swaying mass of couples dancing to the music of a local band, the smell of cigarettes and warm bodies, an arm around her waist that kept creeping down to her buttocks, a pelvis thrust firmly against her own, garlic on his breath, and then another partner and another.

'We still have them,' Suzanne says. 'Just now we are organising. It's a pity you are not here in July, Connie, we could go dancing with the boys again.' She nods to a nearby table where five ageing men are talking animatedly. 'You've danced with some of them.' She waves to the group and the men raise their glasses and Suzanne raises hers and tosses her head and Connie glimpses the teenage Suzanne, the flirt who was prone to play with fire when it came to men.

Flora leaves the table and slips behind the bar, returning a moment later with a remote control in her hand.

'Remember this, Connie?' she asks, clicking the remote, and a familiar melody fills the bar.

Connie gasps, her hand flies to her mouth. 'Richard Anthony! Of course, *J'entends siffler le train,* of course I remember.'

'You played it so often on the jukebox the year Jean-Claude took off for Paris. You were heartbroken.'

'My father told you to stop playing it because it was annoying the customers,' Suzanne adds.

Connie nods, puts her hand on her heart. 'I remember. Oh god he was so gorgeous and, yes, I was heartbroken. We'd been writing to each other, so I came back here thinking he'd be waiting for me. But he was leaving to go to medical school, and said he was in love with the hairdresser's daughter. I was devastated. What year was that?'

'It was the year before we left school,' Flora says, 'a lifetime ago. You cried for days. Remember, we went to church so that you could light a candle and pray that one day you would see him again?'

Suzanne puts her hand on Connie's arm and nods in the direction of the five men. 'Your prayer is finally answered,' she says mischievously. 'The one on the right with the beard,' she says.

Connie gasps, 'That's Jean-Claude? But he's so old.'

'Only a few years older than us,' Suzanne says, 'but we are better preserved, I think.'

Connie stares at the men who are singing along with Richard Anthony – in fact the whole café seems to be singing. Jean-Claude is wearing a black t-shirt with long sleeves, his hair and beard gleaming silver under the café lights – a good-looking man in his seventies. Connie peers at him, searching for the young man, the Adonis with glorious golden skin and full lips, the blonde hair that curled moist and warm at the nape of his neck and muscles that rippled as he hurled himself into the waves. She is back in the dense haze of cigarette smoke in the local cinema – little more than a tin hut in those days – his arm around her shoulders, his thigh pressed against hers, and later, her arms wrapped around his waist as she rode pillion on the back of his Vespa. 'I would never have recognised him,' she says, 'nor him me, that's for sure.'

'He's the local doctor now,' Flora says. 'He's had two wives, five children and now he's single again. You could book a consultation.'

And as they laugh a wave of nostalgia for her youth, for lost opportunities, lost loves, and paths not taken surges up inside her. Her long-forgotten self taunts her, and the old men raise their glasses and cheer as the song ends.

'*Encore, encore,*' they shout, and Flora flicks the remote and the song begins again, and Connie knows that the melody will haunt her for days and nights to come.

\*

Hours later Connie wakes suddenly from a deep sleep and, sitting bolt upright, tries to remember where she is. The display on the alarm clock says it's two-thirty – just four hours since she came to bed. She flops back onto the pillows and closes her eyes, waiting for sleep to reclaim her, counting sheep, counting breaths and trying to ignore the creeping sense of panic that is slowly taking hold of her. She longs now for home, for her own bed, for the safety and familiarity of her own room, for the steady sound of Scooter's breathing from his basket in the corner, and for the feel of the sharp spring breeze off the Derwent filtering through the slats of the blind.

Back at home, coming here had seemed essential. There were many things she knew she wanted to do: reconnect with her children, learn to know her grandchildren better, build her friendship with Farah and her daughters, maybe find a way to sing again. But she had felt incapable of doing any of that without first connecting with herself. How ridiculous it sounds now; psycho-babble Gerald would have called it. And she had so nearly told the family about it, at lunch that day, but their interference and the tension she felt in it had made her hold back.

She throws off the bedclothes, gets up and opens the doors to the balcony. The night air is chilly but clear, the lights of the yachts bob gently in the harbour, and the beam of the lighthouse casts its luminous shaft in steady rotation between the town and the open sea. Beyond the quay, the glow of the street lamps curves around the bay bordering the sleeping town. Beautiful. A peaceful fishing port so very much as she remembered it, but what is she doing here? How can it possibly help?

She has run from her fear but brought it with her, tainting a place filled with the magic of childhood, of love and friendship; an unreal world that has evaporated with the passing of time, a place of memories. But reality is different. There have been so many times in her long marriage to Gerald when she has longed to be free, and never more so than during the last ten years. But what will she do with this freedom? Most of her adult life has been focused on Gerald, being his wife, supporting him in his work, responding to his decisions, living the life he had chosen for them both. But how is she supposed to live this freedom, overhung as it is with grief and guilt?

'Sometimes,' she remembers saying to Farah, 'I feel it's a privilege to look after someone I love, to do for him the things he can't do for himself. But a lot of the time I also feel it as a terrible burden, a curse that's poisoning me, slowly killing the love and replacing it with resentment.'

There had been times when she had simply longed for things to be normal again; to lie beside him and let their past envelop them, recharge the batteries of what had kept them together all those years. And there were the dark days when she had felt the urge to exact revenge for those times in the past when he had hurt or betrayed her. Theirs was, for the most part, she supposed, like so many other marriages, a mix of good and bad times. But the difference in their ages had, she thought, made more difference than she had ever anticipated. Gerald had been born in the early years of the war, while she, and Flora, were among the first of the baby boomers. By the time the sixties really started to swing they had been in their late teens but Gerald was already in his twenties, raised by conservative parents and educated at an elite private school in which traditional ideas about the status of men and women were constantly reinforced. He never questioned his own authority and just assumed that things would be done his way, his needs given priority. He had resisted the changes wrought by the women's movement and clung stubbornly to an earlier era. And Tasmania had proved more comfortable for him than England in that respect.

The onset of illness, coming as he was about to retire, had crushed him; the loss of autonomy, of control of his body, the limits of his mobility ate away at his self-esteem. He loathed his incapacity, was shamed and disgusted by it, and while always grateful for Connie's care it was clear that he frequently resented it.

'Promise me,' he had begged her in the days when he was still fairly self-sufficient, 'promise me you will never put me in a home.'

And Connie, who could envisage all too clearly what this might mean, had promised – against her better judgment.

When things became very bad she had thought he might recant, suggest a home or hospice for his own sake as well as hers, but he reminded her, several times, of that original promise. And she, while understanding his need, was unable to rid herself of resentment for the way it curtailed her life and her chances to know her children and grandchildren better.

It was only when Farah came into the house to help with Gerald's care that she had been able to share this dark side of resentment and frustration, and the desire to lay down the burden and never pick it up again. Farah had understood, and although she rarely spoke of her own loss, the haunting nature of their very different experiences of grief was understood between them and bound them together.

The lighthouse beam highlights the shadowy contours of the sea wall where she, Flora and Suzanne had so often sat as girls, kicking their sandy feet against the stonework. Connie recalls the feel of damp shorts stained green with seaweed, feels the sting of saltwater on bare legs that were always a mass of tiny scratches from the sharp little shells that formed a crust on the wall. Long and meaningful conversations were held on that wall about school and parents and, later, on the subject of boys, love and sex. Suzanne, perhaps by virtue of being one year older, or French, or on her own territory, or all three, had assumed the role of expert on matters of boys and sex, although she showed little interest in the subject of love. So it was on a day when Connie and Flora sat there alone, giggling with embarrassed fascination at a couple seated further along the wall, locked together in a passionate embrace, that they had got into a conversation about love.

'Do you think that when people fall in love they love each other like that forever,' Connie had asked, 'even when they're old?' The question had come from a dark place within her in which she constantly questioned the nature of her parents' relationship; the difficult silences, the hints of resentment, the snide remarks let fall. It seemed so much at odds with their behaviour as a lively, sociable and devoted couple outside their home.

Flora had paused before saying, 'I think that if you love someone, really love them, you can also hate them and different things will tip you one way or the other. Perhaps if you love someone a lot you just can't keep it up all the time,' she said.

Connie gets to her feet marvelling now at Flora's teenage insight into something that she herself has only learned through the course of a long marriage. How did Flora know that? Flora has always been so scared of love, and so often faltered at the borderline of commitment. Did she fear that darker side, or just never meet anyone with whom it was worth taking the risk? Connie sighs, the tiredness capturing her again now, and she turns back into the bedroom casting a last glance across the moonlit bay. Flora is her oldest friend but now they are here together after all this time Connie realises how little she knows of her life, how many gaps there are to be filled, bridges to be crossed before it can really feel like old times once again.

# *Five*

ndrew takes the lift down from his office on the thirteenth floor staring at his own reflection in its mirrored wall, until it comes quietly to rest in the executive car park. He's about to head straight for his car when he changes his mind and strides up the sloping ramp to the street and stops at the top, breathing in the damp air, watching commuters heading for home and wishing he'd never given up smoking. It's eight years now and he no longer craves cigarettes, just the excuse to escape from the office for a few minutes and stand here, hunched and shivering in winter, sweating in summer, smoking in companionable silence with the other outcasts.

'Be at the gallery by quarter past five,' Linda had instructed him this morning. 'I might need some last minute help. And it's good to have a few people in there when the doors open, puts the punters at ease.' She says this of every exhibition at the small, privately owned gallery in Toorak that she manages. 'It's Zachary's latest – amazing work, it'll knock everyone's socks off.'

'Not mine,' Brooke had said without looking up from her iPad. 'I've got a rehearsal.'

Linda had sighed and rolled her eyes. 'But I might need

help with the refreshments and, anyway, you're not *in* the wretched school play.'

'I'm assisting the sound engineer, and you always have the food catered. You just want me there to play dutiful daughter.'

Linda had shaken her head. 'Well, is that too much to ask? Anyway, *you'd* better be there, Andrew – five-fifteen, no later.'

Andrew had been about to invent a reason why he couldn't be there but changed his mind once he knew it was Zachary's gig. It's not that he has any interest in Zachary's work, which is, in his opinion, execrable, and the man himself a complete arse. Andrew can't imagine why Linda is risking her own excellent reputation on him, although of course he *can* and does imagine it, and that's why he is going to the opening – to work out whether this is reality or just imagination.

Andrew checks his watch; it's already quarter to six and Linda has called his mobile twice. She has staff and volunteers, caterers, and various youthful and pretentious hangers-on who see her as their point of entry into the elite of Melbourne's art world, but he knows she wants him there because of his position in the Department for the Arts. She thinks it raises her profile and the profile and credibility of the artists she exhibits. Andrew sighs and is about to walk back down the ramp but changes his mind for the second time, and weaves his way across the street through the slow moving traffic to the posh little café cum bar where he some-times has lunch, orders a double scotch, downs it quickly and then makes his way back to the car.

Half an hour later he is hesitating just inside the entrance to the gallery, which is already packed with the sort of crowd who always seem to turn up at Linda's events: well dressed, well heeled and many of them already on the way to being well oiled. He spots Linda at the far end of the room talking to a couple whose names he really ought to know but can't recall. She is wearing one of those A-shaped outfits she's very into at the moment. It looks like a series of different-coloured tents worn one on top of the other; she says it's called 'block colour pyramid layering' and is the latest fashion. Andrew thinks she may have made this up. Around her neck odd shaped lumps of wood painted in vivid colours hang from a black silk cord. And she's had her hair cut and coloured – today, obviously, because it wasn't like this at breakfast. It's a deep sort of claret red, cut short and dead straight on one side and much longer to an angled point on the other. Andrew thinks it looks awful to the point of ridiculous but doubtless her sycophantic friends think it's incredibly chic. The thought of having to stand beside her and be polite to strangers drains him of energy and he reaches out to grab a glass of wine from the tray of a passing waiter.

As he stands there watching, almost obscured by a pillar, Andrew spots Zachary detaching himself from a small group of admirers. He's recently grown a stubbly, grey speckled attempt at a beard and is dressed, as always, entirely in black: jeans, skivvy, leather jacket rather too tight for his middle-aged spread. To Andrew's eyes he looks like a throwback to the sixties and as though he needs a good wash. He watches as Zachary strolls over to where Linda is standing and she turns slightly, and begins the introductions. As he leans forward to shake hands with potential buyers Zachary slides his other hand down to the curve of Linda's bottom, stroking and squeezing. She looks up at him, smiling, edging closer.

Andrew inhales sharply. He's been here less than a couple of minutes and knows all he needs to know; if he were still in any doubt, he need only look at the expression on Linda's normally rather haughty face to see that this is a woman in thrall to the artist, and it's nothing to do with the paintings. He glances around wondering whether anyone he knows might be watching him watching his wife being groped by this ridiculous poseur. For months, more than a year in fact, he's been on the point of telling her he wants a divorce; several times he has geared himself up to it but he has always fallen at the first fence. But evidence that she is shagging Zachary firms his resolve, gives him, he thinks, a grievance sharper and more focused than just the fact that he no longer loves her, doesn't even like her much anymore, finds her boring, shallow and overbearing. It's not as if she needs or wants him, hasn't done for years, although career-wise she certainly thinks it's useful to be married to him.

Alongside his anger and fear of humiliation he feels a sense of relief. He imagines the house without Linda in it, furnished in his undoubtedly uncool and more comfortable style. He sees it transformed from the stark awkwardness of a show home to a real home where he can scatter his newspapers and books, put his socked feet up on the coffee table, and where the roof will not fall in if he leaves a dirty cup by his chair overnight and doesn't make the bed before he goes to work. What joy, what freedom. On the other hand there will doubtless be a long and painful battle before he reaches such a state of bliss.

He longs to stride across the room in outrage and punch Zachary, to make a scene, humiliate them both, draw disapproval and scorn down on them, then stalk away victorious. The trouble is that he doesn't really feel outrage, just the liberation of knowing that the end is nigh. He remembers his father: 'You have the upper hand,' Gerald would have said. 'Don't screw it up by descending to their level.' He'd had a big thing about dignity, his dad. Had he been here now he would have counselled icy calm, steely politeness and eviscerating language all combined with an implacable expression. That's what Andrew knows he needs now – well, not now, not here, but later, at home, when Brooke has gone to bed he will prove himself to be his father's son. He hopes he has the chutzpah to carry it off; cool and superior he can manage very well but he knows he lacks his father's cutting edge. But there has to be a first time. He parks his empty glass on another passing tray and turns back out of the door, leaving as quickly and quietly as he came.

*

The rehearsal is almost at an end when Andrew reaches the school and he slips into a chair in a darkened area at the back of the hall watching as the teenage actors struggle through their remaining lines in tones that indicate they have had enough for tonight. There's a scene change and a teacher directing the students to move here or there. Eventually they grind on to the end and there is a smattering of applause from half a dozen hangers-on who are sitting down at the front.

The teacher calls the cast and crew together onto the stage for a brief pep talk and Andrew sees Brooke, in jeans and a black t-shirt, her fine reddish hair tied back in a ponytail, wander onto the stage, and his breath stops in his chest at the sight of her. She'll be sixteen in a few months and could pass for more; here among her friends she seems so unlike the rather surly teenager, cut off from him by her headphones, or irritably slamming her bedroom door. As she sits down cross-legged on the boards she seems totally detached from him – like someone from another world, another life. His distance from her strikes him as quite shocking. When did they last have a real conversation? When did he last ask her what she was doing, whether she was happy, what sort of friends she has? Has he asked her anything at all about the play? How long is it since he talked to her rather than just issued instructions or edicts about the time he expects her back, about homework, or exam results? What does she think of him? Andrew feels his neglected love for Brooke forming into a painful lump in his chest. He leans forward, sinking his face into his hands, and sits like this while the teacher talks about interpretation, energy, concentration and the importance of timing.

What will happen to Brooke when he and Linda split up? Will she understand? Will she forgive him, or side with her mother? There is a lot of talking now, the teacher is winding up and reminding them to be on time for the next rehearsal. Someone switches on the auditorium lights and the students get to their feet. Andrew steadies his breathing, gets up and walks down towards the stage.

'Oh, hi, Dad.' Brooke seems awkward, embarrassed by his unexpected presence.

'Hi,' he says, smiling up at her and then at the drama teacher who is reaching for his briefcase. 'I was passing so I thought I'd see if you needed a lift.'

'I thought you were going to the gallery.'

'I did, but my heart failed me,' he says. 'It was all white wine and canapés, and I wanted a cheeseburger. You?'

She nods, relaxed now. 'Cool, but you'll be in dead trouble with Mum.'

He looks up at her, pulling down the corners of his mouth. 'I know, but a cheeseburger and fries with you would more than make up for that.'

'I'll get my stuff,' Brooke says, grinning. And she heads off backstage and returns immediately, a long green scarf wrapped around her neck and her school backpack slung over one shoulder, looking younger now, more vulnerable. She is totally unlike her mother, he thinks, and she has her grandmother's eyes. A flash of memory burns him with longing: his mother reaching out to put her arms around him, to comfort him over something – a lost football match, a cut knee, a failed exam – and he wants that comfort now. He aches for it, for her ability to soothe the sore spot, to reassure him that things will all work out okay. For months he has felt that splitting up with Linda will fix everything, but now that this is within reach he sees that it will take more than this to fix his life – work has become little more than routine, his fitness has slipped and Brooke is almost a stranger. Not to mention dealing with his mother and Kerry once Connie returns from her trip. It all seems insurmountable. All he knows is that escaping from his marriage would be a pretty good starting point.

He glances sideways at his daughter as they walk out across the car park. Choose me, Brooke, he begs her silently. Please choose me. I'll do the best I can, better – much better – than I have ever done before or am doing right now, if you only choose me. He clicks the remote control and the car lights flash.

'Are we going to McDonald's or Hungry Jack's?' Brooke asks, sliding into the front seat.

'Up to you, I'm at your ladyship's disposal,' he says, wondering whether he sounds normal, or pathetic, like the desperate, needy loser he feels.

\*

## Bloomsbury, London

In his flat above the bookshop Phillip Tonkin lights a cigarette and draws lovingly on it, thinking yet again how increasingly hard it is to be a smoker these days; so many places ban it, so many people disapprove. You can't even smoke in a pub now. To Phillip, pubs no longer seem like real pubs without the faint haze of tobacco smoke as you walk in the door, and some old codger in a corner of the public bar constantly trying to relight his pipe. And what about flirting? How do you flirt without smoking? Nothing beats the moment of eye contact as you light a woman's cigarette and then your hands touch. Phillip brushes a fleck of ash off the lapel of his blue linen jacket.

It's hard to come to terms with the fact that a lifelong comforting habit is now socially unacceptable. One of the advantages of living alone is that he has the freedom to smoke whenever he chooses. He's not allowed to smoke in the shop, even though he owns it, because it's a workplace. And even if he tried to have a quick fag in the little back office or the stockroom, Bea would find out and give him hell. She's a tough old coot, but he couldn't do without her – she knows the stock back to front and inside out. She's become a bit of a Bloomsbury institution. Her reputation has travelled far and wide; people come into the shop to have her hand-pick titles for them, even to be interrogated by her about their seriousness as book buyers. Phillip frequently cringes at the way she challenges customers' requests, criticises their choices and bears them off instead to another shelf to sell them something completely different. But they return time and again, like prisoners volunteering for torture, and as they rarely leave without having bought at least a couple of books, Bea is worth her weight in rare first editions.

They were at university together, and their shared passion for books has been the basis of a long, although frequently combative, friendship. Bea's career in publishing that ended with retirement a few years ago has now become a new career selling books. The sign above the shop says *Tonkin's New, Second-hand, Remainders and Rare Books*, but it seems to Phillip that it is less Tonkin's and more Bea these days. To her, all books are rare and precious, with the exception of memoirs written by anyone who has ever been in a reality TV show.

'I've spent my life cultivating writers,' she'd once told him. 'I've seen them at their best and their worst, on drugs and off them, blind drunk, starving in garrets and lounging around in penthouse suites. Turning vegetarian because they can't afford meat, and even selling their bodies to buy a new type-writer or computer. I've had them lie to me, try to bribe me with gifts, abuse me and beg me. Writing books is not for sissies, and I don't make judgments.'

It's not true of course; she is hugely judgmental. Last year he'd discovered she was binning the recently published memoir of a *Big Brother* contestant. More recently the arrival of several complete second-hand sets of a best-selling erotica series had her foaming at the mouth. 'There's plenty of women's erotica if that's what they want,' she had stormed. 'Erotica with proper sentences, diverse vocabulary and actual ideas, elegantly and eloquently crafted, but this . . .' and he'd had to instruct one of the other staff to shelve the books and then keep checking that Bea hadn't smuggled them out to the bins. She's always been stroppy, and now she's become some sort of legend in her own lifetime.

Resting his cigarette on the edge of an ashtray Phillip leans across the desk and pushes open the window. Cool spring air and the sounds of the street float in – the beloved background music of his life. He settles into his swivel chair from where he can see right up the street to the sign outside Russell Square underground station. 'Small pleasures,' he murmurs, sifting through the personal mail he has brought up from the shop; the rest he left down there for Bea. She wouldn't have let him get his hands on it anyway in case he lost track of something. Small pleasures: *The Guardian*, a fag, and Bloomsbury at his feet.

'You're an anachronism, sitting there, smoking, still surrounded by books, peering at the small print,' his ex-wife, Lorna, had told him recently. 'It's the twenty-first century, Phillip. Get yourself a Kindle so that you can adjust the font.'

'Kindle schmindle,' Phillip says aloud now as he rips the plastic wrapper off the latest newsletter from his old school, 'ebooks indeed. Smoking banned and real books being edged out. Heresy.' It's happened with music of course, cassettes first, then CDs, now it's all downloading onto phones and iPods. Thank goodness he's hung on to his vinyl, and stocked up on a lifetime's supply of styluses when he saw it coming.

The fate of *real* books, printed ones, is a constant source of worry to him, not just the potential loss of business in his own shop, but the whole global shift that could mean that real books just disappear. What is a home, a room, any place at all without books, without the smell of print and paper, the heft of a book in the hand, the joy of stroking covers and flicking through pages, of making those sinful notes in the margins, or falling asleep on the beach with an open paperback on one's face. It won't happen in his time probably, but the threat, he knows, is there, already he can sense it, and he frequently dwells gloomily on what this will mean for his grandchildren and their children. There may, he realises, be future generations of Tonkins who will never own a real book, will see them only as museum pieces, and who will never fully understand how their great-great-great-grandfather earned a living.

Phillip opens the newsletter and starts to work his way through it. It always comes as a treat, although he's finding that it doesn't give him quite the same pleasure now that even the alumni list is crammed with unfamiliar names. The articles are about people much younger than his own children, and he has to search for snippets about his contemporaries who seem to be dropping off their perches with uncomfortable frequency. There is an appeal for funds to build a new gymnasium, news of exam results and university scholarships, and profiles of retiring staff and their replacements. He always reads it from cover to cover. Why is there an advert for The Samaritans? This is a school newsletter; is it the students, the staff or the alumni who are prone to despair or suicide? He reads on, grumbling quietly about declining standards, until he reaches the obituaries and finds himself staring at a photograph of a very familiar face.

'Good lord,' he says aloud, peering more closely, 'Gerald Hawkins, good lord. Well, there's a sad thing.'

They'd been at school together and then at Cambridge, but some years later Gerry took it into his head to go back to Australia. Tasmania, for god's sake, end of the bloody world more like, although he'd seen a program about it on television recently and it did look rather lovely. But Australia! Gerry had always seemed more English than the English. Father posted here to the embassy of course, that was when Gerry first came to the school, how they first met: same class, same dorm, rugby team, rowing, sixth form and then Cambridge together, pissing off the porters, smoking dope, and the drinking. Christ, all that drinking, a wonder they survived it really.

Phillip stops reading for a moment, and stares out of the window. They'd exchanged letters for a few years and met once when Gerry had been in London on business, but that was back in the early eighties. Then it all tailed off except for Christmas cards but Gerry just stopped sending them and so Phillip eventually stopped a couple of Christmases later. He remembers the last time they'd met, they'd had lunch in the restaurant down the road, spent hours reminiscing. And now he's gone. Bloody shame. He wonders if Bea knows, but of course she doesn't or she'd have mentioned it.

Phillip returns to the obituary: the academic and sporting honours, the starred first, the Cambridge scholarship, and then his life in Australia. He'd married the lovely Connie of course, children, public service career and, good heavens – member of the State Parliament of Tasmania. So he'd gone into politics after all! Phillip tries to visualise Gerald as a politician – not difficult, he thinks, but Tasmania? Tiny place, does it really have its own parliament? 'Shows how little I know about Australia,' he says aloud. He was a Catholic of course, Phillip remembers now, and there was a religious phase – lots of agonising over contraception and the Church – although with Gerry it was always hard to tell whether those contentious bones that he'd throw into a discussion actually constituted something he was wrestling with, or was just something he did to start an argument. He returns to the obituary. Long illness, what rotten luck. Survived by wife, children, grand-children, and sister. Ah yes, Flora.

Phillip leans his head back and closes his eyes. A punt on the river, Flora and Connie in summer dresses, bare shoulders turning pink in the sun, legs stretched out enticingly between the seats, a bottle of champagne. He can almost smell the dark weedy water, Flora's French cigarettes and the scent of those girls' bodies sweating slightly in the heat. He remembers longing to slide his hand under Flora's skirt and up her smooth inner thigh to the warm acquiescent wetness that he was sure awaited him. Those were the days. Not that he'd had much luck with Flora though. He'd waited until Gerry was locked in a clinch with Connie, and then moved closer, pushing Flora's skirt above her knee, and the moment he put his hand on her bare thigh she'd thrust out her foot and kicked him hard in the balls. Fortunately she wasn't wearing shoes at the time, but just the same it doubled him up and he'd had a horrible feeling he might be going to throw up.

'Don't even think about it,' she'd hissed, leaning close to his ear as he moaned softly over the side of the boat. 'It's not going to happen, not in a million years.' He'd been worried that Gerald might have heard but he was far too involved with the intricacies of Connie's bra to be even remotely interested in his best friend's pain and humiliation.

Of course it would be Flora who'd have advised the school of Gerald's death. He should write her a note of condolence. 'Wonder where the hell she is now?' he murmurs, and then realises that of course the school will know. They'll have at least an email address, and if they won't give it to him perhaps they'll forward a message on to her. On the other hand a letter of condolence should really be written with old-fashioned pen and paper and sent snail mail – more respectful. What he wants is a postal address. And he picks up the phone, dials the number and, swearing at the automatic answering service, he presses the third option for the administration office.

\*

Andrew feels as though his head is exploding. All he wants is for this conversation, argument, fight – whatever it is – to be over. Any thought of emulating his father's icy restraint and cutting language evaporated as soon as it began. It's the night following the exhibition opening and Brooke has gone to a movie with friends.

'Okay,' Linda says now, her voice at a slightly lower octave than it has been for the last hour. 'Yes, I'm having an affair. I didn't plan it, it happened, and it happened because of you and our marriage. You've changed, Andrew – you used to be fun, we used to do stuff together. Now . . . well, I don't know what happened to you but it's like being married to a zombie, you're so remote and cut off. I was bored and miserable and then Zach came along. He's exciting, totally out there, he's creative and clever and funny, and I fell in love because I was bored to death with you and our marriage.'

'Do *not* blame this on me,' Andrew cuts in. 'You're the one having the affair, and not just having it but flaunting it at your poncy launch party, and plenty of other places for all I know. This is *not* my fault. Anyway, as far as I'm concerned this is the end. I want a divorce. Feel free to go and live with that ridiculous wanker if that's what you want, move out, but don't think for a moment that you can take Brooke. She'll stay here with me.'

'No way,' Linda says. 'You can have your divorce as soon as you want, what a blessed relief that will be, but this is my home and Brooke's home and you're the one that has to go. You get a place of your own and Zach can move in here with me and Brooke.'

Andrew's heart is pounding so hard that he feels it may burst out of his chest. 'In your dreams,' he shouts, 'in your fucking dreams! This is my home too, and my daughter is not going to live with that man either here or anywhere else, so you might as well get that into your head right now, Linda. You're the one that's in the wrong. You're the one who's screwing someone else. I am staying right where I am.' He turns away from her and sits on an arm of the lime green sofa that he hates. Arguing has always exhausted him, made him feel less of a man – so unlike his father. 'I'm not having this conversation anymore, but tomorrow I'm getting myself a lawyer and you'd better get one too. And we should agree not to say anything to Brooke until we've sorted the details out between us. Even someone as selfish as you must be able to see that she should not have to be dragged through arguments like this.'

Linda is silent for a moment. 'So I'm the selfish one, am I? Well, that's a laugh. But yes, I agree, we need to keep her out of it, behave as normal. Things are pretty chilly and have been for a while, so she probably won't notice. But don't kid yourself, Andrew, Brooke stays with me. She needs her mother and that's what any judge in any court will tell you.'

Andrew closes his eyes, trying to shut her out. The awful thing, he realises, is that Linda is probably right. If they end up going to court a judge might well favour the mother. But Brooke is almost sixteen, surely she'd be allowed some say in it . . . in which case, what *would* she say? Who would she choose? He hears the sound of a key being inserted in the front door. He gets up quickly.

'She's home,' he says in a low voice. 'Not a word about this. Agreed?'

Linda nods. 'Yep.' She takes a deep breath and straightens her shoulders. 'Hi, Brooke darling.'

Brooke mumbles a greeting from below and as Andrew hears her begin to climb the stairs to the living room he is gripped by a terrible sense of failure, a feeling that Linda will win, that Brooke will slowly be drawn into a new and alien life in which he has no part.

'Hi,' Brooke says, stopping as she reaches the top of the stairs. She looks from one to the other and raises her eyebrows. 'What's going on?'

'Nothing,' Andrew and Linda say in unison, their timing far too perfect to be natural.

Brooke's expression becomes anxious. 'It feels weird, you two seem weird.' She drops her bag on the floor.

'Oh we're always weird, darling,' Linda says with forced gaiety. 'Parents are always weird, you should know that by now.'

And Andrew stands there, feeling as boring and hopeless as Linda obviously thinks he is, staring desperately at his daughter and willing her to read his mind and see how much he loves her and how it will kill him if he loses her.

# Six

lora stands on the hard sand letting the icy water lap around her feet and wondering if she has the fortitude to immerse herself in it. April is proving to be unseasonably warm on a coast that's not renowned for warmth. The water is freezing but inviting, such a clear transparent green, and she can see the tiny shells shifting back and forth in the sand around her feet. She walks out a little further until it covers her ankles, and then a bit further to mid-calf. Her legs are almost numb but the sun is comforting on her back and shoulders. For Flora it is always the knees that are crucial; if she can make it to a depth that covers them she knows she's going in.

Turning around she looks back to the beach to where Connie is sitting on a towel, in a sunny spot between two rocks, head tilted back, facing the sun with her eyes closed. She has done a lot of sleeping since she arrived: jetlag probably but also, Flora thinks, a greater exhaustion, grief and an as yet undeclared relief at the lifting of a burden. How would that feel, Flora wonders, to be totally occupied with caring for someone for years and then to be finally freed? She wonders if Connie has any real sense of that freedom yet and, if she has, whether it thrills or terrifies her. Yes, a lot of sleeping, and not much talking. The latter has been something of a disappointment to Flora, who had anticipated conversations of the sort that it was never quite possible to have on a computer screen or by email. She'd imagined silences too, of course, but long companionable silences in which they would each be in their own worlds but also within the world of the past, its understandings, its memories and its own silences. But it hasn't been like that. There has been awkwardness between them, something cautious and guarded, something more noticeable still when Suzanne is around. The hotel is a place of constant interruptions and mini-dramas. It will get better, Flora thinks, it has to, we just need more time alone, and Connie needs to chill out.

She turns back to face the horizon and takes a small step and then two large strides forward until her knees are covered, holds her breath and plunges in, gasping with the shock and thrashing wildly around to warm herself up, swearing under her breath, until her body temperature drops and she can relax. It's ages since she came to this beach although it's her favourite and the closest to home of the little inlets off the cape. While she loves to walk alone, the beach, she feels, should be a shared pleasure.

They had come here first as children, with her parents and in later years alone, her mother and father preferring the town beach. It seemed like a secret cove; of course other people *did* go there, but there weren't many tourists back in the fifties and those that were around preferred the larger beaches with longer stretches of sand further up the cape. After her first visit to Port d'Esprit, Flora had mounted a relentless campaign to get both sets of parents to agree that Connie could go with them the following year. It was hard at first; her own parents had taken to Connie, who was quiet and polite. They thought her a very suitable friend for their daughter, and even Gerald had conceded that as girls went she wasn't too bad. Connie's parents were hard up though, and her father was touchy, quick to feel insulted. But eventually he had given in, and had insisted on paying her way and making a big fuss about it at the same time. So Connie had come with them to Port d'Esprit, and continued to do so every subsequent year until the summer after the year they finished school. After that Connie won her scholarship to the Guildhall, and Flora made her first – and, as it turned out, her last – step towards entering a convent.

Halcyon days, Flora thinks now. They were free to do much as they wanted, sometimes with Suzanne, but more often on their own, exploring beaches and rocks, fishing with a cork and hook on a line off the quayside, wandering through the streets of the little town. Gerald had grown out of family holidays by then, although he did come one year and spent most of his time grunting irritably or skulking off into town to chat up local girls. Gerald! Flora feels the uncomfortable tightening of resentment in her chest thinking of the way he encouraged their parents' anger and disapproval when she went to India. It was then, while Flora was away for almost two years, that Connie's mother had died in a traffic accident and Gerald stepped into her life. And by the time Flora came home Connie was abandoning her dreams of the opera, and planning a wedding. Flora had long felt that she and Connie were like sisters and now that was about to be reality, but she was torn between joy at the prospect of her best friend being part of her family, and an uneasy feeling that Gerald had kidnapped her. And that was only the beginning. She wonders if Gerald ever had any inkling of the grief he had caused her or the insidious, long-lasting effects of his behaviour towards her some years later.

Looking up to the beach Flora sees Connie sit up and rub her eyes before she looks around, spots Flora, waves, gets up and strolls to the water's edge, yelping as the ripples reach her feet. She looks good, Flora thinks; she's always been sturdy but shapely, and her fine English skin has withstood the ravages of age pretty well.

'Good heavens, Flora, it's bloody freezing,' Connie calls. 'Have you gone raving mad, you could die of hypothermia.'

'It's gorgeous once you're in,' Flora says, wading back towards her.

'Don't splash me,' Connie cries, 'promise you won't splash me,' and she wraps her arms around her body defensively but keeps walking slowly into the shallow waves.

Flora stops, sees her bend to dip her hands in the water and then rub them over her upper arms and neck. In that moment, Connie is eleven again, or thirteen, or even sixteen; this is how she does it, griping, gasping, slowly but surely heading towards full body immersion, and Flora begins to laugh.

'What?' Connie calls out. 'Why are you laughing?'

'You haven't changed,' Flora says. 'Same old Connie, grumble, grumble, gasp, moan and then suddenly you'll be in there, thrashing around and screaming.'

And Connie stops, looks at her for a moment, takes a huge breath, plunges in and comes up gasping, water spouting from her mouth. 'Right,' she shouts, 'you've asked for it, madam. I'm coming for you,' and then she is half-swimming, half-running towards her, and Flora, breathless with laughter and exertion, turns to escape, stumbles, disappears under-water and struggles up again just as Connie grabs her, and instead of the dunking Flora is expecting, Connie hangs on tightly, throwing her head up, struggling for breath, and looks straight into her eyes.

'Oh, Flora, I am so thankful to be here with you. I have missed you so terribly for so long.'

And they cling together just as they had done when they met on the station platform, but this time it's different – something has changed. Time and distance, age and experience, seem to dissolve in the icy water and they are jumping up and down, splashing and squealing like teenagers, freed at last both by what they remember and what they choose to forget.

*

As she drives past the front door and parks at the side of the house Kerry can see that there is no one home. The doors are locked, Scooter is not barking, no signs of life. She gets out of the car and looks around, wondering why she is here. She only decided to come last night, when Chris had suggested they take the kids to the zoo for a picnic.

'You'll have to do it without me,' she'd said on the spur of the moment. 'I'm going down to Mum's.'

Chris, who had been unpacking the dishwasher, had looked up in surprise. 'To Hobart – why?'

'I just – Mum wants me to check it out, make sure everything's okay,' she'd said, and he'd straightened up and looked at her and it was clear he didn't believe her.

'You mean you want to check on Farah.'

She'd flushed then and turned away. 'Somebody has to.'

'No they don't. Connie made the arrangement and she trusts Farah. Don't meddle, Kerry.'

'Can't I just have a day to myself sometimes?' she'd said. 'You're perfectly capable of taking the kids on a picnic.'

'Indeed I am,' he'd said, 'but that's not the point, is it?'

She hates it when he calls her to account like this. In the early days she had admired it, had even felt that it might make her a better, less selfish, more honest person. Now it just pisses her off. He should've been a lawyer instead of a teacher; he'd be fearsome in the courtroom, picking up every inconsistency, every lie, every evasion, torturing witnesses like a cat toying with mice.

'I'm planning to leave really early,' she'd continued. 'I'll be back by tea time.'

She looks at her watch – just after nine, hopefully Farah has taken her children out for the day. Kerry takes the house keys from her bag, snaps open the boot of the car and retrieves two bags of books that she has, over the last couple of years, borrowed from Gerald's shelves. And leaving the boot and the driver's door open she lugs them to the back of the house and lets herself in through the kitchen.

The house is immaculate, spotless; she can't remember ever having seen it looking so perfect. She dumps the bags on the kitchen floor and wanders from room to room sampling the stillness, the fresh lemony scent of some kind of furniture polish or floor cleaner. How does Farah keep it so tidy with two kids? Kerry wonders, gazing at the red plastic crate filled with children's books and a few toys, standing neatly in the corner by the fireplace. Even the cushions and loose covers on the sofa, which is too soft and squishy ever to look neat, appear to have been freshly laundered or dry cleaned. Kerry considers lying down on it; these days she's always tired. But it is not the couch that she wants to lie on, and before she does anything else she wants to see upstairs.

She goes first to Connie's room. The bed linen is stacked neatly alongside the folded doona on the bed, presumably in readiness for her mother's return. The big spare room is still essentially tidy but the toys and books are not packed away like those downstairs. The twin beds are made up, each with a furry nightdress case on it – one a grey and white penguin, the other a pink lion. Some children's clothes are draped over the chair, others are in a neatly folded stack on the chest of drawers. Twins, of course, Farah has twin girls, Kerry remembers – she's met them once. They must be Ryan's age, more perhaps. Well, that's the children, so where is Farah sleeping?

Not in Andrew's old room she sees as she opens the door, and not the other small one which Connie is now obviously using for storage. So it's Kerry's old room that has been occupied by the invading force. Farah has brought her own doona cover, a glorious swirling pattern in shades of turquoise and cobalt, with matching pillowcases. Beside the bed is a pair of black satin slippers embroidered in silver thread and on the night table a pair of glasses, a small dish containing a couple of silver bracelets and a ring, and alongside it three books stacked one on top of the other.

She tiptoes to the bedside table embarrassed by her own intrusion into what is now Farah's room, reaches out a cautious hand and pushes the books around so she can see the titles. One has a red and gold cover with a title in an unfamiliar alphabet, there is a well-worn copy of *Mrs Dalloway*, and a new edition of Daphne du Maurier's *Rebecca*, both of which she knows to be her mother's favourites. Glancing nervously over her shoulder she picks up *Rebecca* and sees that it is inscribed – 'To Farah, I hope you'll enjoy this. Many thanks for taking care of everything for me. Love, Connie.' *Mrs Dalloway* is Connie's own copy, her name scrawled in the top right-hand corner of the title page along with the year, 1974.

Kerry straightens the books, looks around the room, barely recognisable as hers, and tiptoes out closing the door behind her. At the foot of the narrow staircase to her father's study she pauses, then turns away. What's the point? It's several years since he was able to inhabit that room, although as far as she knows Connie has left it just as it was the last time he used it. Is there something of him still left up there or has every vestige of his spirit departed from the house?

Sighing, she goes down to the kitchen, fills the kettle and stands staring out at the garden, waiting for the water to boil, wondering what she is really doing here. What she wants to do is to lie on the old chaise longue in the study. To find something of him there, just as she had wanted to lie alongside him in the last few months and days of his life, on that wretched hospital bed that had been set up for him in the small sitting room downstairs. She had ached for closeness then, but been so repelled by his physical condition that she had struggled even to make herself bend to kiss his cool, sunken cheek or hold his trembling hand. The memory of her inability to accept his illness or help with his care fills her with shame. What a failure she is as a daughter, as a woman. No wonder her mother dislikes her; she, more than anyone, sees through the confident, stroppy exterior to the weak, hopeless person she really is. Some sort of wall has grown up between her and other people, cutting her off from everyone she loves, even her children. She is trapped behind it, disconnected from everyone else, watching what happens but unable to feel a part of it. She's gone through periods like this in the last few years but they have passed; this time, however, it seems to have become a permanent state.

Kerry pours the water onto a tea bag, finds milk in the fridge, and makes her way to the lounge, but the pull of the study is too strong and she is soon heading slowly back up the stairs, along the landing to the narrow little staircase up to the converted loft that her father had described as his eyrie. The room is as it has always been, piled with books and papers, the 1930s telephone converted into a table lamp, the box files, the stacks of government reports, the framed photographs of family, from sepia studio portraits of great-grandparents to snaps of Andrew and herself as children, a photo of her and Chris's wedding, and pictures of them with Ryan and Mia. She picks up a yellowing photograph of her parents' wedding; Gerald in a morning suit, Connie in a full length satin dress with lace sleeves, carrying a bouquet of apricot roses, and then she spots another, a studio portrait of her father taken some time before he got sick. The photographer had captured the best of him, a full head of greying hair, the searching eyes and that cleft chin that Andrew has inherited and she, thankfully, has not. The knowing, half-amused expression, the slightly crooked hint of a smile, his natural air of authority – it's all there. It is a picture of the father she wants to remember, the man whose approval she had so desperately sought but which always evaded her.

It is a picture that restores him, and allows her to ignore the metamorphosis that transformed and diminished him, and finally repelled her.

The old couch where Gerald sat to read, or to snooze on Sunday afternoons, looks very inviting. Setting her cup down on the wonky old wooden stool nearby, Kerry sorts out the faded cushions and lies down. A dodgy spring digs into her hip and she shifts her position, wondering just how long it is since Gerald lay here. Four years, more perhaps? Is it possible that no one has lain here since then? She holds the framed photograph against her chest, folding her arms over it and around herself, trying to recapture him, her mind rambling through the past. All the questions that she never asked, and to which she now so desperately wants the answers, crawl out from the woodwork of her memory. She recalls all the missed opportunities to know him better, to bridge the various stages in both their lives, to reach out as an adult woman, instead of always as a stumbling child. She has spent all her life trying to get to know him, and to make him see her, to notice her, but always being disappointed. What did he really think of her? What would he think of her now? She closes her eyes, willing herself to see him, to feel his presence, but hard as she tries there is nothing. She is cut off from the dead just as she is from the living.

# Seven

*ear Nan,* Brooke types. *Thanks for sending me the photos, those beaches look a lot like the beaches near Hobart, specially the ones with the high cliffs and the pine trees at the back. Sorry I haven't written before. I'm a hopeless case, aren't I? I really enjoy reading your emails.*

She stops suddenly, realising that this is probably the first time she's actually emailed her nan; weird that, everyone does everything by email these days, but she and Nan have rarely been in touch. They talk on the phone occasionally – well, not really *talk* – just chat a bit if her dad is talking to Nan and he calls to Brooke to come and say hello. When Connie first downloaded Skype they'd had a couple of chats but that was a bit awkward, as though after the first pleasantries and bits about what they'd been doing – Brooke going to school, Nan looking after Granddad – they didn't really know what to say to each other. In fact, Brooke realises now, she's had hardly anything to do with her grandmother since she was quite small. Before Granddad got sick, and even when he first got sick, her grandparents often phoned her, and they sometimes came to stay for a few days. They would take her out on a picnic or to the shops and buy her presents. Once Granddad took her in a rowing boat on the Yarra while Nan watched and waved from the river bank, but mostly Brooke and her mum and dad went to Hobart.

She remembers the house back then when it had seemed so big and exciting, those huge cupboards to hide in, and a garden with all sorts of shady corners under big trees. Brooke remembers Granddad teaching her to swim with floaties, and then the summer when he'd said he thought she was ready to manage without them and she had swum right across the pool on her own and everyone had cheered.

There were Christmases too; helping Nan to decorate the tree and then stack the presents underneath it, and waking on Christmas morning to find a stocking filled with all sorts of little treasures before they even got downstairs for the real presents. They went once to a carol service and once to a pantomime, on Christmas Eve. When they got back to the house her nan had brought out warm mince pies and they had all sat outside on the terrace in the mild evening, eating them with custard, and Granddad had even allowed her to taste his brandy.

'Just a sip, Brooke darling,' he'd said. 'You might not like it.'

But it was such a treat that when he tilted the glass she had gulped at it. It was disgusting. Brooke thought she was going to be sick and her throat burned but Nan had given her a spoonful of the warm, sweet custard to take the horrible taste away.

Brooke, sitting now on her bed, her iPad propped on her lap, leans back against the pillows and folds her arms behind her head. She hardly ever thinks about those days now, the times when they were more like one big family instead of three different lots of people all living a long way away from each other and often arguing. In her memories everyone seems nicer than they act now. Brooke feels a surge of longing for those days, a longing for how it felt to be part of that, being the only grandchild, before Ryan and then Mia appeared on the scene.

It was when Granddad got ill that everything changed, or that's how it seems. Not that it was his fault of course, but he did get very sort of crusty and unpredictable, and then so sick that she dreaded going near him towards the end. Nan seemed to disappear around then too, to become someone who just looked after Granddad, who was always distracted – even when she was still talking to you and being lovely, she was never quite there. They didn't go to Hobart so much after he got sick either; her parents, who had always niggled at each other, seemed to get worse and her dad and Auntie Kerry fought whenever they saw each other. Brooke realises now how much everything has changed, how much they've all changed, and how her family, which was something wonderful, has turned into something tense and uncomfortable.

Seeing Nan telling off her dad and Auntie Kerry had been weird for Brooke. Nan seemed as though she'd been taken over by someone else, but if Brooke's honest, she has known that side of Nan before, a long time ago, the side that is strong and firm. On the morning of the day they left, after the funeral and the ashes, when the two of them had talked in Granddad's study, it had been like talking to the old Nan. And as she sits here now, about to get back to the email, Brooke decides she's going to tell Nan what's going on at home. She can't talk about it to anyone, but she *can* put it in the email. Just writing it will help her to find out how she really feels. She clicks the iPad back to life and begins writing again.

*Anyway, here I am, writing now, and there's stuff I could tell you about school and the play and everything but I want to tell you something important and secret. I'd rather talk to you – just us together – but I can't so maybe writing to you will help.*

*Mum and Dad are splitting up. I did sort of think they would last year, and then things got better for a while. But now it's all on again. They're arguing all the time, blaming each other, fighting about money and about the house and, of course, about me, like I'm a piece of furniture or something. Honestly, Nan, you'd think I was only six years old the way they talk about me. They must think I'm pretty dumb, but it's them that's dumb because they talk about it in whispers when they think I'm listening to music. Just because I've got my earphones on it's like they think I'm not really there. But I always use earphones even if I'm not listening to anything. It means I don't get hassled so much. I mean, sometimes I am listening to music even while I'm doing homework but it doesn't stop me working. But these days I'm mostly just using them like a kind of barrier.*

*They don't have huge fights when I'm in the room, just sort of hiss stuff at each other – stuff from fights they've had, or ones they're waiting to have. They save the big fights until they think I'm asleep. I can hear their voices then but not much of what they're saying.*

*The thing is that Mum's having an affair with an artist called Zachary something or other. I've met him and he's really gross. He always wears black. He calls himself 'The Man in Black', it's on his exhibition poster, and he signs his paintings that way too. Mum thinks he's amazing, but just wearing black doesn't make you cool, especially if you've got a beer gut and really bad breath too. I mean, how could she? Dad can be boring, I suppose, but at least he's nice, and he showers!*

*So, the thing is, Dad says he wants a divorce and he wants Mum to move out. He says she should go and live with The Man in Black. She says he should move out and she and Zachary will live here and I must stay with them. Dad says, over his dead body, his daughter will not live with scum like that. So that's one good thing, I suppose. It'd be all right, just me and Dad here, or me and Mum here, as long as I could see whoever wasn't here whenever I want. And as long as I don't have to go to Zachary's house, because it's probably as gross as him, which is why Mum doesn't want to live there.*

*I wish they'd sort it out because it's really hard living with* people who hate each other. I feel like the third point in the tri-angle, and sometimes they use me to get at each other. Some of my friends have parents who've split and they say it's heaps better than before.

But the thing is, Nan, they talk about me like I'm a child, like I don't get to have a say in it. Anyway, I've been on the inter-net and looked it all up and if they do get divorced I <u>would</u> get to decide where I want to go, at least I'd have a say. The judge would talk to me in confidence, and I'm sure he wouldn't say I have to live with that idiot if I don't want to.

Some days I just wish it was all over. But mostly I want them to be like they were, like they used to be when I was little. Do you remember how it was then, Nan? They used to hold hands and put their arms around each other and sometimes they'd be kissing or cuddling in the kitchen. I used to hate this but now I think it was nice and I so want them to be like that again. So really I don't know what to do and that's why I'm telling you all this because I have to tell someone.

I know you can't do anything and even if you think you can, you absolutely mustn't because I'm not supposed to know it's happening. So you have to promise not to say anything to them or I'll be in big trouble and worse still they'll make sure I don't get to hear anything else. So please, please, Nan, promise you won't say anything to them or to anyone else, like Auntie Kerry, although I don't think you would tell her really. Can I come and stay with you when you get back? Like we said? The holidays are in June and wherever I end up I'd still rather be with you.

I hope you won't be upset about all this. I'll be okay but I just want it to be over. Writing this has made me feel a bit better. I know the times are all different over there but please write to me soon.

Lots of love
Brooke xxxxxxxxxx

\*

'I'm sorry but what else could I do?' Farah asks, putting the coffee pot on the kitchen table. 'I came home and the car is there with all the doors open. I thought there were burglars. Connie told me there are no other keys.'

'There are several other keys,' Kerry says irritably.

'But they are all in the house, in the little drawer of the table in the hall. Before she left she told me, "No one else has a key, Farah".'

Kerry sighs. She's in the wrong and she knows it. As they'd been about to leave after staying for the funeral and the ashes she'd taken a set of keys from the drawer. She could have asked Connie who would, undoubtedly, have given them to her, but at the time it had felt good to just take them. She was entitled, after all – wasn't she? I'll be able to keep an eye on things, she'd thought, although she knows it was actually about asserting her right to come and go in the house.

'Well,' she says now, watching as Farah pours very dark coffee from a metal pot that is definitely not Connie's. 'Mum must've forgotten I had one.'

There it goes, she thinks, another little lie. She seems to be telling more and more of them these days, little, essentially unnecessary, lies. They fall out of her mouth before she knows it, at home, at school, everywhere; desperate little grasps at editing the truth to protect herself. It's as though this growing crop of little lies makes her feel as though she's in control of something, like she's grasping at herself because she doesn't know what's happening to her.

They are silent for a few moments. 'If it was as I thought – the house is being burgled – I *have* to call the police.'

'I suppose so,' Kerry says grudgingly.

Farah pushes a cup across the table to her. 'It's Turkish,' she says, 'very strong, maybe too strong. Taste it carefully.'

Kerry shakes her head. 'I like it strong.'

'Perhaps just sip it to see.'

Kerry picks up the small fine china cup – also not one of Connie's – takes a gulp and gasps.

'Christ,' she says, swallowing. 'I see what you mean. That nearly blew my head off. It's good though.'

Farah smiles and sips her own and, as the two of them sit in silence for a moment, Kerry sees that her own hands around the cup are shaking. She sets it down and it clatters onto the saucer, coffee splashing across the scrubbed surface of the table.

'Sorry,' Kerry mumbles, clasping her hands together to stop the shaking. 'Sorry.'

Farah puts down her own cup and leans forward to look at her. 'You've gone very pale, are you all right?'

Kerry shakes her head. 'No, I feel . . .' she hesitates. How does she feel? Sick, light-headed and suddenly very cold.

'I think you should lie down,' Farah says, and she comes around the table to where Kerry is sitting, puts both arms around her upper body and urges her to her feet. 'Put your arm around my shoulders,' she orders, and then proceeds to half-walk, half-drag her to the old sofa in the little alcove off to the side of the kitchen, and lowers her down to it.

Kerry flops onto the edge of the sofa and Farah lifts her legs up, grabs a folded rug from the arm, shakes it out and lays it over her. The room is spinning and there is a strange drumming in Kerry's ears but lying down is good. She closes her eyes briefly, then opens them and sees that Farah is filling a glass of water at the sink. Water, she thinks, opening her eyes again, that would be good, and she leans up on one elbow and takes a drink before flopping back down again.

'Shock perhaps. Did you eat something this morning?' Farah asks, tucking the rug around her.

Kerry shakes her head. 'No, I haven't eaten since last night. I left at half past six, meant to get some breakfast on the way but I kept forgetting.'

Farah looks at her watch. 'And now it's after one,' she says. 'Drink some more water and I will get you something to eat.'

'I'm not hungry, I . . .'

'You should try to eat something, it will help; a piece of toast and some tea. Please do not try to get up.'

It's not a request; Farah's manner implies that she is accustomed to her patients doing as they are told. Not that Kerry wants to move. The room is spinning more slowly now and she feels she is drifting, into sleep or perhaps some other sort of unconsciousness, and then she is up near the ceiling, looking down at herself huddled there on the couch under her father's blanket. It's the one he used when he was still mobile but weakening rapidly. He would sit or lie on this couch, blanket around him, close enough to hold a conversation with whoever was in the kitchen without getting in the way. The blanket is light and very soft, made of a synthetic material, and patterned like the skin of a tiger. She can remember Connie saying that she had searched everywhere for something light because the weight of blankets irritated him. Strangely, while Kerry can clearly see the blanket from above, she can also feel its warmth and softness wrapped around her.

There is a movement beside her and she half-opens her eyes. Farah has moved the coffee table alongside the sofa and is setting down a small tray.

'Kerry,' she says softly, touching her arm. 'Kerry, are you able to sit up a little?'

Reluctantly Kerry turns slightly on to her side and pushes herself into a semi-recumbent position.

'A little more, please.'

And she moves further up and Farah quickly slips some cushions behind her back. 'Good.' She hands her the cup. 'Sip it only, not like . . .'

'Not like the coffee,' Kerry says, managing a wobbly smile.

'Exactly. I should not have given you the coffee, I'm sorry. I think you were already in shock. What happened this morning was not nice.'

Kerry sips slowly, leaning back against the pillows, feeling herself descend from the ceiling and back into her body. 'No it wasn't,' she says eventually. 'I was fast asleep and was woken up to find three policemen looking at me. It was really quite frightening, and then having to explain who I was and that I wasn't robbing the place . . .'

Farah nods slowly. 'It is frightening of course, the most terrifying thing, the shock, then the terror. To be invaded, to be woken like that . . .'

'You mean you . . . ?' Kerry's voices trails away in embarrassment.

'Yes. Always we lived in fear of the Taliban, but it was Australian soldiers who broke into our bedroom.'

'Australians?'

Farah nodded. 'We were told they made a mistake with the house.'

'Were they armed?'

Farah laughs. 'But of course! It is a war.'

Kerry sits up straighter, her head has stopped spinning now. 'That must have been terrifying.'

'Rashid and I had taken the children to sleep with us, we thought it would be safer. But in that moment we both thought we would all be shot. The Australians were very kind. They made many apologies. For weeks we had talked of trying to leave the country; after this we did everything to get away. It is terrible always to be in fear in your own home. How can you raise children like this, always in fear, the terror, the killing – often they see other children killed and maimed.' She gets to her feet, smiling. 'It's good that you're drinking the tea. Please try to eat the toast as well.'

Kerry picks up the plate; the toast has been cut into small triangles and she takes one and pops it into her mouth.

It tastes like food of the gods. Odd – how good something simple can taste when you're feeling wobbly. She remembers how Connie would bring her tomato sandwiches, made with very thin brown bread and lots of butter, or perhaps a boiled egg with toast soldiers, when she was sick. And last year, when she had the flu, Chris had brought her buttered toast with a smidgen of Vegemite. But right now the joy of the toast is soured somewhat by shame. Here she is, firstly being rude and grumpy over something that was entirely of her own making, and then practically fainting with shock at being woken by the police, and all the time she is sitting with a woman whose bedroom has been invaded in the middle of the night by soldiers with AK47s or whatever it is they carry these days.

She looks over to where Farah is making more tea and toast. This is the first time she has ever really thought about Farah. She's seen her of course, said a few words to her when they visited, but they've never actually had a conversation. Her own despair at her father's decline, and the guilt of her failure to bring herself to do for him any of the awful, messy, degrading things that her mother and Farah would do for him, had made her hostile to the nurse who was simply doing her job. Now for the first time she starts to feel curious about Farah's life, both in Afghanistan and in the process of climbing with her children into a rickety boat in pursuit of a safer, better life. She has always seen her as too different, too foreign to connect with. At school, the refugee children mixed easily with the others, and when she met their parents she had a specific job to do which gave her a way of relating to them. Beyond that she could feel no connection. But Farah is just like any other strong and compassionate woman who would fight for the best for her children. They have, she thinks, more in common than she has ever bothered to think about.

Kerry's cold face burns now with a flush of shame; she wants to reach out to her but she feels like a ghost. There is nothing in me that any normal person can connect with, she thinks, and she rests her head back on the cushions and closes her eyes again, listening to the comforting sound of Farah making more tea.

# *Eight*

'But of course you must do something,' Suzanne says, 'of course. You're his mother, Brooke is your granddaughter.'

'So what are you suggesting?' Connie asks. 'That I should call Andrew and tell him I know what's happening, and break faith with Brooke?'

'But you have not promised her anything,' Suzanne says. 'She asks but you have not replied yet, so you have not agreed to keep silent. You are not bound by what she asks you.'

'I think you're wrong, Suzanne,' Flora says, 'absolutely wrong. Actually I think what you're suggesting is unfair – and it could make matters worse.'

'You think I am unfair? I am practical. Brooke is a child and it's Connie's duty to protect her. Stop her doing something stupid.'

'She sounds as though she's a very mature and sensible teenager,' Flora says. 'It's good that she's told Connie what's happening and is confiding in her. She has someone to talk to now, an emotional safety net. She *doesn't* sound like a girl who's about to do anything stupid.'

Connie leans back in her chair, uncomfortable with the tension between Flora and Suzanne and wishing she had waited until she and Flora were alone to talk about this. At first Connie had thought that it was her presence causing a problem but she's been here now for three weeks and it's clear that Suzanne and Xavier are edging Flora out. It's not an orchestrated campaign, just two people trying to find a way to be together and a third who is inconveniently in the way.

'I agree that Connie has a responsibility to Brooke,' Flora continues, bringing Connie's attention back to the conversation, 'but that responsibility is to respect her confidence, and to support her in getting through this.'

'I agree,' Connie says. 'I think I'll email or text her and arrange to call her sometime or somewhere when she can talk freely. Maybe we could chat online – Skype or something. I don't want to undermine her by giving her the impression that I think she can't cope. She's very sensible, she's an observer and a listener, and super sensitive to what's happening among the people around her.' And as she says this Connie realises that she is talking about herself. Brooke is trapped between Andrew and Linda as she had been as a teenager when her own parents' marriage was on the rocks. She has a horrible sense of *déjà vu*. Perhaps, as Andrew's mother, she does have a responsibility to talk to him, but as Brooke's grandmother she feels she has a greater responsibility to keep her confidence.

Suzanne shrugs. 'Well, what do I know? I am not a mother . . .' she flicks Flora a sharp look '. . . not even a retired teacher, but I think there are expectations of parents, and your son and his wife, Connie, are failing badly in this role. So it seems to me that you should step in.'

'The perfect recipe for setting the cat loose among the pigeons,' Flora says sharply. 'Andrew and Linda's marriage is their business – they won't welcome Connie's interference, and Brooke will be in trouble for spilling the beans.'

'In your position, Connie,' Suzanne says, getting up from the table, 'I would be on the next plane back to Australia to take charge of the situation, but you will both think this very *passé* and perhaps interfering. Anyway, I have things to do, and if you two want to get to St Malo before the rain comes you should leave soon.'

\*

By the time they reach St Malo and park the car it has started to rain and they duck into Flora's favourite café, and order *café crème* and almond croissants while they wait for the weather to clear.

'I remember this place,' Connie says, slipping onto a velvet covered bench in a booth that could easily be the one she had sat in with Jean-Claude all those years ago, crying her eyes out because he was leaving for Paris the following day. 'The red velvet upholstery, the ornate mirrors and lamps; in my memory it always seemed opulent but now it looks a little faded. I think I prefer it this way.'

'Faded elegance,' Flora says with a chuckle, 'always rather attractive. The hint of having passed through better days, just like us!'

Connie laughs. 'I wish,' she says. 'Very French, isn't it? I mean, French women age so elegantly, don't they?'

'Some of them,' Flora says, 'but walk through Port d'Esprit on any given morning and you won't be overwhelmed by visions of ageing elegance.' She looks around at the motley crowd of tourists and locals, her mind filled with memories of times spent here over the years. Here, where she had thought she'd grow old. But now perhaps she should simply bite the bullet, move out and take a chance on the future. She could always get a place here in St Malo, help Suzanne out occasionally, maybe teach English or even work in a shop, just earn enough to pay her rent. The money that she had got for her flat when she moved to France will not be enough to buy anything similar at today's prices.

'I don't think Suzanne approves of me,' Connie ventures. 'Not just about Brooke, but in a more general sense.'

Flora smiles. 'You're being oversensitive. Suzanne speaks excellent English but she doesn't have the English tendency to frame things in convoluted ways that soften or play down the message.'

Connie laughs. 'You're right. Australians are a bit the same and I suppose I've never quite grown accustomed to it.'

'But Suzanne can be tough, and she certainly disapproves of me from time to time.'

'And what about Xavier?' Connie asks. 'Does she ever disapprove of him?'

'Not as far as I can see, but his time will come!'

'Do you think she's in love with him?'

'It's hard to tell with Suzanne. I've known her so long, shared the place and worked with her for fifteen years, and I still can't work her out half the time. She's never settled to being without a partner; it's as though she sees being single as some sort of failure on her part. And she's certainly very different with Xavier than any other man she's been involved with since Jacques. She's warmer and more relaxed when he's around, and when he's not there she refers to him a lot – you know, dropping his name into conversations whenever she can, the way people do when they're in love. And I know she wants to expand the business. The little toy shop next door is closing at the end of the summer season, and Suzanne wants to buy it. She says she could turn our flat into two holiday flats, do up the place next door and live in it.'

'Does she think Xavier would invest? Has he got the money?'

'He's not short of it. I think they want to live together, and if Xavier sold his house they could probably afford it.'

'So where would that leave you?'

'I'd go, for sure. Suzanne and I rub along fairly well working together, but it would be really difficult for me if Xavier came into the mix. It's such a relief to be able to talk about this.'

'I can see it's a difficult situation . . .'

'And likely to become more difficult quite soon, I think.'

'Have you thought about what you might do?'

Flora sighs. 'Many times – in fact I was thinking about it just now. Getting a place in St Malo is a possibility, but I often yearn to go back to London. I need to decide where I want to be. I wish we had more time to talk, Connie, there are always so many interruptions at the hotel. I think I need to be away from here to think about it in practical terms. You're not planning to take Suzanne's advice and race back to Australia, are you?'

'Definitely not. I know this must sound selfish but I can't face the prospect of being drawn into this separation or divorce, whichever it turns out to be. The last few years have taken their toll, I'm a mess – grief, relief, sadness, anxiety about the future. But I can give Brooke a bit of support and I think I can do that just as well from here as I could if I was in Hobart.'

Flora nods. 'Of course you can. And you do need to look after yourself right now. Are you still off to England next week?'

Connie nods. 'I'm sticking to my original plan, but I thought I might come back here briefly before I go home if that's all right?'

Flora takes a deep breath. 'Of course, but I wanted to ask . . . well, please say if this wouldn't work for you, but how would you feel about my coming with you to London, just for a few days? Would you mind? It would be so good to be able to talk more, away from here.'

'Mind? I'd love it – really I would. Oh do come, Flora, come for the whole time – if Suzanne . . .'

'Suzanne will cope and I actually think the best thing I can do for both of us is to get out of there for a while. It'll give me time to think about what I want to do. And she'll have a chance to see what it's like having Xavier around full-time, because that's how she'll organise it. She'll moan about me going away, but I think it'll suit her.'

'And when you get back?'

'Who knows? Perhaps I'll be clearer about what I want by then. But I've felt for some time that it's all falling apart and it's not only because of Xavier. I think this arrangement has reached the end of its natural life.' Putting it into words makes Flora feel stronger. The restlessness and anxiety that have plagued her for the last year or so are to do with the way she has tied her life to Suzanne's. It's time – more than time – to work out how she will spend her old age.

'Then come,' Connie says, 'please do come!'

'So where will we be going?'

Connie smiles. 'It might be a bit dull for you – after all, you've been going back and forth to England for years – but I just want to go back to the places where you and I grew up: Tunbridge Wells, the school, home, Ashdown Forest, Brighton, and that part of the south coast. It's just a senti-mental journey for me. It seems to have been such a happy time, especially after Dad left, just Mum and me at home. We were hard up but it didn't seem to matter. I want to wander around those places again.' She pauses, breaking off a piece of croissant and dunking it in her coffee. 'I've spent so long being a wife and a mother and then a full-time carer that I've almost forgotten who I was before . . . well, before Gerald.

'Being married a long time you become so enmeshed with the other person that it's easy to forget who you once were,' she continues. 'This trip is self-indulgent, but it's about finding my old self, first by being with you and then by going back to some of those places. Honestly, I think I put myself on the backburner for too long, and let Gerald lead. It just felt easier that way.'

'I noticed that when I stayed with you,' Flora says. 'I wanted to tell you that at the time, but I didn't think you'd want to hear it then.'

'No, I wouldn't have,' Connie says. 'I would have resisted it. I suppose I became a bit of a cliché, the acquiescent, comfortably married woman. Even when he was sick, he was still the driving force – everything revolved around him. And now he's gone, and I'm trying to find my way to the future.' She pauses, gazing down into her coffee cup, then looks up at Flora, her eyes bright with tears. 'I need to remember what I wanted from my life, who I might have become if I hadn't married him. I did love him, you know, I wouldn't want you to think . . .'

'I know, Connie.' Flora takes her hand across the table. 'I've never doubted that, and you were the best thing that could have happened to him; he was incredibly lucky and I am sure he knew it.'

'I never forgave him, though, for the way he cut you off,' Connie continues. There is a short uncomfortable silence. 'And I'm ashamed that I didn't stand up to him, but you know what he was like, he wasn't a man who could easily admit that he'd been in the wrong.'

'Well, we're here now, we still have our friendship and perhaps this is the time of life when we need it most.'

They are both quiet for a moment.

'Okay,' Flora says, eventually breaking the silence, 'where else are we going?'

'Well, London, of course. Bloomsbury, where Mrs Dalloway . . .'

'". . . said she would buy the flowers herself",' Flora cuts in. 'I always imagined her walking down Marchmont Street to do it.'

'Me too! So you'll really come with me? You won't change your mind and think you have to stay for Suzanne?'

'I won't change my mind.' And she lifts her cup, holding it out towards Connie in a toast. 'Here's to the girls' own tour. Bring it on.'

\*

Andrew holds his razor under the tap, swishing the soap off it and leans closer to the bathroom mirror, running his hand over his chin. The signs of strain are showing in his face, no doubt about that; bags under his eyes, what seems like a small but permanent furrow between his eyebrows, and a generally washed out, pasty look. He pulls back a little, stands up straight, squares his shoulders and pulls in his stomach. He doesn't look all that bad for forty-four, he thinks, but perhaps he should grow his hair a bit. He'd thought the very close cut would suit him and according to Brooke it does, even Linda had given it a nod of approval, but he feels strangely exposed and vulnerable. That's the last thing he needs right now when each argument leaves him reeling, as though he has been slapped around to the point of exhaustion.

Linda is a formidable adversary, he's always known that. She's similar to his sister – perhaps that's what he'd first admired in her. He's always envied that ruthless terrier-like streak in Kerry too, admired it even when she was about to bury her teeth into his ankle – or more likely his jugular. He can hold his own most of the time but he lacks the head of steam that builds so quickly in his sister and his wife. And when he and Linda married he'd assumed he would never be on the receiving end. How stupid was that? He just wants to live in peace. Every day now he reminds himself that he once loved Linda enough to want to spend the rest of his life with her. She is Brooke's mother and that has to be respected, it can't be part of the fight. But of course that's what it's become.

He steps back from the mirror to study his body; he really needs to start going to the gym again, something to make him feel better about himself. There's nothing like deadly emotional combat with someone you once loved to poison the way you feel about yourself.

'You've completely lost interest in sex,' Linda had hissed at him recently. 'I can't remember when we did it last, just after your father died, I think, because I thought at the time, oh yes, this is what people say about life being all about sex and death.'

He knows she was right about that, knows that he had wanted to make love that night in his mother's house, because it was a sort of proof of life. But since then he's felt disconnected from anything physical, lives in his head while his heart and his body feel numb. There has been relief in bringing things out into the open, but he's still in much the same state and all he has the energy for now is fighting for what he wants to salvage from his marriage – namely Brooke.

But he has a few days of breathing space now because Linda is in Brisbane on gallery business. Andrew wonders if she realises that leaving him alone with Brooke is a tactical error. He's decided to tell Brooke what's happening. He knows he should wait for the two of them to be able to do it together, but Linda is insisting that Zachary be there at the same time. It will, she says, show Brooke that the three of them get on okay and they can all be friends. 'In your dreams, Linda,' he says softly into the mirror. Tonight, he thinks, I'll make a nice dinner for the two of us and break the news then. He slips his arms into his shirt sleeves, and walks through to the kitchen doing up the buttons as he goes.

Brooke is sitting at the bench with a bowl of muesli, and reading something on her iPad. Sometimes Andrew wishes he'd never bought it for her; that or the iPod seem welded to her, like additional body parts. She's made a pot of coffee and he pours himself a cup and sticks two slices of bread into the toaster.

'How about I make risotto tonight?' he asks, joining her at the bench. 'Isn't that your favourite?'

Brooke glances up at him; amazingly, she is not wearing earphones. 'Mmmm, okay,' she says and returns to what she's reading on the screen.

'No earphones this morning?'

'Don't need them,' Brooke says. 'Mum's away, no arguments.'

Andrew stops his cup halfway to his mouth. 'What do you mean?'

'Like I said, no arguments, no need to block them out. Same as when there's only Mum and me here.'

'Arguments?'

Brooke gets up from her stool and starts packing books into her bag. 'Get real, Dad. I'm not deaf or stupid. I know what's going on.'

Andrew's throat goes dry. 'You mean . . . ?'

'I know you're splitting up, okay? I wish you'd just get on and do it – all this fighting is driving me insane.'

Andrew slides off his stool. He wants to put his arm around her but stops himself in time. Right now she looks as though being touched is the last thing she wants. He fidgets with his mug and spoon. 'I'm sorry. We were going to get things sorted before we broke the news. Make it easier for you.'

Brooke laughs out loud. 'Well, you stuffed that up, didn't you? It's like the West Bank, bombs flying in all directions. Anyway, don't you think I'm entitled to know? I'm not a child.'

He nods. 'Yes, yes of course, but . . . you didn't say anything . . . I . . .'

'I was waiting for one of you to tell me, giving you a chance to do the right thing.'

'So I guess you know everything then?'

'That Mum's having an affair with that awful Zachary. You both want this place; you both want me to live with you. Yes, I know all that,' Brooke says, continuing to rummage around with her school bag, not looking up. 'And what really pisses me off is that neither of you have bothered to ask me how I feel or what I want.'

Andrew stares at her, then looks away, embarrassed. 'I'm sorry, you're right, we should have told you. We thought we were doing the right thing.'

'Well, you weren't,' she says and for a moment her bottom lip trembles slightly and she looks as though she might be going to cry, but then she seems to get control of it. She stands abruptly and heads to the sink, where she rinses her bowl, her back to him. 'Fight over the house if you want but not over me. I should have a say in where I live and who with.'

Andrew nods. 'Yes, yes, of course. All right, well, look, here's how things are at the moment . . .'

Brooke turns suddenly to face him. 'I told Nan.'

'You what?'

'I told Nan all about it. I emailed her. I had to talk to someone, didn't I?'

'You emailed or you actually talked to her?'

'Both. I emailed her and then we talked on Skype.'

'You shouldn't have done that without . . .'

'Fuck off, Dad. It's not my fault all this is happening. I've got a right to talk to Nan.'

Andrew, shaken first by Brooke's knowledge of the situation, is caught now between the shame and embarrassment of his mother knowing what's going on, and a longing to ring her himself and ask her what he should do next. 'So what did she say?' he asks, hoping that he doesn't sound quite as pathetic as he feels.

'She said I should talk to you, tell you how I feel. She said I should remember that you both love me and want the best for me and that in the long run she believes both of you will see that I should be consulted about my own future.'

He nods, several times, slowly, having difficulty taking all this in. Somewhere in the background he hears his toast pop up and smells a faint scent of burning. He turns to retrieve the toast, thankful that Brooke has chosen now, this time when the two of them are here alone, to talk to him, because it means he has a head start. He nods again, dropping the toast onto a plate and looking around for the butter. 'Yes, okay, that's right, that's good.' His palms are sweating. 'So . . . er . . . have you thought about what you want . . . d'you want to tell me?'

'Yeah, okay,' she says, looking him in the eye now, sitting back down on her stool. 'Well, I don't mind whether I live with you or Mum as long as I can see the other one every week without any fighting about it. But I am absolutely not going to live with that creep Zachary and I am not going to stay overnight in his house or anything like that, never, not ever – absolutely no way – so I don't see how I can live with Mum, unless she's going to live alone. And he'd have to promise not to visit when I'm there.'

A huge wave of relief surges through Andrew. 'So you'd be happy to live with either one of us as long as we live alone – no third parties?'

'Yep.'

'So you and I could stay here together if . . . if that's how it worked out? You'd like that?'

'I just told you, it'd be okay. But it's not my absolutely best choice.'

Andrew's stomach lurches; for a moment there he thought he'd won. 'So what's the best choice?'

'I want to go and live with Nan in Hobart.'

'With Nan?'

'Yes, it'd be great, really cool.'

'That's ridiculous, Brooke. I'm sorry, darling, I know we were wrong in not telling you – I mean, not asking you earlier. But Hobart, no way. What about school? You'll be going into sixth form. Besides . . . we're your parents. Children live with their parents, that's how it is.'

'No it's not,' Brooke cuts in. 'I know people at school who live with aunts or their older sister or their grandparents when their parents split. They reckon it's really good.'

'Have you talked to Nan about this?'

'No, not yet, but I bet she'd say yes.'

'It's ridiculous . . .' he begins, 'the school thing just makes it impossible, the upheaval; it would be very bad for you. You might stuff up and lose a year.'

'*This* is very bad for me,' Brooke says, 'being stuck in the middle here. I could come home sometimes for weekends and in the holidays. The airfare from Melbourne to Hobart and back is really cheap, it's not like you couldn't afford it.'

'But what about school?'

She grabs the iPad and turns it towards him. 'I've found one, it's in Sandy Bay not far from Nan's house, near the river. I could ride my bike. See – small independent college for girls – brilliant, no dickhead boys to cope with – here, look . . .'

'What *is* this?'

'It's the My School website, you can look up all the schools, ninety-six percent participation, that's really good, and they specialise in languages.'

Andrew looks at the screen, the blocks of text in blue-framed boxes, percentages, charts, numbers of teachers, figures in categories that mean nothing to him. Suddenly he feels incredibly old and fragile, as though if he has to have one more argument with anyone about anything he might just burst into tears.

'Let me think about it,' he says eventually. 'You've just sprung it on me . . .'

'Will you talk to Nan?'

'Whoa, Brooke, not yet. I said I'd think about it.' He glances at his watch. 'Shouldn't you be gone by now?'

She jumps up from the bench, and zips up her backpack. 'I've gone. Think about it – promise? I'll leave you the iPad.'

'I promise,' he says.

Brooke bumps her face against his, landing a kiss on his ear, and then strides off up the passage. 'I knew you'd say yes,' she calls from the front door. 'Love ya, Dad.'

'I haven't said yes,' Andrew calls after her, 'I said I'd think about it . . .' but the front door slams and she is gone, leaving him with the iPad.

Andrew shakes his head, staring at the maze of words and numbers on the screen. Then he leans forward, folds his arms on the bench, rests his head on them, and considers whether he might just call in sick and go back to bed for the rest of the day.

# Nine

*F*lora zips up her suitcase and stops in the open doorway to take a last look around the room. She'll be back of course, but this feels like a defining moment and she's struck by the enormity of it. It is so easy to contemplate big lifestyle changes when you're young, and so daunting at her age. She thinks back to other times when she has felt the weight of change pressing on her. A dull and chilly March day in 1958 when she had been dragged by her parents into the throng of thousands queuing for entry to Wembley Stadium. She was ten and had envied Gerald who, being at boarding school, had escaped an afternoon of boredom. Flora had been in her bedroom singing along with The Chordettes to 'Lollipop' on the gramophone she'd got for Christmas, when her mother had called her to hurry up and get her coat on.

'Why can't I stay here?' she'd called back down the stairs. 'I promise not to go out, I'll just stay in and read my book.'

'Absolutely not,' her mother had said. 'Come along, quickly now, Daddy's already started the car.'

Flora had switched off the gramophone, cast a longing look at *Little Women*, and struggled into her coat. Sermons in church were bad enough but this one sounded gruesome and would last for hours. But later, when they were in their seats high up in the stands and Billy Graham began to speak, Flora had known that God was speaking directly to her. The message, constantly repeated, was simple, and the passion of the delivery brought her out in goosebumps. This was no sermon, it was like nothing she had ever experienced. No complicated sentences mumbled in a monotone from the pulpit, no tedious and incomprehensible phrases from the bible; just passion, promises, and a call to action. When it finished and those who wanted to dedicate their lives to God were invited to leave their seats and come to the centre of the stadium, her father had got to his feet and Flora quickly followed.

'Oh sit down, for goodness sake, and don't be so ridiculous,' her mother had hissed, as people began to stream into the aisles and onto the ground. 'Evangelist indeed. He's just a cheap entertainer. I told you we shouldn't have come. Whatever would Father Barrett say if he could see you both?'

Her father had hesitated, begun to protest and then, with more angry urging from her mother, had dropped back into his seat while Flora, struggling to drag him up again, had wept hot tears of despair that she had not been allowed to give herself to God, and was now bound for hell and damnation. Something remarkable had happened that day; God had become real for her and from then on she would both chat and pray to him, ask for advice and confide her deepest thoughts. And a few years later she had known she wanted to enter a convent. The decision was not only about her faith, but also about her fear that she would never fit in with the wider world. She was confused about herself; drawn always to the company of girls and lacking the interest in boys that most of them shared. There was, she felt, something different about her. The only person she'd talked to about it was Connie.

'I read a book about a girl like that,' Connie had said. 'She liked girls the way we – well, most of us – like boys.'

'Really? Can I read it?' Flora had asked.

'I can get it for you,' Connie said. 'I heard Mum talking about it to her friend Grace, so I pinched it from her shelf and read it under the bedclothes. I didn't like it much, didn't understand all of it, but maybe you will.'

'What's it called?'

Connie had shrugged. 'Can't remember, but it's got a green and white cover, and I know just where it is on the shelf.'

A couple of days later she had pulled a brown paper bag out of her satchel and handed it over. 'Maybe don't show it to your mum,' she'd said.

And Flora, who had no intention of doing anything of the sort, stuffed it into her own satchel and opened it later in her bedroom. It was called *The Well of Loneliness*, which was such a sad title that she wondered if she really did want to read it, but that night she smuggled it into bed with her and started reading. It seemed very long, and she found it quite dull. The girl called Stephen was not at all like her, and yet the sense of displacement and wrongness that Stephen felt was very real to Flora.

'Did it help?' Connie asked as she slipped the book in its brown bag back into her own satchel.

'Sort of,' Flora said. 'It made me feel that I'm not the only one.'

'It doesn't matter, you know,' Connie said. 'Mum said there are a lot of girls who are like that. Not just ordinary people, famous people too. There's nothing wrong with you.'

But although Connie's mother's words were reassuring, whatever it was that Flora felt never came up in polite conversation. The chances of finding anyone else like her seemed pretty remote. By the time she left school she had no more information than she'd had at fourteen, but she had some strange and scary feelings towards other girls and prayed long and hard for guidance. The convent seemed like a safe place to be, and she lived in a fever of anxiety until she was admitted.

It was harder than Flora had expected, the God of the nuns was so different from her God; this one seemed more like her parents: distant, critical and frequently punishing. And as she was wondering whether she would take the option to leave at the end of the preparatory year, the decision was made for her in the most unexpected way. She fell in love with Sister Mary Margaret, who was in her thirties, and, even more frightening, her love was reciprocated. Two months later Mother Superior counselled Sister Mary Margaret and put her onto a strict program of prayer, sacrifice and rehabilitation, and Flora was expelled.

It was a relief in many ways and she was able to avoid disclosing what had happened, simply telling her parents that she had been found unsuitable to take the veil. God, she believed, understood and forgave her. But by the late sixties he had been displaced by the Maharishi, who promised to rid the world of unhappiness and discontent and that, she was sure, had to be a good thing.

There have been other, less spiritual and more earthly turning points at which she has felt this same overwhelming sense of change. The death of a friend in India had brought her home to England and then, a few years later, Gerald urging her back to Hobart had given her direction. That was short lived; eighteen months later, bruised by the soured relationship with her brother, and banished from his home, she had come back to London determined on a new start in teaching. And decades later there was the time she had decided to stay here in Port d'Esprit with Suzanne.

As she stands here now, looking out from the window of the bedroom that has been hers for fifteen years, Flora is filled with a sense of despair at what now seems like a series of second rate decisions taken for the wrong reasons. What has she now but herself, her gut instincts and a vague and wavering version of the God that she found along with thousands of others on that March day in Wembley Stadium?

Wisdom has evaded her, she has not achieved great spiritual depths, nor discovered lasting earthly love, despite many attempts. Now, as she teeters towards an unplanned old age, she might as well be stepping into a void.

Outside in the yard Pierre, the kitchen hand, is lugging a sack of potatoes off the back of the greengrocer's truck to take to the kitchen. It's all so familiar, so safe and pleasant on the one hand, so stultifying on the other. She sighs and turns away from the window, remembering the letter that came for her this morning and which she hasn't yet opened. She checks the top of the chest of drawers, the dressing table, her bag and remembers finally that she put it in the pocket of her jacket. The envelope of thick cream vellum is stamped 'Tonkin's Books' in the top left-hand corner, with an address in Bloomsbury. Puzzled, Flora opens it, takes out two sheets of matching notepaper covered in neat but bold handwriting and begins to read. Of course, Gerald's old friend, a letter of condolence, how thoughtful. She reads on through the assorted memories, and sympathies, to the part that suggests that if she is ever in London perhaps they could catch up for a drink. 'I don't think so, Phillip,' she murmurs, and shoves the folded letter into her pocket; she'll show it to Connie when they are on the flight. But then she thinks again. It might be good to meet Phillip, might help both her and Connie to make sense of Gerald and his dramatic effect on both their lives.

'So you are off now?' Suzanne asks, appearing soft as a ghost in the doorway.

Flora folds the letter, puts it back in her pocket, and glances at her watch. 'Yes, the taxi'll be here any minute. It feels very strange . . . leaving like this . . .'

'But you will come back,' Suzanne says. 'It is a little holiday only . . .' her voice fades away.

'I'll be back in about three weeks but it's the beginning of the end Suzanne,' Flora says, taking her hands. 'Things have to change, we both know that,' and she is stunned to see that Suzanne seems to be holding back tears. To Flora's knowledge Suzanne has not cried since the dark days following Jacques's death. She is stoic, a woman who keeps her emotions on a tight rein, but she is visibly moved this morning.

Suzanne nods. 'But it is hard just the same. I have relied on you so long, Flora, I don't know how I will manage . . .'

'You'll manage. And you'll have Xavier, it's what you want.'

Suzanne shrugs. 'Yes, perhaps, I think so, but what if I'm wrong? How can I be sure?'

Flora smiles. 'You always want certainty, Suzanne, but there is none. It's an illusion; we talk about it, cling to the idea of it, but we don't get to have it.'

Suzanne sighs. 'I know, I know. Well, you will be back soon and we will decide then. Perhaps you find a place in town, and we still work together . . . a little . . . sometimes?'

Flora nods. 'Perhaps,' she says. 'But perhaps not – let's wait and see.' And as she says it she knows without a shred of doubt that this part of her life really is over. She no longer belongs here and as she picks up her bag and follows Suzanne down the stairs she feels as though she is about to step off the edge of a cliff without a safety harness.

*

Kerry wanders restlessly between the tables where small groups of children are drawing and colouring images inspired by a short film on Tasmanian wildlife. There are seagulls and mice, a couple of platypuses, some snakes, a few frogs, but most have chosen the wild-eyed Tasmanian devil; in one of the drawings it actually appears to be breathing fire. She pauses, looking now at the children, some totally absorbed in their work, others talking or whispering to each other, a couple chewing the ends of their pencils and gazing out of the window. There have been times in her teaching career when she had thought it might be more challenging and satisfying to teach, like Chris, in high school, but right now she's thankful she's here. Of the limited range of feelings that seem available to her, thankful is about the best.

And she *is* thankful for this classroom and its familiar, delightful, often annoying occupants; thankful for its structured processes, its timetable and the demands that used to irritate her but now force her to struggle each day to keep going, to focus, to believe she will get through. She's thankful for the school and, most of all, for her family, although she is incapable of telling them that. In fact most of the time now she is incapable of telling anyone anything much at all. Every day has become a struggle, every day she tries to reach beyond that invisible wall and every day it seems more impenetrable.

There's a disturbance now at a table on the other side of the room, the tearing of paper, raised voices, a child bursts into tears.

'Calm down,' Kerry says, crossing to the troublesome table. 'What's going on here?'

'Simon says my platypus looks like a cricket bat,' wails the little girl whose name is Lucy Braddock. 'And he says he's going to smash it with a cricket ball.'

Kerry is thankful too, she realises now, for the years of experience that enable her to automatically operate in teacher mode; she calms Lucy, reprimands Simon, and urges everyone to get on with their work.

What she would really like is to lie down on the couch in her mother's kitchen while Farah makes tea and cuts buttered toast into triangles for her. In fact what she would like most of all is for her mother to do that for her but even if Connie had been there Kerry knows that she couldn't ask for that, because for the last few years she has been pushing her mother away, holding her at arm's length so that she wouldn't detect the repulsion she felt at her father's physical condition, and the shame and the anger that it bred in her. How could he do this, how could he desert her? She had spent her life trying to win his approval and attention with very little success and then, as he diminished before her eyes, he also took her mother's attention away from her. It was too much to bear and the pain had to be turned into something else.

Kerry sighs, remembering the silent kitchen, the soft weightless blanket, the smell of toast. That day she had thought she was falling apart, and that night, in Connie's bed, she had dreamed of it happening, saw herself standing upright, a dark silhouette against a light background with a network of cracks swarming across the silhouette until it shattered, leaving shards of broken glass on the ground where she had stood.

'So what happened?' Chris had asked as he walked out to the car to meet her when she arrived home from Hobart.

'Don't know, really . . .' an attempt at a casual shrug. 'Just tired, I suppose.'

'Poor darling,' he'd said, 'come on in and put your feet up and I'll make you a cup of tea.'

Kerry longed to collapse into him, into his comfort, into his love, but the wall blocked her. The previous evening she had fallen asleep really early and Farah had called him and told him she needed to stay the night. It felt right but she knew he would have been worried about her.

'Farah was lovely to me,' she said. 'She thinks I should get a check-up.'

'So, you'll do that, won't you?' he'd said, looking anxiously at her.

She'd nodded.

'When?'

'Oh well, when I have time.'

'*Make* time, Kerry.' He'd moved over to sit beside her then, put his arm around her shoulder, took her free hand in his. 'Please, this week, do it this week.'

She hasn't, of course, because the task seems monumental. How could she explain her symptoms? How could she explain the invisible wall, the disintegrating silhouette? How could anyone understand that?

'Did you call the doctor?' he'd asked a few days later.

And of course she lied – mumbled about blood tests, waiting for results. But that was a couple of weeks ago now, and she knows he's suspicious. She'd lied too – by omission – not telling him about scaring the life out of Farah and waking up to three police officers staring down at her. She'd sworn Farah to secrecy the following morning as they'd gone for a walk with her two daughters.

And as she'd left they had stood facing each other awkwardly until Kerry had felt herself lurch forward and put her arms around Farah.

'Come back if you need to,' Farah had said, stroking her shoulder. 'It's nice and quiet here. Let me know you're coming so I don't call the police again.'

They'd both laughed then.

'Take sick leave,' Chris had also suggested. 'Get the doctor to give you a certificate.'

And she couldn't tell him that she didn't dare to take sick leave because without some sort of structure, some framework for each day, the cracks would start to open up. She will have to do something soon though, or he'll frogmarch her to the surgery. Tomorrow, perhaps, she'll call and make an appointment . . . she could do it today in the lunch break, but no, tomorrow is good. That's it then, she'll do it tomorrow, definitely, first thing in the morning. Only when tomorrow comes it still seems too hard.

*

'Have a look at this,' Flora says, passing Connie an envelope once they are airborne. 'It arrived this morning.'

Connie looks at her and then takes the envelope. She is

caught up in the excitement of setting foot on English soil again. She yearns for a sense of homecoming, of belonging. She looks down at the envelope.

'Tonkin's Books?'

'Just open it,' Flora says.

'Nice notepaper. I miss this, you know – letters, I mean – opening envelopes, the feeling of holding in my hand something that the other person has held in theirs.' She holds the folded letter and looks out of the window to the choppy waters below. 'This is so amazing, Flora, going back after all this time.'

'Yes, it must be,' Flora says, 'anyway, just read the letter.'

Connie fumbles for her glasses, unfolds the pages, reads the letter and turns back to Flora. 'How nice. Phillip Tonkin . . . I feel I should know him but . . .'

'A summer afternoon, a punt on the river at Richmond,' Flora says. 'You and Gerald, Phillip Tonkin and me.'

Connie gasps and her hand flies to her mouth. 'Of course, the one you almost emasculated. How extraordinary, you know I'd completely forgotten about him. He and Gerald used to send Christmas cards but that all stopped years ago. How nice of him to write.' She hands back the letter. 'Especially in view of your last encounter. Shall we go and see him? After all, we're going to Bloomsbury where he has a bookshop, and we would probably have ended up there anyway without realising who owned it,' she laughs. 'You're right, it's an extraordinary coincidence, arriving just on the day we leave. Another day and we might have missed it. It sort of seems as though it was meant to be. Let's go.'

Flora smiles. 'That's what I thought.'

'Another chance to connect with our younger selves.' She pauses, recalling a glimpse of Phillip reeling back in shock, then doubling over the side of the punt. She turns back to Flora, grinning. 'Maybe Phillip wants to try his luck again.'

Flora lets out a snort of laughter. 'I doubt it. He's the same age as Gerald – more or less – and blokes his age are usually more interested in much younger women.'

'I wonder if he ever found out,' Connie says.

'That he was trying to get off with a dyke? Unlikely. Gerald didn't know at the time, and considering how he behaved when he found out, I doubt he'd have included the news in his Christmas cards.'

They are silent for a moment, holding up their cups to the flight attendant carrying the pot of tea.

'That was such a terrible day,' Connie says, sipping her tea.

'When?'

'The day he found out.'

Flora inhales deeply and nods. 'It certainly was. I've been thinking about it quite a lot recently. I still get a sinking feeling in my stomach every time. Perhaps I should have told him earlier but I just assumed he'd realised but found it easier to pretend ignorance. Letting him find Denise in my bed prob-ably wasn't the most thoughtful thing I've ever done.'

'You know, Flora, I really hated that your falling out with Gerald meant that you only knew our family through me. I would love you to come to Hobart, there's heaps of room for both of us in the house.'

Flora hesitates, shooting her a discomfiting look that catches Connie off guard, making her feel on edge.

'I *have* been thinking about that,' Flora says. 'I do want to meet the rest of the family. And what about Denise, I suppose she's long gone now?'

'No, she's still there. She gave up her job and became a cheese maker, and then she got into a relationship with a bread maker who had a stall in the Salamanca markets, a lovely woman called Clare. They bought a big block of land with a small house on it, and then built premises for the cheese and bread businesses. They built it into something quite large, the tourists love it there. And the stall still operates at the markets every Saturday morning, regular as clockwork.'

'What's Clare like?' Flora asks. 'I hope Denise has been happy.'

'Clare was lovely, but she died some years ago now. It was very sad. But Denise has kept the business going. Years ago they found a sperm donor and Clare had a baby, so there's a son. I can't remember his name now, but he's delightful, and he and his girlfriend run the business with Denise. It all seems so long ago. I often run into Denise and she always asks about you. I don't think Gerald ever really understood what we all lost back then. It's time we'll never have back. Death stirs up so much, doesn't it? So much grief about so many things.'

Flora nods. 'Yes, a lot of grieving, not just about his death but for all those lost years – decades of our lives which could have been so very different if only . . .' Her voice trails away and Connie sees the enormous sadness in her face.

They sit in silence, hearing only the sound of the engines and muffled snippets of the conversations around them, and Connie closes her eyes and thinks of home. She thinks of the years of Gerald's illness and what it has done to them, to her and the children and grandchildren, slicing into their lives, dividing rather than uniting them, straining their relationships to breaking point. It ought to have bound us together, she thinks, but now that he's gone there's so much damage to repair. And just as she knows that she has never forgiven him for what he did to Flora, there is something else she has not forgiven.

'He made me promise, you know,' she says, turning to Flora. 'That's the other thing I can't forgive. He made me promise never to put him into any sort of care, no matter how awful it got. He kept making me promise it again and again as things got worse. I know I shouldn't mind, I loved him and it was my duty to look after him. But it was terrible, Flora;

122

the last few years have been a nightmare. It wore me into the ground and sometimes I hated him for it, really hated him, because it changed everything and damaged all of us, separated me from the children and grandchildren. That's the other thing that I simply can't forgive, how he pressured me to make that promise. But sometimes I think it's myself I can't forgive for keeping it.'

# Ten

'How's it going?' Donna asks, joining Brooke on the seat in the bus shelter.

Donna, smelling of cigarettes and a mango face mask she had tried out at morning break, is, as usual, oozing energy. Sometimes Brooke loves that energy, it jolts her out of her own little world, which is pretty depressing these days, and draws her into a social life that she would not otherwise have had. At other times, like now, it just totally pisses her off because Brooke likes being alone with her music or her books, or her iPad – she is never afraid of her own company.

It's started to rain and the strong wind drives it inside so it stings their faces and legs like hundreds of tiny sharp needles. As another great gust of icy wind swoops through the shelter, the two girls huddle into one corner. When Brooke left home this morning it was bright and clear, the wind cool but friendly; now it's just turned midday and it might as well be winter. Donna is wearing a silver anorak over her blazer; if a teacher had seen her leaving the school in that there would have been trouble.

'Is it better since you talked to your dad?' Donna asks.

Brooke shrugs, wishing she'd brought her own anorak this morning. 'Yeah, I s'pose. At least they're including me now, and I think they're trying to be nicer to each other. I wish they'd get on with it though, it's, like, going on forever. They agree about one thing and then they start arguing about something else. I just want it to be over. I mean, I know what I want . . .' she hesitates. She hasn't yet told Donna about her plan to go to Hobart. If she does Donna will freak out and then Brooke will have that to cope with too.

Fortunately Donna is fully occupied trying to light one of the two cigarettes she has pulled from the pocket of her anorak. She draws on it, exhales and offers it to Brooke.

Brooke shakes her head. 'No thanks. Does your mum know you smoke?'

'You're joking, she'd go mental. Anyway, I don't really smoke. I mean, I never buy them, just get them off other people.'

Brooke gives her a long look, wondering whether she wants to start an argument about whether or not that means Donna is not really smoking, and decides against it. 'Who gave you those?'

'Danny Philpot,' Donna says.

'Eeww! He's touched them and you're putting them into your mouth? That's disgusting. *He's* disgusting.'

'He's cute,' Donna says, 'and mega funny.' She sucks smoke into her mouth and blows it out again. 'Anyway, I don't inhale. You don't have to, you can, like, smoke without inhaling and it just *looks* like you're inhaling.'

'But that's *why* people smoke – to inhale,' Brooke says. 'You'll stink of cigarettes and your teeth will go yellow but you don't even get whatever people get when they *do* inhale.'

'Well, it's safer not to inhale anyway,' Donna says with a note of defiance. 'You can't get lung cancer this way.'

'Yes you can, because you inhale the passive smoke, and anyway you can get cancer of the mouth.'

'You cannot, there's no such thing.'

Brooke rolls her eyes. 'There is so! I did smoking for my

health project. You only do it because you think it makes you look cool, but it doesn't, it's just really gross.'

The wind whips into the bus shelter even more strongly now. Brooke peers out searching for signs of an approaching bus, and spots a teacher heading their way under a green umbrella, a huge shoulder bag bumping against her hip, her free hand stuffed in the pocket of her trench coat.

'Spoiler alert,' Brooke hisses, turning back into the bus shelter. 'Whiskers is on the way.'

Donna drops her cigarette on the pavement, grinds it out with her shoe and peers up the road. 'The bus is coming too,' she says, 'she'll have to run for it.'

Miss Whiskin does indeed run, her umbrella swaying, the wind blowing her dark red hair across her face. She reaches the stop just before the bus and looks at them with suspicion.

'Why are you girls out here at this time of day?'

'Mrs Morland fainted and the Head cancelled her senior classes,' Brooke says. 'We were told we could go home.'

Miss Whiskin nods. 'Right. Tacky anorak, Donna,' she says. 'It doesn't conform to uniform standards, and neither does the cigarette you just put out. My classroom tomorrow morning, eight-thirty.' And she pushes past them and steps up into the bus.

Donna pulls a face and pokes her middle finger at the teacher's disappearing back. 'Whiskers' hair is the same colour as your mum's, only it doesn't look good on her – miserable old bag. I like your mum's.'

'I don't,' Brooke says. 'It's horrible, artificial. I hate Mum's hair how she's got it now.'

'But it's so cool,' Donna says. 'She always looks cool, your mum – her hair, her clothes and everything. I wish my mum would dress like that. Your dad's nice too, but he's not really cool, he's just, well . . .'

'Ordinary,' Brooke says. 'I like that. I wish they'd just be ordinary, both of them. Act like ordinary parents.'

'So what's going to happen?' Donna asks. 'Will you have to move?'

'Maybe, but they can't agree about the house, who'll stay, who'll go, who I'm going to live with.'

'I s'pose you want to live with your mum?'

Brooke hesitates. 'I just want them to make up their minds,' she says.

'You should go with your mum,' Donna says. 'She'd probably buy you more stuff if your dad wasn't around. My mum hides stuff and then pretends she's had it for ages. And if Dad sees she's been shopping she lies about how much she spent.'

Brooke nods slowly. 'My mum does that too. Last night we went down into town and Mum bought stuff for both of us, then she goes, "Don't tell your father, he'll never notice".' She leans back in her seat. Andrew has been away in Perth for two nights and is not due back 'til Friday, and, just as when her mother was away before, it's so much nicer when there's only one of them around. Brooke had said that to her nan when they'd Skyped the other day and Nan had said that it was bound to be like that when two people were at loggerheads. Nan had talked to her dad too. He'd phoned her and told her they were close to working things out.

'Well, you see, Brooke,' Connie had said, 'in a relationship both people put up with things that they don't really like. They do it to keep the peace. But when things go really wrong, like they have for your mum and dad now, they're not only upset about the present, but all that old stuff comes up for them too.'

'It's the same for me too, Nan,' she'd said. 'I mean, I'm so fed up with both of them right now that I keep thinking of all the things they've ever done that have upset me.'

'That's why it's best for you to stay out of what happens between them, and just think carefully about what you want for yourself, and remember that none of this is about you. You've been very brave and mature, Brooke,' she'd said. 'I'm so proud of you, and I'm looking forward so much to seeing you in the holidays.'

But Brooke is feeling less brave and mature with every passing day because each time she thinks she knows what she wants, something happens to change it.

'If we get off at the next stop we can have hot chocolate in that place on the corner,' Donna says, nudging her in the ribs. 'Then we can walk the rest of the way.'

Brooke nods and they grab their bags, jump down from the bus and head for the café.

It's half past two when Brooke turns into the private road to the townhouses. Down near her own house a big van is parked in the street and as she walks towards it two men lift an ugly but expensive-looking black leather sofa off the tailboard and set it down on the pavement. Brooke peers ahead through the fine rain. Yuk, bad taste, Mr Perozzi, she thinks, glancing along to where she expects to see the front door open to receive it. But Mr Perozzi's door is closed. The door that's open, and towards which the sofa is now being carried, is Brooke's own front door, and standing on the front step, anxiously watching its progress, is her mother.

Linda steps aside to make room for the delivery men as they shift and turn to get the sofa onto its side. 'Careful,' she calls, in her imperious, gallery manager voice. 'Make sure you don't damage it.'

The men mumble something under their breath and ease the sofa in through the front door. Brooke pauses at the gate; she has a horrible feeling she knows what's happening. Her chest tightens and her heart begins to pound, making her breathless, as though she has run fast all the way from the corner of the street. Linda watches as the sofa disappears safely into the hall, and it is as she turns to follow it that she spots Brooke out on the street.

'Oh my god, Brooke,' she says. 'What on earth are you doing home this time of day?'

'Mrs Morland was sick so they let her seniors go.'

Linda looks awkward, her face is flushed, and she keeps shifting her gaze away from Brooke's. She swallows, takes a few steps forward and stops. 'Well,' she says, 'well, I certainly wasn't expecting you yet.'

'What's happening?' Brooke asks, although it's pretty clear now from her mother's embarrassment that her worst fears are about to be realised. 'Why is that gross sofa here?'

Linda takes a deep breath, and walks towards her. 'Well, it's like this, darling, I mean . . . I'd hoped we'd have this all done by the time you got home. All nicely settled, you know, so we could all talk about it calmly together, but as you're here . . .'

Beyond her mother, in the doorway, Brooke sees a familiar figure in black signing papers on a clipboard. He hands it back to the delivery men along with some money, and they return down the path to their van and drive away. Away, Brooke thinks, from the scene of the crime.

'What's *he* doing here?' she asks, nodding towards Zachary. 'Where's Dad?'

'Darling, you know Dad's in Perth. I just thought I should take the opportunity to finalise things once and for all.'

'Behind his back?'

'Well . . .' Linda hesitates. 'Look, this has been very hard for all of us and we just don't seem to be getting any further. We talk and talk and never . . .' she pauses again. 'I wanted to get back to some sort of normal life with the least trouble and heartbreak for everyone, particularly for you, Brooke.'

'For me? For me! I told you I'd live here with Dad or you but I wouldn't live anywhere with Zachary. That was the *one* thing I asked *not* to happen. And now he's moving in.'

Linda holds up a hand to silence her. 'I know but, darling, you have to be realistic. You can't live here with your father, he's a hopeless housekeeper, you'd never have proper meals or clean clothes . . .'

'I can cook and wash my *own* clothes, in fact I often do, so don't . . .'

'You know what I mean,' Linda cuts her off. 'Besides, Andrew has very long days and is quite often away for two or three nights at a time. And, darling, be honest, it would be terribly dull for you, you know it would. Look what fun we have together, what fun we had last night shopping . . .'

'It's not about *you*, it's about *him*,' Brooke says, pointing to Zachary, who is watching them from the doorway.

'Well, that's not negotiable, Zach's moving in with us,' Linda says, less sympathetic and firmer now. 'I know it's not what you wanted, Brooke, but it's the way things are. We're all going to get along fine. I've moved all your dad's things into that little flat above the gallery. It's been empty for ages, so it's not as though he'll have nowhere to stay until he finds a place of his own.'

'You mean you've told him, he knows about this?'

'Not yet. I'll call him tonight, when we've got everything sorted.' She has her firm, bossy face on now. 'And you have to understand, Brooke, that I need to talk to him first. So no calling him before then, okay?'

'I hate you,' Brooke says, feeling the hatred boiling up inside her like the contents of some witch's cauldron. 'I will never, ever forgive you for this, and as soon as Dad gets home I'm going to live with him.' She pushes past her mother and heads for the front door.

'Hey, Brooke, sweetheart,' Zachary says, sauntering towards her down the path. 'We're gonna be friends, aren't we?' He catches her arm. 'I had a look in your room – those posters are a bit tacky. I could do a mural for you, something around your music or all your French stuff . . .'

Brooke wrenches her arm free. 'If you ever go in my room again I will slash every bit of black leather that you own with a very sharp knife, even if you're wearing it.' And she runs up the stairs to her room, slams the door behind her, throws herself on her bed, gets out her phone and dials Andrew's number.

*

Kerry is sitting in the staff room with her tuna sandwich and a cup of strong black tea, flicking through a magazine but thinking about Chris, who left at the crack of dawn to drive to Hobart to pick up his older sister at the airport. Normally Kerry would have been over the moon at the prospect of Erin's visit but right now she's not sure how she feels. In fact she doesn't think she feels anything at all. But having her around will be a help; Erin is terrific with the children and they adore her. Still, Kerry wonders how she'll cope with the effort of trying to behave like her normal self when she feels more like an automaton. Her phone rings and she pulls it from her jacket pocket and gets up, walking out of the staff room into the passage.

'Hi,' Chris says, 'it's me. Thought I might catch you in the lunch break. How're you going, darlin'?'

'Fine, are you at the airport?'

'Yes, the flight's a bit late so I'm having a coffee.'

'Was the drive okay? You left very early.'

'Oh well, you know me, I love that café where we stop for breakfast. I needed time for bacon and eggs and sausages and all the other things middle-aged men with expanding waist-lines aren't supposed to eat.'

'I wondered . . . if you'd called by the house?'

'Connie's house? No, why would I do that?'

'Oh, just maybe to check out that everything's okay?'

'Well, Farah's there, isn't she? Didn't you call her the other night? She'd have told you if there were any problems.'

'Yes,' she says, 'of course she would. She said everything was fine.'

'Well, then . . .'

'Just me being silly.'

'No, no, it's understandable. Do you want me to drop by there before we head home?'

'No, 'course not, no need.'

'Well, as long as you're okay.'

'I'm fine.' But she can hear the flatness in her tone, and knows it disturbs him.

'Did the doctor say anything about the blood tests? They seem to be taking a long time.'

Alone in the passage outside the staff room Kerry feels herself blush. She still hasn't called the doctor let alone seen her, but – another lie – she'd told Chris she'd been. Just a bit run down, she'd told him, but the doctor was doing some blood tests. 'They do,' she says. 'Perhaps I should chase them up.'

'Do that,' he says. 'You probably just need a tonic or something. Do it today.'

'Okay,' she says. 'It'll be lovely to see Erin. The kids were so excited this morning.'

'Me too,' he says, 'and I think the flight's landing now.'

'Good – well, give her a hug from me and I'll see you both later.'

'And you'll call the surgery about the tests?'

'I will. Gotta run now, the bell's just gone. Drive carefully.' And she hits 'end' and stands there staring at the phone, knowing just how much she loves and depends on him, but unable to feel it.

What she'd like to do is call Farah. They've spoken a few times since the day Kerry fell asleep in the study and was woken by the police. That day seems almost like a dream now. Somehow Farah had seen beyond the physical reality of Kerry lying there on the sofa and recognised that something more serious was happening than just a dizzy spell or low blood sugar. She had persuaded her not to drive back to Launceston that night.

'You should see your doctor soon,' she had said.

'You think there's something wrong with me?' Kerry asked, almost with relief that there might be a simple explanation for the way she was feeling.

Farah had turned away to move a pot from the stove. 'I think you have had a sad and difficult time. Losing your father, your mother being so occupied with him for so long. These things are hard to cope with. You need help.'

'A psychologist, you mean?'

Farah shrugged. 'Maybe, or perhaps a grief counsellor. Perhaps you are depressed.'

Depression was what Kerry herself had been fearing but hearing it from someone else shocked her. How could Farah know? She nodded. 'Okay,' she'd said, trying to wind up the conversation, 'I'll do something about it next week.' But she knew she wouldn't, knew that it was too hard, too scary, too much to contemplate. Best to wait and see if it went away. Thinking back now on the day and the evening she spent with Farah, she knows that even after the 'D' word had been mentioned, she'd had a wonderful sense of peace there in her mother's house, and she longs to get it back again.

# *Eleven*

*C*onnie stands on a high ridge of land, shading her
eyes against the sun, gazing out across the panorama
of vivid green fields bordered by low hedges, dark
clumps of trees, meadows lying fallow, and others with the
first signs of the future crop tinging them with the palest
of pale greens. In the middle distance six triangular white
gables peak above a line of tall trees, their earth-toned roof
tiles blending perfectly into another clump of trees at the
rear. Nearby, scattered glimpses show other, lower roofs that
meld into the landscape and the stark grey spire of a church
reaches upward like a lance. In the distance, the slopes and
hedges, the rough heath and the dark clumps of forested land
spread for miles, merging into the blurred grey-green of the
horizon.

Connie feels a surge of pure joy, as though this place and
the broader landscape have enfolded her with their beauty,
their familiarity and their meaning. She is enchanted by
the rediscovery of something old and precious, something
unchanged since her childhood.

'It's just the same,' she says, turning to Flora, eyes alight,
cheeks flushed with emotion. 'Just as I remember, no more
buildings, not even a mobile phone tower or a telegraph pole,

just the forest and the heath, the fields and that wonderful smoky distance blending into the sky. I can barely believe it. I've thought of this place so often, imagined it taken over by some hideous sports arena or shopping centre, but here it is, just the same.'

Flora smiles. 'Well, it *is* Ashdown Forest,' she says, 'it's been pretty much unchanged for centuries, so by comparison your lifetime memory is just the blink of an eye.'

Connie nods, still drinking in the landscape, still high on the nostalgia of homecoming. Standing here in this spot, the trees around her forming a dark border to frame what might be a painting by Constable, she is filled with a longing to share this with her children and grandchildren, particularly with Brooke, who has been foremost in her mind. 'There were times when I thought I would never come here again,' she says.

'Here to the Enchanted Place or here to England?' Flora asks.

'Both, but especially here. It's always had a sort of magic for me ever since Mum told me it was where Winnie-the-Pooh lived. Every time I read the books to the kids and then to my grandchildren, I dreamed of coming here again.'

'We came here as kids too,' Flora says, and taking a step back, she focuses her camera and snaps Connie in close-up, the landscape hazy in muted sunlight, and beside her the stone plinth with its bronze plaque engraved in memory of Pooh's creator. 'I do love it but it's never had quite the same magic for me as it has for you.'

'Mum and I came here often for walks and picnics; it was an important place in our life together after Dad left. When I was a teenager we'd cycle up here with our sandwiches and books, and stay for hours. I'm sure you came with us sometimes.'

Flora nods. 'I think I did.'

'We did it for years. The last time we came here I was

home on holiday from Guildhall. It was the week before the accident, and of course she died a few days later. We sat here talking about how one day I'd travel the world with the opera and she'd come and visit me. Maybe we'd get a flat in London together, but we'd always come back here.' Connie stops now, gazing down at the place where they had sat that day. 'You were away then,' she says, looking up at Flora.

'I was indeed. I was seeking enlightenment, and devoting myself to Maharishi Mahesh Yogi,' Flora says with a grin. 'And I came home to find you'd got engaged to Gerald.'

Connie nods. 'He was very good to me then, maybe too good. He went to a lot of trouble to find Dad in Spain – not that Dad was remotely interested – so Gerald organised the funeral, everything. But really I wished he'd let me do it. I wanted to, I thought it was the last thing I could do for Mum, but Gerald was dead set on doing everything. He had the best intentions, but it made me feel incompetent, and I didn't know how to resist him.'

'Mmmm. Well, I was amazed when I got home and you announced you were getting married.'

'I do remember that,' Connie laughs. 'I remember you saying "So I suppose we're going to be sisters now?" and I was thinking, "Well, you might look a bit more pleased about it".'

Flora grimaces. 'I was pleased, Con, of course I was. In one way I was thrilled because it meant we'd always be part of the same family. But I was jealous; you were my best friend, we had our own sisterly friendship, I wanted that, and I suppose I was a bit scared that although you'd be part of the family, Gerald might sort of co-opt you into his life. Which, of course, he did.'

Connie nods, silent now, gazing down at the spot where she had sat with her mother that last day.

'Anyway,' Flora says, 'I can't even remember now why this is called the Enchanted Place.'

Connie looks up at her. 'In the Pooh books it's the place where Christopher Robin and Pooh take their last walk together. Christopher Robin is going away to boarding school, and they know, somehow, that things will never be quite the same again.' She points towards the memorial plaque and quotes from memory, '"and by and by they came to an enchanted place on the very top of the forest called Galleons Lap", which is where we're standing now. It was actually called Gills Leap, but Milne changed it, and since then everyone seems to have called it the Enchanted Place. I think it's much nicer because, to me at least, it *is* enchanted.' She's silent for a moment, then turns back to Flora. 'It means a lot that we came here together. Come on, I'll take you to the place where Kanga teaches baby Roo to do his kangaroo jumps, and to Eeyore's Gloomy Place, and if you like we can walk down to Pooh Bridge and play Pooh Sticks.'

They walk on over the pale mauve carpet of heather, down a steep slope along fern lined paths, towards the bridge.

'I can't tell you how wonderful it is to be here again,' Connie says. 'I came back looking for something I couldn't define – still can't. Australia is my home now, and I love it, but there's always a little bit of myself that's missing, that's still back here in England. You must feel like that about Tasmania.'

Flora pauses, thinking. 'Hmmm. I suppose I feel an affinity, but it's different for me. I was just five when we left Australia, and the only time I've been back there was the eighteen months I stayed with you. I often think of it, and I'm curious about it. But it's not the sort of feeling you're describing. England and France have really been my life but perhaps there is a bit of me in Australia. We're like the wild geese, aren't we? Never entirely settled, always seeking out an idea of home.'

'You might find that bit of you if you came back,' Connie says. 'You would certainly find your only remaining family.'

'Yes,' Flora says, 'I guess I would. And I am thinking about that, but I'm not as good as you at expressing myself.' She laughs then goes on, 'I'm getting quite emotional. Suzanne wouldn't approve of that at all. She would send me off in pursuit of some suitable task to stop me dwelling on things and upsetting myself.'

Connie nods and they walk on in silence. 'Sometimes,' she says eventually, 'it seems important to upset oneself, or at least to allow oneself to be upset. It hurts like hell but it also heals. That's why I'm here now with you, churning up the past, burrowing into it like woodworm into precious timber, pricking myself on the splinters as I go, believing if I dig deeper I will somehow discover something I left behind that will nourish me now, all these years later.'

*

At the rear of the shop in the half-glass cubical laughingly called 'the office', Bea, spectacles perched on the end of her nose, is reading a battered, leather-bound journal, while also keeping an eye open for intruders. The shop itself is a place where intruders are welcome – an intruder being a potential customer, a potential victim for Bea's personal crusade to get people to expand their reading horizons, to discover or recapture the joy of turning pages as opposed to flicking a remote control. Today, though, she is on the alert for another sort of intruder – a person or people she would prefer to observe before meeting.

The shop is fitted with CCTV cameras that silently scan the shelves and tables, the corners and crannies, the walkways between the sections. They also scan the ever-changing mix of customers: tousle-haired Nordic tourists with backpacks, men and women in serious suits, nubile young women in skimpy skirts, Hasidic Jews, bag ladies with trollies, men in macs with canvas shopping bags, ageing women in flat shoes, smart baby boomers in stilettos they should have abandoned years ago, polite Asian students, Sikhs and priests, waiters and wealthy American tourists. The shop is, as Bea often tells people, London in microcosm: all human life is here, with the exception of children; very few children end up at Tonkin's unless their parents are seeking shelter from the rain.

Bea is very happy about the minimal presence of children; little people are, in her opinion, unsuited to bookshops. They whine and wheedle, they have sticky fingers and runny noses, absolutely no decent conversation and have been known to drop whole ice cream cones onto a pile of best sellers on the central display table, something which parents see not as sacrilege but as amusing and endearing.

Books are Bea's life; she has edited and published them, promoted them, rejected them, marketed them and now she buys and sells them. Her garden flat, just a short walk from the shop, is full of books on shelves, in stacks, in boxes. When she finally retires, she says, she will have sufficient reading material to occupy her until death.

'You'll find my body there one day,' she told Phillip recently, 'mouldering away, infested with maggots, under a complete set of Gibbons' *Decline and Fall of the Roman Empire*. Reading that will, I suspect, just push me over the edge.'

But today Bea is reading not a book but a journal. Her own journal, one of the many she has kept intermittently through her life and rather more regularly in her youth than she does now, in her seventies. She's been going back through the journals since the day Phillip shoved a copy of his old school's newsletter in front of her, and stabbed his finger at an obituary.

'Gerry Hawkins has died,' he'd said. 'Did you know?'

And Bea had shaken her head and picked up the paper and stared at a photograph of a much older Gerry than she remembered, and her heart had lurched with that blend of nostalgia and regret that is felt when the best and the worst creases of the past have been ironed out by age and time.

She had started to read the obituary while Phillip waffled on about having written to Gerry's sister in France. And while he dashed out to post the letter she had read the whole thing, twice, searching for a fragment of the man she knew amid the biographical details and bland prose.

They had all been at university together, she, Gerry and Phillip, and had remained friends once they graduated, even one year setting off together to Morocco with a few others, in a battered Kombi. They were a motley collection of individuals, declaiming about politics and free love, drinking far too much cheap local wine and anything else they could get hold of – the exception being Gerry, who was in the middle of his very boring teetotal 'I think I might be destined for the priesthood' phase. The thing with Gerry was that you never knew whether he was serious or just wanting to stir things up.

And it was those memories that had sent her, that evening, to search the crammed bookshelves in the spare bedroom for the old journals, and to bring them in to work, one at a time, in order to dip into the memories, in between chiding the shop staff, chivvying Phillip about the state of the accounts and persuading customers that they could buy a lifetime of enjoyment for less than it cost them to have lunch at the pub.

'Got a letter from Flora,' Phillip had said a couple of weeks later, shoving it into her hand. 'She lives at that place in Brittany where we camped – remember? Extraordinary coincidence, she and Connie are in Sussex now and coming up to town next week. They're going to pop in. I can't remember if you ever actually met Connie.'

'Never,' Bea had said, shaking her head and not taking her eyes off the letter. 'Gerry was a master at compartmentalising his life. But I heard an awful lot about her.' She'd heard so much in fact that she was quite sure that she would recognise Connie even though they had never met, and she has never even seen a photograph of her. She remembers everything

Liz Byrski

she has ever heard about Connie, remembers her presence, her subtle insinuation into Gerald's life after the tragic death of her mother that had driven Gerald to acts of emotional heroism. She remembers his stories of Connie's fragility and need and she has imagined this nervous, clinging young woman on whom she had bestowed pale wispy hair, large, haunting eyes and a tragic demeanour. In addition to all this Connie had ridiculous pretentions to become an opera singer. Gerald, while acknowledging that she had both talent and commitment, had been adamant that she did not have enough of either, and was also emotionally unsuited to the rigours of such a life. Connie, he had once told Bea, was a needy and dependent girl, unlike Bea herself – whom he had called a feisty, voluptuous and assertive woman. It was only when he'd announced that he felt obliged to marry Connie because she needed someone to look after her that Bea had paused briefly to wonder whether those qualities that he claimed to admire in herself had actually scared him off. So – yes – she remembers Connie, whom Gerald courted out of sympathy and married out of duty, while Bea suffocated her passion under a pile of bullshit about not needing any man, and certainly not 'a self-centred knob-head like you, Gerry'. She'd actually written that in her journal in red biro illustrated with a roughly drawn heart stabbed with a knife and dripping biro blood. Yes, she does remember Connie.

And now it's the Wednesday of the week when they might pop in, and in between snatching snippets of the past from her journal, Bea watches with suspicion each time two women appear at the entrance to the shop, hover for a moment, and then head together or separately for fiction or non-fiction, biography, academic or travel. She searches the faces for Connie's wispy pallor and aura of neediness that she has imagined for decades. Bea is confident that her antennae will immediately detect this presence in the shop and there will be time to study her before she is required to shake hands, offer condolences, smile affectionately at old Gerald-related jokes and pretend that this is a delightful moment of nostalgia and remembrance.

Overhead Bea hears the thud of Phillip's feet as he runs down the bare wooden staircase from his third floor flat. The sound of his approach is distinctive, because unlike the footsteps of customers or staff going up and down to rare books, first editions and foreign literature on the second floor, Phillip runs. The customers don't run, the staff don't run, only Phillip runs. It is, Bea thinks, a matter of pride, to prove he still can run up and down stairs. He wears soft-soled shoes mostly, like moccasins, with cream or beige twill or linen trousers and usually something blue, a t-shirt or shirt with a blue linen jacket, or a navy sweater in winter. Someone must once have told him that he looked good in these clothes – Bea wonders if it was Lorna, his ex – because he rarely varies his wardrobe, and indeed they do suit him. He is still a good-looking man, quite fit for one in his seventies who smokes and takes only moderate exercise. Bea keeps expecting him to turn up with an attractive woman of more than a certain age on his arm, but he never does.

'Ah! You're there,' Phillip says, appearing in the cubicle doorway. 'You okay for dinner Friday night?'

Bea raises her eyebrows. 'Dinner? I imagine you mean fish and chips while we go through the accounts.'

Phillip shakes his head. 'Dinner, proper dinner. I thought we'd go to the Italian place on Judd Street.'

'We're dating now, are we?'

'It's Flora and Connie, we're having dinner with them.'

'I thought they were coming to the shop.'

'They were, but they're still in Brighton, coming up by train on Friday morning, so I asked them to dinner. Are you on?'

'Wouldn't miss it,' Bea says, shuffling papers on the desk. 'Flora, weren't you and she . . . ?'

'Never,' Phillip says, 'but not for lack of trying on my part.' He hesitates and looks awkward. 'You . . . well, you won't . . . ?'

'Of course I won't.'

'Good. So Friday, then, that'll be lovely,' and he is gone, out through the shop and into the street.

'Hmmm,' Bea says softly. 'Not sure about lovely, but it'll be interesting, that's for sure.'

\*

Andrew, in a window seat, puts on the headphones, tunes to the classical music channel, gazes out onto the rumpled bed of cloud and tries to imagine himself lying in all that cool soft whiteness. The last few days have been truly awful: meetings with his counterparts from other states, stultifying discussions about funding for the arts at state and federal level, and a tedious lunch at Parliament House as guests of the local minister. It was during that lunch that he'd felt his phone vibrating inside his jacket pocket and, murmuring apologies, had left the table to take the call.

'Can't you come back *now*?' Brooke begged when she'd explained what was happening. And he'd had to tell her that he couldn't, that he had to visit two regional arts projects and it would be late on Friday afternoon before he could get back to Melbourne.

'Listen, Brooke, please listen to me,' he'd said. 'The worst has already happened, so just hang in there until I get back. Stay out of his way, don't pick any fights with him or your mother. I'll come and see you on Friday evening, I promise. Do this for me, darling, please. Friday evening.'

She'd been extremely grumpy with him but he'd called her back later in the afternoon and told her that he would look around for somewhere for them both to live. 'I'll call when I land in Melbourne and come straight over,' he'd told her.

'And don't tell Mum that you're going to move in with me. I'll talk to her when I get there.'

And then he'd talked to Linda – well, shouted at her down the phone. How dare she move that prick into his house with his daughter! How dare she do anything in his absence! What gave her the right to move his personal possessions out of his own home and into that grotty little studio above the gallery? And Linda had shouted back, enraged about his calling Zachary a prick when he was actually a sensitive artist. She was adamant about her right to have whomever she wanted staying there because she was the joint owner of the house, so there was little he could do about it. Andrew wasn't so sure about that, but from the other side of the country all he could do was call his solicitor, who turned out to be lounging around in some exotic Balinese resort and not returning calls.

Andrew's head keeps spinning; new dimensions of the disaster that is his domestic life rear up like octopus tentacles wrapping themselves around his brain in a constantly tightening grip, destroying his concentration and paralysing his efforts to devise a plan of action. He is awash with rage and hurt, but his physical distance has disabled him. He feels burnt out, as though he would like to lie down in a darkened room for a very long time rather than go from the airport in a taxi to engage in combat with his wife and her lover.

He wonders what his father would have done in this situation, but the idea of his mother even having a lover, let alone moving him into their home, renders it ridiculous. The reverse would have been a more likely scenario and, anyway, Andrew knows that he is not really his father's son, much more his mother's boy, and for the first time ever he is struck by the hideous sexism of those images: a father's son as someone to be proud of, a mother's boy as someone weak and shameful. The truth is that his mother was always a much finer and stronger person than his father. He was all action and bravado; a rousing speaker, adept at winning arguments, and ruthless in negotiating deals. But Connie was substance, endurance and compassion; and it was only as he aged that Andrew had learned to recognise this, to see the fortitude and wisdom and most of all the compassion that so often went unnoticed. Gerald had needed that hard edge in order to do all that he had done: run for Parliament, win, survive another two elections, lose a fourth, and then slip effortlessly into a high level consultancy and a couple of directorships.

Closing his eyes and trying to concentrate on the music, Andrew reminds himself that his father was not a bad person, but a man who did what had to be done in order to achieve what were largely admirable ends. In politics and in business he was essentially fair and ethical, but he could always justify cutting corners if it guaranteed the desired result, and he was easily able to convince himself that riding roughshod over his opposition was simply the way of things. On the few occasions when someone rode roughshod over him he took it with good grace and didn't bear a grudge. 'That's politics,' he'd say, or alternatively, 'That's business. It's not personal, one has to rise above these things, see them for what they are.'

Thinking now about his father, Andrew recalls hearing two rather different versions of the past. First is the story, cemented into family history, of how Connie's mother, running for a bus, had tripped and fallen into the path of an accelerating car, never regained consciousness and died four weeks later, leaving Connie alone in the world. Gerald had stepped in as protector, advisor and eventually as lover and they married some months later. Andrew had never totally believed that Connie was as needy and helpless as his father's version of events made her sound. It didn't fit with a toughness that he had seen in her as he grew up, an emotional fortitude under that mild and accommodating exterior. So it hadn't come as much of a surprise to him when, towards the end of his life, his speech tortured but still coherent, Gerald had mustered the strength to deliver a few sentences on the subject.

'She's the strong one,' he'd said one day as he and Andrew watched Connie carrying bread out to the bird table. 'She would never have married me if her mother hadn't died as she did. I moved in on her when she had no defences. God knows where I'd have ended up without her.'

Sometime later Andrew had repeated this to Kerry and to his surprise she had let out a bark of sarcastic laughter. 'Well, we all know that, don't we? He couldn't live without her and now he refuses to die without her, however long it takes and even if he destroys her and us in the process.'

At the time he'd been shocked – Kerry rarely had a critical word to say about their father – but later he'd thought she was right. He remembered occasions in the past when he'd felt that Gerald had insinuated himself between them – between Andrew and Connie, between him and Kerry. But in those years his father's illness and dying had somehow insinu-ated itself between all of them, divided their loyalties, and isolated them from each other. They were sucked down into the black hole of need that was Gerald's last years, leaving them reeling, fragmented, cut off from each other.

Andrew shifts in his seat and pulls the window blind down halfway to shade his eyes from the sun. He thinks about Connie and Gerald, young, hopeful and in love. Two young people setting a course for the future just as he and Linda had done, filled with hope and trust and love, and the very different course their lives had taken. Marriage, he thinks, is either a blessing or a disaster, maybe both at different times. He wonders now about his mother, what she might have become if she hadn't married his father, and he's shocked to realise that he'd completely forgotten that she'd wanted a career as a singer. For the first time ever he wonders why she didn't pursue that – was that Gerald's doing? What does she think about it now? Alone in his seat he feels his face flush with the shame of having never shown the remotest interest in what that might have meant to her.

But mulling over his parents' marriage is getting him nowhere. He has to get his head around dealing with his own, and Andrew puts his seat into an upright position, catches the attention of the flight attendant and orders a double scotch, in the hope of reigniting his initial determination to walk straight into the house, grab Zachary by the throat, hurl him back against the wall and king hit him.

# Twelve

*F*lora sits alone on the pier with an ice cream cone, a 99, with one of those short stubby chocolate flakes stuck in it. She's disappointed by this because like many of the people strolling on the pier today she can remember the days when a 99 was much cheaper, much larger and had a full size flake in it. The present version is a rip-off by comparison; it is also quite delicious.

Flora loves the pier; for her it epitomises the essentially English seaside she recalls from the fifties and sixties: slot machines, ice cream stalls, crude postcards, little shops selling shell necklaces and boxes, artists waiting to draw your like-ness in charcoal in a mere ten minutes, and the scent of fish and chips and candy floss mixed into the salty sharpness of the wind off the sea. A noisy, jostling group of children pass her heading for the funfair at the end of the pier, arguing about the merits of the big dipper versus the helter skelter, and what they'll do if they win a furry toy in the shooting gallery.

Brighton had been on Connie's visiting list because she had often come here with her mother, who had also been a fan of Graham Greene's *Brighton Rock*. So she and Flora had booked into a hotel here for a few nights and discovered that the latest adaptation of the book was screening at one of the local cinemas. Connie hadn't liked it much, she'd wanted the original 1940s black and white version – Richard Attenborough as Pinkie, trilby hats, gabardine raincoats, and the menacing shadows of The Lanes at night – but Flora had enjoyed the new version, the setting revived memories of the Brighton she remembered from her teens, when she'd ridden pillion on a scooter behind a boy in a pale blue suit.

Today Connie has gone for a nostalgic drive along the coast to Hastings where her grandmother once lived, while Flora takes time alone to sort out the strange mix of feelings that surround her decision to leave Port d'Esprit.

'I love the place and the hotel, and I think Suzanne and I have done remarkably well together all these years,' she'd said to Connie at breakfast. 'I need to leave now, before it sours. It's odd, isn't it, how you can go on for a long time, years in fact, doing the same thing, putting up with things you don't like, and then something happens and you allow yourself to question it. Then quite suddenly you know you absolutely have to change.'

'Mmmm. We cling to safety, I suppose. Take the easiest option.'

She feels, in fact, that to go back now would be a sort of death, an admission that as a single woman in her late sixties, she is fit for nothing else. A cutting off of hope – although hope of what she doesn't know yet, just something different, somewhere different, something of her own. For the first time in years she has let go of her share of the responsibility of the business, has accepted that Suzanne can and will manage without her – and may indeed be glad to do so. The relief is glorious, and the gaping hole of the future is terrifying.

Flora feels her insides clenching as always when she thinks about the future and she forces her mind away from the subject and onto the conversation she'd had a couple of days ago with Phillip when she'd called to say they would be in London on Friday. She racks her brains trying to recall whether or not she knew a woman called Bea who, according to Phillip, 'goes back to the old days too', and whom he'd said he would invite to dinner with them.

'Do you know someone called Bea?' Flora had asked Connie when she got off the phone.

'I don't think so,' Connie had said, shaking her head. 'Is that his wife?'

'No, Lorna was his wife's name and they apparently split up a long time ago. He said Bea was at university with him and Gerald. I may have met her but I can't really remember.'

'So are she and Phillip . . . ?'

'I didn't get that impression,' Flora had said, 'he just mentioned that she works in the bookshop.'

But a previously unknown friend of Gerald's doesn't surprise her; she'd never known much about Gerald's life, even when he was living at home, and once he left for university she knew even less. What does surprise her now that she thinks of it is that she ever met Phillip at all, but presumably Gerald needed a second female to make up a foursome that day on the river.

Flora feels the cool wriggle of melting ice cream creeping down her wrist and licks it before reaching for her tissues. She finishes off the soggy remains of the cone, gets to her feet and begins to walk slowly back along the pier towards the town. Glancing down at the wooden slats beneath her feet she remembers walking here as a small child, a 99 in her hand then too, staring nervously down through the gaps between the boards at the seawater churning beneath them. Suddenly she had tripped and fallen, hurting her knees, but worst of all she had dropped her ice cream and the flake had slipped between the boards into the sea. She had howled for her lost flake, demanding another.

'You should be more careful, Flora,' her mother had said. 'I'm not wasting any more money on another one.'

But Gerald had bent down, picked up the cone and, after whisking off the specks of dirt with a rather grubby handkerchief, had handed it back to her.

'Here, hold this,' he'd said, and he'd taken the remains of the flake from his own cone and pushed it into hers. 'There,' he'd said, taking her hand. 'C'mon now, Flo, eat your ice cream. I'll look after you 'til we get home, I'll always look after you.'

She stands still now, staring ahead of her, remembering him, a side of him that she had completely forgotten; he would have been about thirteen then, and she had adored him. As a child he had been her hero, and he had, frequently, taken care of her, protected her, stood up for her when she needed it. It was when she was old enough to argue with him, challenge him, suggest he might be in the wrong that he had begun to withdraw that protection.

His death has caused her a deeper and stranger grief than she had initially realised; a grief threaded through with remorse, anger, regret and, perhaps most of all, frustration at all the things left undone and unsaid. But there is still a part of her that grasps at a simple childhood memory of a brother who had once cared for her.

That day he had led her back towards the car ahead of their parents, and on the ride home to Tunbridge Wells she had fallen asleep leaning against him in the backseat, his arm around her. What she remembers is the tenderness with which he had comforted her. Tenderness, she thinks; that's how he won Connie when her mother died. Tenderness; such a seductive quality in a man, and in his youth Gerald had it in spades and used it judiciously. Did he have it in later life? She can't remember now whether she saw it during the time she lived with them in Hobart, but she thinks not. Perhaps time and age had erased that rare and precious quality. And she feels an ache of regret that she had not known him as an older man, and bleakness

because she can't remember when she last felt the tenderness of someone who loved her.

*

Kerry is making a cake, a passionfruit cake that she's never
made before. In fact there are not many cakes that Kerry
has ever made, cakes are not really her thing, and she can't
actually remember the last time she made one, but cake has
become an issue since Mia made friends with a new girl at
the start of the term and the two have been joined at the hip
ever since. Tanya's family lives just two streets away so visits
after school to one home or the other happen several times a
week.

'There is always cake at Tanya's house,' Mia announced
recently. 'Her mum always makes cakes.' And there followed
tales of banana cake, pineapple upside down cake, apricot and
almond, and Mia is still raving about last Monday's chocolate
sponge. Kerry has met Tanya's mum only fleetingly and she
seems a very nice woman, so much so that were it not for her
present state of mind she might by now have arranged to meet
her for a coffee, even teased her about her cake baking; as it is
she's merely thankful that Mia has a nice friend close by.

Last week, as she drove them both home from school, the
seriousness of cake took a grip on her.

'We never have cake,' Mia had said, 'not real cake from the
oven, we only get cake from Coles.'

In the driving mirror Kerry had seen Tanya pull a
disgusted face. 'Yuk,' she'd said. 'That would make me sick.'
She'd caught Kerry's eye then and blushed, remembering
perhaps that only a couple of days earlier Kerry had given
her the task of removing a Coles Swiss Roll from its packet,
after which she had eaten three large slices. The old Kerry
might have challenged Tanya about this but the present
Kerry decided that she should try to do something to restore
domestic honour. And so, today being Sunday, she is making

a cake, and she puts butter and sugar into the mixer, switches it on, and stands by as the machine does its work.

Out in the garden Erin is raking leaves off the lawn and Chris is clipping the hedge, while Mia and Ryan pile leaves and clippings into the wheelbarrow. They look, Kerry thinks, like a real family, connected to each other, while she hovers disconnected on the perimeter. Kerry loves Erin, has loved her since the first time they met sixteen years ago when she and Chris got engaged and took a trip to Galway to meet his family. She had felt immediately at home with Chris's parents and his three sisters but it was Erin, the eldest, and ten years her senior, to whom she had felt then, and still remains, closest, and who has visited them twice before here in Launceston. Erin's two sons are in their twenties now and her husband, a first officer on cruise ships, is often away for long periods. In a few weeks his ship is due to dock in Hobart and Erin will join him there and sail on to New Zealand for a holiday with him.

She switches off the mixer and begins to spoon in the flour, and then the passionfruit pulp, one eye still on the action in the garden. Erin has always had enormous energy which Kerry could usually match, but now it is a daily reminder of how hopeless and helpless she feels. The effort required to get through a normal day weighs heavily on her alongside Erin's ability to keep going, taking everything in her stride. She wants to make her sister-in-law feel welcome, to get back into that warm, sisterly friendship that began when they first met, but enclosed, as she is now, in her own darkness it seems impossible. Erin is cautious around her too, more solicitous than usual, less ready to drop into the joshing manner that has been a feature of their friendship.

And Chris has certainly noticed the difference, too. A couple of days after Erin arrived Kerry had walked out of the shower when Chris, just back from his run, appeared in the bathroom doorway and stood there for a moment just looking at her.

'What's wrong?' she'd asked, the anxiety in his eyes obvious.

He'd pulled a big towel from the rail, wrapped it around her and pulled her towards him. 'What is wrong is that I think you might not be telling me the whole truth – about the doctor, I mean.'

Her breath stopped and she'd struggled to steady herself. She had let out a huge sigh, really more like a groan, and leaned into him.

'Maybe you got the results from the blood tests and you don't want to tell me. Or you never went to the doctor in the first place.'

And so she had owned up.

'So maybe I should make the appointment, and come with you?' he'd said, and she could tell that he was trying desperately to help but also bracing himself for her to tell him not to interfere because she was perfectly capable of doing it herself.

'Yes,' she said, nodding. 'Thanks, I think that'd be a good idea.' And for a brief moment he'd been quite obviously stunned by her acquiescence, and then hugged her closer and said he would go right now and make the call.

Emotional exhaustion, certainly, the doctor had said, possibly depression. It was what she had feared most, the 'D' word that had stopped her from making the appointment herself. Each day she had been waiting to feel better but a diagnosis of depression seemed to banish that possibility. Depression could last for months, years even. She'd read of people unable to go outside the house, incapable of relating to anyone, and no one seemed to know how long they might remain that way. How strange that something so alien can hover over her life and yet she remains detached from it.

'You're taking a very bleak view,' the doctor had told her. 'It can be like that but sometimes it improves much more quickly. You also have an underactive thyroid which will be contributing to the way you feel. That's a real drain on energy, very exhausting.' So, she'd given her tablets for the thyroid, and for the depression, both of which she'd told her would take some time to kick in. 'Weeks, probably,' she said, 'so don't be too impatient. Come back in six weeks and we'll see how you're going.' And she referred Kerry to a grief counsellor. 'Sometimes depression is triggered by the loss of someone you love,' she'd said. 'It might help to see a grief counsellor, think about that and if you decide to go ahead I can recommend someone. Meanwhile, take some time off, look after yourself,' and she'd looked across at Chris: 'You need to make sure she rests,' she'd told him.

Even through the fog Kerry thought this made sense, but she also worried that if she stopped forcing herself out to work, gave up the effort of sticking to a routine, she might disappear further into the abyss. As they drove home she wondered whether it was the feelings that had haunted her during Gerald's final few years as much as his actual death that had brought her to this point.

That was almost two weeks ago and nothing much has changed. And while she's taking the thyroid tablets the anti-depressants remain unopened in the bathroom cupboard. To take them seems like an admission of failure. Having Erin there is a godsend, though, and slowly Kerry has been smothering her pride and accepting more and more of her help. But her predominant state is still one of numbness interspersed with bursts of anxiety and always this debilitating lassitude. Several times she has wanted to call Connie but what would she say? Should she apologise for the way she's been acting for the last few years, and if so what then? How could she explain the complexity of it? It would be hard enough face-to-face but impossible over the telephone to the other side of the world. But she yearns daily for Connie's tomato sandwiches and big mugs of sweet tea, less for the food itself than for what it meant about the love and comfort of childhood, about tenderness and acceptance. And even though Chris, and now

Erin, struggle to find ways of reaching her none of it seems to make any difference.

A few minutes later she is spooning the cake mixture into the tin when Erin appears in the kitchen doorway kicking off her boots and pushing her greying hair back from her face. Kerry loves the way Erin looks; ever since she's known her she's looked like a woman totally at ease with herself. She's fifty-three now and to Kerry she is beautiful, but in a way that doesn't fit with any of the ads for beauty products. She is confident and apparently unconcerned that she is now clearly ageing, something she neither tries to hide nor seems to dislike. She is the same as when they met, and yet she is also different; better, Kerry thinks, more profoundly herself, warmer, wiser and more forgiving. The chance of attaining those qualities herself seems remote.

Erin crosses the kitchen, sticks a finger into the cake mix and then into her mouth. 'Good lord that's to die for,' she says, licking her finger. 'Do we have to wait for it to cook or can I not just eat the mixture now, with a spoon?'

'Definitely not,' Kerry says. 'Your hands are filthy and, anyway, my status as domestic goddess rests on this cake.'

Erin laughs. 'Well, not much chance of it rising then!' she quips and they both laugh.

'I've been thinking,' Erin says. 'The thyroid thing, the depression – would it help you to go away for a while, a week or two? Somewhere nice. I can look after the kids. I mentioned it to Chris but he doesn't think he could get time off until the end of term, but you could go . . . if you feel you could actually face the effort.'

Kerry tries to imagine herself getting on a flight to somewhere peaceful, exotic – Bali, maybe – but the prospect defeats her. It's not just the process of getting there, but the idea of being completely alone in a strange place when just getting out of the door each day is hard enough. She smiles. 'Thanks, Erin, it's a nice idea, but I don't think I can get my head around it right now. I need to be somewhere safe and familiar. That must sound stupid but . . .'

'Not stupid at all,' Erin says, rinsing her hands under the tap. 'It was just a thought. But the doctor did say you should take time off and I know it's none of my business but you've done nothing about that yet.' She sticks a clean finger back into the cake mix and Kerry bats her hand away and slides the cake into the oven.

'I'm thinking about it,' she says, 'really I am.'

It's hours later, two in the morning, when she wakes suddenly, her heart beating furiously from some strange and muddled dream, and sits bolt upright. Chris shifts slightly and turns onto his side and Kerry swings her legs off the bed and wanders silently to the window, opening it slightly to feel the cold night air on her face. She stands there for a while, looking out over the shadowy garden and up at the glorious array of stars in the night sky. She feels huge and bloated, like a great leech that has grown fat on the blood of others and has now turned upon itself devouring her from within, and somehow that feeling seems to relate to the dream. She sees Chris struggling blindly to help her, the children confused – walking wide circles around her – and Erin, who can see it all more clearly because she is to some extent an outsider, trying to tell her something. Behind her she hears Chris stirring, the bed creaking as he pulls himself up into a sitting position.

'You okay?' he asks through a yawn.

She locks the window into its half-open position, walks back to bed and climbs in beside him. 'Erin talked to me about going away . . .' she says, and he reaches over and takes her hand. 'I think she's right, a week perhaps, maybe two, how would you feel . . . ?'

'I'd feel you were doing the right thing,' he says.

'This'll sound stupid after the way I've behaved but I really want to be with Mum, though even if she were here I couldn't,

I doubt she'd want me around. So perhaps I could just go to the house, maybe I could call Farah and . . .'

'Absolutely,' he cuts in, 'do it first thing in the morning.'

'I've never taken time off in term before.'

'So you have an outstanding record of reliability.'

'But . . .'

'No buts.'

'Farah might say no.'

'She won't.'

'And you wouldn't mind?'

'Mind? Glad to see the back of you,' he says, wrapping his arms around her. 'I'll get the whole bed to myself.' And he pulls her closer to him and they lie there spooned together, facing the window, the cool night air on their faces until she falls asleep again.

# Thirteen

'I wonder what Phillip's like now,' Connie says, sitting on the edge of her hotel bed to pull on her shoes.

'Unkempt, vastly overweight, with a shiny and bulbous red nose from drinking too much,' Flora says.

Connie laughs, dropping her shoe, enjoying the image. 'You're so unkind. Why d'you think he'll look like that?'

'Because they always drank too much – but Phillip is single and divorced, so doubtless lives alone, probably in a refined sort of squalor, his surroundings decaying around him. That's the fate of older men who live alone, isn't it?'

'That's a bit harsh,' Connie says. 'I mean, it's a stereotype, isn't it, especially of men of our generation? Do you think Gerald would have gone that way if we'd split up?'

'Undoubtedly,' Flora says, peering closely at herself in the dressing table mirror. 'Mum did everything for him, he never had to cook or clean anything, he scattered his clothes around the place and she or Mrs Peacock collected them up, washed and ironed them, and put them back in the wardrobe exactly where he could expect to find them. She never made any attempt to encourage him to look after himself or take responsibility for anything at home, then you came along and did exactly the same thing.'

Liz Byrski

Connie gets to her feet and pulls on her jacket, sighing as she does so. 'I never intended that to happen,' she says. 'When we got married I was sure I could change him, educate him about how to live. Arrogant, I suppose. I thought it would be pretty straightforward, but trying to change Gerald was like trying to get a tsunami to change direction. In the end it was easier just to give in and get on with it.'

'He thought you loved doing it for him,' Flora says. 'He told me that when I was staying with you. One day when you were out I told him he treated you like a domestic servant and that at his age he should know he had to take responsibility for looking after himself.'

'Did you really?' Connie says, amazed, trying to imagine that conversation. 'I bet he took a dim view of that.'

'A very dim view. Said he wasn't having any of that hairy-legged women's lib stuff in his house.'

'Good heavens,' Connie says, 'I'd no idea. He did improve in many ways, you know, and I guess I should have dug my heels in. Marriage is a strange state . . .'

'Mmmm, well, you don't need to convince *me* about *that*,' Flora says, pulling on her own coat now and looking around for her bag.

'I mean, when you live with someone day after day for years compromise becomes a habit,' Connie says. 'It's the way the relationship works, especially with someone like Gerald; you talk a lot about trivial things like whether the fence needs repairing, or what vegetables to plant. It feels like cementing the companionship, a way to tell if it's still working. If you can rub along, side by side, dealing with all the small things, it feels secure, it can become a substitute for intimacy . . .' she hesitates. 'We didn't have much of an intimate life,' she says. 'I don't just mean sex. Gerald didn't really *do* simple intimacy, and affection was hard for him too. So for me, I think, asking his opinion about small things was a way of trying to get that back, trying to share things with him. But I think it bored and

162

irritated him.' She walks to the door, waiting for Flora to turn off the bathroom light.

'Good thing I'm gay,' Flora says, following her out of the door. 'I'd never have survived living with a man. Shall we go?'

'Okay, seriously, let's guess what Phillip'll be like,' Connie muses as they wait for the lift. 'I'll go rather well preserved but conservative and somewhat unimaginative. Probably thinks of himself as a bit of a ladies' man, nudge nudge, wink wink, and wearing a blazer with grey flannels and . . .'

'Not a cravat,' Flora says, 'please don't let him be wearing a cravat, I'll wet myself if he is.'

'Five pounds says he's wearing a cravat,' Connie wagers.

'You're on. I say he's wearing a baggy corduroy suit with leather elbows, and a viyella shirt with egg on it. Oh lord, why are we even doing this? We're in London, we could be going to the theatre or a movie or having fish and chips.'

'We're doing it for old times' sake,' Connie says, and she shoves her arm through Flora's. 'Now try to behave nicely and let's see who spots him first.'

\*

Phillip is deliberately early, fifteen minutes early in fact. He'd been determined to get his favourite corner table, cosy but not cramped, and he was unaccountably nervous so he'd hurried and installed himself there with a glass of house red which is, as usual, very good. He likes this restaurant and not just because it's only a few minutes' walk from the shop. The menu is interesting and the food lives up to its promise, the staff are friendly, a nice unpretentious place to meet friends. In fact it was here, only under different management, that more than thirty years ago he'd seen Gerald for the last time. He hadn't realised it would be the last time of course, but that's how it turned out. They'd sat here in this corner and eaten one of the huge stodgy lunches it served in those days, steak and kidney pudding with mash probably, or maybe roast beef and Yorkshire pudding, and killed a couple of bottles of wine.

Phillip had been a lot fatter in those days; an indiscriminate eater and drinker, his clothes were uncomfortably tight that day. He'd hated the way he looked, especially compared with Gerry, who was looking lean and energetic, and very well dressed. And as he thinks about it now Phillip remembers Gerry mentioning then that he had his sights on a move into politics. They'd eaten too much and drunk too much, and sat there too long chewing the fat, so that by the time they wandered out into the street it was already dark – one of those depressing winter afternoons when night fell at half past four. They'd said goodbye on the corner, and Gerry had wandered off towards Euston Road and Phillip had walked home. He was still married to Lorna then and he remembers going straight into the kitchen and telling her that he wanted to lose weight, that he never again wanted to feel fat, bloated and ungainly among his peers. Lorna had laughed at him but with some relief, and he was soon munching carrots, lettuce and cottage cheese and wishing he'd never mentioned it. He's glad of it now though, because he's dropped several stones, still plays cricket sometimes and walks a lot. 'Thanks for that, Gerry,' he murmurs, 'you looked as though you'd go on forever that day, and now you're gone and I'm still here.'

Phillip checks his watch, five past seven, no sign of Bea yet, and no sign of Flora and Connie, and at the thought of them the energy that had him worrying about what to wear, what to say and how to behave, and had him here fifteen minutes early, suddenly disappears into some black hole and he wishes he was home in his flat, with sardines on toast and the BBC news. He should just have let them pop into the shop as they'd suggested and now he'll be stuck with them for the evening. Two women in their late sixties whom he hasn't seen for decades; what will they talk about? Two hours, at least, of stilted conversation, all of them wishing they were doing something else. Why is he doing this? Old times' sake, he reminds himself, looking out into the street where it is still quite light. But what old times? They'd barely known each other then, and what would they have in common now, the three of them – just a dead man, and an afternoon in a punt that is probably best forgotten. Old times might be best left as just that, rather than updated.

'Phillip?' A voice takes him by surprise. 'It is Phillip, isn't it?'

And there they both are – the past right there in his face, two women, totally changed but absolutely the same, and as he jumps to his feet a sudden and unexpected surge of emotion makes him catch his breath, and he is transported back to the Phillip he once was, by the company of people who knew that he had once been young.

'Flora? Flora – how wonderful,' he says, 'how amazing, you look just the same.'

'The same only different,' she says, 'as do you.' And she holds out her hand to shake his but he ignores it and hugs her and he feels her hug him back. And over her shoulder he sees Connie, smiling at him, tilting her head to one side as she watches him and Flora, and then stepping forward to hug him herself. How extraordinary, how sudden, this weird sense of connection, this merging of old and young selves, this gift from the past right here in real life, and a feeling that he really does know them.

'You look very different from what we imagined,' Flora says when they are settled in their seats. 'No ravages of drink and debauchery.'

'And we'd lined you up to be wearing a blazer and a cravat,' Connie says. 'The linen has taken us by surprise.'

And in that moment Phillip knows that this is going to be a splendid evening and that the past, in all its various intricacies, is just the past, and this is a clean slate on which their new old selves can begin to write. And now he wishes that he hadn't asked Bea, it was thoughtless and insensitive, and she will bring the past with her, not just the memories but the Gerald baggage. She is a law unto herself and may decide to scrawl indiscriminately all over the clean slate.

*

Bea is deliberately late, fifteen minutes late. She wants to get a look at them before she walks into the restaurant and she's confident that Phillip will have nabbed his favourite table, which means she'll be able to see quite clearly from across the street. It's a pleasant, mild spring evening, people are still hurrying along Marchmont Street on the way home from work, diving in and out of Brunswick Square to pick up a take-away meal, or grabbing last minute shopping in Waitrose. There are tourists too, looking slightly lost, or peering at maps and rummaging through the stalls of second-hand books outside Judd's. Bea loves Bloomsbury, in all weathers and at any time of the year. She has lived here for almost forty years and it has never lost its attraction for her.

This evening, as she walked here along the laneway by Coram's Fields, she'd resented doing this, sharing her place in the world with people who had the power to trample over the past, label it as theirs without even knowing the painful reality of her place in it. But it's too late for that now, she's almost there and she needs to remember that it's all a very long time ago and they were all very different people then. What's the point of raking over the past? A part of her wishes she had refused Phillip's invitation but she very much wants to get a close-up look at both Connie and Flora. Were it not for that she'd be sitting in her flat with a bowl of soup and a good book, and Oscar Peterson playing in the background.

She pauses at the corner and sure enough she can see straight through to where Phillip is sitting with two women. The three of them are laughing and he pours wine into their glasses and they raise and clink them in a toast. She's too far away to see them clearly but neither looks like wispy, weepy Connie. Must try to stop thinking of her like that, not the best start to the evening, and she steps off the kerb and crosses the street, reassuring herself that if it's truly deadly she'll feign a headache and leave early.

'Here she is,' Phillip says, spotting her as she makes her way through the restaurant. 'Over here, Bea,' and he gets to his feet and to her surprise the women stand up too. Flora so much like Gerry, the same searching, grey-green eyes, the same tall, rangy build, a strong handshake – how well those looks last, Bea thinks. Is this how Gerry looked? The likeness is unnerving, destabilising, just like looking into his eyes.

'And this is Connie,' Phillip says. 'I don't think you've ever met.'

The woman who takes Bea's hand is sturdy, with clear fair skin and thick hair once blonde, now streaked with grey. She is shorter than Flora, about Bea's own height, and shapely, her figure still curvy and well defined by her red fitted jacket and a skirt that flares at mid-calf – this is a woman who has never, ever been either pale or wispy.

'No, we haven't met,' Connie says, moving aside so that Bea can slip into a chair, 'but it's nice to meet you now, Bea. Phillip says you were at university with him and Gerald, so I guess this meeting is decades overdue.' And she sits down alongside her.

This surely can't be Connie, it's as though an impostor has taken her place. Bea has to resist the temptation to turn and face her full on, to stare at her and try to make sense of it – to match that old image with reality. People change as they age, she tells herself, taking the wine Phillip pours for her, but do they change this much? Was Connie ever as Gerald had described her? And for the first time in decades Bea allows herself to consider that perhaps Gerald had simply created a description of Connie that suited his own purposes.

'It's good to meet you too,' she hears herself say. 'And I'm so sorry about Gerry, this must be such a sad time.' And she sounds like a normal person, not the raving mad woman she had always assumed she would become should she ever meet Connie. And from the other side of the table, where he is sitting alongside Flora, Phillip smiles across at her and she sees that he is hugely relieved that she is acting like a civilised person, and he gives her a slight, almost imperceptible nod of appreciation, and the waiter hands her a copy of the menu.

# Fourteen

It was late by the time Farah finally got the girls to bed, and by then they were exhausted. It had been a big and emotional day for them, the seventh anniversary of their father's death, and they had all gone together to visit the Muslim cemetery.

'Would you be able to come with us, Kerry?' Farah had asked the previous evening.

Kerry had hesitated, uncomfortable about intruding on their private grief. 'Well, I . . .'

'I know it's so soon after Gerald . . . but I always find it hard. Connie came with me last year and the year before. There is no grave of course, Rashid was buried on Christmas Island. But the Imam had a small memorial built for the people who lost their lives seeking asylum.'

'Then of course I'll come,' Kerry said, although she really dreaded the prospect, but Farah had been so kind to her since she got here, and had welcomed it when she asked to stay on for a couple more weeks, that there was no way she could refuse.

Now, as she hears the murmur of the twins' voices and their occasional laughter as they make their way to bed via the bathroom, she knows it was the right thing to have done, not just for Farah and her daughters but for herself too. Although Farah had told her about the circumstances of her and Rashid's decision to leave Afghanistan and seek refuge in Australia, she knew almost nothing more about Rashid himself, or Farah's Auntie Ana, with whom they had lived here in Hobart.

'She married an Australian in the mid-seventies and they lived in Melbourne for a while, and moved to Hobart about ten years later,' Farah had explained. 'Jack, her husband, died of a heart attack when he was only in his late fifties. When the girls and I were told we could stay in Australia we came here to live with Ana – she had just a small flat but it was good to be with someone from home, and when I started to get some work with the nursing agency Ana took care of the girls. She died two years ago, and she left me her flat.'

Kerry lies back on the couch and closes her eyes, listening to their voices, quieter now that both the girls are in the bedroom. Farah is talking softly to them, as she had done earlier at the cemetery.

'Do you think *plaar* knows we're here?' Lala had whispered, taking her mother's hand as they stood by the modest bronze memorial plaque.

But Kerry could see that Farah was so choked with tears that she could barely speak and so she took Samira's hand and put her other hand on Lala's shoulder and steered the two girls and their mother to a nearby seat. 'I think your dad knows you're here,' she said softly. 'I'm sure he's still taking care of you every day.'

'But our dad has been dead so long,' Samira said, 'and his grave is a long way away, maybe he forgot us?'

Farah swallowed her tears and put her arms around them both. 'He knows, of course he knows we are here. Have you forgotten him?' The two girls shook their heads in silence. 'Will you forget him – ever? No, of course not, and he does not forget you, not now, not ever.'

'Why don't the graves here have headstones like the graves in the other part of the cemetery?' Samira had asked.

And Farah, her voice gathering strength, had described for them the process of the Muslim burial: the cleansing and preparation of the body, and the rituals around it, the purity and modesty of the white cloth in which the body is wrapped, the simplicity of the graves – just shallow mounds covered with grass and wildflowers. And then she had told them stories about Rashid, how much he loved them, how proud he would have been if he could have seen them now, some little anecdotes from his life. And Kerry understood then why Farah had wanted her there; her presence served to lessen the load a little. While Farah supported her daughters, Kerry was there for her. They had talked a little and then sat for a while in silence as the girls wandered off to inspect the flowers on the graves. It had been wonderfully peaceful there, under the big casuarina, both lost in their own thoughts and comfortable in the silence. And Kerry had wondered whether somehow Farah had known that this would also be a good thing for her to do, to be with them in their mourning, while still coping with her own. It had certainly helped, although not in a way that Kerry understood. She knew only that it had left her with a sense of peace, a feeling that she just had to wait for all this to be over. Wait without trying to fight either the grief for her father or her own confusing aching numbness. Just wait.

The house phone rings now, jolting her out of her thoughts. Expecting it to be Chris, she gets to her feet and walks out into the hall to answer it.

'Hello, Farah,' Connie says, sounding as clear and close as if she were in the next room. 'Is that you?'

Kerry's heart thumps in her chest. Her mother doesn't even know she's here. She takes a deep breath. 'It's Kerry, Mum,' she says. 'Is everything all right?'

'Kerry?' Connie says. 'What are you doing there? Is something wrong? Is Farah . . . the children . . . ?'

'Everything's fine, Mum,' she says, trying to sound relaxed. 'But I've been a bit off colour, so I've taken a few days' leave and come down here to stay with Farah. Erin's at home with Chris and the kids.'

'Erin, of course,' Connie says. 'I'd forgotten she was coming. Are you sure it's not anything serious?'

'Absolutely sure,' Kerry lied. 'But it's nice being here, and far enough from work not to feel obliged to go back in.'

Connie is silent for a moment and Kerry's heart beats faster again. She's tempted to say more, to try to explain her behaviour, to apologise, to make excuses.

'Well, that's good. You take care, darling, it's been a very hard time for all of us, I'm sure you need a bit of a break.'

'And how are you, Mum?' Kerry asks, thankful to change the focus. 'Are you having a good time?' And she listens as Connie tells her about France, and London, and meeting up with a couple of Gerald's old friends. She doesn't mention Flora, and Kerry, to whom Flora has been such an unknown quantity for such a very long time, doesn't mention her either.

'Did you want to talk to Farah?' Kerry asks eventually.

'Well, yes, if she's there, I just wanted to check up that everything is okay.'

Farah, who is making her way down the stairs, looks at her questioningly.

'She's here now,' Kerry says, nodding and beckoning to Farah, 'so I'll hand you over. You take care, Mum, and enjoy the rest of your holiday. We're all thinking of you.'

And she offers the receiver to Farah and turns back into the lounge, wishing she'd handled it better but knowing that it could have been worse and wondering how she is ever going to get back to any sort of comfortable relationship with her mother after everything that has happened between them.

\*

Brooke is lying on her bed waiting for a phone call. She checks her phone and then her watch. No message, and it's almost six o'clock – well past the time she'd expected to hear from her father. He was meeting an estate agent at five to sign the lease on a new townhouse, and had promised to call when it was all done. The longer she waits the more restless she becomes. Her bedroom door is locked against possible intrusion by her mother or Zachary. For the past three weeks she has worn her key on a piece of black ribbon around her neck, much to Linda's chagrin and Zachary's amusement. She fiddles with it now as she waits, listening to the rain beating relentlessly on the big dormer window. In the last week the weather has turned suddenly cold and wet and Brooke would love to go down to the lounge and stretch out on the rug in front of the gas heater that's set in the wall and looks like burning logs with real flames. But these days she only goes downstairs when necessary or when Zachary is out. She won't do anything that brings her into contact with him or could be seen as somehow condoning his presence. She would rather stay here, chilly and resentful, rather stick pins in her eyes than have anything to do with him. But at least it won't be much longer now, as soon as her dad calls she'll know the date when the two of them will move together to the nice little townhouse in North Melbourne.

A few weeks ago Brooke had thought things were as bad as they could get and then Zachary moved in and suddenly it all got worse. Just thinking about him being in the house, in the bedroom that Linda and Andrew had shared until quite recently, made her feel sick, and she hated the fact that he touched things that she had to use – taps, cutlery, the TV remote control – and he left his smelly clothes and shoes all over the place. She hated that he sat in her father's chair and occupied what had been his study.

'I know it's difficult, darling, but I do think you're being a bit excessive. And it's very hurtful to Zach. It's not as though he's got some contagious disease,' Linda had said.

'He *is* a disease,' Brooke had said then, and she'd actually thought that her mother was going to slap her because she gasped and raised her hand, but then dropped it again and turned away.

'It's hurtful to me too, you know,' she said then, and as Linda turned back to face her Brooke could see the tears in her eyes. 'I'm trying to do what's best for all of us.'

'No you're not,' Brooke had retorted, shouting now. 'You're trying to get everything just the way you want it. This is *my* home too, you know, mine and Dad's, but you've taken it over and let that man move in. You don't care what's right for me or for Dad,' and she had stomped back upstairs to her room.

But she has hung on, hiding behind her locked door, staying out of their way because her father had asked her to do that. 'The worst has happened,' he'd said on the phone from Perth, and Brooke had thought he meant 'the worst is over'. He'd promised to find somewhere for them to stay and said he'd be there to pick her up on the Friday evening, so she'd made a big effort to stay calm and distant until then. Meanwhile she had packed a large suitcase with everything she needed for at least a couple of weeks, stored all her school stuff in her backpack and waited in silence for Friday evening to arrive. In fact she'd been rearranging the contents of the case earlier that evening when Linda had told her through the locked door that she and Zachary were going out to dinner and then to a movie.

She was both pleased and disappointed about their going out. Pleased because it meant they could get out of the house quickly when her dad arrived, and disappointed because she was hoping that she would be able to watch him throw Zachary out of the house, preferably from the second floor balcony, but more likely through the front door.

She had waited for ten minutes after she'd heard Linda leave, just in case she came back for something, and then she'd unlocked her bedroom door and dragged the huge suitcase downstairs and parked it just inside the front door ready for when Andrew arrived. She wanted a quick getaway, no dawdling, no conversation, until he'd got his car keys and anything else he needed and they were in his car heading off to wherever it was he had found for them to stay.

When he rang to say he was in a taxi and would be there in ten minutes Brooke had put on her coat, hoisted the heavy backpack onto her shoulders and stood waiting by the open front door until she saw the taxi turn in at the bottom of the road. She was down the short path to the gate in a second, stood shifting anxiously from one foot to the other, and almost knocked Andrew over when she threw herself at him as he got out of the cab.

'Whoa, hang on, Brooke,' Andrew had said, signing the cab voucher and handing it to the driver. And then he had turned to hug her. 'Whatever have you got in that backpack? It's enormous.'

Brooke clung to him in relief, determined not to cry like a little kid, or do anything else that would delay their escape from the house. 'It's my school things,' she'd said. 'The rest of my stuff is in my case in the hall so you can just put it straight in the car.'

Andrew looked bewildered. 'Well, let's get inside and sort things out. I need to speak to your mother.'

'They're out,' Brooke said, 'both of them. They won't be back 'til late. But it doesn't matter, can't we just go? Please, Dad.'

'Go where, Brooke?'

'To the place you got for us, like you said.'

Andrew steered her back up the path and into the house. 'Not yet, darling,' he said, parking his case next to hers in the hall and draping his coat over the newel post. 'Oh my god, what has that bastard done with my study?' And he'd walked to the doorway and stood there surveying the black leather sofa and the glass and stainless steel desk that left barely enough room to turn around. 'Where's all my stuff gone?'

'Mum sent everything to the gallery,' Brooke said. 'She said there's a studio on the top floor and you could stay there until you find somewhere else.'

'I knew she sent some things but you mean she sent all my stuff?'

Brooke shrugged. 'Yes. She said she'd told you that on the phone.'

Andrew sat down on the stairs and sank his head into his hands. Brooke was horrified – this was the last thing she needed. He looked as though he was about to cry but she wanted him to be strong, to act decisively, to get her out of this place as soon as possible, not sit there crapping on about his stuff like a big kid.

'Dad, come on, please, we have to go. We can talk about it when we get to the new place. You can tell me about it on the way.'

Andrew had paused for a moment, staring down at the floor, and then seemed to rouse himself. He looked up at her. 'The new place? But, Brooke, we haven't got a new place yet. I've been in Perth, flat out all week. I haven't had time even to think about it yet. It'll take a while, a couple of weeks at least, maybe a month. You can't have thought I would have fixed it by tonight.'

Brooke felt a weird sort of drumming in her ears and her legs started to tremble. 'But you promised,' she said. 'You said you'd fix it and come and get me and you said don't tell Mum I'm moving in with you. You did.'

Andrew got up and went to hug her but the backpack got in the way. He edged it off her shoulders and it fell to the floor with a thud. 'Shh, Brooke, shh. Listen to me. I did say that but it didn't mean that we could move in somewhere today, tonight. We'll go and find somewhere together. Look around, and then there will be a lease to agree on and they'll want to check my references. These things take time. Meanwhile you need to stay here, just hang on like you've been doing, be brave and we'll soon have somewhere of our own. We can start looking tomorrow if you like; see some real estate agents together. But Brooke you *are* going to have to stay on here until I can get something organised.'

Brooke had stared at him in disbelief; she felt as though a part of herself had been burned away and become a little pile of ashes on the floor. 'But I can't,' she cried. 'I can't, Dad, it's too awful. He's just vile and Mum keeps saying I have to be nice to him and he's so gross and creepy, and she let him go in my room so now I have to keep it locked. I can't stay here, I really can't. I can't stay here another night, let alone for weeks.' She was sobbing now, her whole body shaking with desperation.

Andrew had hugged her closer then, and as she began to calm down a bit he put his hands on her shoulders and held her away from him so he was looking into her eyes.

'It's like this, Brooke,' he said, 'I have to be careful how I handle this. I have to do it in the right way because if we can't settle things between us, your mum and I, then we'll have to go to court and someone else will get to say what happens.'

'Yes,' Brooke had nodded, 'and the judge will talk to me and I'll say I want to stay with you.'

'The judge will certainly take that into consideration but only if I can show that I've behaved properly in the circumstances in relation to your care and wellbeing. Taking you away without warning while your mother's out and moving you into a miserable studio with no room to swing a cat, that wouldn't go down well at all.'

'But *she* hasn't behaved properly at all,' Brooke said, her voice breaking with despair.

'Exactly. And that will go in our favour.'

He went on quite a bit after that, about this being a crucial time in relation to the future, about how he couldn't emphasise strongly enough the importance of his appearing to have acted honourably and responsibly. And she had protested and begged and argued for so long that in the end she felt totally dead inside. She put her head down on her arms and just gave up in exhaustion.

'I'll be sixteen soon. Why can't I decide what I want now, because I just can't stay here,' she said eventually.

'I'm asking you to be very grown up and try,' Andrew had said then. 'Try for me, for both of us, so we can get this sorted as soon as possible. I'll find a hotel for tonight, and tomorrow I'll see what the studio is like. We can go together. Maybe I can stay there for a while. Then we'll look around for a place to rent.'

'Can't I come to the hotel with you?'

And he'd relented then and said she should call Linda and ask her if it was okay for her to stay with him for the weekend.

'*Ask* her? Why can't you *tell* her that I'm going to stay with you whether she likes it or not?'

'For all the reasons I've just explained,' he'd said.

'Suppose she says no?'

'She won't.' Andrew had hesitated then. 'Look, Brooke, your mum loves you, and she knows this is hard for you. Try to remember that and make the most of it. Treat her with respect and she'll have to do the same. I don't like this any better than you but I promise it's the best way to do it.'

And so she'd called her mother, who had gone very quiet at the other end of the line, and then asked to speak to Andrew. Brooke couldn't hear what she said, only heard him say that he'd let her know where they were once he'd found a hotel, and that he would bring Brooke back home on Sunday evening, and then the two of them would have to talk. And then he'd got on her iPad and found a place in the city for them to stay together over the weekend.

She didn't see her mother or Zachary for two whole days, which certainly helped, but in the end, of course, she'd had to go back, knowing it could be weeks before she would be able to leave for good. That was three weeks ago and she's still here. The only good thing is that last weekend she and Andrew had found a nice little townhouse near her school and fairly close to his office, and they'd gone straight to the real estate agent's office and he'd filled in the application form and all they were waiting for now was for the agent to check her dad's references.

'So you've changed your mind about living with Nan then?' Andrew had asked her while they were house-hunting.

And Brooke had felt that sudden jerk of shock, because she hadn't given up that idea at all. She saw the new place first as an escape from her present situation, and then as a place to come home to, a place for holidays and sometimes weekends, a place she might eventually live in with her father from time to time, perhaps when she finished school and went to university or got her first job.

'No,' she'd said. 'I still want to stay with Nan, to go to that school. But you won't let me ask her yet.'

He'd looked hurt then, quite crushed, but he hadn't said anything, only nodded, and she'd felt really bad about it.

'After all, Dad,' she'd said, 'you might not want me to stay all the time. I mean, you might meet someone and then I'd be in the way.' And as she said it she'd had a horrible hollow feeling, because she was sure he *would* meet someone and probably quite soon. That had happened to three other people she knew, so it seemed to be a sort of pattern. One parent met someone and the parents split up and very soon, just as it was all settling down, someone new came along for the other parent too, and everything changed all over again. Brooke imagined this happening to her; she saw herself comfortably ensconced in the new place and then one day Andrew would tell her about a lovely woman he'd met, he'd say they were just friends and he hoped Brooke would like her. They would go out together and meet this woman in a café for lunch, or take a walk somewhere, like she'd seen happen in the movies, and then he'd start talking to her about how nice it would be if the three of them lived together. And however hard her dad insisted that she must be honest about how she felt, the woman would still move in and it would be her, Brooke, who would have to fit in, to get her life organised again on the edge of theirs.

As she lies here now thinking about this, Brooke is convinced that this is what will happen, that Andrew may already have met this woman and that even if he's not planning it yet, the prospect is just around the corner. Brooke hauls herself upright. It's the wrong time of day to Skype her Nan but she'll send her an email anyway. Find out when she'll be back, ask if it's still okay to stay in the holidays. She's aching to ask if she can live there, go to school there, but she's promised to wait until Nan gets home for that. She switches on her iPad and starts writing, and she has almost finished her email when the Dad ringtone, one he picked for himself from some movie, starts.

'Brooke,' he says.

And she knows from his tone that something is wrong.

'Did you get the keys?' she asks.

'Darling, I'm so sorry. I got to the office to sign the lease and pick up the keys, and the owner had just called to say he wanted to withdraw the place.'

'What? No, Dad, he can't do that. He just can't.'

'Well, I'm afraid he can, although the agent is spitting chips. As for us, Brooke, I'm sorry, but we have to start all over again.'

# Fifteen

lora wakes at first light to the anxiety that haunts her more with each passing day. She is no nearer to knowing what she wants to do and Connie is not proving as helpful as she'd hoped. She seems to see it in very basic terms.

'You just need to decide *where* you want to be, and who with,' she says. 'Then try to sort out how to do it.'

It is, Flora thinks, characteristic of someone who actually has enough money to decide where she wants to be without having to consider what might actually be possible.

'Once you decide where you want to be you can work out how to manage it. Try to imagine yourself with more money, it might clarify it for you.'

Flora can see that this does, in a way, make sense. In another way it simply frustrates and confuses the issue.

'I want to avoid having to do things on a temporary basis,' she'd said. 'That always gobbles up money and one has nothing to show for it. When Suzanne understands that I really am leaving she'll want things to move quickly. She's very impatient and businesslike.'

'Well, she'll have to wait for you,' Connie had said. 'You've devoted a huge chunk of your life to her business, she has to give you time to adjust and make plans. It's not like you're just deciding whether or not to leave a job; this decision is about the rest of your life.'

And Flora had smiled, thinking not only that Connie didn't know Suzanne all that well, but also that it was good to hear her friend sounding like the old, or rather the young, Connie again – determined, assertive, ready to take control.

Flora gets out of bed and tiptoes to the window so as not to wake Connie, who is still asleep in the other bed of their twin room. London is on the move this glorious spring morning and from their fourth floor window she has a splendid view of Russell Square Gardens where people are hurrying to work along the paths. In the centre of the shallow pond a fountain suddenly bursts into life scattering some small birds and surprising two elderly men who are making their way towards the chairs outside the café. Could she live here? She has longed for London and a couple of nights ago at dinner Phillip had practically offered her a job.

'You'd be terrific,' he'd said, 'and you'd probably stay, unlike some of the younger people we've taken on recently. It's not remarkably well paid, I'm afraid, but it's award rates. And you'd have Bea breathing down your neck, but she's not as terrifying as she pretends to be. I'm sure she'd be much nicer to you than she is to me. Think about it. Come into the shop, I'll show you around and we can talk about it. You're just what we need. Isn't she, Bea?'

This obviously came as a surprise to Bea, whose expression was one of interest mixed with caution. 'Well – yes,' she'd managed, 'yes, Flora, it could work well. You and I together could certainly pull Phillip into line.'

'She pulled me into line once before,' Phillip had said then, 'in a punt at Richmond on a hot summer afternoon in – um – well, a lot of years ago.'

'Really?' Bea said. 'This sounds interesting – do tell.'

'May I?' Phillip asked, looking at Flora.

'Well, if you don't I will,' she'd said.

'Oh, I want Flora's version,' Bea had said, 'don't you, Connie?'

'I was there,' Connie said, smiling, 'with Gerald, just the four of us.'

'Go on then, Flora,' Phillip said, grinning. 'Expose my shame.'

And with the help of a few whimsical embellishments, Flora told Bea the story. 'He was absolutely doubled up,' she said at the end. 'For a few moments, at least, I was pretty worried about how much damage I might have done.'

'Well, it certainly hasn't stopped him leading a full and active life,' Bea managed to say through her laughter.

They were all laughing now. Phillip had tears running down his face at Flora's telling of the story. 'I do feel it was somewhat of an overreaction, Flora,' he'd said. 'And I certainly didn't see it coming.'

Flora had turned to him then and put her hand on his arm. 'There's a codicil to this, Phillip, something you need to know now that you didn't know at the time. You see, I'm a dyke.'

Phillip's eyes had widened, his mouth dropped open. 'You're kidding,' he said, peering at her more closely. 'Really? I never knew.'

'Obviously!'

'And you were back then too? I mean a lot of women . . .'

She shook her head. 'Back then, back before then, from birth, I suppose, although I was about fourteen before I worked it out.'

'Good lord, I'd no idea. I'm so sorry, Flora, how crass I must have seemed. Gerald never said.'

'He didn't know,' she said. 'And he didn't like it at all some years later when he found out.'

'I bet he didn't,' Bea said. 'Gerry and I had many arguments about that. He prided himself on being open minded but he wasn't open minded about that.'

'No, he certainly wasn't,' Connie said, looking sharply at Bea.

'Is that why you and he fell out, Flora?' Phillip had asked. 'I always wondered. When he came back here from Australia once, I asked after you and he said you'd fallen out and hadn't been in touch for years. Never said why though, and changed the subject when I asked.'

'Yes, that's what it was,' Flora had said, nodding. 'Water under the bridge now of course, but it left its mark on both of us.'

'On our family too,' Connie added, 'and especially on our friendship.'

Flora, thinking back over that evening, over the quieter conversation that followed and the genuine warmth and good humour of it all, suddenly feels the effect of Gerald's rejection more acutely than she has for a long time. He had insulted, abused and humiliated her, shown no respect for the person she knew herself to be. She had walked away and vowed not to look back, but of course she has been looking back on it for years, smarting from it, letting it leech away her confidence in her own sexual identity, running from relationships as soon as things got serious. Suzanne's remarks about Connie not being supportive enough crowd back into her head and she pushes them away. But there is some satisfaction in knowing that had he been sitting at the table with them two nights ago, Gerald, rather than she, would have been the one marginal-ised by his prejudice.

'You're up already,' Connie murmurs, yawning, and she drags herself into a sitting position.

'Still half-asleep really,' Flora says, turning to her. 'Cup of tea?'

'Mmmm, yes please. Tea in bed has been sadly missing from my life for donkey's years.'

'Suzanne and I did alternate days,' Flora says, 'but I must admit that even on my days she would wander into my room

184

with a cup before I was up. I try to remember that when I'm annoyed with her about other things.' She fills the kettle, switches it on and gets two cups from the cupboard above the bar fridge.

'Suzanne is going to miss you more than she realises,' Connie says. 'I think that much as she may love Xavier and want to live with him, she'll find her work increases when you move out and he moves in. Have you thought any more about what you would do if money wasn't a problem?'

Flora drops tea bags into the cups and struggles to open a small carton of milk. 'I have, and I'm not sure, but I suppose I'd be more relaxed about taking time to make up my mind, so I might spend a bit of time with you in Australia.'

'Very sensible,' Connie says. 'I'm so glad you want to come back to Hobart, and the house is big enough for us to jog along happily together.' She takes her tea from Flora and empties a sachet of sugar into it. 'By the way, I had a dream last night about Gerald and Bea, can't remember what it was about at all but as I was trying to go back to sleep I remembered something Bea said at dinner. It struck me as odd at the time but then I forgot to mention it.'

'Go on,' Flora says, sitting back on her bed with her tea.

'When you told Phillip why you and Gerald had fallen out, Bea said something – I can't remember the words exactly, but the way she said them it sounded as though she knew Gerald really well. Until then I assumed she was more a friend of Phillip's. Did you hear that?'

Flora shrugs, sipping her tea. 'No, I can't say I did. But they were at uni together, so they probably all knew each other well.'

'Mmmm. Oh well, it just seemed odd. Anyway, it was lovely of Phillip to invite us both to the opera. I wish you'd come too.'

Flora raises her eyebrows. 'Phillip's an opera buff like you and you'll have more fun without me huffing and puffing alongside you.'

'I suppose,' Connie says. 'I'm so looking forward to it and this morning I want to go out and buy something special to wear. I want to dress up. I haven't had the chance to do that for ages so I thought I'd get the bus to Marble Arch and go to Selfridges. It was always my favourite shop. Do you want to come or have you got other plans?'

'I don't think I'm in shopping mood,' Flora says. 'I might go to the bookshop, see the lie of the land and whether I might want to work there. Phillip said he wouldn't be there today so I'd quite like to have a mooch around and talk to Bea while he's out.'

'Sounds like a good idea,' Connie says. 'But you do have to think about what it would cost to live in London – probably phenomenal – and there's the commute of course.'

Flora laughs. 'So what happens to forgetting about financial practicalities and simply deciding first where I want to be?'

Connie colours slightly. 'Well, I'm just saying . . .' she hesitates and changes the subject. 'I was quite touched that Phillip remembered that I was at the Guildhall. He seemed amazed when I said I hadn't sung for years.'

'Didn't you join a choir once?' Flora asks.

'Yes, while the kids were still at school, but I gave it up after a few months.'

'Why?'

Connie shrugs. 'Oh well, Gerald didn't like it much. It was in the evenings and it meant that I was going out to that just as he got home from work.'

Flora is silent for a while, sorting out the contents of her handbag, and Connie gets up and heads for the bathroom.

'I'll grab the shower while you're doing that,' she says.

Flora looks up, taking off her glasses. 'Sure. You know, Con, it sounds as though you gave up an awful lot to please Gerald.'

Connie flushes. 'I know. I keep thinking of the things I should have fought for. But you remember my father and what he was like – he taught me compliance and expected it, so I suppose I easily became accustomed to it with Gerald too.'

The silence is suddenly weighted with tension, and Flora wonders if Connie ever considers how that compliance compounded Flora's own exclusion and the toll it took on her.

'So what do you think about that now?' she asks finally.

Connie hesitates, still standing by the door, staring down at the carpet. Then she looks up, shaking her head almost imperceptibly as if to shake away a thought, and gives a stiff half-smile.

'I think it's time I had a shower,' she says and she disappears into the bathroom, closing the door behind her.

\*

The Marble Arch bus lumbers past as Connie approaches the stop and she runs the last stretch and reaches it just in time. Swiping her Oyster card she drops into a seat near the front, thinking irritably of what Flora had said about how much she had given up to please Gerald. She wants to explore her past here in England and in France; not revisit the long years of her marriage and her life in Hobart.

Since the day she arrived in Port d'Esprit she has revelled in memories – in a whole panorama of nostalgic moments. Her memory of the fishing village was like a blueprint over which a series of contemporary images had been superimposed. There she was, in 2012, walking the same streets, eating at the same places, swimming off the same beaches, all of them updated to the present, just as she, Flora and Suzanne were contemporary and aged versions of the girls they had once been. She could see Flora dancing in the square, Suzanne darting between the pine trees in a game of hide and seek on the cape, and the three of them sitting on the sea wall, hoping to catch the attention of passing boys or, better still, the young fishermen mending their nets on the quayside.

Liz Byrski

It was all there, a delightful mishmash of past and present, a drip feed of memories in manageable, evocative doses. But England was different.

It had been dark when they'd landed at Gatwick and late by the time they arrived at the hotel. The Tudor building that had been a large pub in Connie's childhood was still a pub but also now a hotel, spread across several acres of land with low, single-storey motel rooms, a swimming pool, squash and tennis courts and a gym. Enough of the old building remained, though, to transport her back to Sunday mornings in the saloon when she could sneak in with her parents and sit unobtrusively in a corner with a lemonade and a packet of Smith's Crisps, fiddling with the little twist of blue paper that held the salt, and longing for the day she would be old enough to join the throng of young people sinking tall glasses of lager and sizing each other up by the bar.

Connie had fallen asleep that first night in a strange state of suspension between past and present, acutely aware that she had come home but was also far from home. She woke early to the sound of a mower and, stumbling out of bed, opened the curtains. The scent of freshly cut grass on the damp morning air brought tears to her eyes and transported her back to childhood. The long neglected past that had been smothered by another life elsewhere now flooded back to her. Memories need nurture to keep them rich and fertile, and she saw that hers had become dry and brittle with neglect, fragile as the petals of dead flowers. The scenes the familiar scent stirred up were visceral; her legs felt weak, her chest tight, images spun and swarmed in her head: half-familiar faces, birthday candles and Christmas trees, her hair tightly wound in rags, then later in plastic curlers and later still in pink rollers. Fleeting remembrance of her tears on the first day at school, of cod liver oil and malt, of mittened hands clutching icy milk bottles at playtime, gold stars on an honour board, the discomfort of her first bra, a kiss stolen at dusk under an ancient oak, and of walking beside her mother across the heath towards that enchanted place at the top of the forest. She struggled to breathe through the memories that made her chest tighten with emotion. Beneath the window the mower spluttered to a halt and in the sudden silence, while the gardener perched on a low wall and lit a cigarette, she gulped air again, then slipped away from the window into the bathroom, and let her tears mix soundlessly with the water in the shower, the only witness to this heart stopping interlude of grief and longing.

There have been other occasions like this since then: in the forest, in The Lanes in Brighton, on the seafront in Eastbourne, driving along roads where she had once skipped cheerfully, and standing with Flora outside the narrow semi on the outskirts of Tunbridge Wells which had been her home so long ago. And now they are in London where, back in the sixties, the city was a mere backdrop to the centrality of her own life. How could she have failed to savour it, to learn it in a way that would make it impossible for it to be taken from her? It fills her with regret.

As she steps off the bus at Marble Arch and walks towards Selfridges she inhales once more that sense of the past, seeing young Connie, full of energy and hope and enthusiasm, determined to be herself, dreaming of stepping out onto the stage at Covent Garden to rapturous applause. Those dreams are so long gone it is almost inconceivable that she could ever have owned them. Right now though, her dream is just to find a dress, something special, for this does seem like a very special occasion.

It has to be Selfridges, for it was here that she had come to buy her wedding dress. In a fitting room less spacious than the one in the bridal department Connie remembers that day, imagining herself wriggling into a satin dress with lace sleeves, smoothing down the skirt, waiting for the sales assistant to pull up the long zip, before handing her the circlet of white silk roses, embroidered with the same tiny seed pearls that edged the fine muslin veil. It had been a good life, but it was not the life she had dreamed of living. Had she been afraid of ending up single and alone? Connie stares into the mirror; what if she had let Flora talk her out of marrying Gerald? They would have found a flat together and each would have pursued their own dreams. What sort of life would she have had then? And what about Flora? How might *her* life be different now had Connie not married her brother? But that question she pushes away as she has always done, unable to open herself up to what it might lead to.

Now in a midnight blue dress of crushed taffeta with a stand-up collar, three-quarter sleeves and a close fitting skirt that finishes at mid-calf, Connie sees the woman she has become: a wife, a mother, a grandmother – such precious things to be, such precious people in her life. To regret it would be to regret the people she loves most. She can only regret that it had to be one or the other, and that it doesn't feel as though it was a mindful decision she made herself.

This gorgeous dress is like that other one – destined to be worn only once, for her life in Hobart is unlikely now to provide opportunities to wear it. When Gerald was in Parliament and later in business a formal dress had been a necessity, but the need for one is now long gone.

'I'll take it,' she says to the sales assistant who has popped her head around the curtain. And she doesn't mention that after tonight it will probably spend the rest of its life along-side that other dress, in a zipped plastic sheath at the back of a wardrobe on the other side of the world.

\*

Flora walks slowly down Marchmont Street in the direc-tion of Tonkin's Books, wondering how it would feel to walk here to work from . . . well, from somewhere . . . a bus stop on Euston Road perhaps, or maybe just a few steps up from the Russell Square underground station. Although she had found Phillip's job offer reassuring, the prospect of actually accepting it seems almost too easy and therefore almost too risky. She'd been raised to think that opportunities that fall into one's lap must be suspect, one should have to struggle and fight for something that is really worth having. But it would be stupid to ignore the possibility. Despite Bea's bluntness and apparent eccentricity Flora had liked her – in fact she found those characteristics endearing. And aside from the potential job, if she can catch Bea alone this morning she might also get a chance to talk to her about Gerald.

Bea is on the phone in the office at the back of the shop when Flora arrives but she waves encouragingly and mouths that she won't be long, and Flora waves back and wanders around, gazing at the stacks of new titles on the big central table, looking up and around the open gallery on the second floor, and at the various section signs posted in several languages. The shop, she thinks, is really well laid out, the glass frontage capturing the best of the natural light from the street; it's welcoming and already busy with browsers and tourists. It has the atmosphere of a place where people enjoy what they are doing. Phillip obviously knows his business.

'Gerry and I were among the first of our generation not to be called up for National Service so we went straight to Cambridge and from there I went into publishing,' he'd told them at dinner. Tonkins, he'd explained, had been in the family for more than a century and at that time belonged to his father and uncle. He had been in his early forties when his uncle had died and he had quit publishing and gone into partnership with his father. Books were in his blood, which was one of the reasons that he and Bea had always got on so well.

Both she and Connie had liked him more than they had anticipated, and although Connie had said nothing about it Flora had been pretty sure that her friend had been sizing Phillip up, wondering silently how different her life might have been had she married a man like him, someone who loved books and music, who knew his operas inside out, and seemed free of Gerald's driving and often bullish ambition.

'So sorry, Flora,' Bea says, suddenly appearing beside her. 'I got caught up with a supplier. Anyway, it's lovely to see you. Did you come to look at books or did you want to talk about Phillip's offer?'

'Both really,' Flora says. 'It came out of the blue – I'm not even sure yet whether I want to come back to London, or whether I can afford it. But of course at my age, working with people I like has a lot going for it. And I do have that love of books that you and Phillip have. Gerald never quite got the magic, I'm afraid.'

Bea smiles. 'He certainly didn't have it as a young man,' she says. 'Although he always enjoyed books, he didn't have the same reverence for them as we did. But perhaps he did as he got older?'

Flora shrugs. 'I'm not the person to ask about that. It's so long since I saw him.'

'How sad that you never got over that breach,' Bea says, straightening a pile of paperbacks. 'Those kinds of fallings out always seem so pointless in retrospect, but the Gerry I knew would not have found it easy to apologise, not even to take the first faltering step towards it.'

'You must have known him very well,' Flora says, 'but to be fair I didn't feel able to reach out to him either – I sat around nursing my hurt and my injured pride until it was too late to do anything about it.'

'You had good reason,' Bea says briskly. 'From what you and Connie told us the responsibility lay with him. Anyway, come into the office and I'll tell you a bit about the shop and the work, and then I'll take you on a tour.' She glances at the oversized purple watch on her wrist. 'Are you short of time? If not we could get a coffee and sandwich later.'

\*

It's more than an hour later that they find a table in the only empty corner of the café.

'They make their own bread here,' Bea says, leaning across the table as though sharing a secret. 'The sourdough is to die for. Tell me what you'd like and I'll go and order.'

As Bea joins the queue at the counter Flora sits back thinking over their earlier conversation. It's a beautiful shop in a delightful part of London where she wouldn't be able to afford to live. The rest of the staff are really pleasant, and working with Phillip and Bea would, she thinks, be stimulating and probably fun. They must have one of the best collections of books for miles around.

'Phillip's good to work for,' Bea had told her. 'He gets on well with all the staff; they think he's a bit weird sometimes, but I guess they think that about me too. You'd get the same sort of freedom as I do in running the shop, and I think you might enjoy it. We're looking for someone three or four days a week and our week is seven days, so you'd sometimes have to work weekends, although I imagine that, rather like me, when you're our age and on your own it doesn't make much difference. It would be great to have you here. You'd have to sort out money and all that with Phillip of course.'

Outside the café people are hurrying past heading for the station or Brunswick Square Gardens, darting in and out of shops, or stopping to browse the cheap scarves and jewellery on the stall across the street. On the benches in the nearby park, others are reading newspapers, sipping cardboard beakers of coffee, unwrapping sausage rolls and sandwiches, and tossing crumbs to the pigeons. A typical day in London, this is what her life would be, on glorious days like this, or in driving rain, high winds, frost and snow. There is something about the sort of companionship of working in a bookshop that intrigues her, the friendships she might have with Bea and Phillip, the people she might meet. Is this what she wants?

'Sandwiches won't be long,' Bea says, returning with their coffee. And she slips into her chair and looks straight at Flora. 'I hope you'll think about it and I hope you'll accept,' she says, her dark, almost violet eyes boring into Flora. 'But I imagine you feel like a rest. It sounds glorious over there in Brittany, but I bet it's a real slog, especially in the summer.'

'It sure is. I've enjoyed it, but I know that this is the right time to go. I just have to think carefully about what I want at this time of my life.'

Bea nods. 'Of course.'

'It's odd that we never met before,' Flora says, 'but Gerald didn't really introduce me to his friends. He was five years older so I guess a younger sister was a bit of an embarrassment.'

'I never met your parents either,' Bea says, not looking up. 'And you were in India for quite a long time, but Gerry talked about you a lot.'

'Really?'

'Yes, he was so proud of you for going off like that. He thought it took courage, the sort of courage he didn't have.'

'Proud of me? I thought he was furious with me. He said it was all irresponsible bullshit.'

'Oh, the Maharishi Yogi, yes, he certainly didn't think much of him, he was convinced that he was a shyster. But Gerry envied what he saw as your capacity for absolute belief, and for having the courage to follow that.'

'He *told* you that?'

'Yes. He thought you were wrong-headed in what you believed but envied you your ability to believe so passionately and take risks to pursue it.'

Flora has a strange feeling of the past creeping up on her. 'How extraordinary,' she says. 'I always thought he despised me for it. And, as I found out later, he certainly didn't believe in my right to live my own sexuality.' She pours iced water from the carafe Bea brought back to the table along with the coffee. The coldness seems to burn her throat as she swallows. 'Were you and he . . . well, did you . . . ?'

'Yes,' Bea says, 'we were lovers, for a long time. We were going to get married. In fact we were about to move in together when Connie's mother died . . . and then . . .'

'Then what?' Flora urges her. 'What happened?'

Bea sighs and puts down her sandwich. 'Connie happened. But a very different Connie from the one I met the other night. I thought I knew Gerry very well, but now I think perhaps I only knew one version of him. I don't think he ever told me the truth about Connie. He said that she was madly in love with him, that she depended on him, that he had a duty to look after her as she was so alone.'

Flora inhaled sharply. 'It wasn't quite like that, in fact it was more that he . . .'

'Was he desperately in love with her?' Bea cuts in.

'Well, yes, or perhaps he realised that our parents would think she was the perfect wife, and that would have mattered to him. For all his big talk Gerald was always very much under their joint thumbs, always striving for their approval, and very scared of disappointing them.'

Bea shakes her head. 'I've been a fool,' she said. 'When he told me about Connie I believed every word, believed it ever since. And then a couple of nights ago I met Connie, saw what sort of person she was and somehow, even allowing for her to have matured and toughened up, it just didn't quite make sense.'

Flora pauses, then takes a deep breath. 'Connie was never a needy person. She was doing really well at the Guildhall, she had an amazing voice and could have gone on to a successful musical career. When her mother died I was away, but as Connie tells it, Gerald stepped in and took over. He went beyond helping to actually taking control of everything. What you need to know about Connie then is that a few years before her mother died, her father took off with another woman. Disappeared completely from her life. I've always thought that Gerald probably capitalised on that loss. She wasn't needy or pathetic or anything like that, but I think she was seduced by the idea of a man who seemed to represent a promise of security and loving care. Lots of women yearn for that, especially in those days.'

'That makes sense,' Bea says. 'And he was ruthless in getting rid of me, he dumped me in . . . well, in horrible circumstances. And you may be right about the perfect wife thing. He had often said that I would need to tone myself down when it came to meeting his parents, that they were very conservative.'

'They sure were. I hated Gerald for turning them against me,' Flora says, 'but I know I wouldn't have fared well with them as I got older. I hid a lot from them, but was never prepared to please them by abandoning what I wanted for myself.'

Bea sighs. 'Ah well, who knows what would have happened to Gerald and me if we'd married? Quite probably we'd have torn each other to shreds long ago – two people each determined to have their own way.'

'They said in the shop I'd find you here,' Phillip says, appearing suddenly by their table. 'May I join you?'

'Of course,' Flora says, although she wishes she and Bea had had more time alone to talk. 'Bea's been telling me about the shop and the job.'

The conversation turns to work, bookselling, the rise of ebooks, then the latest literary awards.

'So you'll think about it then? The job, I mean,' Phillip asks her later, as the three of them walk back in the direction of the bookshop.

'I will,' she says. 'Thanks, Phillip, I really appreciate it.'

'My good luck meeting up with you again,' he says. 'Must dash, but come and have a chat when you've thought more,' and he gives her a quick peck on the cheek and heads off in the direction of Tavistock Square.

'Do think about it, Flora,' Bea says. 'And whatever you decide let's meet again before you and Connie leave.' She turns away and then suddenly back again. 'There's something else I should . . .' she begins then stops. 'No – another time. Bye, Flora.' And she hurries away to be swallowed up in the throng of lunchtime customers in the shop.

# Sixteen

rooke inspects the room through the camera function on her phone, searching for the best way to frame the shot. To her it looks amazing from every angle because wherever she points the camera she can visualise her own stuff in place: the bed with her favourite doona cover on it, dressing table over there in the far corner, desk in the opposite corner just under the window that looks out onto the little garden, posters on the walls, shaggy purple rug in the middle. But right now it is just an empty room with white walls, cream carpet and a nice big wardrobe, which all looks pretty ordinary through the camera. Eventually she gives up and takes a picture of the space under the sloping roof, and another of the wall with the window showing the trees outside, and writes a text to go with them.

*Hey Nan – this is my new room. The house is really cool. Only one more week. Love you, Brooke xxx*

The phone makes the whooshing noise that indicates the message is on its way and Brooke slips it back into her pocket. This time next week they'll be moving in. Her dad had said that he would take time off and move during the week but this time it's Brooke who's the cause of the delay. She has exams this week, and as she insists she absolutely has to be there on moving day, they have to wait until Saturday. But it's happening at last, and after what seems like a whole series of let-downs, just six more days seems bearable. They had lurched from one failure to another. After her disappointment at not moving out on the night that Andrew got home from Perth, and the second disappointment with the townhouse, Brooke's frustration level had gone right off the scale.

It's almost six weeks now since Zachary moved in. He has stopped pretending to be nice to her, and Linda has stopped asking her to be nice to him and promising how lovely it will be if they can all be friends. She has even agreed that Brooke can live with her father as soon as he's found somewhere suitable.

'Are you still sure it's this room you want?' Andrew says, appearing in the doorway. 'The other one's bigger.'

'I know, but this is nicer,' Brooke says, sitting cross-legged on the carpet in the space where her bed will go. 'It's really pretty and I like the view of the garden.'

Andrew nods, and walks across to sit down beside her. 'So – happy now?'

'Absolutely,' Brooke says, grinning. 'I love this place, it's much nicer than the townhouse, and it's nicer than home too. It's like a little cottage.'

'It *is* a little cottage,' Andrew says, walking to the window. 'I like the garden. I've always fancied having a proper garden, growing some things.'

Brooke edges closer and leans against him. 'Thanks, Dad. It'll be good living with you. I promise I'll do heaps to help.'

He smiles. 'I know you will. We need to work out a plan for when I have to go away. It's not a place for you to be on your own for several days at a time, but I guess we can deal with that when it happens.'

'I'd be fine here alone, Dad. It'd be cool.'

Andrew screws up his face. 'Your mum won't be happy about it, and I don't think I would. But maybe she'd come here to stay with you.'

'Anything as long as I don't ever have to see The Man in Black again in my whole life, ever,' Brooke says.

'Well, that might be a tough call. Let's wait and see how things go,' Andrew says. 'But at least this is a good start. Anyway, we should work out furniture and whatever else we'll need. We'll have to buy some things – sofa, chairs, kitchen table – and I can't see your mother parting with any of the kitchen stuff. It's going to be a bit like camping at first. But I thought we could go and get some of the small things now, and maybe order some furniture this afternoon.'

'Brilliant.' Brooke scrambles to her feet. 'We could buy a kettle and mugs and get sandwiches and come back here. It'll be like we've moved in already.' She reaches down to drag him up.

'We'd better get a heater too,' he says, looking around. 'A couple probably. These old stone cottages can get pretty chilly in winter.' He straightens his jeans and with a final look around the room he follows Brooke out along the passage into the garden.

*

This is not at all the sort of place that Andrew had in mind for himself and Brooke. By the time their first choice fell through, the weather had changed; it rained for days on end and darker evenings made it difficult to see places after work. They missed several opportunities because they were snapped up before they'd had a chance to view them. The weekends were packed with disappointing visits to properties that were nothing like the estate agents' descriptions. Brooke was moody and impatient and while Andrew understood how unhappy she was, the relentless pressure to find somewhere quickly soon began to wear him down. Her constant questions had started to irritate him and he had stopped returning her calls immediately as he had been doing at the start of this drawn-out saga.

'If you really cared about me you'd have got me out of there by now,' she'd cried, and Andrew had wanted to shake her. Linda was screeching at him over the phone almost every evening about something or other, and now here was Brooke pulling the old emotional blackmail trick.

'Okay,' he'd said in response to her outburst, swinging the car over to the side of the road and switching off the engine. 'Now listen to me, Brooke. I'm doing the best I can as fast as I can but these things just don't happen overnight. I know it's not nice for you being there, it's not nice for me either – living in that freezing rat hole above the gallery. But I *have* managed to get your mum to agree to your coming with me, and I'm constantly checking the internet listings to find places for us to look at. So why don't you just shut up, stop whingeing and help. Get on the iPad and search. You know what we need and what I can afford, so you see if you can do it faster.'

It had taken her ten days to find this place, which doesn't fit any of the criteria they had agreed on. It's further from her school, although it is on a direct bus route. It's a cottage with a garden as opposed to a flat or a townhouse with a small, easy-care yard, and it has all the irritations and inconveniences of an old house; the possibility of insects and mice hiding in those gaps between the floorboards and the wainscoting, and a garden to look after. But it also has charm and character in abundance, a newly renovated kitchen and bathroom, and the garden doesn't look like too much trouble.

'It looks really cute and it's cheaper, too,' Brooke had said. And he'd loved her for that.

He'd loved her, too, for picking a place on which Linda would not have wasted a second glance, a place that looked homely and comfortable, although of course the reality would certainly be that throughout the year it would be either too hot or too cold, and need more cleaning than he wanted to do. But from the moment they had pulled up outside it for the first time earlier in the week, he knew that this was the right place for the two of them to be.

'Do you think you'd be okay here alone if I go and live with Nan?' Brooke had asked.

And Andrew had laughed and said, '*If* that happened I'd be fine, but let's not get ahead of ourselves.'

She'd nodded. 'Good, because if I did and then had to come back to Melbourne to go to uni I'd still love to live here.'

Linda was, of course, horrified when Brooke had shown her the ad for the cottage on the internet. 'It'll be freezing, darling,' she'd said, 'and old places are so dirty.'

'It's beautifully clean,' Andrew had reassured her. 'The carpets and curtains are all new. It's just been repainted, the bathroom and kitchen are renovated, there's nothing to worry about.' And to his surprise Linda had just shrugged.

'Oh well,' she'd said, 'if that's what you both want, it'll be your problem.'

And he'd thought she looked incredibly fed up, and tired. It can't have been easy living with Brooke and Zachary at loggerheads, and Brooke so hostile towards her. But now, as he and Brooke close the cottage door behind them and walk down the path, he wonders how it will be if he does get involved with someone else in the future. How would it be to have his new partner in the house with Brooke? But that's too hard to think about right now.

'So – shopping then?' he asks, slipping into the driving seat.

'Yep,' Brooke nods. 'I texted Nan some pictures. I wish she was here.'

'So do I,' he says. 'We haven't seen enough of her for a long time. I want to put that right.' And as he says that he feels a terrible aching longing for his childhood, for the time when everything seemed so solid and certain and when, however boring, rigid and unreasonable his parents seemed, there was always the comfort of knowing that one of them, usually his mother, would always be there if something went wrong.

\*

It's late on Sunday evening when Andrew drops Brooke home. Together they have made a list of the things they want to take to the new house and he is hoping that Linda isn't going to start an argument over what he can and can't take. He wants the fighting to end and he's already sensed that Linda might be getting close to breaking point. She hates uncertainty but she hates mess even more, and each time he has been back to the house to collect Brooke, evidence of Zachary's mess is all around. All the signs are that while Linda is not starting to regret their separation, she might well be regretting letting Zachary move in with her.

'I know our marriage was falling apart for a long time,' he'd said to her on one occasion. 'But Zachary, well, he's the last person I'd ever imagine . . .'

'Stop there,' Linda had said, holding up her hand. 'I don't need to know what you think of Zach or anything else. That's my business.'

Andrew had shrugged and walked out to wait for Brooke by the car, wondering how Linda was really feeling and whether she was actually allowing herself to imagine what it would be like when Brooke was gone.

'We're back, Mum,' Brooke calls now as she opens the front door. 'Dad needs to see you.' And she heads on up the stairs with Andrew following her.

'Hi,' Brooke says, dropping her bag on the floor and looking around. 'Is he . . . ?'

'Zach's out,' Linda cuts in, getting to her feet. She looks across at Andrew. 'I was expecting you earlier.'

'Sorry,' he says, 'we had stuff to sort out,' and he hands her the list. 'These are the things I'd like to collect next Saturday.

204

I've booked a removal van with a driver and we'll stop by and pick up Brooke and this stuff at about ten o'clock. Just email me if you've got any problems with it.'

Linda takes the list from him and glances down at it. He thinks she looks totally exhausted; some light inside her seems to have been extinguished and he feels a sudden stab of concern for her, but it is gone as quickly as it arrived.

'Okay,' Linda says, looking up from the list. 'This looks fine.' And then she really takes him by surprise. 'You both look worn out. Would you like a drink or a cup of tea or something before you go, Andrew?'

He shakes his head. 'No thanks.' He hugs Brooke. 'Talk to you tomorrow. Ring me when the lit exam is over,' then turns to Linda. 'See you Saturday. G'night.'

'Night, Dad,' Brooke says.

As he makes his way down the stairs he's suddenly aware that Linda is following him.

'Andrew – just a minute . . .'

He stops and turns back, waiting, expecting her to have changed her mind about something on the list.

'I just . . .' She stops and puts her hands to her face for a moment. 'I . . . oh, this is all so awful – I'm so sick of arguing, and I'm dreading Brooke moving out.'

There are tears in her eyes and Andrew is shaken by the sudden wave of compassion that washes over him.

'Yes, I'm sure you are,' he says, going back up one step and putting his hand on her arm.

'Could we . . . ?' Another hesitation. 'Could we talk. Properly, I mean, without arguing? I mean for Brooke's sake – well, for all our sakes . . .'

It's him who's hesitating now. Part of him thinks it may not be possible to avoid arguing over things that matter so much to both of them, but this is a side of Linda that he's not seen for a very long time. Vulnerability. 'Of course,' he says. 'We can give it go.'

'Tomorrow perhaps? We could have lunch? That place near your office we used to go to.'

He nods. 'Twelve-thirty?'

'Fine,' she says. 'And thanks.' She turns and goes back up the stairs.

As Andrew gets to the front door he hears Linda call out to their daughter: 'Brooke, darling, don't go to bed just yet. I thought we might have some hot chocolate and a chat . . .'

'Sorry, Mum, got revision for tomorrow,' Brooke says. 'Lit exam. Night!'

And he pauses in the silence, and hears the crack in Linda's voice as she calls out to Brooke to sleep well, and then the silence again, the deadening grief of it, and he has to fight the urge to run back and comfort her as he used to do years ago, so many years ago, when they were different people in a different relationship.

# Seventeen

Flora is sitting at the table in the hotel room checking the cinema listings and wondering if she would have preferred to be going to the opera after all. Connie's excitement has made her think that maybe she too should have gone off to buy a new dress, and treated it like a special occasion. In their youth she had made an effort to learn more about opera, so that she might enjoy it for Connie's sake, but it remained an act of friendship rather than a personal choice. A good play, the ballet, or a classical concert she loved, but when it came to opera she never quite got it. What she had enjoyed, though, had been Connie's passion; the way she explained the characters and the stories, all the titbits she knew about the idiosyncrasies of the various singers, and the ways in which a different director might have approached it. For Connie it truly was a magnificent obsession, so when Flora abandoned the Maharishi and made her way home, she had been stunned to discover that Connie's attention was now elsewhere.

'But you can't just give it up,' Flora remembers saying. 'You've wanted this since you were twelve, and you were thrilled when you got into the Guildhall.' She can still see Connie's face – the deep blush, the conflicting emotions, the way she dropped her gaze before responding.

'I might not be good enough,' she'd said, mustering enough confidence to meet Flora's eyes again. 'You have to have exceptional talent.'

'And have they told you that you don't have it?'

'Gerald says . . .'

'Bugger Gerald,' Flora had said. 'What does he know about it? The lecturers, what do they say?'

Connie had shrugged. 'They said I was . . .' she'd hesitated, blushing, looking away again. 'They said I was outstanding.'

'Well, then . . . ?'

'But Gerald . . .' Another hesitation, another justification that she was struggling to believe. 'Gerald doesn't think I'm emotionally suited to the life of the opera. I lack stamina.'

Flora remembers that she sank down onto the edge of Connie's bed, put her head in her hands, let forth a chain of abuse about her brother and then challenged Connie over whom she wanted to run her life. She reminded her about the hugely encouraging feedback she'd received on her audition, and of how much her mother had wanted this for her. It all got very uncomfortable after that and it was obvious that her intervention was simply making things harder for Connie, so she'd backed off. But she'd had it out later with Gerald, who had accused her of making trouble because she didn't want him to marry Connie.

'Well, if you're going to ruin her life by stopping her from doing the one thing she's always wanted then no, I don't,' she'd said.

But she'd known by then that the die was cast. Connie, emotionally bereft at thirteen when her father left the country and never contacted her or her mother again, was fair game for a man who professed to love her and wanted to take care of her. Did Gerald love her, or just need her, or were the two things so inextricably mixed that not even he knew? Connie certainly had all the warmth and capacity for love and affection that their own mother had lacked, or perhaps was unable to demonstrate. It was, Flora thinks, what she too most appreciated in Connie – that capacity for love – but it was hard to accept that her friend had relinquished something that meant so much to her for Gerald who, Flora felt, had captured her to fulfil his own needs. It is one more thing for which she hasn't forgiven him. She wonders now if he had always known that. Did it explain why he sent her that ticket to join them in Tasmania? Did he want to justify his behaviour, show her that he had done the right thing by Connie? Did he want her to see that Connie was happy with the big white house and the two bright, argumentative children, happy to be a wife and mother and not mourning her lost dreams of the opera? Was that it? Did he want her there not for herself but as a witness to his success as a husband?

'I can't believe you've done this,' she had shouted at Gerald the week she got back from India. 'Connie had huge talent and ambition but you've made her feel it's not enough. How could you do that?'

'I don't want her to be disappointed,' he'd said. 'She's fragile now, since her mother died, and her father didn't even bother to come back for the funeral. Connie needs someone to look after her.'

'Look after her? That's bullshit!' Flora had snapped. 'If you really loved her you'd encourage her, but the truth is that you want *her* to look after *you*.' It had stung him – she'd seen it in his face, in the hardening of his eyes, in the tight set of his mouth.

'Oh grow up, Flo,' he'd said then. 'You're just having a tantrum because you think I've stolen your friend. You ought to be pleased that I'm making her a member of the family.'

In Hobart she had been surprised to see that Connie was fulfilling the conventional role of wife and mother with some conviction, although Flora thought she also detected an underlying unease in her friend.

'You've changed her,' she'd accused him. 'You knew she could have been a star, but you took her away, starved her talent and her ambition.'

'Don't be so ridiculous,' he'd said. 'You just can't recognise or appreciate a good marriage when you see one.'

His cool, dismissive tone infuriated her and she did what she'd promised herself she wouldn't do – she lost her temper. 'You've crushed something in her,' she yelled at him. 'It's the seventies, Gerry, you don't seem to have got a grip on the concept of liberation.'

That was when he said he wouldn't have any of that hairy-legged women's lib stuff in his house. Things had been tense and awkward between them after that, although they had both managed – fairly successfully, Flora thinks – to hide it from Connie and the children, until that day: the day he found her with Denise. Flora wonders now, for the first time, about her own motives. Was it a conscious decision to let him discover them together? She had certainly thought several times of bringing it all out into the open. Gerald, she assumed, knew about her sexuality. How could he not? She could even understand that he preferred not to refer to it nor hear about it, but did she unconsciously create a situation that would force him to face it? Was that what she'd really wanted?

Flora's flush deepens at what she now thinks might have been her own part in that final schism: forcing a confrontation, shoving reality in Gerald's face in his own house. She gets to her feet in agitation, paces back and forth across the room. Did she want his rage? Want to taunt him and force him to acknowledge her?

'You disgust me,' he'd hissed. 'I want you out of my house right now. I don't want you here perverting my children. And I see it all now, all that stuff about Connie's career, of course you didn't want me to marry her, because you wanted her for yourself.'

The accusation had paralysed Flora. She had loved Connie from their first days at school, loved her as a sister, long before she had come to understand the nature of her own sexuality. Had Gerald really believed that, or had he simply said it to hurt her? Too late now to know that, and speculation can only drive her mad.

The door to the bathroom opens behind her.

'So how do I look?' Connie asks.

And Flora inhales deeply and turns around.

'Oh – are you okay?' Connie says. 'You look like you've been crying.'

Flora shakes her head. 'I'm fine. My eyes are just a bit tired.' And she stands back, tilts her head to one side, and studies her friend closely. Connie is wearing a perfectly fitting, deep blue taffeta dress, black patent shoes with heels that make Flora wince, and a string of pearls. Her hair, so neat, unlike Flora's untameable springy curls, is in its usual bob just below her ears but blow dried rather more carefully than usual.

'You look amazing!' she says. 'Honestly, Con, really lovely. That dress could have been made for you.'

Connie smiles in obvious relief. 'Thank goodness. As soon as I saw it I thought it was perfect, I didn't even try anything else. Then, later, I thought that was ridiculous, and maybe I'd made a horrible mistake.'

Flora shakes her head. 'I reckon you could have tried the entire stock and not come up with anything better. I must take a photo,' and she gets her phone and takes several quick pictures. 'You should send a couple of these to Brooke, I bet she'd love to see them.'

'No,' Connie says. 'Really?'

'Of course, why not? And you'll knock Phillip's socks off.'

Connie grimaces. 'That's not what I was aiming for.'

'I know that, but it'll be a pleasant side effect, won't it?'

She grins. 'It will. But this is for me – you know, another step . . .'

'I know,' Flora says. 'What time are you meeting him?'

'Six o'clock in the hotel foyer.'

'Then you should get a move on. And remember to come home before you turn into a pumpkin.'

Connie laughs, takes a final quick glance at the mirror, picks up her bag with one hand, and with the other holds out an envelope that was tucked underneath it. 'I'm off. If you have time before you go to the cinema would you read this?'

'What is it?'

'Just read it, and we can talk about it later.'

Flora shrugs, and drops it on the table. 'Okay, Cinderella, off you go to the ball. And have a wonderful time.'

Connie executes a small curtsey, but as she walks out closing the door behind her, Flora's spirits suddenly flag. Alone again, the horrible reminder returns: her time away is running out and she is no nearer to a plan for her future.

She sighs, picks up the kettle, fills it in the bathroom, and as she drops a tea bag into a cup and stands there waiting for the kettle to boil, she puts on her glasses, sits down at the table, and opens Connie's envelope. There are several folded pages and, to her surprise, she sees that it's a copy of Gerald's will. The first feeling she has is that she shouldn't be reading this, it's private, between Gerald and Connie and their family, but of course she *is* part of their family too, and she can actually play that part now. Even so it still seems odd. There's all the usual stuff – bequests to each of the children and a trust fund for the grandchildren, and she's surprised that there appears to be so much money. Gerald had made a strong start in the public service, and then as a Member of Parliament – both well-paid jobs, but this much? Perhaps it was the directorships that followed when he lost his seat. But of course, how could she have forgotten! Gerald inherited everything from their parents – everything that should have been shared.

The house had apparently been signed over to Connie some years ago, and she gets the private pension and the

parliamentary superannuation and various other invest-
ments. And there, right at the end, 'a sum equivalent to 500,000
British pounds to my sister Flora Hawkins, in fond remembrance and in some small acknowledgement of the proceeds
of our parents' estate from which she was excluded.'

Flora stares at the words in disbelief, reads them several
times in case she has misunderstood, but no, it's as it
appeared the first time, and alongside that sentence Connie
has pencilled an asterisk with PTO beneath it. Flora turns to
the back of the sheet to find Connie has written a note dated
this morning:

*Dearest Flora,*

*When I left Hobart the solicitor was finalising the paperwork
and the payment of the bequest should be made within the next
four weeks. Forgive me for not telling you this straight away,
it was Gerald's instruction and as his executor I had to respect
that. I'll explain when we talk.*

*Love, Cx*

Flora stares at the words, and then reads the whole will
again. Then she puts the pages down on the table, takes off
her glasses, and stares into the darkness beyond the window.

\*

It's unusual for Phillip to feel awkward about going out with a
woman but that's just how he'd felt as he walked into the hotel
and looked around the foyer for Connie. Awkward because
he wasn't sure whether they were just two old friends going
to the opera together, or whether it was a date, and he was
even more uneasy about what Connie might think. After all,
they *aren't* old friends, all they know of each other they know
through Gerald and the information they'd exchanged a few
nights earlier. But years ago Phillip had fancied Connie madly.
Gerald had introduced them one night in a pub in Soho and

because, at the time, Gerald was having a very full-on thing with Bea, Phillip had assumed that Connie was just a friend. As the evening wore on and everyone got increasingly drunk Phillip had geared himself up to make a move on Connie, but just as he'd shifted closer to her Gerald had moved between them and warned him off. Typical Gerald of course, even in his religious phase he was always juggling women.

Phillip is always able to get his hands on theatre or opera tickets at short notice, and the prospect of going to the opera with someone as passionate about it as he is delighted him, and Connie had jumped at the chance to go with him to *Nabucco*. Years ago he wouldn't have given a thought to the importance of getting it right, but Lorna, and a couple of other women with whom he'd had relationships since his divorce, have taught him things that he wishes he'd known when he was younger, and the importance of getting the tone of an occasion right is one of them. He thought that old friends was probably what Connie had in mind, and that was what he was aiming for. But it had come as a shock to him that when she emerged from the lift looking as though she'd stepped off the cover of a posh magazine for mature women, all his male instincts revived.

As he sat next to her in the front row of the dress circle, he could feel the warmth of her arm against his. She seemed, in fact, to radiate warmth and pleasure, and the occasional discreet rustle of her taffeta dress along with the scent of a vaguely familiar perfume went straight to his head as well as his loins. He knew that he needed to be very careful, because what he also felt was that, despite the interesting discovery that he still had loins, what he most wanted was friendship. He didn't want to confuse things. In his seventies there is so much more than just sex to enjoy, and most of it is less emotionally risky and complicated.

Now, in the interval, as he carries drinks to a table in the bar, he recalls his state of mind that day on the river. Young people, he thinks, simply don't have a clue about what really matters, about the many wonderful and indefinable ways that people can become and remain connected.

'Thank you, Phillip,' Connie says, taking the wine glass from him. 'And thank you for all of this, it's wonderful, everything: the production, the cast, the orchestra and most of all being here in this place, which was so much a part of my dreams. *And* being with someone who's enjoying it as much as I am. My friends and family would generally rather watch the footy, or even synchronised swimming, than spend a night at the opera.'

He laughs. 'Not Flora, surely?'

'Well, no, but it would be her least favourite of the arts. When we were young she tried very hard to enjoy it for my sake.'

'We must be similar,' he said. 'Whenever I come here – and that's quite often – I look at the audience and wonder where they come from, because in my quite large group of friends and acquaintances I can never find anyone to come with me.'

'Philistines,' she says laughing, and they clink their glasses.

'Why did you give it up, Connie?'

She takes a slow sip of champagne and savours it. 'To marry Gerald, of course.'

He shakes his head. 'Well, you must have loved him very much.'

She smiles, looking down into her drink. 'This is a contentious subject. I don't think Flora has forgiven me for choosing Gerald over the opera, even though it let her off the hook in terms of having to sit through it. At the time I wasn't really in love with him. He'd always been like a brother to me, and I was very fond of him.'

'So why on earth . . . ?'

'It's complicated.'

Phillip leans towards her, putting his glass down on the table. 'Really? That's very sad. So you do regret it?'

'I think so, yes. I think – well, I know – I had considerable talent and plenty of stamina. But I let Gerald persuade me otherwise and I wonder now if perhaps I *wanted* to believe him because back then I didn't really believe in myself. I mean, I certainly longed for the career but I was also quite terrified of it. At some level I must have wanted what Gerald was offering more.'

'Which was?'

'Well, that he would look after me always, that we would have a comfortable life, beautiful children, financial security – all that kind of thing. I was only young. My mother had recently died, my father – well, you don't want to hear all that. Gerald loved me and he did all the right things, and I grew to love him too. And while he certainly wasn't perfect he did do all that he said he'd do.'

'So you don't resent him for it, then?'

She laughs. 'I never said I was a saint, Phillip. That's partly why I'm here in England now. I often resented the fact that Gerald got to tick off all the items on his career agenda and I ticked off none of mine. But I have two wonderful children, three grandchildren, a lovely house and, of course, a level of financial security that a lot of people would kill for. So I shouldn't complain – it's just that I see now that I *could* have had both career and marriage. It's not so unusual now, but back then most of us abandoned our careers to marry. The women's movement was starting but it by-passed many of us. You must remember how it was.'

'Of course,' he says, 'of course I remember. Strangely, last night I was watching *The Red Shoes* – Moira Shearer, Marius Goring – the dancer who must choose between love and the ballet. You know it?'

'Oh yes.'

'Well, that was made much earlier of course, in the late forties, and I was thinking that although things had changed by the sixties when we were young, it was still a very difficult choice for women. Having it all was only very occasionally a reality.'

'Exactly, and I did rather better than Moira Shearer's character, who danced to her death under a train, don't you think?'

He smiles. 'You don't seem bitter.'

'Not bitter, but angry sometimes, and I'll admit to disappointment. That's something I haven't overcome.'

'So when did you last sing – I suppose you still do?'

Connie shakes her head. 'No, and I can't really remember the last time. When we first moved to Australia the opportunities were limited. There were the children, and we were busy and later, when Gerald was elected to Parliament, it got busier. I used to help out in his electorate office. We did get to the opera and concerts quite often, but since he got sick . . . well, it's a long time now. Which is why tonight is so special.'

'I see,' Phillip says, nodding, looking down into his glass, 'but it seems like such a big sacrifice. I think that anyone who has a passion for their art pays a heavy price if they sacrifice it for marriage, or anything else. I wonder if it doesn't leave a scar – I mean, to any artist isn't the fulfilment of the gift, the realisation of the talent, what matters most? If that is frustrated . . .' he hesitates, searching his memory for something he'd once read, '. . . I can't get the exact words, but it's a quote, something about if an artist is frustrated in pursuing their talent it . . . he or she gets twisted out of shape.' He is about to go on but looking up he sees the shock on Connie's face. He reaches out to take her hand. 'I'm sorry, Connie, please don't be offended. It's just something I read – a book – Vita Sackville West, I think, but I can't remember the title.'

She has flushed and now bites her lip. 'Yes, I see,' she says. 'I understand what you're saying.'

'It was stupid of me, but it seemed so relevant. A woman who had longed to be an artist had abandoned her dreams to marry and years later she meets a man who knew her in the past, and he asks her why . . .' his voice trails away and Connie stays silent. 'And then . . . and then he says that to her and . . . well, then she's just as hurt and offended by it as you are. I'm so sorry.' He flushes now, furious with himself.

Connie looks at him long and hard. 'I can see that you're right,' she says eventually. 'It sounds dramatic but I rather think it *is* actually right. There is a sort of distortion.'

'Right perhaps, but tactless on my part,' he says, getting to his feet as the bell rings for the second time. 'We should go back.' He's anxious, now, that he has ruined the evening.

'Maybe,' she says, 'but food for thought.' And she smiles and gets up. 'Maybe I should read that book.' And as they walk back to their seats she slips her arm through his. 'It's all right, Phillip,' she says. 'Really it is.'

And he places his opposite hand on hers and thinks that perhaps, despite his poor choice of words, or indeed because of them, they seem to have shared something quite important and intimate; something he will remember for a very long time.

\*

'I can't believe you didn't tell me,' Flora says. 'All that time in Port d'Esprit and then here and you never said a word. Frankly, Connie – it seems quite manipulative. All those conversations about what I wanted to do, when all the time you knew that money was an issue and so it was crucial to what I might decide.'

They have walked to the café in Russell Square for breakfast and Connie is struggling to understand Flora's reaction to Gerald's will, which is so different from what she had expected. She tears off a small piece of croissant and dunks it into her coffee, a habit she'd reverted to in Port d'Esprit where Suzanne still served *café crème* in the old-fashioned French bowls which she'd loved as a girl. She puts the piece of coffee-soaked croissant into her mouth letting the soft milky flakes dissolve on her tongue.

'Look,' she says, 'like I said, Gerald left instructions about how a whole lot of things should be done, and one of them was that I should see you in person and tell you about the bequest at a time when I felt you would be open to accepting it.'

Flora throws her hands in the air. 'So Gerald's still calling the shots! Aren't you capable of reading a situation for yourself, working out what is the right thing to do, or is everything always to be exactly as Gerald wanted?'

While her voice is fierce with anger her expression is hurt, bereft almost, Connie thinks.

'And *he* told you to come and see me? I thought you came because of us, our friendship. I thought you came because it was important to you. Gerald drove a wedge between us that strangled our friendship and now, even though he's dead, he's still directing the movie.'

'Flora, stop!' Connie says. 'That's not fair; you know I wanted to come. Seeing you again was always the most important thing to me. Gerald knew that, he knew it when he got the will drawn up. It was a few years ago, before he lost his speech. He'd decided to make a very simple will that left everything to me to divide up as I wanted. I told him I thought that his family would appreciate something more personal, which reflected his own wishes rather than mine. So he talked to the solicitor and came up with this will. Over time he'd begun to feel he should have shared the proceeds of your parents' estate with you, even though they wrote you out of it at the time. He wanted to make amends for that but he thought you might . . . well, what he actually said was, "She might get on her high horse and refuse it". He knew I'd visit you the first chance I got, so he thought this was the best chance of your accepting it. What more can I say? I would have come here, bequest or not, surely you know that?'

Flora is silent; she sits across the table from Connie looking everywhere except into her eyes. She fiddles irritably; moves a knife a little to one side, her coffee cup slightly in the opposite direction, crumples a paper napkin then uncrumples and smooths it out again. Tension starts to build in Connie's stomach. Should she have done this differently? She can't even remember the last time there was tension between her and Flora, and this reaction is so uncharacteristic.

'It feels wrong,' Flora says, her eyes filled with hurt and confusion. '*I* feel wrong. I ought to be over the moon and I'm not. This may seem unreasonable, Connie, but it makes me uncomfortable that you and Gerald discussed this – as though you were planning how he could get me to gratefully accept his bequest as though that would constitute forgiveness . . . it just doesn't feel good.'

Connie flushes in discomfort, torn between thinking that this *does* sound reasonable and also that, in view of the circumstances, it's entirely *un*reasonable. She says nothing, waiting for Flora to go on.

'You asked me to imagine what I would do if money wasn't an object, when all the time you knew that it needn't *be* an object. I said I'd visit you in Hobart, get to know my family – and I meant it, really meant it. Now it feels like you were setting me up, as though if I go there I'm saying what happened is okay, forgiven, passing absolution on him. Perhaps you think I'm being ridiculous . . .'

'No,' Connie cuts in, 'not ridiculous, but I do think it's a bit unreasonable. *I* don't need you to forgive Gerald for anything, Flora, that's between you and him, or rather you and his memory. I have my own forgiveness issues with him. What he's left you is inadequate in comparison to what we inherited from your parents. He should have shared it fifty-fifty with you at the time, and as he didn't he should have found a way of leaving you an equivalent share at current value which would be more. But – this was how he wanted it.

And yes, I *can* see why you felt asking you to imagine a decision free of financial constraints was manipulative. Perhaps it was. It was my own selfishness. I so want you to come to Australia that I was longing to know if you wanted that too. And I was over the moon when you said that you did. I'm so sorry I've upset you.'

Flora's lips are pressed tightly together. She puts both hands up to her face for a moment and then nods. Connie waits again in the silence. She had thought that Flora might say something cynical about the bequest, perhaps make a joke about it while at the same time being delighted. She had expected breakfast this morning to be a celebration in which they would plan the future. But this has touched a nerve in Flora and Connie sees that it's more complicated than she had assumed.

'Last night,' Flora says, 'while you were out, I was thinking about Gerald a lot, about what he did, what he said to me and the effect it had on me.'

'What do you mean exactly?'

'What he said after he found me with Denise.'

'Look, I know that was awful for you but . . .'

'Actually, Connie, you *don't* know. You only know what he said about not wanting me in the house influencing his children, and about my being jealous of him. You know that because it happened that same day, and I told you about it. What you don't know is that I saw him again, later.'

'When? I thought that was the last time you saw him, when you left the house that day.'

Flora shakes her head. 'I saw him three weeks later. I know you thought I'd left Tasmania, gone to Melbourne before returning to England, but I'd stayed on for a while to sort things out with Denise and of course I had to wait for a berth on a ship, I couldn't afford to fly in those days. Anyway, one morning I bumped into Gerald near the post office. He was horrified. He grabbed my arm and dragged me around the corner, said he was ashamed to be seen talking to me.' She stops, staring down into her coffee cup, then picks it up and sips the coffee slowly.

'Go on,' Connie says. 'What happened then?'

'He said the most vile things, and told me to get out of Tasmania. He said he was going to run for Parliament at the next election and he wasn't going to have that skewered by people knowing he had a lesbian for a sister. He said he would never get elected, that you would all be contaminated by my presence, the children would be bullied and shamed at school, and that even if I didn't care about him, if I cared at all about you and Kerry and Andrew, I should go as far away as possible and never come back.'

Connie is frozen with shock; she opens her mouth but can't begin to speak. Her head is spinning with the awfulness of it and the fact that Flora has kept this from her for all these years. 'I had no idea,' she says eventually. 'But he did run a very hard line on homosexuality in his election campaign. And of course Tasmania was a very different place in those days, and it rallied a lot of people to support him. Back in the seventies and eighties it was a red-hot issue.'

'I know,' Flora says. 'Connie, Gerald abused me to the extent that I was left feeling that I was essentially sick and shameful. I won't repeat all of it, and I've never told anyone else this, but I know you've often wondered why I never really got into a relationship, why I only ever had casual affairs and always ducked out when things started to get serious. Well, that's the reason. Because whenever I get involved with a woman and start to feel serious, to really care about her, I have this terrible fear that I'll just bring shame on her and on myself. It completely overwhelms me. And so I back off at a hundred miles an hour, back to my hole and hide, because Gerald is always in my head, his face in my face, his voice saying the hideous things he said that day.'

222

'But, Flora . . .'

'I know it's decades ago and that people, or most people at least, feel differently now, but that's still there, when I get close to anyone it's like a switch flicks and I run away.'

# Eighteen

ndrew watches as the removal van disappears around the corner. So it's done at last, after all the arguments about Brooke, about the house, about money and possessions and furniture, it really seems to be over. Suddenly, surprisingly, the hostility has dissipated and all he feels now is relief. It must, he thinks, have been the reality that Brooke was moving out that had led to Linda's change of heart, the night he'd taken Brooke home. He'd been profoundly moved by her distress that night, but by the following morning he was back to wanting to pull out of the lunch commitment, and tell her to piss off and he'd see her in court. But part of him, he thinks now it was the better part, had made him hold back and he'd turned up at the restaurant to find Linda sitting at a corner table staring out of the window and sipping a glass of sparkling water. She looked terrible, worse even than the previous evening, vulnerable still, and in the harsh white light from the window her face looked haggard. He almost wanted to hug her but didn't.

'I can't bear this anymore,' she'd said, before he even sat down. 'I want it to be over. I know I've behaved really badly and I don't expect you to forgive me, but I *am* sorry, so let's just decide what happens next.'

She told him to feel free to take everything that was on his list, and anything else he wanted, and had asked him for some time to raise the money to buy him out of the house.

'I think Zach will buy in,' she'd said. 'He's putting his house up for sale, but you know what the market's like – it may take a while.'

'Whatever,' he said, 'take your time. I don't want to put you under any more pressure.' They'd even managed to talk in a civilised way about Brooke's maintenance and what Linda would contribute.

'I want to see her at weekends or at least alternate weekends, and I want her to be able to come over in the week if she wants to.'

'I won't interfere with your seeing her,' Andrew said. 'I'll fit in with whatever works for her and for you but you need to understand that Brooke is adamant that she won't stay with you while Zachary is in the house, so you'll need to think about how you're going to manage that.'

Linda had nodded. 'Well, Brooke may have to be a bit more flexible about that.'

In your dreams, he'd thought, but he hadn't said it.

'I keep thinking about what we lost,' she continued. 'I mean, things were falling apart long before I got involved with Zach. The heart had gone out of it for both of us.'

Andrew nodded. 'Even those few times we began to talk about it we ended up in a mess.'

'You changed . . .' Linda began.

'So you've said,' he cut in. 'I was terminally boring, but frankly I just felt like giving up on everything. We seemed to have come to the end of the road – and Dad getting so sick was part of it.'

'But what happened was between *us*,' Linda said, 'it wasn't to do with your father. It was us, we tried talking about it and got stuck so then we just let it all drift.'

'Yes, but for me that was because I was floundering. Everything changed, I couldn't get a grip on anything, particularly myself. Mum was cut off and distracted, my relationship with Kerry and Chris went down the plughole. I don't understand it but it feels as though Dad's illness somehow infected all of us.'

Linda had shrugged. 'Sounds a bit fanciful to me,' she said. 'I don't think it was anything to do with that, but it's your family . . .'

Andrew hadn't tried to explain because he wasn't sure he knew how. All he knew was that as Gerald's decline became more evident, and more incapacitating, he had felt that his own life was also somehow suspended. He couldn't move forward or back, he was waiting, always waiting, for something to happen, some sort of change that would fix everything and take him – take his whole family – back to where it had once been.

'Anyway,' he said, surprising himself with his conciliatory tone, 'everything will be better if we can keep talking rather than fighting.'

She'd nodded. 'Yes. You were my friend as well as my husband, I'd like to hang on to the friendship.'

He'd been too choked up to speak then, but eventually managed a rather feeble, 'Me too.'

As he'd walked back to the office after that lunch he'd felt as though a great weight had lifted off his shoulders. And now, as he stands in this quaint little rented cottage, staring at the cardboard boxes, the pieces of furniture they bought and those they had delivered from the house, the jumble of stuff all in the wrong place, it seems as though a shaft of light has opened up and the ice that had formed around his heart is starting to thaw.

He stands here now feeling pleasure in the ache of muscles weary from lifting furniture and boxes, and climbing on and off the tailboard of the van. He really should take more exercise. But there's more lifting to do before they're finished. The beds are in the two bedrooms, but more or less everything else is here in the lounge. The familiar torture of flatpack furniture awaits him, but even that seems like fun right now.

'Coffee, Dad?' Brooke calls from the kitchen, and he wanders through and sees her standing by the sink, ripping the packaging off the new coffee machine. She stands back looking at it, and then unwinds the cable and plugs it into the socket. 'This is so cool. Do you know where we put the coffee capsules?'

Andrew pulls the box from a plastic carrier bag and hands it to her.

'Do you know how to use it?'

She rolls her eyes. 'Of course. Everyone's got them these days. Donna's mum's got one.'

'I still feel rather attached to the plunger.'

'Well, you soon won't,' and she fills the machine with water and adjusts various switches. 'It's really easy,' she says. 'Black or white?'

'White, please.'

He watches as she gets milk from the bag and begins to unpack the rest of the shopping and put it away.

My daughter, Andrew thinks, my beautiful daughter. And he can barely believe the pleasure he feels as he imagines them with everything unpacked, everything in its place, living here peacefully together.

'I am so unfit,' he says, 'why don't we start cycling again?'

'Cool,' Brooke says. 'It's a good thing Mum gave me her bike, because mine was too small last time we rode. I think that path we used to ride on actually comes along quite near here.' She picks up her phone and fiddles with it.

'You don't need to look for it now,' Andrew says.

'I'm not. I'm trying to find a photo Nan sent me. Look.'

She hands him her phone and he pulls his glasses from

his top pocket and examines the photograph of his mother. She's in what looks like a hotel bedroom, wearing a dark blue dress and the Broome pearls his father had given her on their thirtieth anniversary. She looks as he remembers her, before all the drama of Gerald's illness changed her. 'Crikey,' he says, 'I can barely believe it,' and he peers hard at the photograph, wanting to see it better, moving his fingers across the screen to enlarge it, and he has a sudden intense longing to see Connie in this dress, to be in that room with her.

'She bought that dress for the opera,' Brooke says. 'She went with Granddad's friend.'

'Really?' He can't take his eyes off it. There is something about his mother in this picture that he had almost forgotten. A look he used to know but which he now realises went missing a long time ago. It's anticipation, hope, he thinks, a look that says that something good could be about to happen. A huge lump tightens his throat; he sees that in the confusion of his own feelings about his father's illness and death and the recent turmoil of his failing marriage, he has simply failed to consider what might be happening to his mother. He remembers a conversation with Kerry on the morning of the day they scattered the ashes, a conversation about the future, just the two of them in a café at Battery Point. They had talked about where Connie should live, what should happen to the house, how they would get her to organise her life in a way that they both thought best. And he feels himself flush with shame at the memory of it, the self-interest involved in attempting to tidy up Connie's life, tidy her away for their own convenience. He opens his mouth to speak, but words seem to choke him and he clears his throat several times.

'She's beautiful,' he says eventually, wishing he could actually express what he feels. 'Really beautiful.'

Brooke nods, puts their coffee mugs on the table, and sits down, facing him. 'Scroll through,' she says, 'there are some more.'

Andrew swipes his finger across the screen; Connie is laughing, waving her arms, and in another doing a sort of mock curtsey. Carefree, he thinks, that's the word: free from the burden of care. Then she's back in her usual clothes, a linen dress, then jeans and a shirt, somewhere on a stony English beach, with another woman.

'That's Brighton,' Brooke says, peering across the table. 'They were there before they went up to London.'

'So who's this?' Andrew asks, pointing to the other woman.

'Auntie Flora, of course,' Brooke says. 'Don't you recognise her? She lived with you, didn't she?'

Andrew enlarges the photograph. 'So it is. Yes, she did live with us for a while but it's so long ago I didn't recognise her.'

'She looks like Granddad, and like you.'

'Yes, yes, I suppose she does.' He remembers Flora's hair now, so much of it, wild and curly, just as it is here, only now it's grey – a silvery grey in the photograph. 'But Flora lives in France, and this is Brighton.'

'She went to England with Nan, they're there now. Did you like her?'

Andrew looks up, wondering. Did he like her? She's been excluded from his consciousness for so long he can barely recall how he felt, and then he remembers running. Running with his leg tied to Flora's leg, both of them running as fast as they could, hanging on to each other, bodies hurtling forward towards a white line marked on the school sports field. 'Yes,' he says, 'yes, I did. She was fun. We won the three-legged race together.'

'Really?'

'Yep, sports day. I'd've been about nine or ten. It was one of those races that you have to run with a parent, and Dad was supposed to be there and run it with me, but he forgot, so Flora stepped in instead. Yes, I did like her. She left very suddenly and for a while I really missed her.'

'I think Granddad was horrible to send her away like that,' Brooke says. 'Horrible and stupid.'

Andrew shrugs. 'Well, he must have thought he was doing the right thing. He was always very fair, so wouldn't have done it lightly.'

'But it *wasn't* fair. *You* would never do that to anyone. Like, Auntie Kerry's *your* sister and you have your stupid fights where you just bristle up at her and she gets all red in the face, but you'd never banish her from the family.'

Andrew smiles. 'No, I doubt that would happen. And I can't see Kerry putting up with that sort of treatment anyway.'

'Well, you certainly wouldn't ban her for that.' Brooke stirs sugar into her cup and licks the spoon.

'For what?'

'For being a lesbian. I mean, I know Auntie Kerry's *not* a lesbian, but if she was, you would never chuck her out for that.'

Andrew looks at her in amazement. 'A lesbian? You mean that's why . . . ?'

Brooke nods. 'Yep. Didn't you know?'

Andrew is silent, trying to take it in. 'I think you must have got it wrong, Brooke,' he says. 'I mean, Flora may well be a lesbian but he wouldn't have thrown her out of the house for that.'

'He did,' Brooke says. 'Nan told me. He made her leave the same day he found out, and he didn't speak to her again. Not ever. You must've known.'

He shakes his head. 'Well, I knew she was banished and they never spoke, but it was never talked about either. Mum used to talk to her and write but we were never told what it was all about . . .' he hesitates, wondering suddenly about his own lack of curiosity. 'She stayed with us for quite a long time, and one Sunday morning I went out to footy practice, and when I came back she was gone. When I asked when she was coming back Dad said she'd left and wouldn't be coming back, that she'd done something terrible and we were just to forget about her.'

'But didn't you mind?'

'Well, yes, I did actually. In fact I think I started to cry, and he told me not to be a baby. He said he'd sent her away for my sake, well, mine and Kerry's and Mum's, and we'd soon forget about her. And . . . and well, I suppose that's what we did.'

'That's horrible. Didn't you even ask when you were grown up?'

Andrew closes his eyes, trying to remember. 'I think I did. Yes, I remember now, I asked Mum, years later. I was still living at home, so I suppose I was about seventeen, and she said, "You need to ask your father to explain that".'

'And did you?'

'Yes.' He remembers it clearly now. 'I went up to his study and he was sitting at the desk writing something, and I asked him why he'd sent her away and why we couldn't see her.' It floods his memory now with images as sharp as if he were standing in Gerald's study, facing him across the desk, watching the flush of anger creeping up his neck and spreading across his face, his eyes fixed on Andrew's own. 'I don't want to talk about this, Andrew,' he'd said. 'And if I were in your position I wouldn't be asking questions. This will not be mentioned again.' And he can hear his father's voice in his ears, and feel the chill of fear at the sense of something dark and dreadful, and his own resolve never to ask again. 'D'you hear me, Andrew?' Gerald had repeated. 'Never.'

\*

Kerry wanders around the little supermarket ostensibly looking for dog food and washing powder but, paying insufficient attention, she keeps missing them. She sighs, stopping for a moment, staring into the freezer filled with vegetables, trying to focus on the task at hand, trying not to think about her mother, trying to find a place in her head that will get the shopping done and get her back home again. She has left Farah and the girls clearing leaves and weeds in Connie's garden, while she has come to get the things she and Farah forgot when they did the shopping earlier in the week. Right now Kerry thinks it would suit her nicely to climb into the freezer and be cryogenically frozen if she could wake up sometime in the future to find she was normal again.

She can remember times when she has cursed her feelings, wished she didn't feel so much, so intensely and so often. But since she slipped into this black hole of depression, this feeling-free zone, she knows that feeling intensely is far better than the alternative. She wonders if she will feel anything ever again, and it seems pretty unlikely – in fact some days it seems impossible. Feelings are all around her, but she is never a part of them, just an observer. She had thought that getting away would make a difference. Chris, Erin, the children all seemed to be thrusting feelings in her face all the time. They were happy, ecstatic even, or sad, or angry, worried, anxious, or spilling over with laughter, and she was a thing apart.

But even though she's been at Connie's for three weeks now, her numbness hasn't really gone away. The one thing that is easier, though, is that Farah doesn't keep asking her if she's okay, or if she's feeling better. Chris and Erin, on the other hand, had constantly looked at her with concern or sympathy. 'How're you doing?' Chris would ask as they woke up each morning, and she could hear his need for her to be better, and his fear that nothing was changing. 'Any better today?' Erin would ask over breakfast, trying to sound casual but her tone was loaded with concern. Kerry had struggled to find something within herself to reassure them, but it just wasn't there, nothing was there, not better, not worse, just nothing.

So it is a bit easier with Farah, who seems to understand that this is not something that is going to be better in the morning, so she doesn't ask. What she does, instead, is to make sure that Kerry works towards getting better.

'I think we could all do with a walk,' she'd said this morning when she had seen Kerry lying on the sofa staring glumly at the blank TV screen. And Kerry, who would have much preferred to stay put, got up, put on her walking shoes and they all walked right down into Sandy Bay, had a coffee and struggled back up the hill again, after which she did feel more able to get through the rest of the dull and wintry Sunday.

'The exercise does help,' Kerry had admitted when they got back.

'Good, because I think we must tidy up the garden this afternoon, and we've run out of dog food so one of us has to drive down to the supermarket.'

What Farah is doing, Kerry realises, is keeping her on track. She is kind and concerned but she expects Kerry to pull her weight, and doesn't count on overnight results.

When Chris called yesterday evening he'd asked if being in the house was helping, and she had wanted to tell him something to make him feel better, to give him some sort of hope.

'I think it may be,' she'd said. 'There are lots of memories, I suppose that's a good thing.' It was all she could think of to say but he'd sounded relieved.

'We miss you,' he'd said. 'I miss you especially, Kerry. I love you, and I'm thinking of you all the time.'

'I love you too,' she'd said, because she knows that she does, she must do, even though she can't feel it. She thinks of him and the children constantly, wanting their hugs, their kisses, their physical presence, without having to try to enter their emotional space. And she thinks of Connie and wonders whether her mother will ever be able to forgive her for being the daughter from hell.

She sleeps a lot and finds herself dreaming of her child-hood, strange muddled dreams in which she is running to catch up with her father who is always just that little bit too far ahead of her. And sometimes she dreams of Andrew, something she hasn't done for years, and in those dreams she's trying to catch him too. He stops and turns around and holds out his hand waiting for her to catch up with him and take it, but however fast she runs she never reaches him. Weird, she thinks, but then maybe not really weird at all.

But it does seem odd when, as she climbs back into the car with her supermarket shopping, her phone rings and it's Andrew.

'I tried you at home,' Andrew says, 'but Chris said you're at Mum's. Is . . . well, is everything okay?'

'Of course, why wouldn't it be?' Kerry says, trying to sound normal.

'You and Chris, I mean, you haven't . . . ?'

'We're fine,' she says. 'I just needed a bit of a break and Erin's there so I came down here for a while.'

'Oh good, I just . . . well, actually, Linda and I have split up, and then when you weren't home I thought . . .'

'Oh god,' she says, 'I'm so sorry about you and Linda, I'd no idea. But, no, Chris and I are okay, thanks, nothing like that. Are you okay?'

'Yes, well, yes and no. It's all been a bit of a mess. Linda's with someone else, and they're in the house and Brooke and I are renting a cottage until she can buy me out.'

'Shit! That's all happened pretty quickly. Are *you* okay?'

'I am now. Relieved really. It's been a long time coming, and the last couple of months have been bloody awful but the worst is over. We moved in here yesterday and it's really nice.'

'And Brooke?'

'It's been hard on her,' Andrews says. 'She loathes Linda's new . . . er . . . boyfriend, but she had to stay on in the house with them both longer than was good for her.'

'You should've let me know,' she says. 'Is there anything I can do?' She can't imagine what she possibly could do even in her normal state and as she is now it seems a ridiculous question.

'No, but thanks,' he says. 'It'd be good to get together sometime soon though. School holidays perhaps? It seems so long since we actually had a conversation without arguing.'

Goosebumps take Kerry by surprise and she shivers. 'Yes, too long,' she says.

'Are you sure you're okay, Ker? You sound a bit odd.'

'Just tired, I think, still getting over Dad. We all are, I suppose. Have you heard from Mum?'

'I spoke to her on the phone about the break-up and she's been in regular touch with Brooke. Helped her through it, I think. Kerry, there's something I want to ask you. Do you know why Dad kicked Auntie Flora out of the house all those years ago?'

'No idea. I asked once, and Dad just said it was none of my business, and we should all be very glad that he'd sent her away for our sake.' As she speaks she can see a vague image of her aunt, a tall woman with a nice smile and curly reddish-brown hair, building a sandcastle with her and saying, 'This bit is the tower where the princess gets locked away.' 'Why do you ask?'

'Well, it's just that Mum told Brooke that Dad found out Flora was a lesbian.'

'What?'

'I know – it's weird, isn't it? I mean, not that she was, or is, but that he reacted like that. Does it make sense to you? I mean, he was always rabidly anti-gay but that . . .'

'I think I remember something . . .' she says, trying to recall how it happened. It was later, years later, and her chest is suddenly tense, her heart beating faster as she remembers another summer. She was fourteen, the summer that Jennifer Mortimer came to stay. Another day, another beach, she and Jen stretched out on towels on the sand. She could feel the heat of Jen's body alongside her, the sides of their hands were almost touching, and although they were apparently dozing and sunbaking, Kerry knew Jennifer was as alert as she was; the narrow space between them fizzled and crackled with electricity. She felt Jennifer's little finger twitch and shift and link into hers and her heart seemed to swell with the thrill of it as her father's dark shadow loomed above them blocking out the sun.

'Kerry?' Andrew asks. 'Kerry are you still there?'

'Yes,' she says, 'yes I'm here, I'm thinking. And I don't know . . . but I think it does make sense. Something happened . . . years ago one summer . . . it's just . . . just so long ago . . .'

\*

'So d'you think she'd fit in?' Phillip asks, attempting to cross his legs and knocking his knee hard against the corner of the filing cabinet in the process.

Bea smiles. He never fails to forget the filing cabinet, she thinks; he must have a permanent bruise on that knee.

Phillip swears and rubs the knee. 'This office is ridiculous.'

'You're telling me,' she says. 'When are you going to get that other room fixed up so I can have a proper office?'

'Okay, okay, I'll get that chap down the road to come in and give me a quote this week.'

'Yes, I do think she's ideal. We've been lucky with staff but the young ones do tend to come and go. We need someone more mature and if Flora says yes it'll be because she's really made up her mind to settle here. I think we'd get on well.'

Phillip nods. 'Me too. So hopefully she'll make up her mind in the next few days and we can get things moving.'

'How was the opera?' Bea asks.

'Magnificent, as always, or almost always, I'm very . . .'

'Actually, I meant how was going to the opera with Connie?'

Liz Byrski

'Ah, yes. Well, it was very nice to go with someone who really knows their stuff and enjoys it. And it was . . .' He stops, as if struggling to find the words he wants to say.

'And it was what?' Bea prompts.

'It was interesting to hear about Gerry from Connie's point of view.'

'Really?' Bea is bursting to know what this means but he will only tell her in his own time.

'Mmmm, I don't know whether I should . . .' Another pause. 'But I don't think she said it in confidence . . .'

'Oh for god's sake, Phillip, stop farting around and tell me whatever it is.'

He fidgets in his chair and sits upright, this time banging his elbow. 'Shit!' He rubs it fiercely. 'Well, you know all that stuff Gerry told you about how needy Connie was, and how helpless after her mother died, and how he felt compelled to look after her?'

'Yes, yes, and how much she relied on him – get on with it.'

'Well, I don't think that was true at all.'

Bea smiles. 'What makes you say that?'

'Oh, just something she said about letting Gerald persuade her that she might not make it in the opera.'

'Flora said something similar – what she was implying, I think, was that it was Gerald who was afraid he couldn't make it without a woman who would stand adoringly alongside him.'

Phillip puffs out his cheeks. 'That sort of makes sense, I think.' He pauses. 'You don't seem surprised.'

'No, but I *was* surprised when I met Connie because she didn't seem to me to be a woman who could ever have been as Gerry described her. It absolutely rocked everything I'd ever believed about the two of them. And then the other day, when I had lunch with Flora, it all started to make sense.'

They sit there in the office, staring at each other.

'So how does that make you feel now, Bea?'

Bea gives a short, sharp laugh. 'Well, Dr Freud, I suppose the answer to that is that I feel strangely relieved. As though something has been put to rest. I realised long ago that Gerry and I would never have lasted in the long term. And I suppose it clarifies something that always concerned me about him – his capacity for self-deception in getting what he wanted or needed. I think I always saw that but tried not to, although it made me uneasy.'

He nods. 'Odd bloke, wasn't he? And I get the feeling he was stuck in a groove, didn't change much over the years. Anyway, your birthday next week. Lunch at The Ivy as usual? Or do you want to go wild and do something different?'

'Different? Good heavens,' she grins, 'why would I do something different? It's the annual highlight in my pleasantly boring social life. Might be nice to see if Connie and Flora would like to come along.'

'Excellent idea.' Phillip gets to his feet without bumping anything. 'I'll check with them and hopefully book for four. I wonder what would have happened to your publishing career if you'd married Gerry. You probably had a lucky escape.'

'I'm beginning to think that myself,' she says. 'And it comes as something of a relief after all this time.'

# Nineteen

'And this is my room,' Brooke says, walking in, trying to see it through the eyes of someone encountering it for the first time. If this were someone else's room she knows she'd think it was perfect, like a room from a novel, the buttery late afternoon light from the window falling in all the right places, the view of the garden with the fading purple bougainvillea sprawled against the back wall, her new bed under the sloping ceiling, the new desk of Tasmanian oak and, beside it, the purple leather typing chair.

'Nice chair,' Donna says, dropping down into it and spinning around.

'But what about the whole room? I just love it to bits.'

'I know, you've been going on about it all week.'

'You don't like the house, do you?' Brooke says. 'Not just this room, the whole house.'

Donna shrugs. 'Well, it's a bit old.'

'Of course it's old – a hundred and fifty years old.'

'Yeah, well, there you go. It's fine if you like old stuff, it's just not really on my radar.'

'*On your radar?* What's that supposed to mean?'

'I just don't rate it, that's all. I like everything new. Your other place was much better.' She spins again in the chair and when it stops she tilts it backwards and swings her legs up, resting her feet on the desk.

Brooke is wishing she hadn't invited Donna to come and see the house. She hadn't particularly wanted to, wanted to keep it to herself and her dad, at least for a while. Donna has been acting weird since she started hanging out with Danny Philpot, changing almost overnight. And what Brooke hadn't realised until she first went to catch the bus from here is that Danny Philpot lives about five minutes' walk further down the same street, in a big flashy house with pillars by the front door. A house that looks as though it's too big for the block it's built on. And he gets on and off the bus at the same stop as her.

'It was, like, out of some magazine, your old house,' Donna says. 'Not as good as Danny's place but pretty cool. I could just see your mum with her crimson hair . . .'

'It's called claret, not crimson.'

'Well, claret then, and one of those cool tent things she wears with black leggings, and those orange glasses, sitting on the lime green sofa being photographed, with that Zachary, all in black leather in the background. She won't like it here, I bet.'

'She doesn't have to come here, and nor do you. Nobody has to come if they don't like it,' Brooke says pointedly, looking straight at Donna. She wants to tell her not to put her feet on the desk but the conversation is already going downhill and she decides not to make it worse. 'I like it, Dad and me, we both love it.'

Donna shrugs and says nothing, just takes a bottle of black nail polish from her pocket and unscrews it.

'Don't do that in here,' Brooke says. 'You might spill it.'

'I won't.'

'You might. Come in the kitchen and we'll sit at the table.'

Donna pulls a face and gets up. 'You are soooooo uptight, Brooke.'

'I am *not*,' Brooke says, 'I just want to keep my room nice, and I don't want your Doc Martens on my desk, or black nail polish on the carpet.'

Donna looks down at her calf length lace-up boots, white with red laces, patterned all over with bright red poppies. 'Only *you* would think these are Doc Martens,' she says, swinging her legs down and following Brooke out to the kitchen. '*Nobody* wears Doc Martens anymore, but you wouldn't know that, would you, because you know nothing. And you hate boots, unless they're boring black leather up to your knee.'

'Oh shut up,' Brooke says. 'D'you want hot chocolate?'

'Why don't we have some voddie instead?' Donna says. She casts a glance around the kitchen and starts opening cupboard doors. 'I bet your dad's got some here. Ah, look, just what we need!' and she pulls the bottle of Smirnoff out of the cupboard and unscrews the cap. 'We can have a house-warming party.'

'No,' Brooke says. 'You can't drink that, Dad'll kill me.'

'He'll never know unless you tell him. It's not like he marks the bottle, is it?'

'That's not the point,' Brooke says. 'Give it to me,' and she reaches out to grab the bottle from Donna's hand, but Donna, slightly taller, ducks away holding the bottle by its neck above her head.

'You are so fucking uptight, Brooke,' she says. 'Danny says you need to loosen up. C'mon, we can get rat-arsed on this and we'll just fill it up with water.' And she tilts the uncapped bottle out of Brooke's reach.

'I don't care what that loser says.' Brooke reaches for the bottle. 'Give it to me.' She feels like crying but something tells her that this is just what Donna wants. For some reason, she is deliberately goading her. 'Why are you being like this?'

'Like what?' Donna says, pulling a stupid face and then taking a big swig from the vodka bottle.

'Stop it!'

'Stop it, stop it,' Donna mimics in a nasty sing-song voice. She's gathering steam now. 'You are so fucking up yourself, Brooke. I bet you don't really like living in this poxy old house. You should've stayed with your mum and that Zach bloke. He's hot, and he thinks I'm hot too – he told me. He was feeling me up in the hall at your other place, and down at Danny's.'

'You're just being stupid,' Brooke says. 'You're making it up.' Donna's eyes look funny, a bit mad, as though she's taken something.

'I am not,' Donna says, swigging more vodka. 'He rubbed up against me, in the hall. And then he felt my arse as I walked off. It's true, but I don't care if you don't believe it.'

Brooke does believe it, but she can also see now that Donna is totally off her head. 'Did Danny give you something when we got off the bus?'

Donna grins. 'He might have. What if he did? Who wants to know?'

'I do. What've you taken?'

'Just half a little pill. Want some, Brookie?'

'No!' She reaches out to grab the vodka bottle just as Donna whisks it away, and somehow it slips between their hands and smashes onto the kitchen tiles.

'Now look what you've done,' Brooke shouts, and thinks she sounds just like her mother.

'Oooh, now look what you've done,' Donna mimics, 'now look what you've done. What're you going to do, Brookie baby, report me to your dad?'

'Yes, actually, I am,' Brooke says, and she crosses to the cupboard under the sink and pulls out a bucket.

'See if I care.'

'Why don't you just piss off, Donna,' Brooke says. 'Piss off and take your stupid drugs and that gross silver anorak with you. Go and see your mate Danny Philpot in that grotesque

Family Secrets

house. I bet you like that, and the big four wheel drive, and the Lexus, and his mum's Beemer. His dad's loaded, go and drink *his* vodka.'

'Loaded is right,' Donna says, rubbing vodka off her legs with a tissue. 'It's a whole lot more fun there than here in a stinky old cottage. Danny's dad always has stuff in the house, anything you want he's got it.' She struts out of the kitchen and picks up her backpack from where she dropped it, just inside the front door.

'The Man in Black goes there too, that's where he gets his gear. He's doing Danny's sister; she's only just eighteen. Did you know that? Does your mum know that? And by the way, I hate this house. It's like some old granny's place, and just as boring as you are. Boring Brooke, that's what they call you, the cat that walks alone, and you think that's kinda nice? You're tragic, Brooke, you really are, a tragic stuck-up cow.' And she grabs the silver anorak and starts twirling it around her head, slings her backpack over her other shoulder. 'I'm off – too dreary here, Miss Tragic.' And she opens the front door and walks off down the path and out of the gate into the street. 'Tragic!' she yells from the pavement, and heads off in the direction of the Philpot house, still waving the anorak and chanting over and over again. 'Tragic, tragic, Brooke is tragic.'

Brooke stands by the window, forcing herself not to cry, watching until Donna is out of sight. She thinks Donna looks stupid in those gross boots – in fact she always looks a wreck.

'That girl really needs some fashion advice,' Linda had said some months ago, and at the time Brooke had thought it mean and felt hurt on Donna's behalf. But she knows it's true. The other girls laugh at Donna behind her back and criticise her tacky clothes and cheap jewellery, and Donna hasn't a clue. Brooke can't remember now, how or why they ever became friends. They don't have much in common, there are other girls at school that Brooke likes much better and whom she goes out with sometimes. She doesn't have a BFF and doesn't want one. One day BFFs are practically in love with each other and a couple of days later they're slagging each other off. It was Donna who had pursued Brooke and it was okay having her around at first, but that's all changed since Danny came on the scene.

Brooke leaves the window, goes into the hall to close the front door and then to the kitchen where she gathers up the broken glass, wraps it in an old newspaper and then mops up the spilled vodka with an old towel. Then she fills the bucket with water and floor cleaner and washes the floor. Back in her own room she throws herself on the bed. She had been longing to move in here and they had spent the whole weekend organising it, and making it feel like home.

'Happy now, Brooke?' Andrew had asked.

She'd nodded, her mouth full of takeaway pizza. 'Very,' she'd managed, and carried on chewing. 'I love it here, Dad. I don't have to go back to the house again, do I?'

Andrew had wiped his mouth with a paper serviette. 'You'll want to go and see Mum, won't you?'

'Only if *he's* not there.'

'Well, he lives there now, so you are going to see him sometimes, Brooke.'

She shook her head furiously. 'Why can't Mum come here? Or I can go to the gallery.'

'But won't you want to stay with her sometimes?'

'Not if he's there. I can't, Dad, honestly I can't. Please don't make me. Mum could stay here.'

Andrew had started to gather up the pizza box and crumpled serviettes.

'Look,' he said, 'your mum's going up to Singapore shortly. When she comes back we'll ask her over, cook her a meal and we can sit down together, the three of us, and work out a plan. How does that sound?'

It had sounded pretty hopeless to Brooke but she could see that he was trying to find a way to sort things out and stay friendly with her mother. 'Okay, but I'm not going to the house.'

'Wait and see what she's got to say,' Andrew had said.

Lying on her bed now, gazing up at the ceiling and the neat round shapes of the spotlights embedded in it, Brooke feels as though something has been spoiled. From the minute Donna stepped inside it was as though she was chipping away at it and at Brooke's pleasure in it. A bank of dark cloud passes in front of the remains of the sun, turning the light in her bedroom grey and dusky. Everywhere is completely quiet; it was always quiet at this time of day in the other house, before her parents got home. But this is a different sort of quiet. She reaches for her iPod, whizzes through her play-lists, selects one and lies back again, closing her eyes. But the music doesn't help; tears ooze from the corners of her eyes and trickle down the sides of her face onto her pillow. The clock by her bed says it's ten to five, and she rolls over onto her side, picks up her phone and dials Andrew's number at work. The call goes straight to message bank and she waits for the beep.

'It's me, Dad. Just wondering when you'll be home. I can make something for tea. Ring me when you get this message.'

He'd said this morning that he'd be home about seven-thirty, but she feels a desperate need to talk to someone. She stares at the phone debating whether or not to ring her mother, but what can she say? Just ringing for a chat? Tell her about the house? But now that Donna has told her this gross stuff about Zachary, Brooke feels as though she has a flashing light on her that will travel through the phone to her mother. There's no way she can tell her mum or her dad, but she can't say nothing either. The weight of it presses down on Brooke as though a great stone is crushing her. All the time she was living in the house with the two of them she was furiously angry with her mum. But now, in this new place, so different from the one where she has lived for as long as she can remember, everything feels strange and lonely.

Brooke dials her mum's number. It goes to message bank. She hesitates. 'Hi, Mum, it's me. Just ringing to say hello . . . um . . . well, the house is great, I think you'll like it now we've got all the stuff in it and everything. My room is mega good. Anyway, ring me and I'll tell you about it.'

She hangs up, listening to the huge, unbearable silence before resorting once more to the phone. It's early morning in England so she hits the speed dial for Connie and waits. It takes ages, ages of international silence. Nothing happens, so she takes the phone away from her ear to redial, but the message on the screen tells her she's out of credit. She can't hold back the tears now, and she gets up off the bed and runs out into the kitchen to the phone on the wall, but when she picks up the receiver she finds the line is dead. Getting it connected is still one of the unticked items on the list of things to do. Brooke hangs up the receiver and slides slowly down the wall to sit on the floor. She feels as though everything that matters has been taken away from her. She longs to be little again, to be the small, special person surrounded by lots of grown-ups; the precious centrepiece of a big family, safe, treasured and loved. But all that has gone, evaporated, starting with her grandfather disappearing into his sickness and taking parts of everyone else along with him. Brooke folds her arms across her knees and rests her head on them and sits there on the quarry tiled floor, cold and still as dusk deepens into darkness, and stays there until she hears the sound of Andrew's key in the door.

# Twenty

he weather has changed. Yesterday they strolled in glorious sunshine among the displays at the Chelsea Flower Show and it had seemed that the changing seasons might just as well not exist and that plants from every possible place from the tropics, to the world's coldest, most hostile climates, were at home there. But it was the English wildflower garden that had most enchanted Connie. Tucked into a corner against a hedge heavy with May blossom, flowers that would normally bloom at different times throughout at least nine months of the year flourished side by side: snow-drops alongside bluebells, wild orchids beside primroses, crocus beside dog roses and violets, narcissus and forget-me-nots, and so many more that Connie could no longer name. Nearby, water tumbled over mossy rocks into a sparkling pool where silvery fish darted beneath the waterlilies. It had seemed impossible that they were in the heart of London.

Flora had bought sandwiches from the café and they had sat eating them on a bench among the wildflowers. Connie was transported back to the past again, just as she had been in the Enchanted Place, and later on the seafront at Eastbourne, where the white crested waves had crashed onto the stony beach behind her and geraniums, marigolds and pansies bloomed in symmetrical patterns in the manicured beds that divided the street from the promenade. She had not anticipated that the most evocative and moving moments on this trip would come, not from gazing at the house where she once lived, or strolling with Flora in the grounds of the school where their friendship was forged, but simply from nature. From the mown grass to which she woke on her first morning, to the tangles of cow parsley where they had stopped to walk on the South Downs, the purple heather of Ashdown Forest, and the unique, earthy scent of the wall-flowers in the beds at the top of The Mall near Buckingham Palace. It is the sights and smells of nature that have trans-ported her into the deepest recesses of memory.

'I'm awash with nostalgic pleasure,' she had told Flora yesterday as a string quintet in a corner of the wildflower garden played a selection of traditional songs. 'Right now I could stay here forever.'

But this morning they woke to overcast skies that soon delivered heavy rain and Connie had made her way by bus to the National Portrait Gallery, while Flora set off in the opposite direction to visit an old friend in Clapham. It's still raining now as she opens her umbrella, crosses the street from the Gallery and runs up the steps to St Martin's-in-the-Field where she waits, watching people hurrying across Trafalgar Square, heads down, hands in their pockets or clinging on to umbrellas buffeted by the wind.

Phillip, hovering on the opposite pavement, waiting for the lights to change, makes a run for it, jumping the stream of water surging along the gutter.

'So sorry, Connie,' he says, joining her on the steps. 'Only just made it.' And together they join the disparate group heading inside for the free concert.

The pews at the front are full and Connie is about to slip into one near the back when Phillip grasps her elbow and draws her into a small stall at the side.

'We can have this to ourselves,' he says. 'Most people don't seem to like sitting in them but I love it – it feels like a private box at the opera. Sorry I wasn't able to manage that for you, by the way.'

'The seats were wonderful,' Connie says. 'It was such a lovely evening, one I'll always remember.'

'Me too,' he says, slipping out of his raincoat as the musicians file in from the side door to take their places. 'I've heard this group here before,' he whispers. 'They're splendid – students all of them – and they usually play with a wonderful young soprano. Look, here she comes.'

The young woman, dressed like the others in black, takes her place at the centre, facing down the aisle. She looks tense, Connie thinks, remembering the thrill but also the terror of performance and the awkward sense of intimacy and vulnerability when the audience is comparatively close without the separating height and distance of a stage. The singer waits, focused, as the musicians settle into position. Her hands are clasped at her waist, her corn gold hair pulled back into a neat bun at the back of her neck. Despite the nerves there is something serene and somehow timeless about her. Connie stares intently, remembering a day like this, a plain black dress, her own hair piled more elaborately on top of her head, and a sea of faces in front of her. It was a Sunday afternoon concert in Canterbury Cathedral and the senior student who was scheduled to sing solo had developed the flu. Connie relives the anticipation of waiting – the tension in her chest, the effort to relax while remaining poised and alert – as this young woman waits now, for her cue, and the moment when she must become the music.

The audience is still now, no fidgeting, not a cough or a whisper, while they wait, men in suits, young women on their lunch breaks, hikers with backpacks, elderly Americans in plaid trousers and plastic macs, Japanese tourists, and a couple of street dwellers huddled in a similar nook on the opposite side of the church, escaping the rain. Huge white candles flicker in black iron holders on each side of the musicians, and behind them diffused white light pours through the triple-arched windows above the altar mixing to a softer hue with the golden light from the huge chandeliers suspended from the creamy domes of the ceiling.

Connie is captivated by the restrained elegance of the church, and the apparent composure of the young soprano. She hasn't looked at the program but as the first notes of 'Musetta's Waltz' float up from the instruments she gasps, putting her hand over her mouth, waiting for the first familiar words which will follow. She sees the singer's body change in readiness, the measuring of the breath. And then it happens, her voice floats out, perfect in tone and volume. Confident and with the promise of incredible range, it fills the church with its magic.

*Quando me'n vo'*
*Quando me'n vo' soletta per la via*

Connie's heart and mind sing with her. Once again she too is the young soprano, full of ambition, high on adrenaline, all fear evaporating as her voice carries her into every corner of that cathedral, just as this singer's voice fills St Martins on this wet and chilly May day forty years later. She relaxes now, sitting back on the bench, tears running uncontrollably down her cheeks, transported back in time by the beauty of the voice and the music, back to that first solo performance, when her future had stretched ahead of her like a broad path beckoning her on through fields of wildflowers.

Phillip glances at her with concern. He reaches out and takes her hand in his, squeezes it, and she grips his in return, holding on as though to a lifebelt. And for the next forty-five minutes, through 'Songs of the Auvergne', 'The Jewel Song' from *Faust*, 'The Song to the Moon', and more, she holds on without letting go, even at the end, when the soprano and the musicians take their bows to rapturous applause, and the audience rises raggedly to its feet, coats are dragged on and bags picked up, and they shuffle softly down the aisles towards the exit, infused with the magic of the music. But still she sits in silence, in remembrance and a strange sort of grief, and Phillip sits with her.

'Thanks,' she says eventually, brushing some tears away. 'I needed it to be really over.' And he nods and takes her arm and suggests that they should make a move, perhaps get something to eat in the crypt café. And as they step outside Connie draws deeply on the damp air, exhausted by her own total absorption in the performance and the emotional toll it has taken on her. The rain has cleared now and Phillip steers her to the circular glass lift that takes them down to the crypt, where he leaves her at a table while he collects bowls of soup, a plate of crusty bread and two glasses of red wine from the counter.

'Food for the soul, I hope,' he says, unloading the tray. 'How are you feeling now?'

'Exhausted and a bit wobbly,' she says.

'I thought you might be reliving something.'

She tells him about Canterbury Cathedral. 'I couldn't believe my luck. I was horribly nervous, it was my first solo public performance.'

'What did you sing?'

'"Musetta's Waltz",' she says, smiling, 'and "The Song to the Moon", and then "Danny Boy" and the "Twenty-third Psalm". It was terrifying and wonderful all at the same time.'

'And *you* were wonderful?'

'Apparently I was,' she says, blushing. 'So I was told. It was pretty amazing.'

'Was your mother there to hear you?'

'No, it was the year after she died. Gerald was there though.'

Liz Byrski

Phillip looks up warily from his soup. 'And he thought you were wonderful?'

Connie is silent for a moment. She smiles, and then begins to laugh.

'What is it?'

'Gerald thought it was a pretty good performance, but he felt my voice and interpretation were "somewhat immature" – as if he would have had any idea what he was talking about.'

Phillip has stopped eating. 'So how did that feel?'

'Pretty awful. It was the high spot of my life as a music student and everyone had been telling me how well I'd done. He waited 'til we'd left the others to say it. I think now that he didn't want to say anything in front of people who actually knew what they were talking about. Foolishly I believed him rather than them. It was the turning point. My heart was never in it in quite the same way after that.'

Phillip shakes his head. 'I wish I'd known. I might have knocked some sense into him.'

Connie laughs again. 'Probably not. You know Gerald – he never entertained the idea that he might be wrong about something. Years later when I told him that I still resented the way he'd talked me out of my career, he said, "But we've been happy, haven't we? You've been happy?" And of course he was right – I had.'

'All the same . . .' Phillip begins.

'Look, I have resented it. Especially when he got sick and I could see what the years ahead would involve. I was in my late fifties and Gerald had just retired. I thought it was my turn, and I'd been offered a job in a very nice private school for girls quite near where we live. Music is one of their specialities and they wanted someone to start and run a choir. I was so looking forward to it. Gerald wasn't very keen on the idea but I told him it was my time . . . we knew he was sick by then, just not what it was or what it would mean. But the

254

diagnosis came a couple of weeks before I was due to start, and the very next day he had his first serious fall . . .' She hesitates, moving her spoon back and forth in her soup, gazing down into it in silence. 'And so I knew that I wouldn't be able to do it. I wouldn't be able to be reliable, that the job of caring for him had begun and it would last until . . . well, until he died.' She pauses again, flushing, and looks up. 'This sounds awful, but I was so angry and resentful that I could hardly bear to speak to him. I had always been there for him, and I'd waited for my chance to do something I wanted and then suddenly I was losing my own life to his *yet again*.' She puts down her spoon. 'I hope he didn't know it and I tried hard not to let him see it, but that resentment stayed with me to the end. It's strange, really, there had been so many things that I'd forgiven, things that I felt were really unreasonable and demanding on his part. And yet the one time when it *wasn't* his fault I couldn't forgive him. Trying to hide that from him, and from the children and grandchildren, became a terrible struggle. It's stood between us – separated me from them, and that's affected every one of us.'

# Twenty-one

erry sits at the kitchen table scrolling through the photographs that Andrew has sent to her phone, photographs her mother had sent to Brooke. She has looked at them several times a day since she and Andrew spoke on Sunday evening. Now it's Thursday and she's still drawn back to them, still trying to see more deeply into the pictures, to work out what she actually knows about her mother.

'Do you think you ever saw Mum and Dad as other people see them?' she'd asked him on the phone a couple of days ago. 'I don't think I've ever even considered who they were outside those roles and all the assumptions that go with them.'

'I've tried,' he'd said, 'a few times, but more now, now that Dad's gone. I feel I knew him more clearly than Mum, because he was always a person of extremes, always telling you what he thought, what mattered, how we ought to see things. I think of Mum and what I get is reassurance and love, and I suppose safety, and I feel guilty because I think my relationship with her has been just that, always wanting but never really taking the trouble to get to know who she is, other than just Mum.'

'That's what I'm feeling too,' Kerry had said. 'But I'm wondering about Dad too. I was always so desperate for his attention . . .'

'Looking for his approval?'

'Yes . . . and never feeling I got it. Unlike you.'

Andrew laughed. 'If I did have it I never knew. He always had me on the end of a piece of string – he'd tug it to get me to do something or behave in a particular way, and I'd do it but I never felt it got me anywhere with him or won me any approval.'

'But he adored you,' Kerry said. 'You could do no wrong. "My number one son", he called you. He was incredibly proud of you.'

'Well, he only had one son, and if he *was* proud of me he never really let me know. He never thought I was tough enough, or smart enough, or capable of making difficult decisions.'

Kerry was silent.

'Are you still there, Ker?'

'Yes, yes, I'm thinking. It looked so different to me. I was very jealous.'

'And I was jealous of you. He called you his "little princess", he was always stroking your hair and telling you how lovely you were, and letting you sit on his knee. I wanted him to hug me and he hardly ever did.'

'Why haven't we talked like this before?' she'd said eventually.

'You never think of it, do you? I suppose I took everything for granted, and then Dad got ill . . . and everything else seemed to go downhill too.'

'I want to talk to you properly – face to face, spend time together. Will you come over in the holidays – you and Brooke? She and I used to be real chums but I've lost touch with her. I feel I hardly know her.'

'We'll come,' he said. 'Give Mum time to get back and over

the jetlag. We'll come then. But why do you think Mum told Brooke about Flora and not us?'

'Maybe because it was easier for her,' Kerry says. 'She probably hoped Brooke would tell us, and thought that by the time she got home we'd have sorted out how we felt about it. Not that there was any real sorting out to do.'

'I wonder too if she felt bad about never having told us – I mean, all those years, she must have known it wouldn't have mattered to us. So I guess she was just being loyal to Dad.'

'And I wonder how Flora feels about *that!*' Kerry had said. 'Messy, isn't it?'

Staring now at the picture of Connie taken in Brighton with Flora, Kerry sees someone complete and separate, not simply a daughter's projection tinted and tainted by time. And she feels – yes – she actually *feels* something. It's a longing to reach out to Connie, and have her reach out in return. It's like a bullet entering her chest in slow motion and emerging from the other side, then gone. But it is – was – a feeling, the first she has had since the fierce burst of anger she'd felt when she stopped the car and got out the day they were driving home after the funeral. A real feeling, a tiny crack in the wall.

'What are you looking at, Kerry?' Samira asks, peering over her shoulder.

Farah has gone out to see a patient who needs to be checked every four hours, and Kerry is alone in the house with the twins.

'Some pictures of my mum,' she says, turning the phone so that Samira can see.

'I like your mum,' Samira says. 'She's always nice to me.'

Kerry nods. 'She's nice to me too.'

'Do you miss her?'

She hesitates. 'I do, I miss her a lot. I've missed her for about ten years.'

'That's silly. You can't miss someone when they're here.'

'Actually, I think you can,' Kerry says. 'You can be at a distance from them even if you're close by.'

Samira shakes her head. 'I don't think so,' she says with great authority. 'Like, I miss my dad more than anyone because he's dead and he's not coming back.'

Kerry smiles at her. 'I know what you mean. I miss my dad too, but I really think I miss my mum even more than him. I know that sounds funny.'

'That's totally weird,' Samira says. 'Who's that other lady?'

'It's my Auntie Flora,' Kerry says, studying Flora's face, trying to see more than just the family likeness, seeking memories here too.

'Is she nice?'

'I think she is, but I haven't seen her since I was younger than you are now, so I can hardly remember.'

'Did you miss her?'

'I don't know,' Kerry says. 'I haven't really thought about it until now.' And Samira shrugs and races off to the lounge where Lala is calling her to see something on the television.

The trouble with a photograph, Kerry thinks, is that it captures a mere second, a look, an expression, and freezes it in time. A look that may not even be characteristic. What sort of person is this long distance aunt? What does she care about? What makes her laugh or cry? She thinks of Flora, isolated from her family and her best friend all those years, for simply being who she was. She remembers the beach, the chill of a shadow blocking out the sun, her eyes flying open, how she snatched her hand away from Jennifer's, her father's eyes dark with anger, and the steely control in his voice.

'Come along, you two, time for a swim or a walk. I'll come with you.'

And she'd scrambled to her feet, her face blazing with fear and shame, heart pounding, knowing he must have seen their linked fingers. In the ten days since Jennifer had arrived to stay, a current of electric sensuality had developed between them. They dared not speak of it even to each other though no words were needed. But that afternoon she was terrified. Once on her feet she thought her legs would crumple under her and she shivered despite the warmth of the sun.

After that they were never alone. Her father was on holiday and they went everywhere as a family. Only Andrew was exempt, and Kerry knew that as soon as they were out of the door he would be off on his bike to meet his girlfriend at Battery Point. The tension was paralysing, but somehow they got through the final few days until it was time to deliver Jen back to her parents.

'I'd like to talk to you in my study, Kerry,' her father had said when they got back. 'Right away, please.'

And she had followed him upstairs, fear churning her gut, and perched awkwardly on the edge of the chair facing him across his desk.

'I will not have that girl in this house again,' he'd said, 'and I want your promise that you will have nothing more to do with her. Nothing at all.'

'But, Dad . . .' she'd begun.

'I don't want to discuss this, Kerry. And if I were in your position I wouldn't be butting in or asking questions. This is not negotiable. If you can't promise me that then I shall have to talk to her parents, tell them what you were doing.'

'But we weren't . . .'

The icy chill of his look silenced her. 'I want you to tell me that it will never happen again. I want the best for you, Kerry, in every possible way – a good career, a fine husband and a happy marriage with beautiful children. Your behaviour has put all that at risk. And you will say nothing of this to your mother. She would be deeply hurt if she knew about this.'

It's many years since Kerry has given this exchange even a passing thought and now, as she digs into this little pocket of memory, she is torn between feeling it cruel and ignorant, or simply laughable.

Humiliated and shamed she had walked out of his study and down the stairs. Her cheeks burned with her usual embarrassing blush, tears pricked her eyes, and she wanted to roll up in a corner and die. As she reached the foot of the stairs Connie walked in from the garden towards the kitchen and caught sight of her.

'Oh, Kerry darling, you're upset.'

'I'm fine,' she'd said, gritting her teeth.

'I can see you're upset. You and Jennifer were having such a lovely time, but she can come other times, you know, whenever you like, and anyway school starts again soon so you'll see each other every day.'

She'd opened her mouth to speak but couldn't, and ran instead into Connie's arms.

'Poor darling, come on, let's make some tea and take it out into the sunshine. I've got your favourite cookies . . .'

And life was normal again, except for that terrible secret she now shared with her father. She maintained a sort of friendship with Jennifer but they never visited each other's homes again. There was a tension between them, his tension, which could never be released.

'We were just girls being girls,' she'd told Andrew on the phone the other night. 'Usually it's a passing thing, part of teenage discovery, but Dad obviously didn't see it that way.'

Kerry stares again at the photographs of Flora, remembering that on the few occasions she has thought of her it has been with fierce disapproval. She flushes with shame as she recalls her self-righteous and hostile remarks to Connie about her. All these years they had believed Flora guilty of some terrible sin or crime when all she was guilty of was being herself in a way that harmed no one else. It shocks her now that they had been encouraged to forget about Flora, and they had shown no curiosity about that. She'd always known that Connie kept in touch with her, but why has she not asked her mother about it? And how could Connie go along with it for so long and never talk to her or Andrew about it? None of it seems to make sense, until she thinks again of that day on the beach and, later, facing her father in the study. And she remembers his words, his orders, the expression on his face and the way it paralysed her. He had always had an extraordinary power to silence them when it suited him, to remove what he didn't want to see or hear, and she remembers the thing he always used to say: 'I don't want to talk about it.' And the thing about not asking questions, said in a way that made her feel completely powerless, always followed it: 'If I was in your position I wouldn't be asking questions.' She'd heard him say that to her mother, and it was only when she'd been at university in the late eighties that she learned that this was the means some men used to silence women – the power of concealed threat – and once again it takes Kerry's breath away.

*

Early on Saturday morning Andrew wheels the bikes out of the shed and leans them against the wall, thinking that cycling was just one of the many things that had fallen by the wayside in the slow disintegration of his marriage. This ride means a new start. Although a real new start would mean a new job too – the present one feels like a ball and chain that he drags behind him with little enthusiasm and dwindling energy. It was his father who had steered him towards the public service and it has served him well for years but it has never really been what he wanted. At university he had wanted to study art history or literature or both, but Gerald had dismissed this with a grunt and a wave of his hand.

'And what sort of job will that get you?' he'd demanded. 'Do you want to end up mouldering away in some university? What sort of career is that, where's your ambition?'

Andrew had rather liked the prospect of mouldering in a university, he saw himself in an office full of books, preparing lectures, becoming an expert in some obscure corner of the history of art, or early colonial writing. Anything, really, that would allow him to live a quiet life with books. Alternatively he would have enjoyed something physical and had floated the idea of agricultural college. But Gerald had decided that economics was the way of the future and he managed to make it sound interesting.

'You can go anywhere with an economics degree,' he'd said.

Andrew knows now that his father was right – it could take him places, had already done so. It's just that they are not the places he wants to go. It's time, he thinks, to take a risk in order to find the sort of life he wants for himself, not the one that Gerald had wanted him to have. He doesn't want to spend the rest of his life living out his father's vision.

'Are the bikes okay?' Brooke asks, appearing beside him in her cycling gear.

'They're fine. I just need my helmet and then we'll get going. Remember when we last did this?'

'Yonks ago,' Brooke says. 'We went with Mum to that café she likes. When she comes back we could see if she wants to do it again. I bet Zachary doesn't ride a bike.'

The thought of Zachary on a bike strikes them both as hilarious and they double up with laughter. Andrew runs inside, collects his helmet, phone and wallet, and they set off slowly down the shallow slope, getting used to the feel of the bikes again.

'That house really is embarrassingly awful,' Andrew says as they cruise to the end of the road. 'Is that where Donna's boyfriend lives?'

Brooke nods. 'Yep. Gross, isn't it?'

Andrew slows down and comes to a stop. 'That looks like Zachary's car. It can't be, surely?'

Brooke looks away and then back at him and he sees her face is flushed.

'Why are you looking like that? *Is* it his car?'

'Yep. That's his. Donna says he goes there sometimes.'

Andrew slips back into the saddle again and starts to move on. 'How odd. Do you know why?'

Brooke ignores his question. 'Let's get going,' she says, 'I want my breakfast,' and she pulls away, cycling faster so she can put more distance between herself and the house.

Andrew follows her with a distinct feeling that something is wrong. She's been strange, subdued, since the day he came home to find her sitting on the floor in the darkened kitchen. The row with Donna had really upset her but he's convinced he hasn't quite got the whole story yet.

'Is there anything you haven't told me about all that business with Donna?' he calls, pulling alongside her.

'Dad! We're cycling. Don't spoil it by talking.'

Andrew smiles and speeds up, thinking how much she has grown in so many ways since they last rode together. Back then it was always him saying 'don't talk, pay attention to the road, don't talk'. And they ride on side by side in silence and then speed up as they get on to the river path. It's a glorious morning, the air is blistering cold on his face but the sun cuts through the trees casting jagged patterns on the concrete. More of this, he thinks, more of this is what I need, a more natural, active life, and as they ride on through the sunlight his heart suddenly soars with a sense of possibility – the possibility of being different, being true to himself after so many years of doing what is expected of him. His breath comes faster and he feels the pull of his calf and thigh muscles, the tightening in his chest that warns him how unfit he is, but it's glorious here, the wide road on one side, the long stretch of grass down to the water on the other, his lungs bursting in the clear cold winter air. He pedals faster, cycling as hard as he can, passing Brooke, needing to push himself to the limit.

'Slow down, Dad,' Brooke yells, 'look where you're going!'

And her voice is the last thing he hears before his front wheel cracks into the concrete bollard and the bike rears up, spinning away from under him as he is thrown sideways, off the cycleway onto the road, and into the path of the oncoming traffic.

*

'I can't tell you how good this feels,' Chris says, grasping Kerry's hand as they edge their way through the Saturday crowds in the Salamanca markets. 'I thought . . . well, I thought lots of things but the worst was that it was all my fault and that you were going to leave me.'

'Typical man,' Kerry says, nudging him. 'It had to be all about you! It was never your fault.' She laughs, leaning closer to him, wanting to feel the solid warmth of his body that she has missed so much. She had called him the previous morning and suggested that he and Erin drive the children down after school and stay until Sunday evening. 'I want to come home,' she'd said, 'but it might be fun for us all to have a weekend in Hobart together.'

Last night, when everyone else had gone to bed, she'd tried to explain to him how it had changed.

'I haven't been able to feel anything for weeks – well, months really,' she'd said. 'I could see things happening around me and I knew I should feel happy or sad or hurt or touched, I knew what the feelings ought to be but I just couldn't actually feel them. It was like being behind a wall with everyone else on the other side. But on Monday I was looking at photos of Mum and Flora and I felt something, *really* felt it. Like something moved through me and I felt it in my chest, something had changed.' She'd paused, wondering whether he understood, and saw that he was confused but hopeful. 'You see I'd had a feeling, I actually felt something again.'

'Okay,' Chris had said cautiously, 'and then what?'

'Well, a couple of nights later I was thinking about something that happened ages ago when I was about thirteen and this girl, Jennifer, came to stay.' And she'd told him about Gerald's reaction.

'Seems a bit over the top,' Chris had said.

'Exactly. And I kept thinking about it and I felt myself go quite cold with shock at the awfulness of it. And eventually – this sounds weird, I know – but I just started to laugh. Not just pretended to laugh, I *actually* laughed with my whole body, but most of all with my mind, Chris.'

'Well,' he'd said, obviously still trying to understand, 'that sounds good, but why?'

'I laughed because it was so horrible and cruel that it suddenly seemed ridiculous. I laughed about Dad and what he did to Auntie Flora. I laughed about all the years she's been a sort of pariah – a symbol of darkness. An example of what might happen if one of us overstepped the line in any way. And there was this thing he always said to shut us up. It brings me up in goosebumps remembering it. He did an awful thing to Flora, Chris . . .'

'Well, by our standards he did, but your dad wasn't a bad person . . .'

'I know. But he was a bully and he did a cruel and awful thing, so awful that it suddenly seemed funny and I started laughing at . . . at the crassness and stupidity of it all, the waste, the terrible hurt. I laughed and I couldn't stop. In the end I had to lie down on the floor and wait for the laughing to end. And I realised that I was feeling things again, that wall had come down.'

She could tell that it didn't make much sense to him but she could also see the enormous relief in his face, and feel the intensity of his feelings in the way he held her and kissed her. And she decided not to tell him about the really dark moments, the dreams, that fragile silhouette, crazed with cracks, shattering into shards of dark glass.

Later, when she'd leaned over to kiss him, she felt the salt of his tears on her lips.

'It feels just like us again,' Chris says now. 'It's been difficult for a long time and you've been different . . .'

She nods. 'I'm sorry, it must've been really hard for you. All of it, especially these last three months, but I think I'm getting back to normal now.'

'Normal?' he grins. 'You were never normal! You were always outstandingly crazy and infuriating and perfectly wonderful, which is why I married you. It's really good to have you back. Let's just take things one day at a time.' He puts his hand to her face. 'Good lord, you're freezing, and your ear is so cold it'll drop off.'

Kerry nods. 'It's bitter, isn't it, despite the sun? There's a stall up here where they sell hand-knitted beanies. I'm going to get one, and the kids probably need them too.'

Salamanca Place is packed as usual on a Saturday morning, and they squeeze on through the crowd, steering Erin, Farah and all the children to the beanie stall. Kerry watches as Chris insists on buying everyone a beanie and soon they are trying on different colours and patterns while he takes pictures on his phone.

Since he and Erin arrived with the children yesterday afternoon Samira and Lala have taken charge of Mia, making a space for her in their bedroom, letting her rummage through their clothes. They are acting like big sisters and Mia is making the most of it, lapping up the attention, and walking between the twins holding both their hands. Chris snaps them discussing whether she should have a pink or purple beanie. Kerry laughs as he photographs her encouraging Ryan to get a dark green one with red stripes, and then Erin and Farah giggling together like little girls – as though they are all one big family.

Sorting out the beanies takes a while and when Chris has paid for eight of them and they are all kitted out they make their way through the crowds to a café and order several different pizzas. It's just as the pizzas arrive that Kerry's phone starts to ring.

'Ignore it,' Chris says. 'This is all so good, just ignore it.'

She ignores it for the first few rings and then pulls it out of her pocket just as it stops.

'Brooke,' she says, staring at the phone. 'I don't think she's ever called me before. Do you think something's wrong? Maybe I should . . .'

Chris shrugs. 'Okay, but best go outside, you won't be able to hear anything in here. Don't be too long or I'll eat your share of the one with anchovies.'

Kerry weaves her way between the tables, finds a spot that is sheltered from the wind, presses 'call back' and waits, stamping her feet against the cold and turning up the collar of her jacket.

Brooke answers, speaking so fast that Kerry can barely understand her. 'Slow down, Brooke,' she says, 'slow down, take some deep breaths and then tell me what's happened.'

Brooke slows down and Kerry listens as she tells her about the bike ride, about Andrew being thrown off the bike and onto the bonnet of a passing car. Brooke gasps for breath and goes on: the ambulance, the emergency ward, the cut on Andrew's head and his arm, and his neck, the brace on his neck . . .

'Whoa, hang on, Brooke,' Kerry says. 'What was that you said about his neck?'

Brooke repeats it and Kerry's shiver has nothing to do with the cold. 'Is he conscious, Brooke? Can I speak to him? Can you hold the phone for him?'

There is some fumbling and faint voices in the background, and then she hears Andrew's voice, the apologies, the explanation, the embarrassment and, most of all, the fear.

'I'll be on the first flight I can get,' she says. 'And I'll call Brooke back to let her know when that'll be. Try not to worry,

Andrew . . .' she hesitates, 'love you.' Her heart is racing and she can feel fear surging through her and has to pause and feel that, really feel it for its own sake, before she does anything else. Months with nothing and now the intensity of her fear for her brother propels her over the crumbling remains of that paralysing wall. Opening the restaurant door she steps inside and waves to Chris, beckoning him to join her.

'He *sounds* okay,' she says when she has explained what's happened. 'And he *says* he's okay, the cuts on his head and arm hurt, and his bum – his mobile was in his back pocket so when he landed on his bum bits of it got embedded in one buttock, but it's his *neck*, Chris. The doctors think he could have broken his neck. They won't know until they've done an MRI, and Brooke's really rattled. They can't get hold of Linda, who's in Singapore, and Andrew's worried about Brooke having to cope alone. I've told him I'll get the first flight I can.'

Chris puts his arms around her. 'Of course,' he says. 'I'll come with you. We'll see if Erin and the kids can stay here with Farah for a couple of days, until we know what's happened. There's no way I'm letting you go alone, not after all you've been through. Come on, we'll tell the others and go straight home, get online and find a flight.'

Kerry nods, ignoring the tears that are running down her cheeks. She puts her hands up to his face. 'You're the best,' she says, 'I love you to bits. You do know, don't you, that none of what's happened was ever about you?'

And they hurry back through the restaurant, gather up the others and the remains of the pizzas, and head out through the crowded marketplace to the car and back to Connie's house.

# Twenty-two

'It's quite ordinary-looking, isn't it?' Connie says, as they clamber out of the taxi, trying to remember how she'd envisaged The Ivy. 'I was expecting something . . . well . . . grander, I suppose – after all, it's one of the most famous restaurants in the world. Not that I'm complaining. I always feel like a fish out of water in places that are grand or glamorous.'

'Subtlety and tradition, Connie.' Bea smiles and grips her elbow as they hurry across the street, out of the rain, while Flora follows with Phillip. 'The glamour of The Ivy is the clientele, and today that's us! You'll love it, it's understated and down to earth, but very special. And you may catch a glimpse of the ghost of Noël Coward or Virginia Woolf, or even Laurence Olivier.' She shakes out her umbrella and closes it. 'Phillip has brought me here on my birthday for as long as I can remember. Perhaps that's a lack of imagination on both our parts but I wouldn't swap it for anywhere else. It always feels like a special occasion.'

'And it always has to be the same table,' Phillip cuts in, as he and Flora join them. 'I think the sky would fall in if we had to sit somewhere else. We saw Tony Blair in here once, and last year Helen Mirren was almost within groping distance but I managed to restrain myself.' And he steers them inside and Connie checks out the customers as he speaks to the maître d' about their reservation. She feels an ache of envy over his friendship with Bea, it's so rich with familiarity and knowing, more comfortable than many marriages. In fact it appears more comfortable than her own marriage had been, but then this is not a marriage and so it's free of the complications and expectations of that kind of relationship.

She remembers a summer evening a couple of years ago when, in the room that had become Gerald's bedroom, she had heard his breathing settle to the rhythm of sleep and had switched off the light and crept out, closing the door behind her. It was still early and she hadn't been ready to go to bed, nor had she wanted the distraction of a book or the television. She wanted company, intimacy; not sexual intimacy – she'd given up on that long ago – but a male friend to talk to and relax with, to give her a hug or hold her hand from time to time. And she needed someone who could understand the spiritual and emotional loneliness and the burden of guilt she felt in her own ingratitude for what she had. Farah, she thought, was the only person who could possibly understand this.

Through the open door she caught the scent of the honeysuckle and moon flowers that she had planted years earlier alongside the pergola, and she followed that scent to the garden where the last vestiges of light were fading. In the blissful stillness and silence she had walked across the lawn to gaze out over the darkness of the river glittering with sprinkled reflections of the city lights. There she had sat on the low rock wall beyond which the land dropped sharply away, and wept. She wept silently with loneliness, and with despair that Gerald's illness was devouring the people she loved most. Her family was like an old piece of porcelain crazed with tiny cracks and ready to shatter. Kerry's feisty energy had turned to bitter impotence and hurt, Andrew's calm thoughtfulness to chilly distance and Chris was struggling with the change in Kerry. And Linda, well, they had never been close, but now she seemed more critical and superior than ever, while Brooke was turning inwards to protect herself as her mother seemed to pick on her as a way of getting at Andrew. Only Ryan and Mia seemed unscathed. She had wondered how long it would last, and whether it was too late even for Gerald's death to rescue them.

Connie stares down at the menu without seeing it, thinking of going home, of being alone. Her stomach lurches as she recalls the prickly emotions of the last day she spent with her family, the day they had scattered Gerald's ashes. How can I mend this, she wonders, will we ever recover from the last ten years?

'Have you decided on an entrée, Connie?' Phillip asks. 'The oysters are always magnificent . . .'

And she draws a deep breath and actually looks around the restaurant. Bea was right, she does love the atmosphere, the modest art deco style, the soft lighting, and the sense of tasteful restraint; it touches a part of her that remains essentially English. But her pleasure in it is overhung by the knowledge that all this will be over in a few days. She had wanted to recapture the past but she had never anticipated that it would evoke such curiosity about and longing for the road not taken. She is not ready to go home, not ready for this to finish.

The waiter hovers alongside her and she drags herself back into the present – it's Bea's birthday, not a time for self-indulgent raking over the past or brooding about the future. She looks up and smiles.

'I'll have the scallops and then the risotto, please,' she says, putting down the menu. 'What are you having, Bea?'

*

Bea orders the Mediterranean fish soup followed by gnocchi and sits back watching as Phillip and Flora order their food.

This birthday feels special. So many old friends have gone already, died in their fifties and sixties, but she is seventy-three, still working and feeling as though she will go on doing so forever. What she wishes now though is that she could go on doing so with Flora. It's rare at this age, she thinks, to encounter someone who seems like a kindred spirit, someone with whom you feel totally at ease, as though you've known them your whole life. How different things might have been had she known Flora all those years ago. How delightful it would be to make up for that now.

The waiter arrives back at the table with a bottle of champagne in an ice bucket and Phillip nods to him to open it.

'So,' he says, when their glasses are filled, 'a toast to you, Bea, happy birthday, my dear and oldest friend, and many happy returns.'

And they raise their glasses to echo his toast and for one extraordinary moment Bea feels she might shed a tear. 'It's lovely to be celebrating with you, but you'll be gone in a few days and I'm really going to miss you,' she tells Connie.

'You and Phillip must come to Hobart,' Connie says. 'Separately or together. I have heaps of space.'

'Well, unless Flora decides to stay on and run the shop we'll have to come separately,' Phillip says.

'I need to go there first anyway,' Flora says. 'There's a lot of catching up to do. I have a family to meet, and I have to convince them that I'm a completely harmless old black sheep.'

'I think meeting an aunt who is a black sheep might be fun – intriguing, really,' Phillip says. 'Don't let them think you are completely harmless, it might disappoint them.'

'I've always wanted to go to Australia,' Bea says, 'especially Tasmania, and now there's that amazing new art museum full of weird and wonderful things.'

Connie nods. 'It's carved into the rock. The construction alone is worth a visit and . . .' She stops abruptly and Bea,

274

sitting opposite her with her back to the entrance, sees her expression change, sees laughter fade into puzzlement. Connie sits up straighter, peering past Bea, tilting her head to one side to get a better view.

'Are you celebrity spotting, Connie,' Bea asks, sipping her champagne, 'or did you see a famous ghost?'

Connie is silent for a few seconds. 'Not a celebrity . . . for a moment I thought . . . but it must be a trick of the light . . .'

'You obviously need more champagne,' Phillip says and he reaches across the table to fill her glass, but Connie ignores him, leaning back in her chair as though backing off from something.

'What is it, Connie? What's wrong?' Bea asks, seeing that Flora's expression has also changed. 'What's . . . ?' and she jumps as a pair of hands cover her eyes.

'Happy birthday,' says a voice behind her. 'Guess who?'

\*

Flora had seen the woman come into the restaurant, seen her speak to the maître d', but then she'd been distracted by the conversation at the table. It was only as the woman seemed to be heading in their direction that she'd had a flash of recognition . . . familiar, she'd thought, but who . . . ?

The woman is tall, with familiar grey-green eyes, reddish hair curling around her face, late forties, perhaps. She stops behind Bea's chair and smiles at Flora and Connie over her head as she slips her hands over Bea's eyes, and in a moment of horrible clarity Flora knows exactly who the woman is and that something truly awful is about to happen. She hears Connie gasp, then feels her stiffen beside her, sees Phillip turn and almost leap from his chair. And as Bea takes the woman's hands in hers and moves them from her eyes, Flora sees the shock and distress in her face.

'Surprise indeed . . .' Bea says, clearly shaken, getting to her feet.

And before she can say any more the woman hugs her, smiling at Connie and Flora over Bea's shoulder, while Phillip looks from one to the other as if working out what to do. Connie's gaze is riveted on the two women and she seems not to notice as Flora moves closer to her and puts a reassuring hand on her arm.

'So sorry to gatecrash,' the woman says, smiling apologetically, hugging Bea. 'I thought it would just be lunch with Uncle Phil as usual.'

Bea's face is flushed. Connie's seems to have turned to stone.

Bea looks at Flora and panic crosses her face. She clings to the younger woman's arm. 'Flora, Connie . . .' she hesitates, smiling. 'This is my daughter – Geraldine.'

A waiter appears alongside Phillip, takes the champagne from the ice bucket and reaches out to top up their glasses.

Phillip swings around, almost knocking the bottle from his hand. 'Not just now,' he says sharply.

Bea, looking straight at Connie, grasps her daughter's hand and draws it through her arm.

'Is there something wrong?' Geraldine asks. 'I don't want to intrude. I just thought it would be nice to surprise Mum . . . it was just . . . just a surprise . . .'

Connie takes her bag from the back of her chair and slings it over her shoulder. 'It certainly is a surprise and indeed a shock,' she says in a voice that cuts through the tension like an ice pick. She turns to Flora. 'I'm leaving,' she says. 'You should probably stay here and get to know your niece.' And she wrenches her hand free from Flora's and makes her way briskly between the tables and out through the restaurant door.

# Twenty-three

'This is soooooo boring,' Brooke says, 'not a bit like I imagined. Nothing's happened for ages, not since they moved you up here and that doctor came. I thought there'd be things happening all the time. Emergencies and stuff.'

'Well, there was quite a bit happening when we were *in* Emergency,' Andrew says. 'There was a lot happening to me at any rate: needles, oxygen, stitches in my bum, bandages, blood pressure machines . . . do you want me to go into cardiac arrest so you can see them put those electric pad things on my chest?'

Brooke sighs and he imagines her rolling her eyes but he can't see that because he is flat on his back and his head is fixed in position with a neck brace and cloth bags filled with something that feels like pellets.

'Duh! 'Course not, but I thought the whole place would be, like, exciting, you know, like *Grey's Anatomy.*'

'It's Saturday afternoon in Melbourne, Brooke, not a stormy night in Seattle, but I'll try to do better next time. Get a pair of handlebars lodged in my chest instead of just bits of a phone in my bum.'

'Shut up, Dad. You know that's not what I meant. It's just that it's all so slow, we're just waiting all the time.'

'That's hospital for you,' Andrew says. 'It's mostly waiting. Waiting for a doctor or a nurse, a meal, medicine, a bedpan or something bearable to watch on TV, or just to be able to go home. The rest of it is uncomfortable, or excruciatingly painful and life threatening, so I'm happy to settle for boring.'

To Andrew the accident itself is a bit of blur. In fact he doesn't remember that he landed on a car, but he does remember hitting the road, feeling confused and wondering what had happened, and then seeing Brooke running towards him, and feeling it would be unwise to move. There was blood from the cuts on his head and arm, but the worst pain had been in his bum. Then there's not much more he remembers until they got him up here to the spinal unit.

'Shall I try phoning Mum again?' Brooke asks.

'Could do. It is a bit weird that she hasn't called back.'

Brooke dials and waits. 'Still no answer. No point leaving another message, I already left three. Are you sure you can't remember where she's staying?'

''Fraid not. The only place I stored it was in my phone. But Kerry and Chris will be here soon, so it doesn't really matter. They'll look after you.'

'Dad! I told you, I don't need looking after.'

Brooke has been absolutely brilliant, ever since they got here about eight-thirty this morning. He has a vague memory of her at the roadside, calling the ambulance, talking to the police, and arranging to drop their bikes off at home with a guy in a flatbed truck who had pulled over to help. And once they were in Emergency, she did all the talking, and filled out all the forms in her neat round writing, so he only had to sign them. It was almost midday when he was finally moved up here to the ward, and then the doctor, who had introduced herself as Helen Reese, came and broke the news about his neck. That had really panicked Brooke, and it had put the fear of God into Andrew too although he tried not to let her see that.

'But he says his neck doesn't hurt,' Brooke told the doctor, tears running down her face. 'If he'd broken it, wouldn't it hurt a lot?'

'Not necessarily,' the doctor had said. She was a quietly spoken woman in her forties and Andrew was thankful that she could see that reassuring Brooke was as important as reassuring him. 'Lack of pain isn't a reliable indicator in these situations. Quite a lot of people sustain a break or fracture and feel no pain. So we just have to keep your dad flat on his back with his head straight until we know what's happened.' She'd turned back to Andrew then. 'We need an MRI, Mr Hawkins, and I'm afraid that means some-time Monday. Meanwhile we'll keep you as comfortable as possible.' She looked down at the notes and grinned. 'I see you had an argument with your phone as well as your bike.'

He'd laughed. 'That's the most painful part of me right now,' he said.

'But think of the fun you can have showing off your scar,' Dr Reese said, and they both laughed, which made the stitches hurt more. 'You don't actually need to stay here, Brooke,' she'd said then. 'Perhaps your mum . . . ?'

Andrew had cleared his throat. 'Her mother and I are separated. She's in Singapore and we can't get hold of her. But I'm going to call my sister – I'm sure we'll organise some-thing for Brooke.'

'I'm fine,' Brooke said. 'I want to be here with Dad.'

'I'm sure you do, but we actually need to have a contact person – a next of kin who is over sixteen,' the doctor said.

'I'm perfectly capable . . .' Brooke began.

'I can see that,' Dr Reese said, 'but you must be exhausted. You and your dad both need someone else as back-up over the next few days.'

When she'd left the nurse brought Andrew some tea and helped him drink it through a fat plastic straw.

# Liz Byrski

'I could do that,' Brooke said and took over the straw before cutting a cheese sandwich into tiny pieces and feeding them to him. He hadn't eaten since the previous evening and the food helped, stopped him feeling quite so light-headed, and he managed to swallow it all flat on his back without once choking.

'You should go and get something to eat now, Brooke,' he'd said then. She too had missed out on the planned breakfast but he'd seen her tucking into a huge muffin when the morning tea was brought round earlier. She'd disappeared for about half an hour and came back armed with magazines and a couple of Mars Bars, which were his favourite chocolate, and a plastic knife from the café which she used to saw one into bits for him. He dozed off after that, and Brooke had either been buried in the pages of *Hello!* or *Madison*, or plugged in to her iPod. Then she'd helped him with another cup of tea and gone out for a walk in the hospital garden. But in the last hour or so her boredom and frustration have reached irritating heights, and her whingeing and moaning are wearing Andrew down. This morning she was a super thoughtful and efficient young adult; now she has reverted to grumpy teenager.

'Look here, Brooke,' he says now, 'you've been great. I don't know how I would've got through any of this without you. But right now you're being a pain in the arse. I know it's boring but it's no picnic for me either. Kerry and Chris will be here soon, so do you think you could shut up for a while, or go for a walk again or something?'

Brooke is silent for a moment. 'Sorry,' she says, her tone subdued now. 'I'm a bit frightened, that's all. I want them to do stuff to help you and nobody is doing anything.' She takes his hand and he feels a tear drop onto it. 'I do love you, Dad, you have to promise to get better.'

'Of course I'm going to get better, whatever that bloody MRI shows. And I'll get through it because you're around to

make sure they look after me. But just take it easy in the meantime, will you? Maybe get yourself a coffee from the machine or go out and get some air. Nothing's going to happen tonight so you won't be missing anything.'

She was sitting in a low chair at the side of his bed and although he couldn't see her he could sense that she was nodding. 'I'll go for a walk then,' she said. 'Is there anything you want before I go?'

'No, I'm fine, thanks. And, sweetheart, I love you too, and I promise everything is going to be okay.'

*

Everything is grey as Brooke walks out of the hospital and crosses the road into the nearby park. It's trying hard to rain, she can feel the first few drops that stop and start, then stop again. The grass, the flowers, everything, even the people, look grey in the stormy, late afternoon light. She wanders along the path kicking at some leaves, swinging back and forth between anxiety and terminal boredom and wondering why everything in her life has suddenly been turned upside down and inside out. There is a buzz in the back pocket of her jeans and she pulls out her mobile and swipes the screen to read a text from her Auntie Kerry.

'*Just landed. Will be with you very soon. Kerry xxx*'

'*Brilliant!*' she texts back. '*Can't wait to see you. I'll be hanging inside the main entrance. B xxx*.'

She sighs with relief and slips the phone back into her pocket, checks the time and adds forty-five minutes for them to get here from the airport. Six-thirty they'll be here, she thinks, and she closes her eyes, wrapping her arms around herself and imagining Kerry enveloping her in one of her huge hugs.

As soon as Brooke was old enough to recognise and take notice of people other than her parents, she had fallen for her Auntie Kerry. And once she could move around independently she would lurch or stagger across the room and collapse into Kerry's outstretched arms, attempt to clamber onto her knee, or clasp her leg and hang on to it like a limpet until her arms were prised free. Kerry was different from her parents and grandparents, all of whom cossetted her and admired everything she did. While her mother groomed and guided her, constantly corrected her, turned her straight hair into curls or plaits, read stories, and did all the things mothers were supposed to do, her aunt teased her, argued with her, growled like a fierce dog, ran around the room flapping her elbows and quacking like a duck, tickled her until she screamed for her to stop and then screamed for her to start again. She threw her into the air, pushed her higher than anyone else did on the swings, and chased her around the garden pretending to be a wild bear. And although Brooke only ever saw Kerry when they all went to her nan and granddad's place for holidays, it was always as though no time had passed nor distance intervened since the last time they had seen each other. It was like that every time, until suddenly it wasn't.

Brooke was seven when things started to change. They went to Hobart one summer and when Kerry put on her bathers to go into the pool Brooke noticed that she had a very fat tummy.

'I'm having a baby, Brooke,' Kerry had explained. 'I'm so excited. Here, put your hand on my tummy and you'll be able to feel it moving.' And she had grasped Brooke's hand and held it against the side of her huge belly.

Brooke had flinched away at first but Kerry hung on to her hand, so she stood there, staring and waiting and finally feeling something moving around. All she knew about babies was that they were boring; they cried a lot, made messes with their food and pooed in their nappies, and everyone made a huge fuss over them when they weren't really interesting at all.

'There,' Kerry had said, 'did you feel it?'

Brooke nodded.

'He's turning over making himself comfortable.'

'Is it a boy then?' Brooke had asked.

Kerry had shrugged and grinned at her. 'I don't know for sure, it could be a girl, but I've got this feeling, Brooke, that it's a little boy. Won't it be lovely to have your very own cousin to play with?'

Brooke had paused, thinking. The prospect of a baby was not appealing; she liked being the only child in the family and didn't want a baby coming along to mess things up. 'No, I don't think so,' she'd said as firmly as she could, so as not to be misunderstood. 'If you don't mind, Auntie Kerry, I'd rather not have a cousin.'

Kerry had looked both shocked and hurt and it was Uncle Chris who broke the silence; he had swept her up into his arms, laughing. 'You don't want any competition, do you, Brooke? Can't blame you for that, but you know we'll all love you just as much when the baby comes. And we'll be needing you to help out and teach it all sorts of things that you can do already.'

Two months later they were all back in Hobart to see the baby whose name was Ryan, and who did all the boring, messy and disgusting things that Brooke had expected, and drew gasps of delight and wonderment from all the family. Kerry was far too occupied to chase Brooke around the garden, or do the duck thing, or do anything at all that they used to do together. She wanted Brooke to sit in a chair and hold Ryan on her knee, to have her photo taken, and then she would feed him or change his nappy, and talk about boring stuff like whether he was smiling or just had wind, and then she'd feed him again and was always too tired to play with Brooke.

For a long time Brooke had believed that it was all Ryan's fault that everything had changed and she had continued to treat him with disdain. But then she began to notice that other things were happening. She knew Granddad was sick;

everyone talked about it. He had to rest a lot and he was obviously getting worse. His hands started shaking and he often dropped things; he sometimes choked on his food, and his voice sounded sort of wobbly. The next time she saw him he was using a stick, then two sticks, and then a wheelchair, and he was lying down a lot on an old sofa that had been moved into the alcove off the kitchen. It was Nan who had told her that he had an illness and wasn't going to get better.

'It makes him very weak and we have to take special care of him,' Connie had said. 'We all have to try and support him as much as we can. Sit on the stool beside him, don't try to sit on his knee, because he's not strong enough to hold you. He can still read to you, but a bit more slowly now.'

The next time Brooke saw him he could no longer hold the book and struggled with the words. By this time Ryan was almost three and Kerry was pregnant again, and had very little time for Brooke. She always seemed a bit cross and distracted, and Brooke had watched and listened, and waited for things to change, but they didn't. And so she had transferred her affections to Chris, who was always the same, always cheerful, always listened to her and talked to her and told her about the children at his school and how terribly badly behaved they were, unlike Brooke herself.

In the last couple of years, though, Brooke has matured enough to understand that there was more to the change in Kerry than could be blamed on Ryan. Granddad had been ill for a long time, long before she herself had been aware of it, and he was getting much worse. She knew he was going to die and had kept expecting it, and she was shy of him because the person she had known was gone, and in his place was someone who couldn't speak or feed himself, and seemed unaware of anything or anyone around him. She was scared of going into his room and finding him dead, and she stayed away from him as much as possible. Brooke thought about how it would feel to see her father disappear little by little until he became a stranger, and while that helped her to understand why her aunt had changed, she still couldn't completely forgive her for it. The distance between them remained. And so it had been hard for her when Andrew, flat on his back in the hospital bed, had asked her to call Kerry.

'You simply can't deal with all this without some support, Brooke,' he'd said. 'We don't know how long I'll be here. And you know, it's not really your mum's job to turn up for me now, although I'm sure she'd come for you.'

And so, reluctantly, Brooke had dialled Kerry's number and told her what had happened, and then Andrew had spoken to her too.

It's dark outside now and Brooke, bored with wandering around in the damp evening air, heads back into the hospital foyer checking her watch for about the hundredth time – ten past six, not long now. She drops down onto a long bench seat inside the entrance where the taxis drop people off. It's a good spot, she thinks, if she stays here she'll see them arrive. Quite suddenly she feels overwhelmed with relief and exhaustion, she's so tired she can barely keep her eyes open, and she rests her head back against the wall and closes her eyes. Her limbs are heavy with fatigue, and she feels herself drifting into a replay of the moment when she saw Andrew's bike rear up and his body sail, as if in slow motion, across the low brick wall and land with a thump on the bonnet of a four wheel drive before bouncing off onto the road. She can hear it now too, the screech of brakes, people yelling. She can feel the fear – a hard knot of pain in her chest as she leaps from her own bike and runs towards him screaming.

'Brooke, Brooke,' a voice says, and she feels a hand on her arm. 'Brooke, are you okay?' And her eyes fly open and sitting beside her now, in the vast hospital foyer, is Kerry, putting a hand up to stroke her hair just as she used to do. And behind her, smiling down, is Chris.

'Hey there, sleeping beauty,' he says. 'How're you doing?'

And in a great surge of relief Brooke throws her arms around Kerry's neck and bursts into the tears that have been building up since that first awful moment on the bike path.

\*

'So tell me about your mum,' Kerry says some time later when they have seen Andrew settled for the night and taken a taxi back to the house. 'She's in Singapore and not answering her phone? Doesn't sound like Linda. She's always on her phone, fiddling with messages and emails and returning calls.'

'I know,' Brooke says, 'it's weird. I left three messages and she hasn't called back.' She reaches into a cupboard to pull out plates for the fish and chips they have stopped to pick up on the way home.

'Lost her phone perhaps?' Chris suggests, opening a bottle of wine that he has selected from Andrew's rack. 'Or maybe forgot to take it?'

'She usually puts all the details up on the corkboard in the kitchen when she's going away,' Brooke says. 'But I'm not asking *him* to look for them. Claudia at the gallery will know where she's staying too but she won't be there 'til tomorrow.'

'Do you actually want her to come home though, Brooke?' Kerry asks, giving her a long look. She thinks that Brooke looks totally wiped out, her face is grey with exhaustion, her eyes red. 'I mean, I'm not going back to work before the holidays anyway, so I can stay on with you for a while if you like.'

'But Linda needs to know,' Chris interjects. He looks at Brooke. 'I know that all this – the break-up as well as what happened today – has been pretty grim for you, Brooke, but we don't want to make things more complicated by keeping Linda out of the loop.'

Brooke watches as Kerry starts to unwrap the bundle of fish and chips. 'I think Mum needs to know,' she says eventually, picking up a stray chip and putting it in her mouth. 'But it would be better if you could stay,' she says, looking at

Kerry. 'If she came here to stay with me Zachary would be hanging around too.'

They sit down at the table and share out the food. Chris pours wine for himself and Kerry. 'You too, Brooke?' he asks, indicating the bottle, but she shakes her head. 'He sounds like a bit of a tosser,' Chris says, 'and not at all the sort of bloke I'd expect Linda to go for.'

'He's really vile,' Brooke says. 'And the worst thing is there's this girl at school, a sort of friend, or at least she used to be, who goes out with a boy called Danny who lives right near here, just down the end of the road. She says Zachary goes there to buy drugs and . . .' she pauses, blushing. 'Oh well, just to get drugs and stuff.'

There is silence around the table and Kerry glances across at Chris with raised eyebrows. She puts her hand on Brooke's arm. 'What stuff, Brooke?'

'What?'

'You said he goes there for "drugs and stuff" – what are you trying to say?'

Brooke looks from one to the other. 'Well, you know, just stuff . . .'

Kerry shakes her head. 'What aren't you telling us, Brooke? Because whatever it is I think it's really serious and you're worried about it.'

Brooke blushes, looking down at her plate. 'I . . . well, I haven't told Dad . . . I mean, I didn't know how . . .'

She pauses, obviously very aware now that both of them have stopped eating and are waiting for her. She puts down her knife and fork and buries her face in her hands. Kerry shifts her chair closer and puts an arm around Brooke's shoulders. 'If you tell us, we can help you decide what to do and if you need to tell Andrew.'

Brooke nods without looking up, and draws in her breath. 'Donna, this girl, says that Zachary is . . . that he's having a . . . well . . . you know, having sex with Danny's sister.'

Kerry looks up sharply at Chris, who pulls a face and sips his wine. 'Do you know how old this girl is?' she asks.

'She's older than me,' Brooke says, looking up at her. 'I think she finished school last year.'

Chris lets out a slow whistle between his teeth, shaking his head, and Kerry sits up straighter, pausing before she speaks.

'And why did you think you couldn't tell Andrew?'

Brooke shakes her head. 'Because he'll have to tell Mum . . .' she pauses and then the words tumble out almost faster than Kerry can grasp them: '. . . and she'll know I told Dad, and she'll be so upset, and she'll think it's just me being horrible because I hate Zachary so much, and then she'll really hate me and I've been so horrible to her anyway, and it'll all be my fault, and she won't ever want to see me again.'

# Twenty-four

*I*t's almost four o'clock by the time Flora leaves The Ivy and starts to walk back to the hotel. The rain has stopped and a watery sun brings shimmering light to the pavements.

'We'll get a cab and drop you off,' Phillip had said.

But Flora preferred to walk. It's not far to Russell Square and she needs time alone to think about what's happened. The last few hours have turned everything on its head and she's determined that nothing, absolutely nothing, will spoil this for her. She strolls on, joyful and still a little bewildered by the suddenness with which things can change. After all these years alone, out on a limb, cut off from her family, she had been looking forward to a holiday in Hobart and the adventure of getting to know her niece and nephew and their children. And now another family has simply fallen into her lap, and despite her concern for Connie, all Flora can feel is the sheer joy of discovering this connection and what it means.

When Connie walked away from the table Flora had followed her to the door. 'Don't, Connie, please don't go,' she said, grasping her elbow. 'Stay; this is family, *our* family, we need to know more, need to get to know Geraldine and . . .'

'She may be your family, Flora, but she's certainly not mine,' Connie said, pulling her arm away. 'How can you

possibly expect me to stay? The shame of it, the embarrassment. How can you even bear to say her name, and as for Bea,
how could she do this to me . . . ?'

In that moment Flora wanted to shake her. 'This is not about
*you*,' she began, 'and Bea didn't know, you could see that . . .'

But Connie had pushed open the door and walked out,
turning back to look at her. 'Why didn't she tell us, Flora? How
duplicitous was that, pretending to be a friend, but hiding
this? No; what you do is up to you but I want nothing to do
with this.' And she had turned and walked away, crossing
the street and disappearing rapidly around the corner.

As Flora watched her go she felt a fierce stab of anger
and resentment. Connie was right, this was *her* family, and
nothing, not their lifelong friendship or the family on the
other side of the world, was going to get in the way of it.
Taking a deep breath she turned back into the restaurant and
made her way to the table where Bea and her daughter and
Phillip were still sitting. They turned to her in concern.

'I'm so sorry,' Geraldine said, getting to her feet. 'It was
incredibly thoughtless of me. But I was talking to Mum on
the phone yesterday and I suddenly thought how lovely it
would be to get on a train and come up here for the day to
surprise her.'

Flora stood facing her for a moment. They were about the
same height, and their eyes met easily, eyes just like her own.
It was like looking into a mirror image of herself as a younger
woman, and uncannily like being eye to eye with Gerald. She
put her hands out to take Geraldine's, and the connection
was so overwhelming that a lump rose in her throat stopping
her voice; all she could do was search the younger woman's
face. 'No apologies,' she managed to say eventually, 'you have
every right to surprise your mother on her birthday.' She hesitated, trying to get her voice and her shaking hands under
control. 'This is extraordinary and wonderful, and I'm just so
happy to meet you, Geraldine.'

As she thinks of it now Flora is filled once more with the joy of that moment, and stops to savour it. There is a bench nearby at the entrance to a small park and flicking the worst of the rain water from it with the corner of her raincoat she sits down, wanting to savour it again, to fix it in her memory.

She had seen Bea glance at Phillip with enormous relief, and then look back at her. 'I'm so sorry about Connie,' Bea had begun. 'I would never . . . I mean, I hadn't even told Geraldine that you and Connie were here. We rarely talk about the past, it's not as though she even knew Gerry . . .'

Flora had looked at Bea and Phillip and then, glancing up, caught sight of her own reflection in a nearby mirror. Three old people, in reasonably good nick, each of them recognisable from their younger selves, bound together by the past in the most extraordinary way. And she was filled by an overwhelming longing to be part of this, to stay part of it, to hold it and build on it and not let it slip away from her. 'Well, perhaps it's time to talk about the past now,' she said, 'and there's so much I need to know.'

Sitting on the wet seat in the sunlight Flora opens her bag and takes out her glasses and a packet of photographs, photographs that Geraldine had brought with her for Bea.

'You keep them, Flora,' Bea had said after they had looked at them together. 'Geraldine will get me more copies.'

They are family photos taken over Easter in the garden of the Cornish farmhouse which Geraldine's husband, Robert, had inherited from his father. Robert is burly and bearded with a weathered complexion and dark, interesting eyes; he looks, Flora thinks, exactly as a Cornish farmer should: solid, earthy and kind. In the pictures Robert and Geraldine are with their children – Ethan, who is eighteen, Lucy, sixteen, and dark-haired Molly, who is thirteen and looks just like her grandmother.

'This is all so amazing,' Geraldine had said as they looked at the photographs together. And she reached out to take

Flora's hand again, across the table. 'I have a real aunt, an aunt of my own, not just one of Robert's. This is so exciting – I can't tell you how it feels.'

'You don't need to,' Flora had said. 'It's the same for me – a niece, a great-nephew and two great-nieces; I should pinch myself to make sure I'm not dreaming.'

'I was going to tell you, Flora,' Bea said, 'the first time you and I had lunch together, ask you if I should tell Connie, but I chickened out. I kept thinking that I would tell you if you were going to stay here and work with us, but if you weren't it would be easier for Connie not to know. How do you think she'll . . . ?'

Flora put her hand on Bea's arm. 'Don't, Bea. This is not about Connie, and while I love her dearly I don't need her approval to get to know this side of my family. Let's not spoil this now by worrying about it. I'll talk to Connie later.'

Flora shifts on the damp bench and runs her fingers over the photographs again. Then she slips the pictures back into the envelope and into her bag, gets to her feet and walks on towards the hotel, feeling entirely different from the way she did before this happened. She has always seen herself as a solitary figure, a woman walking life's streets alone; now she is a woman with a family; walking alone but not alone, a woman who is part of something greater than herself. It's a feeling she's never had before, not even during that time she spent in Hobart where everything was so much of Gerald's making. Today she had felt instantly accepted into the heart of Bea's family; it all seemed so easy and so right. And as she turns into the foyer of the hotel Flora knows that whatever happens next, nothing can take away the pure magic of what has happened.

*

'Well, you certainly took your time,' Connie says as Flora lets herself into their room. 'You must have had a lot to talk about.'

'We did,' Flora says. 'I'm sorry you felt you couldn't stay. It would have been lovely to share it with you.'

'Lovely for you, you mean.'

'Connie . . .'

'Well, what do you expect, Flora?' Connie says sharply, her voice tense with hurt and anger, her expression cold and pinched. 'That I would sit with Bea and with Gerald's daughter, and pretend it was all wonderful?'

Flora sighs and tosses her handbag onto her bed. 'Of course not, we all know something serious happened, something difficult and embarrassing . . .'

'Embarrassing? Is that what you think – embarrassing? How about insulting, offensive, humiliating . . . there's plenty more I could think of. Those women, Bea and her daughter, ride roughshod over my feelings, over my marriage and my family, and all you can say is that it was embarrassing?'

Before she walked into the room Flora had counselled herself to stay calm; she would reason with Connie, listen to what she had to say and treat it with respect. But her good resolutions are already being rocked. She crosses to the table, picks up the kettle and heads to the bathroom. 'Look, I'm going to make some tea and we can sit down and talk this through.'

'How *could* you, Flora? How could you let them do that to me and then stay there with them? Doesn't our friendship mean anything to you?'

Flora slams the kettle back on the table. 'Right!' she says, her voice rising with the heat of anger. 'Let me explain a few things to you, Connie. First – nobody has done *anything* to you. None of this is about you. Geraldine decided to give her mother a birthday surprise – that's not about *you*. Bea and Gerald were together, they were going to get married until he decided he wanted to marry you and dumped her. Poor you? I don't think so! He cut her off completely, wouldn't return calls, and six weeks later when she found she was pregnant and tried to contact him, she discovered he'd buggered off back to the parents in Tunbridge Wells to organise a wedding in a beautiful church, and a reception at an extremely posh and expensive country club. When she finally went down there and forced him to meet her he told her to go away and get an abortion, gave her three hundred pounds and told her never to come near him again. So, while you chose your wedding dress in Selfridges, and you and I discussed flowers and hymns, Bea wrestled with her future in a very different way. I know it's a terrible shock, and I understand that you are hurt by it, and I do feel for you in this, but who's hurt you, Connie? Bea and Geraldine, or Gerald himself? Who's the loser here, you or Bea?' She stops abruptly, then picks up the kettle again, fills it at the bathroom tap and plugs it in to the power point by the dressing table.

Connie drops down into the armchair by the window and sits, her chin resting on her hand, staring out across the park.

'She was laughing at me,' she says eventually. 'All the time – that first dinner, then when we met for coffee and went to the shop, she was secretly laughing at me. She must have been or she would have told me.'

Flora closes her eyes in frustration, but moderates her tone a bit as Connie has moderated hers. 'Do you have any idea how ridiculous that sounds?' she says. 'Bea was going to tell me and ask me whether to tell you, she was agonising about how and when, or whether it was kinder to say nothing.' She stops, looking at Connie, who is still staring out of the window. The kettle boils and she makes the tea and carries the cups over to sit facing her. 'No one has set out to insult or humiliate you, unless you choose to take it that way. No one is laughing at you; in fact all three of them were upset and concerned for you. Be hurt, be humiliated and offended and sulk all you want, but don't expect sympathy from me. Empathy, yes; it's a shock, it's a difficult and painful situation, and you have to explain it to Kerry and Andrew . . .'

'What?' Connie swings round to look at her. 'Kerry and Andrew? There's no way I'm involving them in this. They will not know about this, Flora, I'm not telling them and neither will you.'

'They have a half-sister, Connie, and they have a right to know.'

'No, absolutely not. How do you imagine they'd feel if I went home and told them this?'

'Well, if they are the nice, sensible, generous people you've described to me, I think they'll cope all right. They'll be surprised, although perhaps not amazed that Gerald had a secret past. If what Brooke's told you is right then they've adjusted pretty easily to the idea of an ageing lesbian aunt, so I suspect they may find a half-sister quite intriguing. I'd be surprised if they take it as a personal insult. I daresay you're more concerned about how you'll feel telling them rather than how *they* will actually feel.'

Connie shakes her head. 'I can't believe it,' she says. 'It makes . . . well, it makes a mockery of everything, our relationship, our marriage, everything. And to think that I threw everything away for . . . for it to end up like this.'

'Like what? Nothing has really changed, has it? You still have your family, you have some new friends and now a delightful de facto step-daughter if you choose to accept her. And look, there's something else I'm going to say while we're having this conversation, Connie. The longer we're here the more you keep talking about what you gave up to marry Gerald, and while I understand the circumstances in which you did, the fact is that *you had a choice and you chose him.* You admit that you grew to love him and that your family means everything to you, but you seem to imagine that you would have had a better life if you'd followed your career. I think you imagine yourself centre stage at Covent Garden, a dressing room filled with bouquets, and maybe married to someone different, maybe someone more like Phillip. Perhaps that's how it would have been, but the fact is it might not. You might have ended up struggling from one suburban concert hall to another, never quite making the big time, exhausted and short of money, married to a total loser who drank himself into oblivion every day. Dreams are important, Con, but so is reality, and sometimes dreams turn to nightmares. You're never going to know, and you can't get it back. But you have the present and the future, you have your home and family and plenty of money, and you can make the future the way you want it, but only if you let go of this illusion of what might have been.'

They sit in total silence, drinking their tea, both watching the rain that has begun again. It's Connie who breaks the silence.

'Can we not talk about this anymore?' she says quietly. 'I need to think about it, about everything.'

'Of course,' Flora says, incredibly relieved at the prospect of respite. What she would like is to talk about Geraldine and her family, to share the photographs, to talk about how what happened today has affected her, but that, she knows, is not going to happen. Not tonight, possibly not for some time; for now a lull in the storm is the best she can expect. 'Let's go out, maybe see what's on at the cinema?'

It's dusk by the time they leave the hotel and the rain has started again. 'This weather,' Connie says irritably, 'it's so unreliable.'

'Stop being so grumpy,' Flora says as they walk to the cinema. 'If you keep it up you'll be on your own.'

Connie mumbles some sort of apology and they walk on, until they are in sight of the first cinema. 'Nothing with guns or drug deals,' she says.

'Okay, and no cowboys or parallel universes.'

'No gratuitous sex or violence and no cute kids with super-natural powers.'

'And no baseball heroes, or horse whisperers.'

'No Romans with sandals.'

'Or car chases.'

'And definitely not a rom-com.'

'That's Hollywood out then,' Flora says, laughing. 'Oh! This looks more like us. Judi Dench, Tom Wilkinson.'

'Bill Nighy,' Connie says. 'I would even watch a western if Bill Nighy was in it. *The Best Exotic Marigold Hotel.*'

'It's about old people,' Flora says. 'Our sort of old people. I mean, our age group. I read the reviews.'

'Okay then,' Connie says. 'Let's do it.'

And they join the queue, buy their tickets and ice creams, take their seats, watch the ads and the trailers and as the lights go down Connie leans towards Flora. 'Some of what you said was right,' she whispers. 'The rest I'm not sure about but anyway I'm sorry I went for the jugular with you.'

Flora shrugs. 'It's okay. It was like when you used to have hissy fits at school and I had to hose you down. Practising to be a diva, I suppose. We'll get through this. Now shut up and watch the film.'

\*

Connie wakes early, restless and uneasy. She has had a night of strange fragmented dreams which she can now barely remember but which have left her with a sense of something unfinished, and vaguely threatening. She's so uneasy she gets up, showers and dresses before Flora is awake. She sits on the window seat, drawing up her knees and clasping her arms around them, and sees that in Russell Square the fountain is already hard at work, and the old men are in their usual seats outside the café. It's Sunday, no commuters hurrying to work, and she sits quietly watching the birds darting into the sparkling water, and the couples strolling arm in arm through the square. And she knows that despite her love for the places of her youth – the Kent and Sussex countryside, the Forest, the villages and towns, the windy coast and stony beaches, and London so dense with history and so rich in its cultural life – England is lost to her. Time and distance have intervened and whatever she came here to do is done. For the first time since she left Hobart she really wants to be back there, to be home. *What's wrong with me?* she wonders. Yesterday I was devastated by the prospect of leaving, and now everything seems different. This all began with such a great sense of promise but Flora was right about one thing at least: she has become obsessed with what might have been, resentful about its loss.

Yesterday as she got to her feet in the restaurant, steadying herself against the table, sweat broke out on her forehead, her throat went dry, and outrage surged up within her until she felt it would choke her. She had to get out of there as fast and with as much dignity as possible and once on the street she had walked, with no sense of where she was going, for more than two hours until she was cold and exhausted.

This morning all that seems to matter is to be home again, back pottering around the house, doing the sort of small cleansing, healing things that will make it her place again, in her own way. On Thursday she and Flora are due to fly back to France and, a week later, she will be on her way home. Too long, she thinks; I need to go straight home.

It's just after six-thirty and Flora is still sleeping. Connie gets up from the window seat, scribbles a note to Flora and, closing the door softly behind her, walks briskly along the carpeted passage to the lift, and then out through the hotel foyer into the sharp morning sunlight.

\*

The sound of the door disturbs Flora and at first she simply shifts in the bed, yawns and lies there without moving. Memories of the previous day seep slowly into her consciousness and she keeps her eyes closed in an effort to hold off talking to Connie. But the unease will not let her rest and she sits up slowly and sees that Connie has gone out, leaving a note on the bedside table. Flora reaches for her glasses.

*Flora, I need some time alone. Call me if you want to meet up somewhere later. Cx*

Flora sighs with relief. She too needs time to herself, she has something to do and is relieved to be free of revisiting yesterday's conversation for a while. Good call, Connie, she thinks, we both need time and space. Flora is already sure about what she is going to do this morning. She gets up and collects the newspaper that has been delivered to the door, then makes a cup of tea and sits with it on the window seat contemplating the sense of certainty and purpose that is not only entirely new to her, but fills her with the thrill of anticipation.

# Twenty-five

'I hope I remember the way,' Kerry says on Sunday afternoon as Chris steers Andrew's car out of the hospital car park and turns into the street. 'Seems like forever since we were last at Andrew's place.'

Chris passes her his phone. 'Find it on GPS,' he says. 'Better than getting a bum steer right from the start. Shit, this is the one thing I hate about Melbourne, junctions where you have to get into a right lane if you want to turn left.'

Kerry fiddles with the phone, wondering whether her curiosity about Zachary outweighs her unease about this visit, and decides it probably does. They had tried calling the house several times but the phone seemed to be off the hook, so she and Chris had volunteered to go there and find out from Zachary where Linda was staying.

When they'd arrived at the hospital that morning Andrew's doctor had been with him and Andrew himself was looking considerably better than the night before.

'He's doing well,' Dr Reese had said, 'but I'm afraid there's a delay with the MRI. We've only got two machines and one's out of order, so there's a backlog. It looks like Monday afternoon at best before we can get Andrew in there.'

Brooke's face had fallen dramatically. 'But shouldn't Dad go first?' she'd said, and Kerry could hear from her voice that she was close to tears. 'I mean, his neck . . . doesn't he get some sort of urgent status or something?'

'Everyone who's waiting at the moment is urgent, Brooke,' Dr Reese had said, 'some of them in a worse situation than your dad, and some are in acute pain. So while he is, of course, a priority, there are some people who are higher up the list.'

'Don't worry about the delay,' Kerry said when the doctor had left. 'We'll stay – at least I'll stay until we know what's happening, longer if necessary.' She looked across at Chris. 'I guess you'll need to go back in a day or two at the most.'

He nodded and said he would call the Principal at home this afternoon. 'She owes me one – well, several actually, since I covered so much for her last year. But I should prob-ably try to get back by Wednesday. Meanwhile our two will just have to miss a few days at school and stay on with Farah and Erin at Connie's place.'

'That's the other thing,' Kerry had said to Andrew. 'Do you want to let Mum know?'

'Not yet. Not 'til we know the MRI verdict,' Andrew had said. 'If we tell her now she'll want to rush back and if my neck is okay we'll have frightened the life out of her for no reason.'

'She'd want to know anyway,' Brooke had said. 'Wouldn't you want to know if it was me?'

'Of course I would, but it's a bit different. She's on her own on the other side of the world. And she really needs this holiday. I don't want her to wind up in an unnecessary panic about me. I promise we'll let her know as soon as everything's clear, and you can be the one to tell her if you want.'

Earlier in the morning Brooke had seemed in reason-ably good spirits. Kerry could see that she was very relieved to have them there with her. She'd enjoyed showing them the new house and they'd been able to persuade her to tell Andrew what she'd heard about Zachary.

'Linda has to know about this,' Andrew had said. 'And you and I can tell her together when she gets back, Brooke. There's no way she'll blame you, sweetheart, don't worry about it. I think your mum has already started to wake up to what he's really like.'

'And try to get a sense of whether anything else dodgy might be going on,' Andrew had said to Chris when Brooke slipped out to get him some chocolate from the machine in the passage. 'Go inside if you get the chance. And if he's not there you could try his house. It's supposed to be on the market but he might have gone back there for something.' Chris noted down the address.

'I know this is very posh,' Kerry says now as they drive in through the imposing entrance to the enclave of townhouses, 'but I wouldn't like to live here. It seems a bit soulless.'

'Mmmm. Linda's choice more than Andrew's, I should think,' Chris says. 'She's always been very concerned about appearances, but I did quite like her, and I bet she'll be shattered when she hears about Zachary.'

It's almost midday and the blinds on both floors of the house are closed, but there are two cars parked on the driveway.

'You stay here,' Chris says, 'probably won't take long.'

'But I want to see him,' Kerry insists, opening her door. 'And we do need to check that everything's okay – like Andrew said.'

'You're just a nosey tart,' Chris says, giving her a peck on the cheek. 'C'mon then.'

There is no response the first time they ring the bell so Chris tries again, and then again – this time keeping his finger on the bell for much longer. There are sounds of life from within. He presses the bell once more.

'For fuck's sake, wind ya neck in,' a man shouts.

Chris grins and winks at Linda. 'Wait for it!'

There is a thud of footsteps on the staircase, a key turns in the lock and the door is flung open.

'It's Sunday morning, for Chrissakes. Who the fuck are you?'

A man – unwashed, unshaven, hair on end, wearing a grubby black t-shirt and black cotton boxers, stands glaring in the doorway, his gut bulging above the waistline of his pants. Kerry gets a blast of stale alcohol and body odour. How on earth could Linda have fallen for someone like this? Chris turns on what Kerry always thinks of as his best, parents' evening smile.

'You must be Zachary,' he says. 'Chris McGinty, Andrew's brother-in-law, and Kerry, my wife, Andrew's sister. We're trying to get hold of Linda.'

Zachary grunts irritably, but Kerry sees a flash of anxiety cross his face.

'She's in Singapore, back Wednesday or Thursday.' And he moves to close the door.

Chris shifts his weight and puts his foot inside the door. 'We know that, mate, but she's not answering her phone.'

'Brooke wants to talk to her mum,' Kerry adds. 'She thinks Linda might have left the hotel details on the corkboard in the kitchen.'

He grunts again. 'She forgot to take her phone. She rang from the hotel and wanted me to check the messages but I've got a lot on, haven't had time.'

'Ah, we thought that might have happened,' Chris says, maintaining the charm. 'So d'you think you could have a look for the hotel details, please?'

Zachary looks them up and down with distaste. 'Stone the crows. On a Sunday morning.'

'It's past midday.'

He sighs irritably. 'Wait there, I'll go and have a look,' and he turns and starts up the stairs.

'Go with him, Chris,' Kerry whispers, and Chris pulls a face, waits until Zachary is more than halfway up, then runs up behind him.

'I said, fucking wait there . . .'

'Sorry, mate, need a pee,' Chris says.

Zachary grunts again, and points in the direction of the toilet.

Kerry waits until he has moved away from the top of the stairs and creeps quietly up. What greets her takes her breath away. Empty bottles, dirty glasses, ashtrays brimming with cigarette butts and the remains of spliffs and a black lace bra draped over a lamp. From where she's standing she can see a couple of Eskys in which a few crown corks, more cigarette butts and some empty cans are floating in discoloured water. And underneath the dining table a man in stained and faded jeans and a torn t-shirt is fast asleep.

Zachary, lighting a cigarette in the kitchen, looks up and sees her.

'Bit of a mess,' he says, looking around as though he's only just noticed it. 'I'll get it cleaned up by the time Linda gets back.'

'You'd better,' Kerry says. 'I wouldn't want to be in your shoes if she sees it like this.'

He shrugs. 'No real damage.'

Kerry gives a loud, false laugh. 'You're kidding. How do you think you're going to get the stains off that sofa, and what about the scratches on the table?' She looks down at the wood blocked floor, nudging a couple of cigarette ends with the toe of her shoe. 'And then there are the cigarette burns on the floor.'

Zachary shrugs again. 'Yeah, well, let me worry about that. Just do us a favour and don't mention it to her.' He leans over to the corkboard, unpins a post-it note and hands it to her.

Kerry has never had much time for Linda, and she can't imagine how she ever came to be involved with Zachary, but she can't contain her anger and disgust any longer.

'You are a complete bastard,' she shouts, her voice echoing off the walls. 'You couldn't even take time to check her messages. I'll be telling Linda everything I've seen and I hope she chucks you out the minute she gets back and sends you the bill for the damage. You're disgusting and you have no respect.'

'Now look here . . .' Zachary begins.

'What's goin' on?' A girl appears up on the mezzanine naked except for a black thong. 'Who's she?' she asks, pointing at Kerry. 'Why's she shouting like that?'

'Get back in there and put some clothes on,' Zachary says, and turns to Kerry and Chris. 'Sorry about that . . . she's er . . . well, look, Linda doesn't need to know about that. I mean, I wasn't . . .'

'I'm sure you were,' Chris cuts in, 'and Linda's certainly going to hear about it. We'll take her phone too,' he says, reaching out across the worktop for the Blackberry. 'Come on, Kerry, let's get out of here.' And he puts his hand on Kerry's shoulder and steers her down the stairs ahead of him.

'Good riddance! Fuck off,' Zachary shouts, running down the stairs and slamming the front door behind them.

'Bloody hell,' Chris says, grabbing Kerry's hand as they walk down the path. 'Would you ever have believed it?'

Kerry shakes her head, unable to speak, so angry that she can't get words together into a sentence. Chris opens the passenger door for her but she leans against the side of the car and buries her face in her hands. 'Poor Linda,' she says eventually. 'Whatever will we say to her, Chris? It'll break her heart.'

Chris puts his arms around her. 'I don't know, love, but we'll work something out with Andrew. We'll help her. You were wonderful in there, darlin', bloody marvellous. My Kerry back again, I was so proud of you.'

*

Lying flat on your back the whole time, gazing at the ceiling, not being able to see anything that's going on around you, is,

Andrew thinks, mind-bendingly boring. He's not in any real pain, although the cut on his bum is a bit sore, but strangely he's not really worried about his neck. He has a gut feeling that it's going to be okay, in fact he feels he could rip off the stupid neck brace right now, just discharge himself and go home, but he is still pretty dopey. They're giving him drugs of some sort to keep him this way, so he doesn't move about too much. Everything feels better now that Kerry and Chris are here and he doesn't have to worry about Brooke. And it's really quite peaceful now, without any of them around, and he closes his eyes again and the sounds of the ward start to drift away.

It's Chris who wakes him, putting a hand on his arm. 'Andrew,' he whispers. 'You awake, Andrew?'

Andrew forces his eyes open. 'Yep,' he says, yawning, fighting the urge to sit up straight and talk. 'You were quick.'

Chris glances at his watch. 'Not really. You've been asleep. We just got back and Kerry took Brooke straight down to the café for a sandwich, so that I can talk to you. Look, mate, we got the info on Linda's hotel, and a whole lot more, and I need to tell you about it before Brooke comes back.'

Now Andrew really wants to sit up; being flat on his back makes him feel useless.

'Christ,' he says, when Chris has described their encounter with Zachary and the state of the house. 'It's worse than I imagined.'

'And there's more,' Chris continues. 'On the way back we decided to check out the other address, the one you said Zachary was selling.'

'Yes, he's selling it so he and Linda can buy me out of the townhouse. I drove past it one day – nice-looking place, they should get a good price for it.'

'They won't get anything,' Chris says, 'and Linda's in for another shock, I'm afraid. It's not for sale and it's not going to be because Zachary doesn't own it. He was supposed to be looking after it for a mate who was working up in the Pilbara on a mine site. Zachary was supposed to check it out once or twice a week, make sure it was okay. But this guy, Frank, came back unexpectedly and found Zachary living there. He'd been kicked out of the place he was renting, because of damage, and the owner's taking action against him for that and non-payment of rent. Anyway, he'd been in Frank's place for a few months and it was a pigsty. They had a big bust-up and Frank kicked him out. It sounded to me as though that was round about the time that he suddenly moved into your place. He's been in trouble before too, but Frank wouldn't tell me what about – I suspect he's not entirely squeaky clean himself. I can't imagine how Linda ever got herself into this.'

Andrew hesitates. 'No, he's certainly not what you'd expect but we were in a mess and she was miserable. I suppose Zachary managed to say the right things at the right time. Poor old Linda.' He pauses, thinking. 'Look, I don't want Brooke to know about this, okay?'

Chris nods. 'I think I should meet Linda's flight and go with her to the house. We can't let her go there unprepared, and she shouldn't go alone. I'll ring work and tell them I need the rest of the week.'

'That'd be great,' Andrew says. 'It's really good of you, mate. Depending on the MRI I might be able to go with you, but either way I'm not going to be able to handle all this on my own. And I want to keep Brooke out of it. Kerry won't say anything to her, will she?'

Chris shakes his head. 'No, we thought that too. We've just told her that the place was a bit messy but that Zachary had found the hotel details, and that we'd got Linda's phone. Kerry told her not to call her mum until Linda could speak to you at the same time.'

Andrew closes his eyes for a moment, thinking of Linda and the shock that awaits her. It would be so easy to ignore it all and leave her to it but he wants to help her. The mess of their marriage hasn't all been Linda's fault. 'Linda's a good person, really,' he says now, looking up at Chris. 'We were just wrong for each other. Not at first, perhaps, but in the last few years, totally wrong. We should never have let it end like this.'

Chris puts his hand on Andrew's arm. 'I know, mate. I'm sorry about what's happened for you guys, but you'll sort something out for yourselves and for Brooke. Gerald's illness has stirred everyone up. I'll be glad to see Connie back – but she really needed this trip. Once she's home I reckon we'll all start to get ourselves back together again.'

# Twenty-six

'You should do nothing, Mum,' Geraldine says. 'Flora said to leave it to her. She's the best person to deal with this, she and Connie have known each other for years. And frankly, the state you're in this morning you can only make it worse. One minute you're full of sympathy for Connie, and the next you want to punch her. Come on, let's go out and get some air, a walk is what we need. No point sitting around hoping we'll hear something,' and she edges Bea out of the door.

'I suppose you're right, but I feel so useless,' Bea says as they stroll up the street. 'And perhaps we should be going in the opposite direction rather than towards Russell Square, because if we bump into Connie I probably *will* punch her. The rudeness, and the selfishness, as though she's the only one who's affected by all this.' She shakes her head. 'That's my trip to Australia down the drain. I never wanted to meet her and I was very much on edge about it at the beginning, but she was entirely different from what I'd expected and I really liked her – and I felt that she liked me too.'

'I'm sure she did, and still does,' Geraldine says as they turn to walk in the opposite direction, 'but it *was* a difficult situation for her.'

'Well, I know that, it was difficult for all of us, but stomping out like that, and the way she spoke to Flora. But really it's the way she treated you that pisses me off more than anything. None of this is your fault. It's just a difficult situation created by Gerald. We're all stuck in it and we should be helping each other not declaring war. Look at Flora – it was a shock for her too, but she was so thrilled to meet you, wasn't she? I so wish she wasn't going.'

They walk on in silence, past the small park, past a rival bookshop, the hotels, the museum, the church, the florist, and all the places that are part of Bea's sense of Bloomsbury as her natural home. She is so hurt by and angry about Connie's behaviour that she can't put it out of her mind. It's not the spoiled birthday lunch, because that had ended up being wonderful after she'd left; wonderful to sit there with her daughter, with Phil and Flora, and talk about their family, and to see Flora slowly being drawn into that. Bea could see how thrilled she was, how she could barely take her eyes off Geraldine, how much she wanted to get to know her, how she had devoured those photographs. Bea had wanted to tell Flora what Geraldine meant to her; that she'd had no family of her own until her daughter was born. She had grown up in an orphanage remembering little except the small dank room in Hackney where men came to visit her mother, and disappeared with her behind the dusty old velvet curtains and then emerged leaving money on the mantelpiece. She'd been five when her mother went out one day and didn't come back and a few days later Bea was carted off to the orphanage. She never knew what happened to her mother, didn't even know her name, or her father's.

Of course Flora's background was very different, privileged really, but from what Gerald had told her about their parents there was little love lost in that family. He had been terrified of his father, terrified of falling foul of him, of being cut off from the family, and the inheritance. And recently, when Flora had told them how he had banished her and then told their parents about her so they too cut her out of their lives, it had made complete sense to Bea.

She'd realised long ago that Gerald's apparent confidence and sense of his own authority was rooted in a fear of his own irrelevance. He had always feared being left alone with no one to act as mirror of that image he needed to create of himself. It had taken her decades to understand that this was why he needed a woman who would support or indulge that, rather than someone like herself who would constantly challenge him or cut him down to size. Banishing Flora and then spilling the beans to their parents was Gerald's frantic attempt to appear to be doing the right thing, to be an upright man, a responsible husband and father in their eyes. And so he had established himself firmly within the fold, effectively ensuring that the family's wealth would flow eventually to him. For, as Bea had always known, Gerald's priority was to maintain the social status which, at Cambridge, had been vital to his sense of his own importance. Being part of a respected and prosperous family held him together and it was essential to his future. And she understands now why he was so careful about keeping her away from his friends and family – whatever he'd promised her at the time, he'd always known that his family would never accept her. While so many of their university friends were rebelling against their parents and families, Gerald was clinging firmly to tradition as his source of strength.

Bea, on the other hand, had grown to adulthood with no family attachments and had succeeded only thanks to the insight of Mary Small, a teacher in the rather rundown East London secondary school who had seen promise in her. As Bea had prepared to be forced out into the workforce at fifteen, Miss Small had encouraged her to stay on, take her GCE exams and then complete sixth form. She was, the teacher thought, university material, and she offered Bea a home with her, to enable her to complete her education. Mary Small fed, housed, clothed and cultivated her, and grew to love her like a daughter, and that love was returned. Mary was the family Bea had never had; she dissipated her sense of aloneness, and showed her the only love she had ever known until then. Mary had died unexpectedly of a heart attack in the sixties, shortly before the death of Connie's mother. But Gerald had shown none of the empathy or support, nor offered Bea the practical help, that he had lavished on Connie just a few months later. Mary Small didn't count as 'family' in Gerald's universe, despite the years of care and financial support, and the fact that she had left Bea every-thing she owned. Bea would have liked to explain to Flora that her sense of aloneness was why she had kept her baby, and used the money that Gerald gave her for an abortion to equip herself for the birth. Is it this, she wonders now, this understanding of what it means to be alone, that gives her such a sense of kinship with Flora?

'Is it worth me staying up here another night?' Geraldine asks, linking her arm through Bea's. 'Just in case Connie softens a bit and wants to meet? I can ring Robert, he won't mind.'

Bea shrugs. 'About the chances of Connie I've no idea,' she says. 'But I'd love it and I bet Flora would like to see you again, so if you really think Rob will be okay about it then do stay.'

'I'll call him while we're having breakfast,' Geraldine says. 'He'll be fine. He's nearly as thrilled as I am that I've actually got an aunt as well as a mother!'

*

It's ten to four as Flora walks down Marchmont Street on her way to Russell Square, thinking, as she so often does in this part of London, of Virginia Woolf walking these streets and of Mrs Dalloway who 'said she would buy the flowers herself'. What an extraordinary individual Woolf was, she thinks, how completely individual, how courageous and how infuriating, and what a terrible snob. She thinks she will start re-reading Woolf. And she feels a joyful sense of liberation that she will now have the leisure to do this, that she can read the books and essays again without the constant interruptions at the hotel, or the anxiety of having to teach them. It's a very long time since she taught literature to sixth formers, most of whom were waiting out the final torturous months of school and hankering for the wider world. Finding ways to hold their interest had made Flora's passion into a chore that was only occasionally rewarded by a truly bright student who fell in love with Woolf or Henry James, George Eliot or the Brontës. But now I can read them all again, she tells herself, and it seems like luxury.

A clock chimes four as she turns into the square and she can see Connie sitting outside the café, reading a magazine. 'Shall we meet at four?' she had texted earlier, and Flora had replied, 'Fine – usual place?' So here we are, she thinks now, and heaven knows where we'll be at the end of this conversation.

'Have you ordered yet?' she asks as Connie looks up.

'A pot of tea for two and scones,' Connie replies. 'Okay?'

'Perfect,' Flora says, sitting down, anxious now about where to start. There is so much she wants to say, but her pleasure is stifled by the need to protect Connie's feelings, and in a moment of sudden clarity she realises she resents this. She resents having to measure and moderate her words and opinions in order to accommodate Connie's sensitivity. All those years of letters and emails, of smiling conversations through the computer screen, have been constrained by the need to watch what she said. She has tried to avoid needling Connie's divided loyalty or challenging her descriptions and interpretations of things Gerald has done or not done. When she'd left Hobart she had vowed to herself that she would not do anything to come between

315

them, not undermine their marriage or Connie's view of her husband. They had a life and a family on the other side of the world and so she had become, she can now see, a repository for Connie's confidences, a good and patient listener, never rocking that boat but increasingly less than honest in delivering her 'outsider's' opinion. Perhaps, despite her good intentions, she has, in this respect, not been a good friend. Face to face she might not have held back, but the technology that allowed them such ease of connection has its own limitations; a code of conduct that Flora had felt was essential to their continuing friendship.

But she is weary of it now. Gerald is dead and she has accommodated Connie's grief, and her post-mortem construction of him and their marriage, long enough. Underlying that is the nagging voice that always reminds her that Connie was content to let the estrangement continue, never once fighting on Flora's behalf. Her rudeness and lack of consideration for Bea and Geraldine had shocked Flora; it had a ruthlessness about it, as though she felt no responsibility to consider anyone's feelings but her own. And later, her refusal to accept or respect Flora's own stake in this, to acknowledge that she was a part of both sides of the family, had been profoundly hurtful. Her behaviour had been more characteristic of Gerald than the Connie that Flora thought she knew, and it had freed Flora of any latent sense of responsibility for 'protecting' Connie from her own opinions. The time for accommodation has passed, she thinks, and truth, hard as it may seem, is top of the menu for this afternoon tea.

'I've made a few decisions,' Connie says as the waiter appears with the tray of tea and scones.

'Good; wise ones, I hope,' Flora says, and Connie looks up sharply, as though surprised that Flora might be implying that she would make an unwise decision.

They wait in silence while the waiter unloads the tray onto the table.

Tension stretches between them like a tightrope that both must negotiate if they are to meet in the middle.

'I'm not going back to Port d'Esprit with you, Flora. I'm going to go straight home.' Connie picks up the teapot and begins to pour.

'I think that's a very good idea,' Flora says, relieved to be able to start the conversation on a supportive note.

'You do?'

'Yes. I think you need to go home. You had to get away when you did and now you need to go home.'

'Well, I'm glad you're not offended by *that* at least.'

Flora hesitates and then decides not to let this salvo go. 'Why would I be offended by such a reasonable decision?'

Connie sits back and picks up her cup and saucer, sipping her tea, testing its heat. 'Well, I think you were offended yesterday by my decision to leave The Ivy.'

'I thought it was a selfish and hurtful thing to do, and yes, I *was* offended.'

'And you obviously don't care how hurtful the whole thing was to me.'

This is escalating faster than she had anticipated. 'Look, Connie,' Flora says, 'we went through all that yesterday evening. I don't think we need to pick over the scabs.'

'Well, I suppose we're never going to agree about that; anyway, it's over now, so we'll just have to put it behind us. I've managed to change my flights. I'll be leaving late on Tuesday.'

Flora nods. 'Well, I'm sure they'll all be glad to see you back again.'

'The school holidays start in a couple of weeks, so Brooke can come and stay.' She pauses. 'I guess you'll head off back to Port d'Esprit and then organise your flight over to Hobart? I hope it won't take you too long.'

Flora clears her throat. 'Well, I've got some news too, which means it'll be a while before I can get over for a visit.' She looks up at Connie. 'I rang Phillip this morning and told him I'd decided to take the job. He was delighted. I'll be starting there sometime in June, as soon as I've sorted things out with Suzanne and found somewhere to live.'

'The job? But you said you'd come to Hobart.'

'And I will,' Flora says. 'I'd love to, but it will have to be later in the year, when Phillip and Bea and I have organised when each of us can go away.'

'But you can't,' Connie says, her face white with shock. 'You said you'd come sooner, come and live with me. You were going to meet up with Denise again. I told you, the house is plenty big enough for both of us, or you and Denise might . . .'

'Hang on, Con,' Flora says, holding up her hands. 'I said I'd have a holiday in Hobart and think about the future, and I *will* come for a holiday, but I've decided about the future *now*. I'd certainly like to see Denise but I don't have any urge to rekindle the relationship with her after all these years, and I *never ever* said I was going to live there with you.'

'But it's your *home*, you were born there,' Connie says, a high colour developing now on her cheeks. 'I thought that's how it would be. I mean, it's okay for you to come back now . . . now that Gerald has gone.'

'Connie, I was only five years old when we left Hobart, and since then I've only spent a rather uncomfortable eighteen months there, more than thirty years ago. England is my home – England and France, a bit of both. I want to spend time with you and to meet the rest of the family, but I could never live there again, not now. Gerald robbed me of that possibility years ago, and I haven't been waiting for him to die so that I could go back. It's too late now.'

'But you said . . .'

'I said I would come for a holiday while I made up my mind what to do. Well, I've made up my mind now and I'd still like to visit.'

'You're staying here because of *them*,' Connie says angrily, 'Bea and her daughter. I suppose you think they're your family too.'

'Well, they are. I *do* want to meet Geraldine's husband and her children, and they've invited me down to Cornwall to do that. But it's not just that. I need an income and I can earn it here. I'll enjoy working with Phillip and Bea, I belong here, Connie, just as you belong in Hobart.'

Connie is silent for a moment, shaking her head. 'I can't believe you're being so selfish,' she says.

Flora can't resist a slight laugh at this. '*I'm* being selfish, am I? Well, okay, if that's how you want to see it. But try to understand what this is like for me. For years I've had no family, now, suddenly, I have two – yours and Geraldine's – and I hope to make the most of both of them.'

'So when *will* you come?'

'As I said, I'm not sure yet, probably quite a bit later in the year. Have you decided what you're going to tell Andrew and Kerry about all this?'

Connie's eyes open wide, and she looks at Flora in amazement. 'I told you yesterday, I won't be telling them anything at all. It's nothing to do with them.'

Flora is so shocked that as she opens her mouth to speak she catches her breath and has a spasm of coughing. 'You *have* to tell them,' she says, her eyes still watering from the cough. 'Geraldine is their half-sister, they have a right to know. They'd want to know.'

'Never,' Connie says. 'They must never know. This is nothing whatsoever to do with my family, Flora.'

Flora sits very still staring at her across the table. This is a side of Connie that she had not seen until yesterday, a side she doesn't like at all. Is this who she really is now, Flora wonders, this rigid, self-righteous person who wants everything her own way? It's as though she's channelling Gerald. How can she have convinced herself that Flora would live there? How can she not see the damage she is about to do? 'So, effectively, you will do to Geraldine what Gerald did to me – pull up the drawbridge and cut her off from that side of her family?'

'It's not the same,' Connie says.

'Why not? Explain it to me.'

'I shouldn't have to. And, Flora, you are not to tell them either, not in an email nor when you come to visit. Not ever, do you understand?'

Flora stares at Connie, thinking that despite the years of their friendship there is so little that she knows of who she is now.

'I can't agree to that,' she says. 'I won't be involved in that sort of deception. Gerald's behaviour damaged my life, Connie. It isolated me, ruptured our friendship, and cut me off from my family. Have you ever stopped to think how hard it has been for me? And the hardest part was not about Gerald but about you – the fact that you never fought for me. You just gave in and went along with Gerald's cruelty and selfishness. I have struggled to get past this and forgive you, Connie; it wasn't easy but I got there in the end. Now you're asking me to be part of something equally dishonest and selfish, and I won't. I won't meet your family while hiding this, so I won't be heading your way until I can be completely honest and open with Kerry and Andrew about Geraldine and her family.'

# Twenty-seven

'So here's the plan,' Andrew says, looking straight at Brooke.

She waits expectantly, thinking he looks a bit dodgy, as though whatever he's going to say might be one of those sanitised parent versions of the truth designed to 'protect' her by keeping her out of the picture. They've obviously decided something without her.

It's Tuesday lunchtime and they are back at the house, drinking tea and eating sandwiches that she and Kerry had made when they got back from collecting her dad from the hospital. She'd been ecstatic when the MRI showed that his neck was intact and the doctor said he could go home. Brooke helps herself to another sandwich and waits for him to say whatever he's going to say. She's dreadfully tired and Kerry says it's a combination of relief and delayed shock, but Brooke doesn't care because everything is okay now, back to normal. Better than normal, really, because Auntie Kerry and her dad and Uncle Chris all seem to be friends again, just like they were years ago, and last night her Nan had rung from England to say she'd be back on Friday – almost two weeks earlier than she'd planned. 'That's brilliant, Nan,' Brooke had said, 'I can't wait. It's going to be great staying with you.'

She'd almost rushed in and asked about living there but something had made her hold back. And afterwards, when she was lying in bed, she realised that it wasn't just the fact that her dad had told her that she was to wait 'til Nan got back before talking to her about it that had stopped her. It was that she realised she might not want that after all. She thought of her dad, the bike ride, how it had felt – like the start of something, a new life really. About how, as they'd been cycling along she'd imagined them doing that often, and even if her mum wouldn't cycle with them she might meet them somewhere for breakfast or coffee. She imagined herself getting on the bus to meet her mum and go shopping, and going back to stay with her at night or over the weekend. What she wanted, she'd thought then, was just to visit Nan, stay with her sometimes, practise her French, have a little life there as well as her big life in Melbourne.

Andrew looks down at his sandwich. 'Kerry wants to be back in Hobart in time to help Farah and Erin get the house ready for Nan,' he says. 'And she wants to meet her at the airport. So we thought we could get you both on a flight to Hobart tomorrow morning, and Chris and I will meet Linda at the airport late in the afternoon and tell her about Zachary. We need to be there for her because she might need some help back at the house. Then we'll fly over to join you at the weekend.'

Brooke is silent for a moment, then shakes her head. 'I think I should go with you to meet Mum.'

There is silence around the table. Brooke can feel the tension and senses that they all want her out of the way. 'I want Mum to know that I'm not grumpy with her anymore. And . . . well, I need to say sorry for being horrible to her.'

The three adults exchange glances. It's clear they are into the protection racket again.

'Look,' Brooke goes on, 'I know she's going to be upset and I know there's stuff you're not telling me because you think I can't take it. Well, I can. I want to see Mum and I think she'll want to see me.'

Silence again. Andrew messes with his sandwich, clears his throat as though he's about to speak and then changes his mind.

'Brooke's got a point,' Kerry says. 'We thought this would be the right thing but it's not. She needs to see Linda and vice versa.'

'Yes . . . yes, okay, that makes sense,' Andrew says wearily, fiddling with his neck brace. And Brooke thinks that he looks as though coming home has been more than he can handle.

Chris nods. 'Good decision.'

Kerry leans forward and puts her hand on Brooke's shoulder. 'But you must understand that Linda is probably going to be very upset.'

'I know that, Auntie Kerry, and that's why I think I should be here.'

'Sometimes I think you're fifteen going on thirty-five,' Chris says.

'Tell me about it,' her dad says, rolling his eyes.

'Linda will be so happy to see you there, Brooke,' Kerry says. 'But I'm going back to Hobart tomorrow morning. It'll be a crush with all of us there this weekend, and I want to help get it sorted. And I have some bridges to build with Mum. I really want to be at the airport to meet her on Friday morning, just like you want to be there for your mum tomorrow.'

\*

Connie watches as her suitcase disappears out of sight behind the flaps of the conveyor belt, then slips the boarding pass into her bag, rides the escalator to the next floor and joins the queue of people lining up to pass through the security checks. She waits, numbed into patience as the sea of passengers in front of her crawls onwards, until she can put her phone and iPad in a plastic tray, her handbag in another, and as she passes through the detector to collect them on the other side, she feels she is passing through the point of no return. She has walked away from an unacceptable situation, and each time she reminds herself of this she feels first a sense of relief and then a deep unease.

On Sunday afternoon she had left the café seething with hurt and anger. There was nothing more she could say to Flora and she couldn't bear to sit there and listen to her speaking about those people as her family. But all she could do was to give Flora time to realise how unreasonable and hurtful she had been, and there was one very clear way to demonstrate that to her. She had walked briskly back to the hotel, booked another room for herself, told the desk clerk to let Ms Hawkins know her new room number and asked for a porter to help her move her things. It would, she thought, be the sort of shock that Flora needed to make her see sense, and it would elicit an apology, which would be the start of a rather different conversation.

Connie had made herself comfortable, sitting on the new bed with her book resting on her knees, and waited. But Flora didn't come. In fact there was no word from her as the evening wore on. Was this to be a battle of wills? Connie wondered. How long would it last? Something had to happen before she set off for the airport on Tuesday. She undressed, got into bed and lay there stiff with hurt and anger until she eventually fell into a troubled sleep riven with disturbing dreams that she was unable to remember the following morning.

She had ordered room-service for breakfast and ate it miserably, the anger having abated in the night, leaving her feeling bleak but still immovable. It was ten o'clock when the chambermaid appeared to clean the room and Connie opted for fresh air. She crossed the street into the square and walked back to the café. They had used it as a meeting point all the time they had been in London, so if Flora wanted to find her she'd know where to look. And she sat there, trying to read the paper, waiting and hoping to see Flora walking towards her past the fountain. But still Flora didn't come. And so Connie decided to do some last minute shopping.

Later she hovered briefly in the hotel lobby, considering her next move, but soon decided that it was not her job to make the first move. Flora was in the wrong and it should be she who offered the olive branch. She took the lift up to her own room where she began to pack her suitcase. But time was running out, and so, in what felt like desperation, she called Phillip and asked him to meet her for dinner. He sounded uneasy at first, as if he feared being dragged into her argument with Flora.

'I just don't want to spend my last evening in London alone,' she said.

And so he agreed to meet her at the restaurant where they'd had dinner that first night. When she arrived he was already ensconced in his corner, and stood up to greet her.

'Yes, I have seen her,' Phillip said when, after ten minutes of slightly awkward but uncontentious conversation, Connie asked him if he'd seen Flora. 'I think you know that she came to see me on Sunday about the job. And this morning she came to the shop to see both Bea and me to sort out the details.'

She nodded, hoping for more, but Phillip turned his attention to the spaghetti that the waiter had just put in front of him.

'So did she say anything about what happened?'

'Connie, you said you wanted company on your last evening,' he said. 'The rest you need to sort out with Flora.'

She'd flushed with embarrassment. 'I'm sorry, you're right, but could we just talk about the situation – what happened at The Ivy about . . . well, about . . . ?'

'You mean about Bea and Gerald's daughter?'

It shocked her that he coupled their names together so lightly and she caught her breath, and simply nodded.

'If there are things you want to know I'm not sure that it's my place to tell you.'

'It's just that nobody's told me anything.'

Phillip gave a dry laugh. 'No one had a chance.'

'I know, I know, but you must see what a shock it was, how insulting and hurtful. And then Flora siding with Bea and . . . and . . .'

'Can't you even bring yourself to say her name, Connie?'

She swallowed and looked away. 'Why should I have to?'

'Why should you not? None of this is her fault. You seem to see yourself as the victim in this. If that's so then it's a choice you're making, and while I understand that it was a shock and you find the situation difficult, there are no different *sides* in this; it's not war, unless you declare it. No one set out to hurt or insult you, far from it. Frankly, Connie, this is what you make of it.'

'And frankly, Phillip, you are sounding remarkably like Flora,' she'd said sharply. 'I thought we were friends – our conversations, the night at the opera. I trusted you.'

He put down his fork then. 'I thought we were friends too, Connie; we still can be. But friendship doesn't guarantee agreement on everything.' He paused a moment, apparently studying her face which she knew was flushed with emotion. 'Bea is a dear friend – my oldest friend – and I love Geraldine like a daughter. It was painful to see them hurt and insulted.'

Connie's heart was beating very fast, so fast that she was giddy, and her face was burning. It was unbelievable that they were all ranged against her like this. She had expected more of Phillip, who had seemed to understand her so well, who had made her feel attractive, sexy even, something she hadn't felt for years. 'It's me that's hurt by this,' she says, her voice shaky now.

'I'm sorry you're hurt. I understand that it's been a terrible shock, but are you able to put yourself in their situation, think about what it means to them?'

She shrugs. 'What else did they expect, that I'd be over the moon and welcome a new illegitimate addition to my family?'

'I assume they thought, as I did, and as I believe Flora did, that you would be shocked and upset, but that you'd understand. All those years ago Gerald walked away, and then years later you walked away too. Can you imagine how that felt?'

All Connie could feel then was confusion and, briefly, a stab of fear that perhaps she was in the wrong, but she pushed that thought away as fast as it had arrived. 'And so I suppose you agree with Flora that I should go home and announce this to my children and expect them to accept this woman as their half-sister?'

'She *is* their half-sister, whether you and they accept her or not.'

She pushed her plate away and dropped her napkin on top of it. 'I need to go,' she said, standing up. 'This is just making things worse. I enjoyed the time we spent together, Phillip, it helped me to feel normal again. What you said about the roads not taken, the way you said it, it helped a lot. So I'm sorry we've ended up like this.'

Phillip got up and walked around the table to face her. He put his hands on her upper arms, and leaned forward to kiss her cheek. 'I'm sorry too, and I hope you'll find your way through this, Connie, I really do, for everyone's sake, but most of all for your own.' He picked up a rectangular package in Tonkin's gift-wrapping with the signature black ribbon. 'A small gift,' he'd said, handing it to her. 'The book I mentioned when we were at the opera. Perhaps it will occupy some of your journey home.'

\*

The following morning, after a poor night's sleep, Connie had put the last few things into her suitcase and was wondering how to kill the remaining hours before she left for the airport.

She flicked through the papers looking for a movie or an exhibition but nothing really attracted her. Sighing, she tossed the paper aside and walked to the window, where she saw Flora making her way through the square towards the café. Connie leapt to her feet, pulled on her shoes, grabbed her jacket and headed for the lifts.

'I wondered if you'd be here,' Flora said as Connie sat down on the other side of the table. 'That's why I came.'

'I came yesterday hoping to find you here,' Connie said.

Flora hesitated. 'I'm sorry that . . .'

'It's okay,' Connie cut in, 'you don't need to apologise. I realised you just needed time.'

Flora cleared her throat. 'I wasn't apologising,' she said, 'I was about to say that I'm sorry you found it necessary to move out of the room, and that it seems we're going to part on these terms.'

Connie's anger started to rise but it was tempered by the chill in Flora's tone, the distance, her air of resignation. 'It doesn't have to be that way,' she said.

Flora looked at her, tilted her head to one side. 'No,' she said, 'it really doesn't.'

There was silence as the waiter arrived with Flora's coffee and Connie ordered one for herself. Clearly there was to be no apology and Connie, shaken by its absence, was left with nowhere to turn.

'I think all we can do is to accept that we have totally different views about what's happened and what should happen from here on,' Flora said. 'We should try and respect each other's position, and then talk later, when you are home, when we've both cooled down.'

Connie nodded, watching the birds darting in and out of the fountain, shaking their feathers. 'All right,' she said, 'let's do that. Although I don't see a way back from this, Flora, as I won't be changing my opinion. And it seems that you aren't prepared to make any concession to my situation.'

'You know, Connie, you always did take the slightest dispute and push it to the absolute limits. And you always felt you were the injured party. Are you aware of that? I've been making concessions to your situation since the day I arrived home from India and found you engaged to Gerald. I've kept my opinions to myself when you've told me about Gerald the saint and Gerald the sinner. I haven't interfered, I haven't challenged you and I didn't challenge him when he told me to leave. None of that was easy. I could have stayed in Hobart and been a bloody great thorn in his side but I didn't, out of respect and love for you. Meanwhile, you did nothing, you let Gerald have his way and you never fought for me. But Gerald's gone now, and I'm sick of accommodating your situation. You came to France and I was thrilled to see you again, but I knew it would be different, because we had both changed. Our friendship needed work – it needed updating, it needed me to forgive the fact that you let Gerald determine what would happen. I thought we were getting there but . . . well, now I don't know. I have my own life, Connie. I haven't spent all these years waiting for you. Now I find I have some family here and I am going to enjoy them. I want us, you and me, to get back what we once had, before Gerald changed everything but, frankly, the way things are now, I can't see how that's going to happen.'

*

The boarding call jolts Connie from her thoughts, and she gets to her feet, checking her hand baggage and throwing her coat over her arm. So this is it, this is the end, she thinks. London, England, all that it represents is over, soured by things that happened decades ago. And she joins the line of passengers waiting to board, trying to think of this moment as a new beginning, but unable to rid herself of the bitter taste of the last few days.

# Twenty-eight

'Why don't you go and sit down,' Chris says. 'There're plenty of seats over there and you'll still be able to see her coming through.'

Andrew nods, hobbles over to the seats and cautiously lowers his injured nether regions. When the doctor had told him that he could go home he'd been over the moon and couldn't get out of the hospital quickly enough. Rashly, he now understands, he'd thought he would be fine to just get up and go. Reality was more painful and disorienting. His neck was very sore and he has to wear the brace for another week – not that he feels like removing it now, in fact he feels his head might drop off if he does. His bum is very sore and the stitches are starting to pull and itch – the doctor has arranged for him to have them removed at the hospital in Hobart next week – and the remaining legacy of three days on his back is a sense of unworldliness. The last thing he wants is to have to help Linda get through the next couple of days.

'Are you okay, Dad?' Brooke asks, wandering over to him. 'Do you need water or anything?'

He shakes his head cautiously. 'No, I'm fine, thanks. Just finding it all a bit weird. Um, when you talked to Nan, you didn't say anything about living there, did you?'

331

Brooke sighs. 'No, I didn't, you said not to.'

'Good. You see, I know you really want it . . .' he hesitates. It's hardly the time or place to start this conversation, with Chris hovering by the barrier and Linda about to materialise off her flight, but he's into it now. 'But I'm really not happy about it, Brooke. I think you need to stay here for school, it's a bad time to change . . .'

'I know,' she nods.

He's surprised but carries on. 'And I don't want to get heavy about it but your Mum and I are both here even if we're not together. I don't think Zachary's going to be in the mix anymore, so I think . . .'

'Yes,' she says, 'I know. I should stay here with you, see Mum, stay with her sometimes.'

'Oh,' Andrew says, surprised by this sudden change. 'I thought we'd be having an argument about this.'

She shakes her head. 'I need to stay here. I want to be here with you. I like it in the cottage. And, anyway, who's going to look after you next time you fall off your bike?'

He laughs. 'I was thinking *I* should face up to my responsibilities and look after *you*. But I'd also miss you dreadfully if you moved over there. For the last few years I've been disappearing into work so I didn't have to deal with the situation at home. I want to change that now, maybe even change my job.'

Brooke leans against him. 'I love being in the new house with you. Except for the Donna thing, it's the best it's been for ages. Anyway I'd miss you, and Mum too, and if you're not living together you might start behaving like normal parents.'

Andrew thinks it may be the painkillers that make him want to burst into tears but he swallows the urge and takes her hand. 'Well, I think we'll both be trying to do that. Although I suspect that what's happened over the last few years is not uncommon. It was just Zachary that brought things to a head and made it worse for all of us.'

'I was thinking,' Brooke went on, 'that maybe I could just stay with Nan in the holidays, when you and Mum are both at work? I love it there, and Nan and I like lots of the same things.'

'The flight's coming through now,' Chris says, sauntering over to them. He looks at Brooke. 'You did text her about Andrew's neck brace, didn't you, Brooke?'

'You've asked me that three times, Uncle Chris,' Brooke says, 'and I've told you that I did – I told her that Dad's neck was okay but he was wearing a brace and is still a bit wobbly. She texted back that she'd pop over and see him. Remember?'

He grins. 'Sorry, darl, yes I do remember now. Just a bit jittery. I've always been a bit scared of your mother so I want to make sure we've got it right. And she's in for a much worse shock than a neck brace, I suppose.'

Brooke slips her arm through his. 'It'll be fine,' she says, smiling up at him. 'She'll be upset, but it'll make it easier for her to kick Zachary out.'

Chris turns sideways to look at her. 'Sometimes, Brooke, you really knock my socks off. Other times you annoy the hell out of me but this isn't one of them.'

Brooke grins. 'It was great you and Auntie Kerry coming over, like . . . well, like things used to be. Oh look, there she is!' And she pulls Chris back towards the barrier leaving Andrew on his seat.

Linda is pushing her way determinedly through the crowd of arriving passengers, smartly dressed as ever, claret hair making her stand out from the crowd and, Andrew thinks, a little flushed and bright eyed, as though she might have had a few drinks on the flight. She stops abruptly as she spots Brooke, and Andrew can see from her face that this was exactly the right decision. He gets to his feet and makes his way towards them.

'How wonderful,' Linda says, hugging Brooke, then patting Chris on the arm. 'What a lovely surprise, but what . . .' she hesitates, her pleasure changing to anxiety. 'Oh my god, is Andrew worse or something, is that why you're here?'

'I'm just a bit the worse for wear,' Andrew says appearing alongside her.

'Oh my god – you poor thing, Andrew, you look awful.' She puts her hands on his upper arms and stares into his face. 'Should you be up? Shouldn't you be in bed?' She pauses again. 'Something's wrong, isn't it? That's why you're all here.'

Silence. The two men exchange a look.

'We want you to come back to our place,' Brooke says. 'Stay the night, you can have my bed.'

Linda looks from one to the other. 'Why would I do that? There *is* something wrong, I can see there is. It's Zach, isn't it? What's he done now?'

Andrew looks desperately at Chris, who shrugs. 'Your call, mate.'

Brooke picks up Linda's computer bag and takes her mother's arm. 'He's gone ballistic, Mum, but it's all going to be okay. Let's get your luggage and go home and then we can tell you all about it.' And she steers Linda away towards the baggage carousel.

Andrew and Chris exchange a different kind of glance. 'Imagine what she'll be like at thirty,' Andrew says.

*

As the train begins to move Flora and Bea edge their way along the central aisle to their seats, and Flora, a good foot taller than Bea, lifts their bags onto the rack, and settles into her seat, excitement vying with a little trepidation about what lies ahead.

'I thought we weren't going to make it,' she says. 'I love trains, still think they're the best, most romantic way to travel.'

'Me too,' Bea says. 'A train always seems like the start of an adventure. Although I guess it only feels like that because we don't have to go to work on one every day.'

'I may have to,' Flora says. 'Depending on where I end up living.'

'I bet you'll find somewhere that's not too far away. Phil and I have quite good contacts. While you're sorting things out in France I'll start putting out feelers, then when you come back we can have a look at what's available. If you'd like some company while you do it, I mean.'

'I'd love company,' Flora says, 'and now that I've made the decision I feel really good about living in London again.' She shifts in her seat, stretching her long legs out at an angle. 'But right now I'm just excited about going to Cornwall.'

Bea is silent for a moment. 'I'm so sorry about Connie. I suppose she's well on her way by now?'

Flora nods. 'She may be in Singapore as we speak. She was going to make an overnight stop to break the journey.'

'So how do you feel about it all, about . . . ?'

'Disappointed,' Flora cuts in, not waiting for her to finish, thankful for the chance to talk about it. 'Disappointed in her. You know, the day after it all happened she moved out of our room and took one on another floor. She did it while I was out with you and Phillip at the shop. I think it was supposed to make me feel guilty, but all it did was make me cross. If she thought I was going to beg her to come back she was absolutely wrong.' It's a relief to say it – to hear herself saying it and sounding rational after the hurt and confusion she's felt since Connie left.

'It does seem a bit childish. What *did* you do?'

'Nothing. Just ignored it. Behaved as though nothing had happened. And you know what? I kept thinking that it was the sort of thing Gerald would have done – stalked out all haughty, booked a new room and waited for the offending party to seek him out with a grovelling apology. The old Connie, the Connie I knew, would never have done that, but then she would never have walked out of the restaurant in the first place. That's part of the problem, I think.

We each thought that the other would be the same person we knew all that time ago, but that was unrealistic. We wouldn't have expected it if we hadn't been in touch all that time; we would each have assumed that the other would be in some ways different. But we were often in touch on the phone and later we could see each other online and that's deceptive. I held a lot of myself back all that time and so, I think, did Connie.'

Bea nods. 'So where to from here?'

'I love Connie, I always felt she was like a sister, and I want that back, but not if it comes at the expense of getting to know you, Bea, and Geraldine and her family. I shouldn't have to choose and I hope that when Connie's home and had time to think about things a bit more, she'll see that too.'

'And if she doesn't?'

Flora hesitates. 'If she doesn't then I suppose we'll still be in touch, still be friends, but in an even more limited way than before.' She stares briefly out of the window, then turns back to Bea. 'I've told her that unless she's honest with Kerry and Andrew about this, unless she tells them they have a half-sister, then I won't go to Hobart.'

'Oh, Flora, you don't have to do that for us,' Bea says, leaning forward anxiously.

'I'm not doing it for you, Bea. I'm doing it for myself. Gerald forced me out of his family, and alienated me from our parents. He pretended I didn't exist. I know Connie hated that, but she colluded with it by never taking a stand. I'm not now going to collude with *her* in pretending that Geraldine doesn't exist.'

'Well, it's a high price you're paying,' Bea says. 'I hope you won't regret it.'

'I believe I'm doing the right thing, so if I end up the loser then I'll just have to deal with it. The guy with the refreshment trolley is heading our way. D'you want anything?'

They order cups of tea and biscuits and consume them in

silence, as the grimy backyards of the suburbs give way to small, colourful gardens, grassy banks and rolling country-side. Flora gazes out of the window, the steady rhythm of the train helping her to organise her thoughts. There have been several times during her recent weeks with Connie when she has been jolted by the impact of Gerald's way of thinking on the woman she once knew, and none has been more obvious than Connie's reaction to the present situation.

The Gerald that Flora remembers managed his family by command and control. He issued orders, even if they were sometimes masked as requests. And he controlled what was done and how, what was discussed, who knew what and what was kept silent or hidden. It had reminded her of their own father, who only had to say, 'I don't want to discuss this, you will not refer to it again' to put an end to questions, challenges and arguments. As a child she had found it first terrifying and then oppressive, and when, as an adult in Hobart, she saw Gerald doing the same thing, it had shocked her. Since then it has surprised her when, in her emails and conversations with Connie, it's been clear that Gerald's system is still in place, even after he was no longer physically and mentally able to exercise control of it himself. The hardest thing for Flora is that some years ago, when Gerald was a complete invalid, when he couldn't communicate and no one knew how much, if anything, he understood, Connie had maintained the wall of silence that kept Kerry and Andrew believing that their aunt was guilty of some terrible crime – if they even thought about her at all. And what Flora wonders now is just how much of Gerald has been absorbed into Connie, and whether she is in fact capable of recapturing her old self, which had been one of the reasons for her visit.

Flora sighs. She finds it hard not to keep returning to this, although what she really wants now is just to look ahead: ahead to the coming weekend in Cornwall, and then beyond to the strange liberation of winding up her life in Port d'Esprit. She has sent two emails to Suzanne letting her know what she has decided, and that she will be back to pack up her things. Suzanne hasn't replied and that doesn't surprise Flora. Suzanne had already decided what she wanted before Flora left; all this does is make it easier for her and Xavier to go ahead with their plans. A different sort of friendship will grow from this, Flora thinks; one enriched by their years of living and working together, but no longer distorted by that.

How strange that Connie had assumed that she would want to live again in Australia, to pack up all the fine muddled strands of her past here and file it away, even try to recapture a relationship with Denise. Had she *really* assumed that? Had she thought it would be a possible or easy thing for her to do? Or was it perhaps just a projection of what she wanted for herself – someone to fill the gap left by Gerald's death? Flora pictures Connie now, perhaps dozing in her seat above the clouds, and wonders how she is coping with all that's happened. And she knows herself to be the fortunate one for she has found something new, new people, a new life, a new family, while Connie must try to repair what she left behind. But she has her children and grandchildren. And Flora hopes that they will still have their friendship, but only Connie can decide that now. And she closes her eyes and feels a lump in her throat, for what they have shared and what may now be irrevocably damaged, or perhaps completely lost.

# Twenty-nine

*C*hris goes in first, cautiously unlocking the door with Linda's key, although it's pretty obvious there's no one there, just an overflowing garbage bin on the path and a few empty beer cans scattered among the rose bushes. But there is no car in the drive, no sign or sound of life, just silence and the debris of the party or parties.

'All clear, I think,' Chris calls from inside, and Andrew follows him in. 'I'll check upstairs,' Chris continues.

Brooke peers in through the front door and picks her way past a crate of empty bottles and a tatty pair of stilettoes. 'Look, Mum,' she calls. 'Zachary's sofa's gone from Dad's study.'

Linda joins her at the study door. 'Oh my god, what a mess. And what's that sticky stuff on the floor?' She pauses. 'Everything of his has gone.'

And Brooke thinks she can hear the relief in her mother's voice.

Last night, once Chris had told her mum what they found at the house the previous weekend, Linda was ready for a fight and wanted to come back here straight away, but they persuaded her to wait until this morning.

'More chance of his not being there,' Andrew had said, pouring her another gin and tonic. 'And right now the gin is talking. By the time you've finished this one you'll be crying, so we're going to wait until tomorrow.' He'd been right about the crying. It began halfway through that drink when Brooke told her what she had learned about Zachary. She'd dreaded having to do it and her dad had said he'd tell her, but Brooke knew she had to do it herself.

'I'm really sorry, Mum,' she said, watching as Linda's face crumbled. 'I didn't know what to do, I didn't even tell Dad at first . . .'

'And thank god you did,' Linda had said, her words slurring a little. 'Brooke, you have nothing to be sorry for. I'm so sorry I put you through all this. You've been brave and generous, darling, but you must hate me.'

Brooke, always embarrassed by the evidence that anyone, let alone her mother, has drunk too much, blushed at this. 'I'm here because I *love* you,' she'd said quietly.

There was quite a bit more crying and some raging anger before they finally persuaded Linda to go to bed and soon after that they pulled out the sofa bed and Chris flopped down on that.

Brooke was just coming out of the bathroom heading for her own room when Andrew flicked off the kitchen lights and followed her along the passage.

'Are you sure you'll be all right on that bedroll on the floor? You can have my room, you know.'

'Honestly, Dad, sometimes you're really hopeless. You've just come out of hospital and you're wearing a neck brace and have stitches in your bum. Do you really think I'm going to let you sleep on a camping mattress?'

'Well, I . . .'

She gave him a gentle shove. 'Shut up, it's fine. It'll be good for me to be in there with Mum in case she wakes up and is upset. I can talk to her. That mattress is pretty comfortable too.'

'Okay.' Her dad stood there for a moment, nodding, then stretched out his arms and pulled her to him. 'You were brilliant tonight, Brooke, right from the minute Mum arrived. Thanks for staying and for being here for her and for me. I'm sorry for . . . well, for everything, things are going to get better from now on, I promise.'

She'd nodded then, exhausted suddenly by all that had happened, not just that evening but by the burden of the last few months, and within minutes she had flopped down onto the mattress, pulled her sleeping bag over her and was asleep. She hadn't stirred until she heard the men's voices floating out from the kitchen this morning.

Now, from the top of the stairs back at what used to be her home, she stares around her at the chaos. The mess in the study is nothing compared to this and Brooke's legs feel weak with shock. She makes for the breakfast bar and hauls herself up onto the only stool that doesn't have food or liquid spilled on it.

'Well, at least he . . . or someone else . . . has cleared up the vomit,' Chris says. 'And the body under the table has disappeared.' He walks over to Brooke. 'You still okay, kiddo?'

She nods. 'Suppose so, but it's just so sad. All Mum's stuff, she's going to kill him. Look at it . . .' Brooke's voice trails off as she takes in the scene: stains all over the furniture, cigarette burns, sticky stuff spilled on the table, stamped out cigarette butts on the floor, the kitchen strewn with old food, dirty glasses and crockery.

Chris looks at her for a moment, then runs back down to where Linda and Andrew are talking in the hall.

'It's pretty awful up there, Linda,' Brooke hears him say. 'You might prefer to just stay here. Let Andrew and me deal with it.'

Linda takes a deep breath and shakes her head. 'Thanks, Chris, but I need to see it, and the bedrooms too.'

And Brooke hears her mother's steps on the stairs and slides off the stool to meet her.

'Oh my god, how could he!' Linda gasps. 'How *could* he do this? Didn't he have any respect for me?'

'It's not about you, Linda,' Andrew says, coming up beside them. 'This is just who he is.'

But Brooke can see that he is profoundly shocked at what he sees. They go up to the mezzanine, from where the chaos below looks worse than ever, and open the doors to the bedrooms. The beds are a mess, the linen stained with alcohol, a lamp smashed, and Linda's jewellery spread out across the dressing table, some pieces crushed and trodden into the carpet.

'How did he manage to make so much mess in one week?' Linda says. 'I mean, he was always high maintenance when it came to keeping the place clean and tidy, but this . . .'

'I reckon he had people back again after Kerry and I left,' Chris says. 'There are more bottles, more mess, it's worse than when we were here on Sunday morning.'

Linda sinks down to sit on the edge of the bed. 'Why couldn't I see it?' she wails, looking at Andrew and Brooke. 'You saw it, both of you, I know you did, you saw through him but I just believed in him.' She sinks her head into her hands.

Andrew sits down beside her and takes her hand. 'Look, you were unhappy and lonely. We both were. Zachary would have sensed that, it was something he could prey on and he was very good at it. But he's gone now, and we're still here, Brooke and me and Chris and Kerry, the rest of the family. You're going to get back from this, Linda.'

Brooke wanders out to her old room, which bears no resemblance to the place she left behind. It's sad, but in a way it's also a relief. It's over, not just the awful stuff with Zachary but the long months of her parents sniping at each other, the tense painful silences, the furious looks, the snide remarks, the excessive, artificial politeness. They're never going to get back together but at least they might be friends now, and that will make things a whole lot better.

Chris sticks his head around the door. 'Come on, Brooke,' he says. 'Let's get those two out of here and back in the car. Nothing to be gained by hanging around.'

Brooke nods and follows him to the other bedroom.

'You all go,' Linda says. 'I'd better start on clearing this place up.'

'Don't be ridiculous,' Andrew says, getting to his feet. 'We're taking you and Brooke back to the cottage, and then Chris and I are coming back here. I've ordered a locksmith for midday, to change the locks – just to be on the safe side. And I've organised some heavy duty cleaners to come in then too. This time tomorrow you can come back, have a look around and work out what you want to do. You can stay on at the cottage while Brooke and I are in Hobart. But there's no way we're leaving you here alone now.'

He steers Linda down the stairs and out to the car.

Brooke takes a last look around at what used to be her home. 'I hate him,' she says, turning to Chris. 'I hate him so much that I want to kill him.'

Chris takes her hand. 'Me too, but we've got to help your mum get through this. Your dad and I are relying on you to look after her this afternoon, make her rest, or take her shopping or something while we get this lot sorted out. Now, let's go, we'll find somewhere nice for coffee, then drop you off and then Andrew and I will come back. And I can promise you, Brooke, that tosser is not going to get away with any of this if I have anything to do with it.'

\*

Connie is thankful that she'd taken the travel agent's advice and stopped off in Singapore. A good sleep followed by a swim has made a world of difference and as they begin the descent to Hobart she feels she has energy left for the culture shock of home. But as she stares down through the thinning clouds sadness takes over. Thank goodness for Farah and the girls, and then on Saturday Brooke will be there too. Her head spins with jumbled thoughts – so much to do in the house, all the things she left undone. Gerald's study to be cleared out for a start; how she dreads the thought of that. Are there other secrets tucked away in there, secrets from their years together, things she'd rather not know, just as she would rather not have known about Bea's daughter? And then there's Flora, stubborn, selfish Flora. What happens now?

Three months ago she was convinced that now Gerald was gone, Flora would come home. It had never occurred to her that for Flora Tasmania was no longer home, and that she did not share a vision of them living here together like sisters. What can she say to the family without revealing the wounds inflicted that day at The Ivy, wounds that are still both raw and perplexing?

The winter sun is sharp and brilliant as she descends the aircraft steps and follows the other passengers across the tarmac and along the covered walkway into the terminal. And that's when she sees her – Kerry, waving to her, smiling, walking towards her, and Connie is swept forward on a great surge of love and relief.

'But what are you doing here?' she asks once they have retrieved her bags and are heading to the car park. 'Is something wrong?'

'No, Mum, everything's fine, but a lot's happened and I wanted to be here to see you, to talk to you, before I have to share you with the others.' She swings Connie's bag into the boot and then opens the passenger door for her. 'How would you feel about not going straight home? I'd like to talk to you before we get back. You see, it's not just Farah and the girls there, but Mia and Ryan are there too, and Erin as well. Could you cope with going for a coffee somewhere, or even some lunch if you're not too tired?'

And as she looks more closely at her daughter Connie sees that there is a difference and it's in her eyes. The eyes that have for so long burned with hurt or anger or both are actually smiling. Something in Kerry has changed, but she also obviously has something on her mind. 'What a good idea. I'm fine so why don't we go up to that little café on Mount Nelson? It's near home anyway and I've always loved the view.'

The café is busy but they find a single vacant table tucked in a corner by the window and order coffee and muffins, and Connie, who declined breakfast on the flight, immediately tucks into hers.

'You're not eating,' she says, looking up. 'What's the matter, are you all right, Kerry?'

Kerry nods, wrapping her arms around herself, rocking nervously on her chair. 'Yes . . . well, actually no . . . Mum, I'm so sorry for everything, for the way I've been for ages, while Dad was sick, for not supporting you, for everything really. I was a mess and I dumped it all on you.' Her eyes are full of tears and she brushes them away.

'Darling, don't be upset,' Connie says, taking her hand across the table. 'It wasn't just you, it was me too. I handled it all so badly. I was so worn down by it all and I wasn't there for you . . .'

Kerry shakes her head. 'You were amazing, Mum, I don't know how you did it, and all I did was stand on the sidelines all grumpy and hurt because I wasn't getting attention from either of you. I reverted to being a spoiled teenager.'

Connie nods. 'It's over now, Kerry. It was a nightmare for all of us, and now we have to sort ourselves out and try to get back to where we were before it all . . .'

Kerry puts up a hand to stop her. 'No, Mum, I think you were going to say "where we were before it began", but it goes back further than that. I need to tell you that I know what you did, that you spent your whole life deferring to Dad, and I know you did it for us, for Andrew and me. To avoid rows and people taking sides, and that was a big sacrifice that went on for years, and I'm sorry – I'm so sorry that I never appreciated it. A lot of the time – well, for years really – I was just angry with you for always giving in to him, never taking a stand. I felt you were devaluing yourself. And at the same time I was doing the same thing, always running after Dad, trying to get him to approve of me . . . I'm forty-two, for goodness sake, and at the end, that last day when he died, I felt utter despair because there was no chance that it could ever happen. And all the time you were there . . .'

'Don't, Kerry,' Connie says, leaning closer across the table. 'Don't do this to yourself. I know what was happening for you, but he did approve of you, darling, and he loved you so much and was very proud of you, of both of you. But he never found it easy to show that or say it, or to dish out any praise. The more I think about him the more he puzzles me, Kerry. I feel now, after all these years, as though I hardly knew him. Perhaps I didn't and perhaps that's what kept me on my toes, doing everything he wanted. Now I think he was frightened, frightened all his life.'

'Frightened? But of what?'

Connie smiles. 'Of everything . . . of life, of not being able to control things. Not any one specific thing, but life gener-ally. Perhaps he grew up in fear and never grew out of it. Perhaps that's what made him need to feel he could control the things and the people closest to him.' She shakes her head and picks up her cup. 'Perhaps that's silly . . .'

'No,' Kerry says, frowning with concentration. 'Actually, I think it makes sense.'

They talk more, about Gerald, about the past and about childhood.

'Do you remember the summer that Jennifer came to stay?' Kerry asks eventually.

'I do,' Connie says. 'I always liked Jennifer and you were such good friends and then that summer it all seemed to fall apart in the last ten days or so. I never knew why.'

Kerry hesitates, starts to speak then stops, then starts again and tells her about the day on the beach, almost holding hands with Jennifer, and of Gerald's shadow falling across them, blocking out the sun. 'It was nothing, you know what girls are like, how intense it can get with your best friend.' And she went on to talk about Gerald's warning and the fear it instilled in her.

Connie is silent, realising now where this is leading.

'Did you know?' Kerry asks.

Connie shakes her head. 'I didn't. I wish you could have told me, I would have talked to him.'

'I know,' Kerry says, 'but what I don't understand is why you never talked to him about Flora, and why you never told us, Andrew and me. All that time you let us think she was some sort of criminal. I mean, you must have known years ago that Andrew and I would be fine with it, so why . . . ?'

Connie takes a deep breath, and shakes her head. 'I can't really explain it,' she says, hearing the crack in her voice and pausing to stop herself from crying.

'It's difficult . . . it's been difficult with Flora, who has obviously been deeply hurt by that. I wish I could give you some good reason but the truth is that I was a coward. I never forgot his rage when he turned Flora out, and I just didn't want to open it all up again. As for telling you two – I thought of it often but once again took the easy way out and said nothing.' She sighs. 'I've spent all my life saying nothing about things that matter to me, and now suddenly I'm telling everyone what I think in no uncertain terms, and it's not working out all that well.'

Kerry tilts her head to one side. 'What do you mean?'

Connie feels herself flush and looks away. 'Oh, nothing, it doesn't matter, Kerry. I'm so sick of it all, the past, everything I got wrong. I don't want to think about that now, I want to think about the future and about having everyone back together this weekend.'

\*

Much later, when Kerry, Farah, Erin and the children are in bed, Connie pulls a big scarf around her shoulders against the chill of the wind and goes out onto the bedroom balcony. Beneath her the darkness of the land slopes away to the lights along the river bank curving off towards the city, setting the water alight with their reflections, ruffled by small waves. Everything is familiar, the scent of pine trees east of the boundary, the nocturnal squeaks and rustlings in the garden, the occasional sound of a revving engine in a nearby street, and the old breath of the house itself.

Learning that she was returning to a full house had come as a surprise, as had the news that the rest of the family would be arriving on Saturday, but the welcome from Kerry, Farah and Erin as well as her grandchildren and Farah's daughters had banished her earlier bleakness. And Kerry had been right to take her to a café first, Connie thinks now. So much happened in her absence and they had talked for almost two hours. The news of Kerry's depression had come as a shock. The more she thought about it, the more she felt she ought to have spotted it, and that if she had paid more attention to her daughter instead of Gerald, she could perhaps have helped her. Kerry had told her more about Andrew and Linda, and about Brooke's discovery of Zachary's activities. 'She's been marvellous,' Kerry had said. 'Linda and Andrew may have stuffed up their marriage but they managed to raise a pretty special daughter who's come through looking like the only real grown-up among us!'

As she stands there a light goes out and she glances along the façade of the house to her right. Kerry's old room, which Farah now occupies. Farah. Connie sighs. She hasn't really had a chance yet to talk to her, to talk as they had done during those last few years of Gerald's life. But of course there's plenty of time.

'Stay on for a while, Farah, please,' Connie had asked her on the phone when she called to say she would be home earlier than planned. 'Brooke will be over soon, it would be so nice if you and the girls would stay a few weeks more.' It sounded, she knew, as though she wanted company for Brooke, but in fact she was asking for herself. The house with no one in it was too much for her to contemplate just now.

'What I said about Farah . . .' Kerry had said this morning as they walked away from the café and out to the car. 'It was awful. I didn't mean it, you must know I didn't. I was searching for something else to hit you with, Mum. I'm so ashamed of myself.'

The welcome back at the house had done much to restore Connie's sense of herself. Only Scooter seemed less than thrilled to see her again. Obviously punishing her for her long absence, he had given her a haughty look and stalked off to his bed, ignoring her for the rest of the day.

Later she'd watched with pleasure as they ripped open their gifts, and as the wrappings fell to the floor she remembered the shop in Port d'Esprit where she had bought the traditional Breton dolls for Mia, Lala and Samira, and the game of boules for Ryan, and the dusky interior of the silver jeweller's shop in St Malo where she had found the heavy silver bracelet for Kerry, and a finely etched one for Farah. It all seems such a long time ago; a faded dream shadowed by all that had happened in those last few days in London.

'So when's Auntie Flora coming to stay?' Kerry had asked earlier, and Connie, caught off guard, had flushed and pretended to search for something in her handbag.

'I'm not sure yet,' she'd said, attempting lightness. 'She's leaving Port d'Esprit and going back to England to live, so she needs to sort that out first.'

The wind is colder now and Connie goes back into the bedroom and starts on the tedious task of unpacking her bags, tossing some things into the linen basket, stacking others into drawers and onto shelves or slipping them onto hangers. A small package drops out from the fold of a jumper and she stoops to pick it up, wondering at first what it is, and then remembering the book that Phillip gave her that last evening and which she has not even bothered to unwrap. Later, she thinks, I can't be bothered with it now, and she tosses it into a drawer. Whatever I thought I was doing over there, it's finished now. And she sits down abruptly on the edge of the bed.

The last few months seem just an interlude, balm on that muddled, guilt inducing bruise of grief and relief. What now? She had allowed herself to believe that she could slip Flora into the space that Gerald had occupied for so long. But that was just wishful thinking. Who is she now that she's alone? Her children have survived significant dramas without her help and free of her interference, and they have questions about the past; questions that force her to face up to an image of herself of which she's always been aware, but of which she now feels ashamed. 'I was stuck,' she says aloud. 'All those years I was stuck, paralysed by what Gerald wanted, and I'm still stuck. As stuck in the past and as fearful of the future as I was when he was alive, and somehow I have to find a way to change, to break the mould that he created and find my own way. Find out who I am when I'm not reacting to him. Find out what it's like to be in control of myself.'

# Thirty

It's Thursday morning and the house is empty, the silence, the stillness, almost unnerving. Andrew stands at the front door, watching the tail lights of Connie's car as she stops at the end of the drive, then turns out into the street. Since he, Chris and Brooke arrived on Sunday the place has been all action – in fact it's felt like a big party, and perhaps that's what it was, a celebration of their all being together, different, kinder, more aware of each other, an unspoken agreement to repair what had started to fall apart. And now they're gone. Kerry, Chris, Erin and the children left at dawn on Tuesday for Launceston: Chris to get back for the last few days of term, Erin to pack up ready to join her husband's ship, the children to return to school and Kerry to find her way back to herself in her own home. Farah has gone to work, her girls to the last week of school before the holidays. Andrew was glad he had not insisted Brooke go back to school for the last week of the term. The exams are over and he's sure it is the right thing for them both to be here now, and he's taken some extra leave so that he can stay on a bit longer too. He smiles to himself as he remembers how he'd imagined a big battle over her living in Hobart, but she's such a smart kid, wise beyond her years, and had made her own decision. Now

Liz Byrski

she and Connie have gone shopping and, for the first time since he was released from hospital, Andrew is alone.

He closes the front door and wanders slowly through the house, taking it all in, living his history there in a way he's never done before. In the kitchen he recalls breakfast on school days – cereal, toast, eggs, arguments about sports gear and whether he has put his homework in his bag. He remembers Connie teaching him to make a cake and Gerald showing him some experiment with sand and water and the mess they made on the kitchen table. He stares at the couch with its tiger-patterned blanket, picks it up and feels his father there, smells him, hears his increasingly shaky, unstable voice, feels the touch of those weak and trembling hands. Through the sitting room with its memories of *Dr Who* and test matches on the television, and years of Christmas trees surrounded by presents, into the other living room which had become a bedroom, pausing only to glance at the place where his father spent his last years. It's empty now, the hospital bed, the trolley and hoist, the cupboard where the medication was lined up, all gone. Then up the staircase to his own old room, so different now that it's hard to relate to, and then he pauses at the foot of the staircase to Gerald's study, takes a deep breath, and goes up for the first time in more than a year.

In here it's as though time has stopped. Stopped perhaps five or more years ago when his father was no longer able to manage stairs, no longer able to do any of the things he had done here until then. Piles of papers on the desk, books dusty on the shelves, framed photographs of them all at various ages and stages, the colours already fading, the computer so obviously superseded, and Gerald's eccentric collection of old watches, displayed on rolls of felt on the top of a low bookcase. Andrew stands on a small rust coloured rug in front of the desk where he had often stood waiting for instructions, judgments, praise or punishment. Where he had stood waiting for the caning that Gerald had once threatened for some now forgotten offence, a punishment that was never administered. Decades ago his father had smoked in here, brought work home, done the crossword, dozed on the chaise longue that was uncomfortably short for his long frame, and doubtless hidden when the pressure of parenthood was more than he could handle.

Andrew stares at the chaise, sits on it and lies back, discovering the same uncomfortable broken spring that Kerry had found the day she had lain here. He locks his hands behind his head, resting back on the faded cushion. He has a strange feeling that Gerald is still there, his spirit caught perhaps in the deep folds of the curtains, or watching him from the top of the tallest bookcase. 'So, Dad,' he says aloud. 'What now? Do you know what happened? Well, Linda and I split up. I know you'll think that's all my fault because you liked her so much. You two got on well, didn't you? She was your sort of person, you said so the first time I brought her home. You were right in a way and that might have been part of the problem. But it was only partly my fault and you don't need to know all the details. Anyway, I think it's sorted now. And then I fell off my bike, yeah I know, not the first time. I'm okay, but I landed on a car and then on the kerb, my butt is stitched up and I almost broke my neck. Riding too fast, you see, not paying sufficient attention to the conditions of the bike path and . . . smash, there I was, bouncing around like a shuttlecock. I know you'll want to give me a lecture, I can almost feel you bursting with frustration that you can't tell me what you think. But it doesn't matter, because I know what you think, and you're right – irresponsible, reckless and, worse still, Brooke was with me, very bad parenting.' He pauses, looking around the room for something, lord knows what, a sign, the twitch of a curtain, a paper dislodged from the desk fluttering to the floor, but nothing happens.

'Well, you're right, of course, you were often right, and even when you were wrong I believed you . . . mostly. But there were times . . .' he pauses, sighs, listens, '. . . times when – oh well, it doesn't matter now. You did your best, what more can a boy ask of his father than that he does his best? You loved me, all of us, but you were incapable of saying it and you often had a funny way of showing it. I've wondered if you were happy, Dad – ever. Did your heart sing with joy when you looked at Kerry and me as mine does when I look at Brooke? I don't think it did, and I'm sorry if you didn't have that because it's a feeling like no other.'

Andrew takes another deep breath and stands up. 'I know so little about you and that's my fault as well as yours.' He hesitates, feeling suddenly awkward, embarrassed, as though any minute Gerald will emerge, laughing at his stupidity and telling him to bugger off and do something useful. He looks around again. 'I loved you, I should have told you that when I still had the chance, and you should have told me too. But it's too late now. So I just came to say goodbye, and . . . well, rest in peace, Dad.' And he stands for a moment in the silence and then walks quickly to the door, runs down the stairs and out through the kitchen into the bright cold air of the garden, buries his face in his hands and, for the first time since Gerald's death, he sobs violently for what seems like a very long time.

Back in the house he splashes cold water on his face and then wanders through the rooms again, feeling lighter than he has for a long time, feeling his spirits lift as though he has shed a burden. In the lounge he runs his finger along the shelf of CDs, searching for something other than Connie's classics and jazz, and finds it, something of his own left behind years ago. Smiling, he slips the disc into the slot, turns up the volume and waits, feet wide apart, head thrown back, grasping the remote control in lieu of a microphone. And here come the drums, then the guitars, and he is Freddie Mercury striding across the stage at Wembley Stadium, in a white singlet. He knows the words, he knows the moves, all he needs now is for Freddie to break out the first line, and he's there with him, strutting, swinging, singing 'I want to break free . . .'

*

Suzanne is not at the airport; there is no sign of the yellow Renault, which, Flora reminds herself, is just a year old and jointly owned, unlike the hotel's Citroën van, which belongs to Suzanne. So how will they sort this one out?

She signals for a taxi and the driver slings her bag into the boot as she slides into the backseat. It's almost six o'clock, a mild, clear evening with a light breeze. The pavement tables will be packed, the wait staff rushed off their feet, chaos in the kitchen, Gaston yelling at the sous chef, Suzanne putting the fear of God into the staff but bestowing welcoming smiles on the customers. What a joy not to have to step straight back into all that. Flora wonders how Suzanne and Xavier have divided the work between them, whether he is pulling his weight. He's a man who likes his own way as much as Suzanne likes hers. It's probably been a fiery few weeks as they've settled in together.

She winds down the window and watches the familiar countryside unfold, seeing it this time with the eyes of one who has arrived only to leave again. She knows she will always be drawn back to this part of France, the traditions she has learned to love, the small bright towns and fishing ports, the pines along the cliffs, the wide sandy beaches and craggy outcrops. Perhaps she will bring her new family here one day; the coast itself is not dissimilar to where they live now in Cornwall. She would like to come with Geraldine, she thinks, and Bea and the children, introduce them to Suzanne, walk them to the furthest tip of the cape and swim with them off the beach where she and Connie swam on that unseasonably warm day not so long ago. Back then she had thought that one day Connie's children and grandchildren might come here too, but the prospect of that now seems to be fading into the distance.

But she can't dwell on that for long because the weekend in Cornwall comes back, jostling for her attention. They had welcomed her with genuine warmth, plied her with questions about her life, about France and Australia, and when she, Geraldine and Bea were alone they had talked about Gerald, the one that she and Bea had known and the man that Flora thinks he may have become.

'And my step-brother and sister,' Geraldine had asked, 'do you have any idea what they're like? I know it's years since you saw them but do you have any photographs?'

'I thought you might ask that,' Flora had said, and fetched her iPad from her bag. 'These are some pictures of the family that Connie's sent me over the years.'

She'd felt strangely uneasy about sharing the photographs without Connie's permission, but the desire to connect the two sides of the family with each other in even the smallest possible way was too strong and she didn't hold back.

'He's so like me,' Geraldine had said, peering closely at a photograph of Andrew, 'and is that his daughter?'

Flora had nodded. 'That's Brooke, taken a couple of years ago.' She flicked to the next photograph of Kerry and Chris with Ryan and Mia. 'Kerry is much more like her mother.' She'd heard herself speaking as though she really knew them, and the words stuck in her throat.

She turns her attention back to the road now as they head into Port d'Esprit along the main street, past the post office, the church and the square and turn finally onto the quayside and make their way towards the hotel. It's just as she expected: busy with tourists and locals – Jean-Claude and his cronies as always at a corner table, and in an opposite corner Nico, the baker's son, playing accordion. Flora gets out of the car and is paying the driver when she feels a hand on her arm.

'Flora, *Dieu merci*,' Suzanne says, hugging her. 'I can't tell you how thankful I am to see you.' She picks up Flora's case and steers her across the wide pavement, between the tables, in through the restaurant to the office off the kitchen and closes the door behind them. 'I have made a terrible mistake,' she says immediately. 'Flora, this man, I cannot work with him, he does not listen to me, always he does what he wants and it is different from what I want. *C'est impossible*. You must stay, Flora. Somehow we work out how to live, the three of us.'

Flora's lips twitch into a wry smile. This is so typical of Suzanne, her needs always come before anyone else's, even before the pleasantries that one might expect in these circumstances. She slips off her jacket and lays it over the back of the office chair. 'Thank you, Suzanne,' she says. 'Yes, I did have a good holiday, it's nice of you to ask.'

'Yes, yes,' Suzanne says, waving a hand dismissively, 'of course I am glad about this, and yes, you look well, you have had a rest, which is good because we are so busy, booked for the next two months. So – you are here, and I know I can rely on you to . . .'

Flora puts up her hand to stop her. 'Hang on, Suzanne,' she says. 'You actually can't rely on me for anything. I've just come back to pack up my things. I'm flying back to London the day after tomorrow.'

'But no, this is your home, Flora, and the business, it needs you. I need you.'

Flora sits down on the swivel chair and turns gently from side to side. 'You have Xavier now. It's what you wanted – to buy the place next door, convert our flat and live with Xavier. You told me it was what you both wanted. And I knew that it was time for me to go, not just for your sake but my own. Time to do something different. I have other plans now.'

'No,' Suzanne says sternly, putting a hand on the arm of the chair to stop her swaying. 'I was wrong, I am sorry, Flora,

357

I was very wrong. *Mon Dieu*, how wrong. I love Xavier, yes, but I cannot work with him.'

Flora knows Suzanne well enough to detect the note of desperation that underlies her confident tone. She grips the hand that is steadying the chair. 'Did you read my messages?'

'Yes, of course,' Suzanne replies, 'but now there is no *need* for you to take this bookshop job. You can stay here, as we have been so long, *à deux*, a great working partnership. It is what you want.'

Flora shakes her head. 'It was good, Suzanne, very good. But it's over now. It's time for me to go, get a place of my own, live in England again.'

The conversation is long and increasingly painful. Meanwhile, Flora can only imagine Xavier cruising between the tables, stopping to take a drink with some locals, signalling a waiter to fetch something for him. She listens as Suzanne tells her the same things over and over again until she finally runs out of steam and sits down suddenly on the small sofa in the corner.

'So you see . . .' Suzanne says with a shrug, 'there is no other way.'

'There is always another way,' Flora says, 'and you are resourceful, a wonderful *patronne*, full of energy and ideas, and you'll find that way. You will hire someone, or two people perhaps, rearrange things a little, and in a while, a very short while, it will seem normal, and you will wonder how you ever did it any other way.'

'But . . .'

Flora shakes her head. 'I'm going back to London. That's how it is.' She knows that the firmness of her tone will be strange to Suzanne, that she will struggle to match the Flora she has known for years with the one speaking to her now. She is different, she has the confidence that comes with choice, and with the satisfaction of feeling grounded elsewhere.

'I have a great job with good people, Suzanne. And better still I have a family in England now. It's time to go home again.'

*

It doesn't take long to pack her things and tie up the loose ends of the last fifteen years, to catch up with people and say her goodbyes. On the last morning she slips out early and rides her bike to early mass for the last time, sitting at the back of the church, wondering whether or not she will take communion, thinking that what she would really like is a chat with God rather than a formal mass. A chat of the sort she had had as a young woman when she had been considering life in the convent. But she seems to have lost the knack. I want that back, she thinks, walking slowly down to the communion rail. Help me, please, help me to get that back. And she swallows the host and sips the wine, crosses herself and returns to her seat and stays there, for the rest of the service and for some time after, sitting in the silence, waiting until it feels right to leave.

Once outside she unlocks her bike and rides slowly around the town for the last time. She waves to the pharmacist as he rolls back the blinds, and swerves to miss the slosh of water from a waiter's bucket as he swills it across the pavement, then she turns back to the quay and swings the bike down the side way into the backyard, and parks it against the kitchen wall.

Gaston is taking a tray of croissants from the oven. He smiles and rolls his eyes. 'You don't change your mind?' he asks hopefully.

She shakes her head and glances at her watch. 'I leave in a couple of hours. But why are you baking croissants, hasn't Nico delivered this morning?'

Gaston puts down the hot tray and wipes his hands on his apron as Pierre slides the croissants off the tray into the baskets ready for the tables.

Liz Byrski

'Monsieur Xavier,' he says with a shrug, 'he thinks we will make our own. It is, how you say in English, *authentic*? I say to him, Nico *père* has made our croissants for years, Nico *fils* delivers them – how is this not authentic? But he does not answer.'

Flora smiles and pats his arm. 'Suzanne will stop it very soon, I'm sure,' she says. 'Just hang on a week or so and you'll see.' She nods towards Pierre. 'Can I borrow him a moment?'

'Of course,' Gaston says. 'But one moment only.'

'I have something for you, Pierre,' Flora says, and beckons him to follow her out into the yard where she points to her bike. 'I'm going back to England,' she explains in French. 'I won't need this anymore and I want you to have it. Perhaps it will help you get to work on time.' And she smiles and pushes the bike towards him and Pierre grasps the handle-bars in delight.

'*Vraiment?*' he says, a huge smile splitting his long, pale boy's face.

'Yes, really,' she says. 'You're doing well, Pierre. Madame Suzanne will never tell you this herself, but I will tell you now that she thinks highly of you. She will think even more highly if you get to work on time.' And she pats him on the shoulder and goes back inside.

'So, you will come back to see me?' Suzanne says later as she walks out with her to the taxi. 'You will come for a holiday?'

'Of course,' Flora says, close to tears now. 'I'll come so often you'll probably get sick of me.'

Suzanne shakes her head. 'Never,' she says. 'And I can never repay you, for all the years . . . for . . .'

And she turns suddenly and runs back inside through the restaurant and Flora sees her disappear up the stairs. It is the first time she has seen Suzanne cry since her tears after Jacques's death, and it moves her deeply. But she turns back to the taxi and climbs in, this time beside the driver.

'*Allons y,*' she says, and he slips the car into gear. As they move slowly on down the quay she leans back in comfort and watches as the past slips away behind her, sadness jostling for attention with a growing sense of excitement about what lies ahead.

# Thirty-one

'The room I'd really like,' Brooke says cautiously, obviously wondering how this will be received, 'is Granddad's old study.'

There's a silence in which the proverbial pin could have been heard to drop. Andrew draws a breath, wondering how Connie will take this. His father's study has been sacred ground for so long. 'Oh, I don't think so, Brooke . . .' he begins.

'Would you really, dear?' Connie asks. 'I thought you'd prefer Andrew's old room.'

Brooke looks from one to the other, then shakes her head. 'Really, Nan, if I'm going to spend the holidays here from now on, and if you're really okay with it, I'd have the study, but maybe you want to keep it as . . .'

'As a memorial? Of course not,' Connie laughs. 'It's just that it's a bit cut off from the rest of the house and small compared to the other rooms.'

'Perhaps you prefer Kerry's room?' Farah says. 'I can move to . . .'

'No, please, Farah, don't move,' Brooke says. 'I really would love the study. It's cosy – like a tiny apartment up there, all on its own with its own little shower and toilet. I think it would be heaven.'

Andrew looks at Connie and raises his eyebrows, wondering how she really feels.

'Well, then, that's what you shall have,' she says. 'But it needs clearing out.' She looks at Andrew. 'Do you think . . . ?'

'Of course, Brooke can help me. If we sort through the books and papers, and the small stuff, I can get Ted next door to help me with the furniture.'

'Should you be doing that?'

'I'm fine,' Andrew says, 'much more comfortable since the stitches came out.'

'So I can really have it?' Brooke asks.

'Of course you can. Do what you like with it. I'm sure Granddad would have loved to see you up there.'

'I think we might chuck out the chaise,' Andrew says. 'I sat on it the other day, there's a broken spring.'

'Oh, please let me keep it,' Brooke says. 'It's so cool. I don't mind the broken spring.'

Connie tilts her head on one side and looks at Andrew. 'When were you up there?'

'When you two were out shopping the other day.'

'But why?'

'Just having a last chat with Dad,' he says, feeling himself flush.

'But when we got back,' Brooke says, 'you were singing to Queen. You should've seen him, Farah, it was really embarrassing.'

'All right, all right,' Andrew says, blushing.

'I thought it was rather nice, you singing like that. When you were much younger you used to do it to Boomtown Rats – "I Don't Like Mondays". I've got a photo somewhere . . .'

'Well, we won't bother looking for *that*,' Andrew says. 'But on the subject of photographs, you didn't show us any of those friends of Dad's that you met in London. Phillip, was it? And I can't remember the woman's name.'

'Bea,' Brooke says.

Connie gets up abruptly. 'I didn't take any. Silly really, just never thought of it at the time. Anyway, that's it then. You two can start on the study as soon as you like. It might need a coat of paint, but there's plenty in the shed.' She looks at Andrew. 'How long do you think you'll stay?'

'The end of the month if that's okay with you.'

'As long as you like,' Connie says.

'So, let's go and see what we want to do with the study,' Andrew says.

'What's going on?' Brooke asks as they make their way upstairs. 'Why did Nan say that about the photos?'

'What do you mean?'

'She had photos of Granddad's friends, she sent me some when she first met them, but she didn't show us them with the other pictures at the weekend. And now she's saying she never took any. Why's she lying?'

Andrew narrows his eyes. 'Are you sure?'

'Positive. I can show you on the iPad when we get upstairs.'

'Okay, show me the evidence, Sherlock,' Andrew says, closing the study door behind them, and Brooke sits down beside him on the chaise, flicking through the photo gallery.

'Here we are then, Watson,' she says. 'This is the night they first met those people, at a restaurant in Bloomsbury where they were staying. This is Phillip, and this woman here is Bea – Beatrice, I think. They were both at university with Granddad.'

Andrew studies the photograph. The four of them are sitting at a table, looking towards the camera, laughing. Phillip, lean, grey haired, casually well dressed in a blue jacket and paler blue shirt, and Beatrice, plump, older probably than his mother, and with thick silver hair cut in an edgy style. She is wearing purple and a string of large orange beads. They look as though they are having a great time.

'How odd,' Andrew says. 'Got any more?'

'Heaps,' Brooke says, and together they go through pictures taken in a bookshop. 'He owns that shop,' Brooke says, 'and I think that Bea works there. Yes, look, in this one she's there in the office at the shop.'

There are pictures taken outside the shop, in cafés, and in a park somewhere near a fountain, and with each one Andrew feels a growing sense of anxiety. Why is his mother lying about the photos?

'She must've forgotten she sent them to me,' Brooke says.

The next photograph he's seen before – Connie in the dark blue dress doing her mock curtsey.

'That's the night she went to the opera with Phillip,' Brooke says.

'This is totally weird.'

'Yep, and it's also weird that while Nan was away she mentioned Auntie Flora all the time in her messages and now she doesn't even want to talk about her. Just keeps changing the subject.'

Andrew's head is spinning. It disturbs him that Connie is lying; she has always been so insistent on the truth. But of course his mother must have lied about lots of things in her life – who doesn't tell a lie to save someone's feelings, or to stop oneself looking a fool, or to hide something embarrassing or shameful? So what sort of lie is this? What could be so important, or embarrassing or shameful or whatever, that Connie would lie about the photographs?

'Look, Brooke, don't say anything about this. I want to talk to Kerry about it, I'll call her. But not a word to Nan.'

'Of course not, Dad! You know, lots of times when Nan emailed she said Auntie Flora would be coming here – she even sounded as though she thought she'd be coming to live – but now, well, she just keeps avoiding the subject.'

'Yes, I noticed that too. It is a little odd, isn't it?' he says. 'And one more thing, Brooke, while we're sorting out this room, if you find anything dodgy just . . . just give it to me and don't mention it to Nan.'

'Dodgy like what?'

He shrugs, awkward now, embarrassed that he even has to say any of this. 'Well, you know, personal stuff, anything that might upset Nan.'

'What, like love letters or porn or something?'

Andrew gulps. 'Well, that's unlikely, I think, but . . .'

'Not really,' Brooke says, obviously right into it now. 'I saw this woman on TV the other night talking about how she found a whole box of love letters when she was clearing out her dead husband's study and . . .'

'Okay,' he says, 'stop right there. I don't want to talk about this. Just don't say anything to Nan about the photos, and if you find anything, anything at all, keep quiet and give it to me.' He grins to break his own tension. 'Okay, Sherlock?'

'Okay, Watson. But it would be pretty exciting if we did find something, wouldn't . . . ?'

'Brooke! Shut up.' And he grabs her, claps his hand over her mouth and pretends to strangle her when she tries to speak. 'If you find anything just keep quiet. It's our secret and if you tell anyone, anyone at all, I'll have to kill you.'

And she nods furiously and collapses in giggles. 'You're a weirdo, Watson.'

\*

'We didn't decide about a room for your friend Flora,' Farah says as she chops vegetables for soup later in the day. 'Kerry's room is the nicest and so you must want her to have that. The girls and I will go back to the flat before she arrives, unless you prefer us to leave sooner.'

Connie, who has just opened the mail, pauses to read a letter from someone in the nearby university who wants to start a choir. 'Sorry, what was that, Farah?' she says, fixing the letter to the fridge door with a magnet.

'Your friend Flora,' Farah begins again. 'We should prepare a room for her. You must let me know when she is coming, Connie, and the girls and I will move back to the flat.'

Connie hesitates. She's been home almost two weeks and has been waiting to find the right moment and the right way to say this. 'I don't want you to go at all, Farah,' she says. 'In fact I was going to suggest that you rent out your flat and you and the girls come and live here with me.'

Farah puts down her knife. 'Live here?'

'Yes, I think it would be lovely. Brooke will be here a lot of the time now, and she loves Lala and Samira. And it might be easier for you. I could be here when they get home from school when you're working, be here if you want to go out in the evenings. You don't seem to have a chance to get out much. You need to make a life of your own here.'

Farah blushes. 'But I have made a life here, Connie,' she says. 'I have a home of my own, I have my girls and my work. And I help at the Muslim family centre.'

Connie blushes, her neck prickling with heat. 'Oh, Farah, I'm so sorry, I put it so badly. It's just that I remember what it's like to be a mother; a lot of work and sometimes you need a backstop. I could be that for you, and you for me with Brooke. Maybe it would give you a bit more free time – you work so hard.'

Farah is silent for a moment, and Connie's heart thumps hard. She is nowhere near ready to be alone in the house, but this is where she wants to be.

'It's kind of you, Connie,' Farah says cautiously, 'very kind. And it would be a lovely place for us to live. But this is your family's home, how would they feel about it? Kerry and Andrew?'

'I don't know, I haven't asked them, but I don't think they'll mind. Why should they? You're part of the family now anyway.'

'If we were to do this I would pay rent, I would share the

cost of food and utilities, and share the work. That is the only way I might be able to do it.'

'Well, none of that's necessary but if it's what you want . . .'

'It is the only way I could agree to it.'

Connie feels as though the breath has been knocked out of her. '*Could* agree? I actually thought you'd be pleased. I mean, the girls like it here, you'd have much more space, the pool, the garden. I thought it would be easier for you and it would be lovely for me.'

'Connie, I'm honoured that you invite me into your family home like this,' Farah says, 'truly honoured, thank you, but it's a surprise. I need time to think, to talk to the girls, and both you and I need to be clear about how it would work.'

Connie nods, looking away out of the window. 'Yes, yes I suppose you're right,' she says. 'But will you think about it and talk to Samira and Lala?'

'Of course,' Farah says. 'I think they would like it very much. But what about Flora? You told me on the telephone that she will come to live with you. How would she feel about me being here, about the girls? Don't you want to talk about it with her?'

Connie turns away from the window.

'Connie, what's the matter?'

'It's nothing,' she says, shaking her head. 'Nothing at all . . .' and she drops into a chair, rests her elbows on the table.

'Forgive me but I think it is too soon for you to decide something like this,' Farah says, sitting down beside her. 'You need time, now that you are home, to see how you feel, and we both need to think about how it would work.'

Connie nods slowly, unable to speak at first. 'You're right of course,' she manages eventually, 'we should think more about it, but . . .' she puts her head in her hands. 'That's not how it's going to be, Farah – with Flora, I mean. Things have changed and I'll tell you but, please, don't say anything to anyone else . . . and would you stay, please, in the meantime? Stay at least a little bit longer?'

# Thirty-two

*O*n a sunny afternoon in the second week of June, in a small terraced house in Shepherds Bush which she is house-sitting, Flora checks her email – again. She's been doing this with increasing frequency since she got back to London, but day after day Connie's silence seems to grow in significance. It's almost two weeks since they parted in the foyer of the Bloomsbury hotel the morning Connie left.

'We'll email, won't we?' Connie had asked, appearing suddenly anxious and uncertain after her rigid stance of the last few days.

'Of course we will,' Flora had said. 'We'll work this out somehow, Connie. We can't let one disagreement ruin things after all these years.'

Connie had nodded, smiling a tense smile. 'No, no we won't let that happen. I'll let you know when I'm back.'

And they had hugged each other, not speaking but holding on tightly, willing each other not to cry. And then Connie had turned away and walked quickly across the lobby to the taxi where the driver was lifting her suitcase into the boot, and Flora stood and watched as it drove away, and then made her way slowly back to her room.

Two days after she should have got home Connie hadn't emailed, so Flora had sent a brief message asking if she was home safely, hoping the flight wasn't too awful. 'Let me know how you are,' she had said at the end, but Connie hadn't replied to that nor to the message she'd sent from France and another when she moved into this house. So what next? she wonders. Does Connie intend to ignore her completely?

The elderly corgi who lives in the house waddles over to her, leans against her legs and gazes up pleadingly. Flora scratches between her ears and the dog takes this as a signal that a walk is imminent. She grabs Flora's sleeve, chewing at it in antici-pation, and Flora pushes her gently away and goes out to the hall to collect the lead. The house and dog belong to a friend of Bea's who is visiting her daughter in America, and had been desperate for someone to take care of both in her absence.

'C'mon then, Tinkerbelle,' Flora says, and the dog yelps with excitement as she opens the front door. 'Tinkerbelle,' she says aloud, shaking her head. 'What sort of person names a barrel-shaped corgi Tinkerbelle? Even if she wasn't always barrel-shaped it's still a pretty nauseating name for a dog.' Tinkerbelle wags her tail furiously as if in agreement and skips nimbly down the front steps.

The house is delightful, a nineteenth century terrace immaculately cared for and with a glassed extension that makes the most of the sunny walled garden with its patch of lawn surrounded by big pots of red and white geraniums. She has it for four more weeks, by which time she hopes to have found somewhere similar to rent or perhaps buy, if Gerald's bequest will stretch to that. London feels like home again.

It seems strange now that just a few months ago she had felt close to despair at the lack of choices open to her, and then, suddenly, everything changed. The only fly in Flora's ointment is Connie's silence, and the longer it continues, the more anxious she becomes.

*

Connie stands silently in the kitchen listening, waiting for them all to be gone. First Farah, dropping the girls at a friend's house, and then on to visit patients; then Andrew, following in her car, off to meet an old friend from university days for breakfast. Then silence. She takes a deep breath; how can she have made such a stupid mistake? She has to talk to Brooke while Andrew's out of the house, and she heads up the main stairs and then the narrow flight to Gerald's study where Brooke is packing Gerald's books into boxes, and listening to music on her iPod.

Connie stops in the doorway, looking around the room. 'Goodness, you've made such a difference already. Where's all the other stuff?'

Brooke grins, and turns off the music. 'Great, isn't it? Some of the papers took a long time, we did that on Monday. Dad took all of that and the small stuff and the rubbish down to the garage yesterday. Those boxes over there are full of files. Dad says he'll go through them some other time. He just wants us to get it all out so that he can move the furniture.'

Connie nods, thinking how much lighter it looks up here now, how, without all the clutter, you can see the charm of the room, the way the light falls, and of course the dust. 'I haven't been up here for ages,' she says, sitting down on the chaise. 'It needs a good clean. I'll come and help you with that when the boxes are gone, and you'll need new curtains.'

'Well,' Brooke begins cautiously, 'Dad said that if you were okay with it I could have a Venetian blind, one of those with the wide wooden slats.'

'Of course I don't mind, that would look lovely. I want you to make it your own, Brooke, and I can see now why you chose it. I'd got so used to resenting it that I had forgotten what a nice room it is.'

'You resented it?'

Connie nods. 'Yes, silly, I suppose. How can you resent a room? But I did. Granddad spent so much time here.

He used to shut himself away for hours pretending he was working when he didn't want to spend time with me or the children. He did work some of the time, of course, but a lot of it he'd be reading those . . .' she points to the shelf of paperback crime novels, just where Brooke is standing, 'or listening to the radio or sleeping.' She shrugs. 'Anyway, this'll be a lovely room and, fortunately for you, escaping up here will not be seen as dereliction of duty. Well, probably not anyway.'

Brooke smiles. 'I can't wait to get it done, but then it'll be time to go home and back to school.'

'The long holidays will roll around soon,' Connie says. 'Perhaps we'll all have Christmas here again this year.' She pauses – 'I think there's an aerial socket in that corner, behind the desk. We could get you a TV, then we won't have to fight over what to watch.'

'Wow, that would be brilliant,' Brooke says. 'Thanks, Nan. Are Farah and the twins staying on?'

'For a while at least. I asked her to move in permanently, but she thinks we both need time to see how it might work – all of us living here – before we decide. I suppose she's right. Brooke, there's something I wanted to ask you. The photographs I sent you while I was away, do you still have them?'

'Yes, of course, they're on my iPad.'

'Do you mind?'

'Of course not, as long as you don't delete any.'

They look steadily at each other and Connie, flushing, looks away. 'Ah, well, I was hoping to get rid of some,' she says with an awkward laugh, thinking she must look like a guilty child.

'No, Nan,' Brooke says firmly, withdrawing the proffered iPad and putting it on the windowsill behind her. 'They're my photos now, you sent them to me.'

Connie's face is burning now. 'Well, I don't know about that,' she begins. 'It's just that . . . that . . .'

'That you deleted some of your own, and then remembered that I must still have copies?'

'Well, okay, yes, that's right, and I just wanted to see them.'

'Oh! Okay,' Brooke says, 'I'll email them to you.'

Connie feels ridiculous. She gets to her feet and walks around looking at the books still on the shelves, looking at anything to avoid looking at Brooke. 'I'd really prefer it if you . . .'

'Why did you lie to Dad about the photographs?'

'Lie?'

'Oh, come on, Nan, you know you did. You wouldn't show us the day you got back and when you finally got round to it a whole lot of them, the ones with Granddad's friends, were missing.'

'Really, Brooke,' Connie says, 'this is not . . . this is . . . for goodness sake, I feel as though I've been dragged up in front of the headmistress.'

'Why did you delete them, Nan?'

Connie sinks back down onto the chaise, shaking her head, putting her hands over her face.

'Oh, Nan, I'm sorry, I didn't mean to upset you. I just want to know what's going on. You really liked those people at first, now you've wiped them out, haven't even mentioned them. And Auntie Flora – you were so excited about her coming to live here and now you don't even want to talk about her.' She crosses the room and pulls up a chair facing Connie. 'Please don't cry.'

Connie looks up at her. 'I'm not crying. It's not your fault, Brooke, you're right. But I can't tell you why. I just can't.'

'Something happened, didn't it, in England?' Brooke says. 'Something that involves Auntie Flora, and those people?'

Connie nods.

'So tell me, it can't be that bad.'

'It is,' Connie says, fighting the urge to talk about it, to let Brooke know exactly how awful it is. 'It's really bad and if I told you . . . if I told you . . .'

'You'd have to kill me,' Brooke jokes.

Connie smiles. 'Well, not exactly, but I'd have to make you promise not to tell anyone else, not Andrew or Kerry, no one.'

'Then don't tell me,' Brooke says, angry now, standing up again. 'Don't tell me because I'm sick of things that can't be talked about. I'm sick of whispered arguments that I'm not supposed to hear. I'm sick of Dad telling me stuff that I can't tell you or Mum, and Mum telling me stuff I can't tell Dad, and Dad and Auntie Kerry telling each other stuff that no one else is supposed to know. I'm sick of all those things we couldn't say in front of Granddad in case he could still possibly hear and understand, and sick of Granddad's secrets, whatever they are. Why couldn't we have known about Auntie Flora years ago? How cruel was that, sending her away from her family, letting everyone believe that she'd done something terrible? And, Nan, don't think that I don't know that you used me to tell Dad and Auntie Kerry about that so you didn't have to tell them yourself. Well, thanks very much for that – I really walked into it, and it turned out okay, but you really shouldn't have done it.'

Connie sits upright on the couch, frozen. She feels weak and nauseous, but daren't relax in case she falls apart. She sees Brooke bite her lip, and she comes over to sit beside Connie on the chaise.

'I'm sorry, I probably shouldn't have said all that but it's true, and I'm sick of it, sick of adults telling me how important it is to be open and honest, and that if you are everything can be sorted out sensibly, but doing exactly the opposite. I've had a horrible time – Mum and Dad arguing or not speaking then splitting up, and Mum having an affair, and having to live with that toad for weeks, then moving house, and then finding out he was a pervert and not daring to say anything and him trashing the house, and the accident. It's been awful, Nan, and I wasn't even allowed to tell you about Dad nearly breaking his neck. And while all that was going on I was expected to do my exams and behave as though nothing had happened.'

Connie manages to reach out an arm and put it around her shoulders, silent still, not knowing where to start. 'I'm so sorry, darling,' she says eventually. 'You're quite right, it's not the way to do things. It's Granddad's way. I think it made him feel in control of things, but it's divisive. I suppose I learned it from him, but it's not how I want to do things now. I'm really sorry about my part in that, particularly in what you said about my telling you about Flora. It was a very wrong thing to do. I've been having a bad time myself, but that doesn't change anything. You're so mature and sensible, Brooke . . .'

'No,' Brooke cuts in, 'don't say that. I'm sick of being told that, too. I'm still a kid . . . sometimes I just need to be a teenager. I'm sick of having to be a grown-up for adults who are behaving like children.'

Brooke lets out an enormous sigh and leans against Connie and they sit there in silence. Then Brooke gives a stifled little snort of laughter.

'What is it?' Connie asks.

'I was just going to say, please don't tell Dad how rude I was to you, but that doesn't really work with what I was saying before, does it?'

Connie laughs. 'No it doesn't, but you weren't rude. You were honest, so there's nothing to tell. But there is a lot for me to think about, more than you could possibly realise.'

Brooke brushes strands of hair back from her face. 'I won't delete those photographs, Nan, because I think whatever it is that happened probably affects all of us, otherwise you wouldn't want to hide them. And you might get over it, and then you'll wish you had them.'

Connie relaxes with a sigh, and leans back, shifting her position on the chaise and encountering the broken spring. 'Shit!' she says, moving again. 'Shit, that hurt.'

Brooke laughs. 'I don't think I've ever heard you swear before.'

'Oh, I can do much better than that,' Connie says, 'as you'll soon discover now you're going to be here more. You're right about the photographs, about everything, really.' She gets up and heads for the door, then pauses. 'This morning I was going to do something I should have done before I went away, reply to all those lovely messages people sent me about Gerald, but I don't feel I can start on it now. D'you fancy coming for a walk with me and Scooter, going for coffee somewhere and eating something that's really bad for us?'

Brooke gets up, puts her arms around her, and hugs her. 'Sounds like heaven,' she says. 'Let's do it.' And she follows Connie down the stairs.

*

It's later that afternoon when Connie remembers the book and at first pushes away the thought. But she doesn't like the way she left things with Phillip, and can't stop worrying about what he must think of her. Perhaps it's a legacy of her life with Gerald, the need to please a man and have him think well of her, but she is uneasy with the way she behaved toward him that last evening. He was, after all, there at her urging, and was trying to help, even if his basic loyalties lay elsewhere. She should at least send him an email to thank him for the book, but she'll have to read it first – she doesn't even know the title and can't remember whether he had told her who the author was.

Upstairs she retrieves the package from the drawer and removes the gift-wrapping. It's a paperback, the cover background a blurry black and white photograph of some trees and a hedge and superimposed over it the back view of a woman in a dusty rose tinted coat and matching broad brimmed hat. Very 1980s. *All Passion Spent* it's called, and Connie tries to remember what she knows about Vita Sackville West, which is not much at all. She sits down on the edge of the bed and sighs. Maybe she could send the email without reading it, but then he'd made such a thing of it she can hardly mention the book without reference to its contents.

Connie kicks off her shoes and swings her legs up onto the bed, leans back against the pillows and begins to read. Lady Slane's husband, an eminent statesman, has died and her adult children are arguing bossily about how she should spend the last years of life. Connie's mouth twitches in a smile, and she settles herself more comfortably against the pillows. But Lady Slane, who long ago sacrificed her dreams of an artistic life to marry and have children, has plans of her own. She takes a lease on a small house in Hampstead that she has admired since her youth and ignores the disapproval of her family. Connie scrunches her toes in delight as this unlikely eighty-eight-year-old heroine moves in with her maid, sets up her easel in the garden, and variously takes afternoon tea with her landlord, a builder and another tradesman, each in his own way devoted to the practical and visual arts.

At this point, Connie reluctantly puts the book aside. Time has flown without her noticing and she goes downstairs wondering where everyone is and then remembers that Brooke and Andrew have gone to buy blinds and other bits and pieces, and Farah is meeting the girls from school and taking them on to dancing class. She sighs with pleasure at the stillness, the lack of need to hurry, the sudden delight of having the house to herself, something she has, until now, wanted to avoid. And she fills the kettle and stands by the window waiting for it to boil, thinking of Lady Slane freed in her old age to do whatever she wants.

Connie makes herself some tea and carries it back upstairs, trying to remember what it was that Phillip had actually said about the book – something about a tree, wasn't it? She picks up the book and begins to read again and then she remembers. A man from the past turns up, a man Lady Slane had met only a couple of times during her life as a diplomatic wife in India, a man who has admired her greatly. Lady Slane takes tea with Mr FitzGeorge, a friendship starts to grow, they talk of many things, they walk together on Hampstead Heath. They talk of the past, the occasions on which they met, they speak of her husband and family and how she abandoned her desire to become a painter in order to marry. 'I remember looking at you and thinking, that is a woman whose heart is broken,' he tells her.

Shocked, Lady Slane assures Mr FitzGeorge that she has had everything that women want: a husband, children and a comfortable position in life. 'Except that you were defrauded of the one thing that mattered,' he says. 'Nothing matters to an artist except the fulfilment of his gift . . . he grows crooked like a tree twisted into an unnatural shape . . . life becomes existence – makeshift.'

Connie puts down the book and stares at her reflection in the mirrored door of the wardrobe facing her. Makeshift? A tree twisted into an unnatural shape? Is that who she is? Is that what she has let herself become? And, just like Lady Slane, she puts her hands over her eyes, to shield herself.

# Thirty-three

ndrew is lying in bed trying unsuccessfully to go back to sleep. Outside in the passage Farah is whispering to Lala and Samira to be quiet, but they're having trouble containing their excitement about going on a ferry trip. He hears her hurry them down the stairs, their excited voices rising as they head for the kitchen. He closes his eyes and considers going back to sleep, but his mind has started buzzing again. Being here in the house with Gerald gone is so very different, he feels free at last from the constraints of the past that stopped him from venturing along paths that attracted him. The past is peeling away, pushing him towards something new and, most of all, towards a new sense of himself. There is a tap at the door.

'Are you awake, Andrew?' his mother calls, and comes in with a cup of tea.

He sits up. 'Tea in bed, what a treat. What have I done to deserve this?'

'Nothing yet,' she says. 'But I'll think of something.' She sits down on the edge of the bed. 'You haven't got plans for today, have you?'

He shakes his head. 'No, just going to see if Ted is around to help me move the furniture down from the study.'

Liz Byrski

'Well, Chris could help with the furniture. They're coming down for the day. They'll be here mid-morning.'

'Really? They were here just a week ago, taking Erin to the ship.'

'Yes, but I called them yesterday evening and asked them to come. I need to talk to you – all of you together.'

'About what? Is anything wrong? You're not sick, are you?' He puts down his cup and leans forward to peer into her face.

'I'm fine,' Connie says. 'Just been doing some thinking and now I need to act on it. And don't bother asking me; I'll tell you all at the same time and not before. Drink your tea, dear, and maybe you could pop out for some milk and perhaps some Danish pastries for when they get here. Take Brooke with you, she'll be better at choosing them.' And she pats his arm, gets up and disappears down to the kitchen.

\*

'So what's going on?' he asks Brooke later as they drive to the bakery.

'Er . . . we're buying Danish.'

'I meant what's going on in a macro rather than a micro sense,' Andrew says. 'Seems we're having a family meeting.'

'Mmmm, seems like it.'

'Okay,' Andrew says, 'you *know* something, don't you, so tell me.'

'Dad, I don't know anything, honestly. I have a thought but I'm keeping that thought to myself.'

'So you definitely know something – it's about Flora and those other people, isn't it, the ones in the photograph?'

'I *don't* know, but that's the thought. All I know is that Nan wants to tell us something and we all have to be there.'

'So it must be something important for her to get Kerry and Chris to drive down here again so soon.'

Brooke's phone rings and she pulls it out of the pocket of her anorak. 'Hi, Mum . . . Oh, nothing much, just in the car with Dad going out to buy some Danish . . . what? Oh yeah, I know, he's not allowed to choose them . . . Nan told me . . . yeah, he always gets the ones that have been in the display cabinet too long . . . dry, yeah, I know . . . well, men don't see those things, do they? So how are you, Mum, did you get some new furniture yet?'

Andrew rolls his eyes. 'What's so special about choosing pastries?' he mumbles, but Brooke ignores him. He drives on, wondering about Connie and this meeting. What could be so serious that she would destroy photographs, and what's it got to do with Flora?

'Mum says hi,' Brooke says, pointing at the phone.

He waves at the phone. 'Hi from me. Tell her I'll be back at the end of next week if she needs any help at the house.'

Brooke passes on the message and hangs up.

'I don't like this secrecy,' he says.

Brooke bursts out laughing. 'That's just what I told Nan the other day. Too many secrets, too many people deciding what other people can or can't know.'

'You told Nan that? What did she say?'

'She said I was right and that she'd think about it.'

Andrew nods. 'So you *do* know something after all.'

'Stop hassling me, Dad, I've told you, I don't know what's going on.'

'Stone the crows,' Andrew says, banging his fist on the steering wheel. 'Well, it's obviously something serious, something big.'

'Yep,' Brooke nods. 'She probably discovered Granddad had a love child.'

He laughs. 'Now you're just being ridiculous,' he says, pulling up outside the bakery.

*

Connie steps out of the shower, drags a towel off the rail, and walks back into the bedroom drying herself. The luminous numbers on the bedside clock say it's nine-thirty; not long now. She'd woken at six and was up, dressed and walking Scooter vigorously along the footpath by twenty past, desperate to do something to take the edge off her anxiety, trying instead to concentrate on the conversation she'd had yesterday about the choir that was being started at the university. 'I'd love to be involved,' she'd said, 'and I do have some experience . . .' and by the time she put down the phone she'd agreed to join the organising committee as well as being part of the choir. But even this couldn't hold her attention or calm her nerves this morning. Back home from her walk she'd made tea for everyone and, despite Farah's protests, breakfast for her and the girls, and then for Brooke and Andrew. Now they've all gone for a while and she has time to spare, which is the last thing she needs. She sits down on the bed, wrapped in the towel, and ponders whether to check her email now or leave it a little longer.

Since that confronting conversation with Brooke, and then her encounter with Lady Slane, Connie has been in a spin cycle of anxiety and indecision. Time and again she has gone over everything that both Flora and Phillip said to her, and as she has done so her image of herself has taken a beating. The more she chewed on the bone of her discontent the more her sense of righteous hurt and anger began to wither, so that now it seems just selfish and inconsiderate. She doesn't like the picture of herself that now runs through her head like a movie on constant replay. She sees that none of what happened at The Ivy was directed at her. She can understand Bea's dilemma over whether or not to tell her, and Flora's overwhelming desire to embrace her niece. The situation was of Gerald's making, and it throws new light on his motives and his behaviour both then and in their life together. She's not yet sure what that actually tells her about him that is new, rather, it seems that she must open her eyes to what she has always known but had chosen not to see.

Connie wants reconciliation but the price seems so high, for the price is telling Andrew and Kerry and the impact that the news of a half-sister might have on them. Andrew, she thinks, will be shocked to find he is no longer his father's eldest child, but he will probably take it in his stride. But what about Kerry, who has spent so much of her life craving her father's attention and approval? What about the hurt and anger, which has now transformed into something more peaceful – contentment, perhaps, or acceptance? Connie's head spins with possible disastrous scenarios, but time and again she returns to Brooke's words, her frustration over secrets and lies, and the duplicity that creates among people who should be able to trust each other. I no longer need to do things his way, Connie tells herself, I have to find my own way.

Finally, late yesterday afternoon, she had taken the plunge and emailed Flora, then called Kerry and asked if she and Chris could drive down this morning as she had something to tell them. They are already on their way, and now more than ever she needs to hear from Flora. She takes a deep breath and opens her iPad. The little white envelope icon has a small red circle beside it with the number 1 in it and Connie's heart does a somersault. She steps away from the bed and finishes drying herself so fiercely that it hurts, then turns her back on the screen, and stands in front of the open wardrobe searching for something to wear, anything to postpone the moment when she must open the message only to discover that it is just a message from someone else. Her email to Flora had been full of apologies, of explanations, of ramblings about what had happened and her own part in it, and when she'd read it again before going to bed she'd cringed at its excess, but it was gone by then, too late to do anything about it. All she could hope for now was that Flora would take time to read it, see honesty and genuine regret and forgive the rest. The wardrobe does not distract her, and dragging on her dressing gown for warmth, she clicks the envelope.

'*Dearest, dearest Connie,*' Flora begins, '*What a joy and a relief it was to get your message . . .*'

Connie flops back on the bed with something between a sigh and a sob. Then she hauls herself up to a sitting position to read the message that is as long, if not quite as emotional and rambling, as her own had been. It is filled with Flora's pleasure in hearing from her, there are no recriminations, just news of the house in Shepherds Bush, of the longer term house-hunting, of life in the bookshop and, of course, the visit to Cornwall.

> *And yes, I do have pictures of them all and am attaching them, as you asked. I can't tell you how good it feels to know that you've found the courage to do this. I know it's been incredibly hard for you but I'm sure you're doing absolutely the right thing now.*

Connie opens the photographs and stares into the faces; first Geraldine, so uncannily like her father, although her smile has an unmistakable trace of Bea about it. The two older children are like their father, and the youngest girl is, Connie thinks, a miniature version of Bea, plump and dark haired with a devilish glint in her eye. She reads Flora's message again, wishing she could call her, speak to her now, but it's the middle of the night in London so that will have to wait.

\*

'These are really good,' Kerry says, tucking into a pastry topped with custard and apricot. 'Where did you get them?'

'Just down the road,' Andrew says. 'Brooke was charged with selection – consensus is that I can't pick good ones.'

'That'd be right,' Kerry says through a mouthful.

She looks so good, Connie thinks, so very different from

the Kerry who, for longer than she can remember, has stared at her with those hurt and accusing eyes. I could have helped her, Connie thinks now, I could have helped her years ago; all that longing for Gerald's approval, the endless disappointment. Perhaps I could have saved her, saved them both, from that.

They are watching her now, waiting, curious, impatient.

'Come on then,' she says. 'I know you're all wondering what's going on.' And as they settle down she has a terrible moment of panic that this is not, after all, the right thing to do, that she had been right in wanting to hide the truth, to protect them from it. But they are waiting now and there is no turning back.

'I have a lot to tell you,' she says, and she hears the wobbliness in her voice and clears her throat to get control of it. 'It's a long story . . .'

'Just start at the beginning, Mum,' Kerry says gently.

'Actually,' Connie says, 'I think I might begin at the end, with the most important thing of all, and work back from there.' She pauses, heart pounding. 'What I have to tell you all, but particularly you, Kerry and Andrew, is that, when I was in London, I met some of your father's old friends, and . . . and I discovered that . . . that he had a child with someone else; a daughter born just before he and I married, and so you . . . you . . .' her breath disappears quite suddenly and she gulps, hesitates, '. . . you have a half-sister.'

There is a moment of such pristine silence that Connie stops breathing. Kerry gasps, her hand flies to cover her mouth. Andrew darts a fierce look at Brooke, who lifts her shoulders and shakes her head furiously. Chris gives a wry smile, clears his throat and looks away, and outside in the silent garden Ryan hurls a ball for Scooter and he runs after it barking furiously.

*

Brooke looks from one member of her family to the other and finally at Connie, sitting rigid and upright in her usual chair, hands twisting nervously in her lap. She sees the movement of her throat as she swallows and takes a deep breath as though in readiness for the storm to break. Brooke slips down from her spot on the window seat and sits decisively on the broad arm of Connie's chair, leaning into her so that their arms touch and she can feel her grandmother's tension.

It's Andrew who speaks first, shaking his head, looking across at Kerry, raising his eyebrows. 'Well, there you go, proof of something I've been thinking about a lot in the last couple of months – that I never really knew him. Perhaps none of us did.'

The colour is returning to Kerry's face. 'A half-sister,' she says. 'And you knew nothing of this before?'

Connie shakes her head. 'Nothing at all.'

'And those people you met . . . ?'

'Yes, Phillip and Bea, university friends. Bea was with Gerald, they were about to move in together. Then for some reason Gerald changed his mind and shifted himself into my life. He dumped Bea, and six weeks later she discovered she was pregnant. He had moved back to live with his parents, but she managed to find him. He gave her money for an abortion and told her to go away, not to contact him again. She took the money but kept the baby, and she sent him a copy of the birth certificate. He never replied and she never heard from him again.'

'Did you meet her?' Brooke asks. 'The daughter, I mean, I know you met Bea.'

Connie looks up at her, her colour deepening, and Brooke sees that she has asked an awkward question. 'I sort of did,' she says. 'I'll explain that later.'

'So what's her name – our sister?' Kerry asks.

And Brooke, still leaning against Connie, feels her tension increase.

'Her name is Geraldine.'

Kerry gasps. 'But that was what you wanted to call me.'

Connie nods. 'I wanted to call you Geraldine, but your father was against it. I could never understand why. I thought he'd love to have his daughter named after him. We argued, he stormed out of the house and came back three hours later with the certificate showing that he'd registered you as Kerry Ann.'

Brooke watches as conflicting emotions cross her aunt's face. Kerry sinks her head into her hands and Chris, sitting beside her, puts his arm around her shoulders and pulls her to him.

Kerry looks up, looks around at them all. 'It's all right,' she says, 'I'm not crying. It was just exasperation, disgust . . . well, everything really.' She sits up straight. 'Andrew's right,' she says, looking across at him. 'There is so much that we didn't know about Dad, and so much that we should have challenged and changed years ago. All that stuff about what we weren't allowed to talk about.' She shakes her head. 'It doesn't mean I don't love him, I just wish I'd . . . oh well, it doesn't matter now.'

Andrew lets out a short dry laugh. 'Bastard!' he says, shaking his head. 'Oh! I mean Dad,' he says, 'not her, not our sister.'

And Chris throws his head back and laughs, and Kerry joins him.

Brooke leans forward to Connie. 'You were incredibly brave, Nan,' she whispers, 'really cool.'

Connie softens, leans towards her, grasps her hand. 'It was you really, Brooke,' she says, 'you made me see sense.'

'A half-sister,' Kerry says again, still laughing, her eyes bright with curiosity. 'Well, what's she like? It's quite exciting, really. D'you have any photos, Mum? When do we get to meet her?'

# *Thirty-four*

*Sandy Bay, Hobart, October 2012*

Flora stands at the bottom of the garden, staring out across the river. Home at last, she thinks, after all these years and so much angst, but it's not home at all, not anymore. She had wondered how it would be, whether she would feel alienated and ill at ease, or able to experience it for what it was: her birthplace and a part of her childhood. Her memories of it as an adult are always overhung with the pain of her leaving in the seventies and the events leading up to it.

Two days ago, before she'd left England to fly here, she had walked down to Holy Trinity Church in Shepherds Bush and slipped quietly into a pew to have a chat with God. 'Please help me, help *us,* all of us, get this right,' she had asked. 'Don't let us mess it up. Give me patience and generosity if the going gets tough. Let Connie's courage not fail her at the last minute. Let us be the family we really are.'

Any priest, she thought, would have been shocked by the direct requests, arrow prayers shot up in panic, selfish instructions and demands. But Flora has never managed to adhere to the rules for a relationship with God as set down by the church. She remembers it now and looks automatically skyward. 'Thanks,' she says, 'I think it's going to be okay. Thanks for listening, and I really will try to do better, be a better person in future.'

'Is it as you remember?' Connie asks, appearing alongside her now.

'It seems more beautiful,' she says, 'and almost unchanged.'

Connie nods. 'Up here you really could be back in the old days, but you'll see a difference when I take you into the city.'

'It's really good to be here, Con. I was starting to think it was all over for us.'

'Me too,' Connie says. 'Without Brooke giving me a good shaking I might still be floundering in self-righteous indignation. But it's over now, thank goodness.'

'Mmmm. It can't have been easy for you but I kept believing that your generous spirit would work it out eventually. And look at them now.'

They turn in silence, watching the family gathered around the table on the deck, Kerry, Andrew and Chris talking animatedly with Geraldine. And on the lawn nearby Brooke, Lala and Samira sit cross-legged with Geraldine's eldest daughter Lucy, pulling at blades of grass and falling around with laughter.

'She's a lovely woman, Geraldine,' Connie says. 'I feel terrible . . .'

'It's all over,' Flora says, 'really it is, for all of them – Geraldine, Bea, Phillip . . . they understand, there's nothing more to say.' She can see the relief in Connie's face but suspects that she will continue to live for some time with the emotional aftermath of her behaviour.

'It's our family, Flora,' Connie says, 'as it should always have been. And angry as I am at Gerald I'm still sad that he's not here to see how it could have been, how it *will* be.'

Flora nods. She understands the sentiment but can't bring herself to wish that Gerald were there. 'All we have to do now, all of us, is to take careful steps towards keeping together a family spread across continents. I think it's pretty exciting.'

Connie nods. 'Bea says she'll come after Christmas, maybe bring little Molly with her.'

'And what about Farah?'

'Farah has me on trial,' Connie says, smiling. 'She says we need to see how we manage sharing the house when everything has calmed down. The New Year, she says, we'll make formal arrangements about money and the division of labour.'

'Quite right too,' Flora says, 'it's a way to avoid misunder-standings in future. Trust me, without that Suzanne and I would never have lasted as long as we did.' She sits down on the low rock wall above the steep edge of the escarpment.

'What I can't understand,' Connie says, joining her on the wall, 'is why, after the way Gerald treated her, Bea named her daughter after him.'

'I asked her that, and she said that when she did it she thought he would come back to her. In fact she kept hoping that he'd turn up one day, cap in hand. It was years before she finally stopped believing.'

They sit in silence, kicking their heels against the wall as they had so often done on the harbour wall in Port d'Esprit.

'We've had some of our best conversations sitting on walls,' Connie says.

'We have, and never an argument; those we save for cafés and hotel rooms.' Flora has been thinking for weeks that she needed to talk about the fact that Connie never put any pres-sure on Gerald to change his mind. But now she's here she knows that the future is more important than the past. And perhaps, after all, Connie simply knew best – Gerald was not just unlikely but unable to change.

'Remember Port d'Esprit, the couple kissing on the wall, and what you said about love?' Connie asks.

Flora looks puzzled, shakes her head. 'Sorry, no I don't.'

'Well, I asked if you thought that when people fall in love they love each other like that forever. And you said that if you really love someone, you can also hate them and different things will tip you one way or the other. *And*, you said, perhaps if you love someone you just can't keep it up all the time.'

Flora raises her eyebrows. 'Really? I said that?'

'Really. I've thought of it often and wondered how you knew that then – after all, we were only about thirteen at the time.'

Flora turns to her in amazement. 'Are you serious? I haven't got a clue. It would be bullshit that I made up on the spur of the moment. Honestly, Con, I can't believe you've been thinking about that all this time, taking it seriously. No wonder it was easy for Gerald to talk you into things.'

'But you seemed so sure of yourself . . . and I've always believed . . .'

'No,' Flora says, 'don't say that, I was just a kid . . .'

'But how did you . . . ?'

'Connie, are you really telling me that you have thought seriously about something I said about love when I was thirteen?'

'Well, yes, because . . .'

'Because nothing. I knew *nothing* then and I know even less now. Do you know *anyone* who knows less about love than I do? Give me a break.'

There is a pause.

'Is this going to be our first argument sitting on a wall?'

'Maybe,' Flora says, grinning. 'I think I quite like it.'

Behind them two younger generations talk and laugh, sounding as though they have always known each other, and Connie feels the shadows of the years lifting on their laughter and floating out and away over the sunlit river.

'Anyway,' she says, 'I just wanted to tell you that you were right. Everything you said about love that day was right. I understand it now.'

394

# Acknowledgements

*amily Secrets* was born on a wet afternoon in Hobart when I read Vita Sackville West's wonderful novel, *All Passion Spent*, and began thinking of a novel about a woman who had just lost her husband. So thank you, Vita – I can barely believe it took me so long to discover it. Special thanks, too, to Imelda Whelehan and David Sadler, for not only making me so welcome in your lovely house in Sandy Bay, but also allowing me to steal it and make it (with minor adjustments) into Connie's family home.

My sincere thanks are due to those people who generously made time to talk with me about the writing of this book: Lynnley McGrath, Mary Rawlinson, Robin Lawrence and Kennan Taylor. Your help was valuable in assisting me to bring credibility to various aspects of the story and I appreciate it greatly.

I am so lucky to work with the wonderful people at Pan Macmillan who are now friends as well as colleagues. The amazing Cate Paterson has guided me through eight novels – I can't imagine how I would do any of this without you, Cate. Emma Rafferty has once again brought her extraordinary insight to bear on the editing of this novel and helped me to make it very much better than the draft she first read.

Liz Byrski

And Jo Jarrah's forensic attention has now, as always, saved me from my own mistakes of which there are always many. Special thanks, too, to publicity whiz Jace Armstrong for getting me into all the right places – in all sorts of ways. And finally, thanks to the terrific sales and marketing teams, who get the book into all the right places, and to all staff at Pan Macmillan whose consistent support, efficiency and goodwill make publishing with them such a pleasure.

# MORE BESTSELLING FICTION FROM LIZ BYRSKI

## In the Company of Strangers

Ruby and Cat's friendship was forged on an English dockside over sixty years ago when, both fearful, they boarded a ship bound for Australia. It was a friendship that was supposed to last a lifetime but when news of Cat's death reaches Ruby back in London, it comes after a painful estrangement.

Declan has also drifted away from Cat, but he is forced back to his aunt's lavender farm, Benson's Reach, when he learns that he and Ruby are co-beneficiaries.

As these two very different people come together in Margaret River they must learn to trust each other and to deal with the staff and guests. Can the legacy of Benson's Reach triumph over the hurt of the past? Or is Cat's duty-laden legacy simply too much for Ruby and Declan to keep alive?

## Last Chance Café

Dot despairs at the abandonment of the sisterhood – surely pole dancing can never be empowering? Margot is resentful that her youthful ambitions have been thwarted by family – her ex-husband is on a pilgrimage to try and walk away his grief, their daughters are coping with unemployment and secret shopping binges, meanwhile Margot's sister Phyllida discovers that her husband dying is the least of the shocks awaiting her.

Liz Byrski takes her fallible characters on the journey we are all on – what does it mean to grow older? And is there ever a stage in life when we can just be ourselves and not feel pressured to stay young?

## Bad Behaviour

One mistake can change a life forever.

Zoë lives a contented life in Fremantle. She works, she gardens and she loves her husband Archie and their three children. But the arrival of a new woman in her son Daniel's life unsettles her.

In Sussex, Julia is feeling nostalgic as she nurses her friend through the last stages of cancer. Her husband Tom is trying to convince her to slow down. Tom means well, but Julia fears he is pushing her into old age before she is ready. She knows she is lucky to have him. She so nearly didn't . . .

These two women's lives are shaped by the choices they made back in 1968. In a time of politics and protest, consciousness raising and sexual liberation they were looking for their own happy endings. But back then Zoë and Julia couldn't begin to imagine how those decisions would send them along pathways from which there was no turning back.

## Trip of a Lifetime

How do you get your life back on track after a sudden and traumatic event? This is the question Heather Delaney constantly asks herself as she eases herself back into her busy job.

Heather is not the only one who is rocked by the changed circumstances – reverberations are felt throughout her family and friendship circle. And then along comes Heather's old flame, Ellis. Romantic, flamboyant, determined to recapture the past and take control of the future, he seems to have all the answers. But can it really be that easy?

## Belly Dancing for Beginners

Gayle and Sonya are complete opposites: one reserved and cautious, the other confident and outspoken. But their very lives will converge when they impulsively join a belly dancing class.

Marissa, their teacher, is sixty, sexy, and very much her own person, and as Gayle and Sonya learn about the origins and meaning of the dance, much more than their muscle tone begins to change.

## Food, Sex & Money

It's almost forty years since the three ex-convent girls left school and went their separate ways, but finally they meet again.

Bonnie, rocked by the death of her husband, is back in Australia after decades in Europe, and is discovering that financial security doesn't guarantee a fulfilling life. Fran, long divorced, is a struggling freelance food writer, battling with her diet, her bank balance and her relationship with her adult children. And Sylvia, marooned in a long and passionless marriage, is facing a crisis that will crack her world wide open.

Together again, Bonnie, Fran and Sylvia embark on a venture that will challenge everything they thought they knew about themselves – and give them more second chances than they ever could have imagined.

## Gang of Four

*She had a husband, children and grandchildren who loved her, a beautiful home, enough money. What sort of person was she to feel so overwhelmed with gloom and resentment on Christmas morning?*

They have been close friends for almost two decades, supporting each other through personal and professional crises – parents dying, children leaving home, house moves, job changes, political activism and really bad haircuts.

Now the 'gang of four', Isabel, Sally, Robin and Grace, are all fifty-something, successful . . . and restless.

## NON-FICTION FROM LIZ BYRSKI

### Getting On: Some Thoughts on Women and Ageing

*Published as an ebook by Momentum Books*

Why are we so obsessed with staying young?

In a culture that advocates the pursuit of endless youth and physical beauty how can we embrace the reality, the pleasures and the rewards of getting on? And what does the 'fight against ageing' mean when all women must eventually face the double-standard of ageism and sexism?

Once past fifty, older women begin to sense that they have become invisible. From the visual displays in the mall to the pages of magazines and the television screens at the heart of our homes, young women with perfect skin, bouncy, enhanced breasts, pouting lips, long straight hair and perfect teeth gaze down on us.

The ageing population is traditionally viewed as a problem; a drain on financial resources, health, housing and community services and a burden on younger generations. But living longer and living well are the triumphs of a civilised society. It is also the future that all generations want for themselves.

Can we change the conversation on ageing? Getting old is tough, but it's also an opportunity to celebrate how far we have come and to shape a different future. In this essay, Liz Byrski examines the adventure of growing old in the twenty-first century: the new possibilities, the joy and the sorrow of solitude, the reality of grief and loss and the satisfaction of having travelled so far.